FALL OUT

M.N. GRENSIDE

FALL OUT

M.N. GRENSIDE

Urbane
PUBLICATIONS

urbanepublications.com

First published in Great Britain in 2020 by Urbane Publications Ltd
Unit E3 The Premier Centre Abbey Park Romsey SO51 9DG
Copyright © Mark Grenside, 2020

A CIP catalogue record for this book is available from the British Library.

ISBN 978-1-912666-75-1
MOBI 978-1-912666-76-8

Design and Typeset by Michelle Morgan

Cover design and illustrations
www.Figgydo.com

Printed and bound by 4edge UK

URBANE

urbanepublications.com

TESTIMONIALS

"A terrific debut thriller set in the film world, written by someone who clearly has worked in it. The story starts with the murder of a screenwriter and a very special screenplay he has sent to five specific people. Their common link? They all worked on a movie that abruptly stopped shooting years before. The story has all the ingredients of a classic page turner, drawing you in with its fast-paced narrative. Fall Out mixes danger and death, hidden clues and intrigue that rival the Da Vinci code and a wonderful set of engaging characters from the producer Marcus Riley to the resilient designer Melinda 'Mako' de Turris. With stunning attention to detail, Grenside transports us through the gilded locations that we can only dream of visiting. The final reveal, set in a remote cave deep in the Philippine jungle blew me away, all the more because it is based on fact!

I'm already looking forward to the follow up novel, but in the meantime if you want a fast-paced stand out different thriller, I can't recommend Fall Out enough. I Loved it."

EMMA FORBES, BROADCASTER

"I predict great success for this wonderful debut thriller and I hope the beginning of a franchise of books about the adventures of producer Marcus Riley and designer Mako de Turris. Fresh in style, fast paced, sparkling dialogue and a fabulous collection of characters. The premise of a screenplay with cleverly hidden clues that can prove deadly to the reader morphs into a fabulous reveal that is based on one of the greatest crimes ever committed. Truly fascinating historical fact buried in a thrill a minute read, all revealed with a lightness of touch that gave me a shiver of delight. I cannot recommend it enough."

**DAWN AIREY, FORMER CEO CHANNEL FIVE,
DIRECTOR OF CONTENT ITV, CEO GETTY IMAGES**

"Fall Out is a tautly written, entertaining thriller that will keep the reader turning the pages right till the very end. It almost reads like a movie and Mark's background in the business comes through on the page. It feels authentic and informed but never overbearing. Although the story revolves around the movie business, the construct reveals one of the greatest twists I've seen and I doubt the other readers will see it coming. As the clues to the initial crime emerge we follow Marcus and Mako from California to Cannes, Switzerland to the Philippines in pursuit of the hidden secrets that underly the mystery until the final reveal, on the old set of 'Apocaplypse Now' in the Philippines, when everything becomes clear. To borrow movie parlance, it sits somewhere between 'The DaVinci Code' and 'Indiana Jones.'"

ALAN MOLONEY AWARD WINNING PRODUCER, INCLUDING BROOKLYN, AND THE OSCAR NOMINATED ALBERT KNOBBS

"Riveting. Page-turning. A jaw-dropping rollercoaster of action and surprise. And best off all, it's based upon shocking true history. A real gem."

DAMIEN LEWIS, INTERNATIONAL NO. 1 BESTSELLING AUTHOR AND MULTI-AWARD-WINNING REPORTER.

"A gripping thriller twisted around an incredible piece of recent history… and an equally fun glimpse into how our industry works! A well-researched ride."

ROBERT HALMI, JR., EMMY AND MULTI AWARD WINNING PRODUCER INCLUDING LONESOME DOVE, TIN MAN AND MERLIN

"A breathless and breathtaking debut. In 1972 Frederick Forsyth's 'Day of the Jackal' set the standard for meticulously researched, fast-paced international thrillers that still stands 50 years later. It is a tribute to Mark Grenside's debut novel that it can be mentioned in that company.

Mark Grenside has a background in film and TV and is a natural storyteller. His book reads like a film script; the dialogue is razor sharp and it's easy to visualise each scene as the action unfolds. It was over too quickly but I am looking forward to the successor and, maybe, the film or TV series.

NIGEL FOSTER, SERIAL ENTREPRENEUR

Fall Out brings the high-stakes world of international film and television to the page with a verve and an industry expertise that invites comparison to John le Carre or Lee Child. Grenside delivers a high-voltage drama, weaving together a hidden treasure plot equal to Indiana Jones, with the suave jet-set world of James Bond. Marcus Riley and 'Mako' de Turris are destined to become our 21st century Bogie and Bacall or Hepburn and Tracy."

ANNE KREAMER, FORMER INTERNATIONAL TELEVISION EXECUTIVE AND AUTHOR OF *RISK/REWARD*, *IT'S ALWAYS PERSONAL* AND *GOING GRAY*.

M.N.Grenside has written a splendid, page-turning first novel and he is to be congratulated. It is set against the entertainment industry of which he clearly has knowledge. It also displays a very high level of historical knowledge, something I am well acquainted with. The pace is fast and the plot is intriguing and this novel bodes well for a series and likely screen adaptation. I look forward to both developments happening."

PETER CLARK, FOUNDER OF TALK RADIO

"I love this book—and I have read it six times! In 30 years in book publishing, I have seldom found a thriller that is so satisfying or this much fun. *Fall Out* is a rich (and believable) mix of history, movies, travel, and unforgettable characters. When you've read this book, you'll join me in longing for the next. Marcus and Mako are wickedly interesting people."

SHERRYE LANDRUM, AUTHOR AND EDITOR

"A wonderfully fresh debut novel and hopefully the beginning of a franchise based on the two leads, film producer Mark Riley and whipsmart designer Melinda 'Mako' de Turris. Written in a very visual style, fast paced, and with dialogue that crackles, Fall Out is set in the movie business by someone who clearly knows it. The story is liberally sprinkled with clever clues and unexpected twists and turns. The writer has created a group of diverse and believable characters in a deeply satisfying read, taking the reader to wonderful locations and a mind-blowing history lesson, all wrapped up in a page turning thriller. It may be a cliché, but I found it hard to put down. Read and enjoy!"

SIMON OAKES, CEO OF HAMMER FILMS

"Clearly a spellbinder! What's so compelling is the knitting together of historical events into a thrilling novel whose center of gravity is modern day Hollywood and the effort of a producer to film a story that some very powerful people would kill to keep it from being exposed. What's riveting about Grenside's tale is that so much of it appears to be backed by his beautifully researched history. FALL OUT is brilliantly written for a world where the unthinkable, turns out to be true. I can't wait to see the film!"

CHARLES S. BONAN, CHAIRMAN, STARSTREAM MEDIA AND AWARD WINNING PRODUCER OF THE BUTLER.

To my beloved wife, Kirsten,
who inspires, supports and puts up with me.

CAST OF CHARACTERS

MAJOR ITO OKOBUTO
GARRISON COMMANDER

GENERAL YAMASHITA
COMMANDER 14TH ARMY IN PHILIPPINES

YONO TAN
EXECUTIONER

MARCUS RILEY
FILM PRODUCER, RECIPIENT OF SCREENPLAY

MELINDA 'MAKO' DE TURRIS
DESIGNER

GARANCE
Ms.DE TURRIS' HOUSEKEEPER

SAM WOOD
SCREENWRITER

JAX WOOD
SAM'S EX WIFE

BILL BAINES
STUNT CO-ORDINATOR

CARA BAINES
FLORIST AND WIDOW OF STUNTMAN BILL BAINES,
RECIPIENT OF SCREENPLAY

ROBERT KELSO
DIRECTOR, RECIPIENT OF SCREENPLAY

CHRISTO MURRAY
COMPANION TO ROBERT KELSO

LOUIS MCCONNELL
AGENT AND ENTREPRENEUR,
RECIPIENT OF SCREENPLAY

JONATHAN REENA
ENFORCER FOR LOUIS MCCONNELL

RAFAEL SATO
BANKER

BENJAMIN
LOUIS MCCONNELL'S BUTLER

TYLER GEMMEL
ASSOCIATE OF LOUIS MCCONNELL

LORNE MADDOX
ASSOCIATE OF TYLER GEMMEL

FERDINAND 'HARIBON' GUINTO
PHILIPPINE ENTREPRENEUR

DATU
DRIVER HARIBON GUINTO

RIZAL
EMPLOYEE HARIBON GUINTO

JOSELITO
EMPLOYEE HARIBON GUINTO

CONSUELA RAMON
HARIBON'S 'YA-YA'

STEFAN DE TURRIS
RETIRED FILM BONDER AND ART COLLECTOR,
RECIPIENT SCREENPLAY

ROBIN VALLINGS
DE TURRIS FAMILY LAWYER

NU-WA DE TURRIS
WIFE STEFAN DE TURRIS, MOTHER OF MAKO

GILES
CHAUFFEUR STEFAN DE TURRIS

MARY
HEAD NURSE STEFAN DE TURRIS

 **PROLOGUE**

NOVEMBER 1944

Major Ito Okobudo reminded himself that when the time came, he should put his fingers in his ears. It was not to block out the screams of the dying men, which was a sound he was well used to, but rather to protect his eardrums from the staccato crack of machine-gun fire as it ricocheted and echoed off the unforgiving stone walls. In such a confined space he was pretty certain it would damage his hearing.

He looked disdainfully at the assembled crowd. All he had to do was nod. The six guards behind him would snap back the tarpaulin covering the tripod mounted machine gun and the carnage would begin.

"Congratulations to you all," the Major beamed, immaculately attired in his formal dress uniform, his swagger stick in his leather gloved hand, his close-cropped hair already dripping with sweat.

Three hundred and seventy haggard faces gazed blankly back at him; a labor force mainly drawn from Australian, American and British prisoners of war. The majority did not understand Japanese and those that did gave scant regard to the thanks. As if there had been any choice?

"We are all gathered here today as a final mark of respect to the completion of our work; forever a testament to Japanese dedication and skill…."

Next to the POWs the Japanese engineers repeatedly bowed, bobbing as if ducking for apples while murmuring gratitude for the praise being bestowed upon them by the Major.

The work had been carried out for General Tomoyuki Yamashita; a man with a reputation for savage efficiency and no tolerance for disobedience or disloyalty. A man who had to be shown respect.

The only way now to enter or exit the cave was to be lowered on a wooden gantry via the airshaft over 100 ft above them. A hole had been cut into the cavern ceiling and opened out at the crown of the great rock. The platform, winched down manually by four men on the surface, could take 25 people at a time. It had taken nearly an hour to assemble everyone, hence Major Okobudo's impatience.

Had the cave been empty the cold of the walls would have made the space cool, even chilly. But today the stench and sweat of the slaves added to the body heat of so many officials crammed into the confined space had turned the vaulted chamber into a hot, humid hell-hole.

"*Dai Tenoheika Banzai*. Long Live the Emperor," cried out the Major as he finished his speech. It was 11:57 AM.

The assembled engineers toasted the Emperor's health with a few drops of sake that the guards had carried in their backpacks especially for this occasion. The exhausted prisoners, not understanding, simply shuffled their feet.

Major Okobudo's orders had been clear. Assemble all those involved. At midday precisely, all were to die and their souls to forever stand guard over the empty cave.

The thin Major stood below the shaft; at his feet were a wooden case of artillery shells and a tin box. Inside the box was the serene smiling face of a stone Buddha and a roll of parchment. These items were coming with him; his passport to freedom. He looked down at his watch. It was only moments until midday. Suddenly there was a noise from above and all eyes swiveled upward. The gantry was slowly descending. Although the Major was indeed going to step onto it to leave, he had not commanded it to come down yet. Furious, he turned around, ready to order the immediate execution of whomever had dared not wait for his order. A solitary figure stood on the platform. The Major recognized him instantly.

Sixty-year-old General Yamashita was a short compact man, bull-necked with a closely shaved head. He was wearing a simple khaki uniform but on his feet were black riding boots set off with solid gold spurs. He would present them a few years later as a gift to his American defense attorney after being sentenced to death for war crimes…. and would take his secrets to the grave.

The General raised his arm and the platform halted forty feet above those assembled. He looked down on the crowd, his left arm still raised. After a short pause he gently waved as if giving a sort of benediction, his cold gaze finally resting on Major Okobudo.

In a moment of terror, the Major realized it was a sign of farewell. The General's order was going to be carried out to the letter. Everyone involved must die. The Major watched the platform slowly rise, and a familiar figure reached out to help the General step off the platform and hand him a gas mask.

"Tan," whispered the Major incredulously, recognizing his own bodyguard, someone he had believed utterly loyal to him.

Tan heaved over the parapet the dead bodies of the four guards Major Okobudo had left on the surface to operate the winch and take him safely away once the shooting had started.

Moments later cyanide canisters rained down. The General's own hand-picked men peered down through their gas masks at the panicked workers, now screaming in terror.

Major Ito Okobudo fell to his knees in despair and saw the large stone Buddha head. In the commotion it had been kicked over by one of the soldiers desperate to escape his fate. It had rolled out of the box and the stone ringlets glowed in the disappearing crescent of light from above, as the large rock rolled into place with a final crash, obliterating the sunshine like an eclipse. Ignoring the panic-stricken cries and writhing of those around him, the Major grasped the stone bust tightly for a moment, trying somehow to hold onto it and his life. His hand twitched and fell to the floor. Silence returned to the cave once more.

Days later a cluster of black and purple flowers began to grow outside the cave walls; on the other side rotted the bodies of the dead.

PART 1
THE SCREENPLAY

 # CHAPTER 1

VENICE BEACH, LOS ANGELES

PRESENT DAY

The End

© Sam Wood 2020

Sam cradled his newly completed screenplay in both hands, savoring the moment. *FALL OUT* was a hit waiting in the wings, and he knew it. A script about greed, a secret fortune, broken friendships, betrayal, and murder. But success would come later. First, it was going to be read by a specific target audience. Who would realize that *FALL OUT* was a road map to their past? Would the guilty see the clues and be flushed out?

Despite all his years in LA, Sam still had the weather-beaten face of a man born and raised in the Australian outback. He looked down at five freshly bound copies laid out on the desk in front of him, each with the name of a recipient in bold type at the top and a quote from French philosopher Honoré de Balzac directly beneath.

He thought for a moment, smiled wickedly then picked up the phone. He was disappointed when he had to settle for leaving a voice message. "Bet that comes as a bolt out of the blue. Well my old mate, the game is up."

Whistling softly, still savoring the drama he was setting in motion, he placed each screenplay inside its own manila envelope and attached the address labels.

The remains of a Bundaberg Rum and Coke gently fizzed in

a silver pint mug next to his laptop. Although it was only 11:00 AM, he had been writing all night and a healthy slug of booze had always oiled his creative gears. Sam took a last mouthful to polish it off, then sunk back in his chair, the heels of his palms rubbing his tired eyes.

Getting up slowly and gathering the five scripts, he ambled out of the sparsely furnished room that he used as an office and went downstairs.

Apart from a cleaning lady, who ghosted in and out three times a week and tried to avoid her employer when he was working, he lived alone. His ex-wife, Jax, now lived happily up the coast in the rain of Seattle.

Sam pulled back the glass door to his deck. A Frisbee arced above his view of Venice Beach and he breathed in the aroma of Jody Maroni's Sausage Kingdom a few yards away. That smell pulled him back to meat pies and the girls at Bondi Beach when he was a young struggling writer in Sydney.

It's not the girls you nailed that matter, he thought to himself, it's the ones that got away that haunt you forever....

"Brunch and a delivery service for these," he murmured breaking the memories and venturing out onto the boardwalk.

A few miles away the assassin pedaled his bike down the ribbon of concrete locals called 'The Strand'. It snaked for 22 miles along the shoreline from Pacific Palisades, through Venice Beach, continuing all the way along the coast past Los Angeles International Airport to the Redondo Beach Pier. Dusted by sand, this ribbon of concrete hugged the shore and was *the* place to skateboard, rollerblade, jog or cycle as well as show off your torso. The only real race was how quickly you could pick up a fellow rider or runner.

He was Asian, slightly built, his well-toned body weighing less than 150 pounds and barely 5'4" tall. He was zipped into black

Lycra cycle clothing, wearing full rather than open fingered gloves and wrap-around dark sunglasses. With an iPhone clipped to his belt and earphones screwed in under his helmet, he looked just like any one of the riders that crisscrossed the city. Despite being superbly fit, he was in his late sixties, and no one would ever consider him life threatening. That was why he was so good. His targets never expected such a small man to be so lethal.

He was heading for the white three-story house on the shoreline at the far end of Venice Beach, which was rumored to have once belonged to Dudley Moore. The only thing he cared about was being the last visitor to its current owner.

Twenty minutes after leaving the house, five envelopes safely in the pouches of the local delivery service, Sam was back. He unlocked the sliding glass door, ketchup oozing from the hotdog he had picked up on the way home.

Wiping his hands on the paper napkin that came with his breakfast, Sam approached the Ken Done painting of a shoal of brightly colored fish that hung on his living room wall. He pulled it away to reveal a wall safe. Quickly turning the combination lock, he swung the door open.

He pulled out the bank statement he had received a few months earlier showing a credit in his Santa Monica bank account of $300,000. That final revelation a few weeks later had lit his creative fuse. The *bang*! was ***FALL OUT***.

He stared at the statement.

"Twenty years. You bastards."

The cyclist reached into his backpack for a small double-jointed wooden-handled knife. With a flick of his wrist, a thin stiletto blade appeared. He quickly gashed his forearm. Impressive to look at, but no serious bleeding. Nevertheless, to minimize the chance of leaving behind any blood droplets, he pulled out an aerosol can of 'liquid skin' and sprayed it over the wound, sealing the cut with a transparent film. He calmly rolled his wrist once more, the blade disappearing into its handle as he returned it to his backpack. He stamped on and buckled the front wheel of his bike, then threw his cell phone to the ground, shattering its screen. He pulled the bicycle pump from its cradle below his seat and stuffed it in his bag, then walked towards a bright yellow front door.

Sam's mind wandered back to his arrival in Hollywood with a manuscript for a historical thriller in hand. It got him an agent, Louis McConnell, but no publishing deal. Louis had, however, quickly secured Sam his first commission, a script for a low budget movie for a young producer in the UK named Marcus Riley.

Making that film had been good fun, so Sam had been thrilled to get a call a few years later from Louis, asking if he wanted to work with Marcus again on a movie to be shot in the jungles of the Philippines.

THE LAST COMPANY would be forever known as the 'movie that never was' because shooting ended abruptly halfway through. The name was still whispered in the canyons and corridors of Hollywood; like a ghost, it had haunted Sam's career and those of most everyone involved.

Sam now knew why **THE LAST COMPANY** had never been finished. They had stopped shooting for a reason. Part of a plan; cold and calculated. He had even vented at one of those he thought involved.

He was startled by the buzzing of his front door intercom.

"Wrong house, mate. Didn't order a courier," boomed the Aussie voice through the speaker while Sam inspected the image on the video screen.

"Not a delivery sir. Just wiped out after hitting something in the road. Right outside your house. I'm sorry to trouble you, but I need some help." The cyclist held his broken phone in front of the video camera. The gash in his forearm could clearly be seen. "Busted my phone, gashed my arm, bike wheel buckled. Can I just make a quick call?" He paused and then flashed a smile. "Even though I tripped over something by your house, I promise I won't sue."

"Smart-arse," smiled Sam and buzzed him in.

The cyclist entered the hall as Sam came towards him.

"Can I use your bathroom first? Clean this cut?"

Sam hesitated.

"I always carry Band-Aids in here." The cyclist patted his backpack. "Don't want to leave any blood on your floor".

"Sure." The writer pointed at a door to the cyclist's left, ten feet from the entrance.

"When you're done, come on through to the living room. Might as well have a beer, no more pedaling for you today. And help yourself to the phone."

Fool, thought the cyclist.

Sam was never on alert. At well over 6 feet 6 inches tall, not much scared him. They had last met years ago, but with the wrap-around glasses, the small man was confident he would not be recognized…. not in time anyway.

The cyclist slipped into the bathroom. He quickly opened the bag and pulled out a large Band-Aid and covered the cut. He carefully put the two protective wings that covered the sticky underside of the dressing back into the bag.

Next he pulled out the bicycle pump and a small aluminum thermos from the backpack. The cyclist unscrewed the top of the flask and upended the tube. A cloudy white cylinder about four inches long and an inch across slid out. There was a band of tape at the top and the bottom with smoke curling around the canister like a ghostly snake.

He flicked open his knife and slid the thin blade along one side of the cylinder. It was two halves of dry ice, held together by the tape. Opening the cylinder revealed a hollow cradle in which lay a small black-jacketed bullet. The bullet itself was just a frozen mixture of water and sugar. The dissolved sugar in the ice gave the projectile density and mass.

Next he picked up the pump. Pulling the handle up with a soft snick revealed a small chamber into which he expertly dropped the bullet. Pushing the top of the cylinder forward it clicked shut, dropping a small trigger at the same time. The gun crafted in his workshop was made from titanium, contained an air pressure of 3000 pounds per square inch, firing at over 1300 feet per second or twice that of a normal .22 air rifle. To prevent the bullet from melting from barrel friction, it was encased in a black nylon sabot. Checking again there was no evidence of blood from his wound, he left the bathroom and walked quickly and purposefully into the living room.

Sam turned to greet him and smiled. He glanced quizzically at the pump then back to the cyclist. As a look of recognition flashed over Sam's face, the cyclist fired. With a sharp clap, the bullet tore into the left ventricle of Sam's heart, dropping the big man in an instant.

The cyclist unclipped the iPhone from his belt and quickly plugged it into Sam's music system via a cable from his bag. He reached up to the painting on the wall and pulled it back to reveal the wall safe. The information from his employer had been correct.

Flipping the two earphones from the iPhone inside out, he attached what were really two microphones inside suction cups to the front of the safe and turned on the music system. As he slowly rotated the combination dial, the headset relayed the sounds of the tumblers falling into place through the massive speakers. The safe swung open in moments. He pulled the contents out and shoved them into his bag.

Stepping over Sam's body, he stopped and bent down to check that there was no pulse. Satisfied, the cyclist grabbed Sam's watch, wallet and some cash, tossing them in the bag along with the black nylon sabot that had just moments ago housed the lethal bullet. He took out his blade and carefully eased it into Sam's bullet wound. Sharply pushing it in the last inch, he twisted the blade and removed the remnants of the bullet, leaving what would appear as just a major stab wound. Standing up he purposely knocked over some furniture in the living room, disconnected the iPhone and its attachments and slid open the veranda door a fraction. Drawing out the knife once more, he inserted the blade into the door's lock and with a twist broke the barrel inside. Looking around for anything else of value a thief would take, he picked up Sam's laptop and the silver mug, also shoving them into the backpack. Evidence of a brief struggle, but nothing too dramatic.

The cyclist exited the house and lifted up the damaged bike. He carried it down Speedway and rounded the corner onto Pacific Avenue where the black Range Rover he had left there earlier was still parked. He slung the bike into the back.

He quickly drove down Pacific Avenue towards Quarterdeck Street, where he could clearly see the Grand Canal. Stopping the car, he slipped two diver's weights into the brightly colored bag, tucked it into a slightly larger grey and green camouflage duffle bag. He never even considered keeping the cash. Money was not what drove him. Quickly checking that no one was watching, his arm arced as he lobbed the bag containing the bank statement, cash, valuables and the laptop far out into the water. As it sank, the camouflaged bag faded from view long before it reached the bottom. He was confident it would stay buried for eternity in the silt of the canal.

He got back in the car and disappeared into the warren of streets of Venice Beach.

 **CHAPTER 2**

HOLLYWOOD

EARLIER, SAME DAY

"So, are you going to pull the trigger?" Marcus Riley asked.

His throat was dry and his heart was beating so hard he could feel it and was sure the others would. The two men looked at him impassively.

"Are you going to answer that?" one asked, staring at him seemingly annoyed.

Marcus realized his cell phone was vibrating loudly, grimaced, apologized, and let the call go to voicemail.

"You first," Marcus said as calmly as possible. "Is the movie green lit; are we a go?"

Marcus was in the President's office of a major Hollywood studio, far from home in London. A few months ago he had mortgaged everything to buy the film rights to a new trilogy that had surpassed the success of *The Girl with the Dragon Tattoo* series. The books had been released anonymously on the internet. Against fierce competition from the major studios, he'd won the bidding war. Then disaster struck. The author was outed as a pedophile, and the books went from red hot to radioactive. One by one the studios that had originally competed with him, and in true Hollywood style of compromise had then seemed eager to be his partner, had walked away. This meeting was his last throw of the dice.

"Marcus. As you know it's a committee decision, but I wanted to tell you myself. I'm afraid it's a pass."

Marcus desperately tried not to show this news was a body blow.

"The project is just not right for us now," the President continued with genuine compassion in his voice.

"Looks like we missed a bullet," added the junior executive wearing a purse-string smile. The meeting was over.

Marcus's face was expressionless as he left the room, desperate to get out of there and be alone but the younger man followed him to the elevator. When the doors opened, he looked at Marcus and murmured dripping with condescension, "Fingers burnt, huh, playing with the big boys? You should have stayed on your side of the pond making Godfather knock-offs with a cockney accent." The man extended his hand towards Marcus.

Straightening up to his full height, Marcus looked down at the outstretched hand. "Do you validate?" he asked dropping his parking ticket into it.

As Marcus drove his cheap rental out through the wrought iron studio gates, he went over his options. There were few. The best seemed to be to get blind drunk. He was teetering at the tipping point; nearly broke, his judgement was suspect, and he'd just been dismissed by the entire Hollywood system. He pulled into a liquor store parking lot.

"A bottle of Chivas Legend Special Reserve," he said, pointing at the most expensive whiskey in the shop.

"Celebrating?" the girl smiled.

"Death of my career," replied Marcus. "Just want to give it a good send-off."

Two hours later he collapsed fully clothed onto the thin mattress of the bed of his motel room.

It was dark when he woke up with a hangover so bad his hair hurt. He sat up checked his tousled brown locks in the mirror and pulled his long fingers down the sides of his cheeks. He stuck out his tongue and pulled down his eyelids, the green iris flecked with brown, but the whites of his eyes were bloodshot. Not a good look at twenty. Bad in your forties.

"Great career farewell," he murmured.

He gulped down a glass of water and four Tylenol and picked up the phone to check his emails. A voicemail icon flashed reminding him of the badly timed call from that morning. He dialed to retrieve the message.

"Hi Marcus, Sam Wood here. Tough out here, eh? They tell me you're not staying quite at five-star hotels these days," said the broad Australian accent. "So, I am sending you my latest script… see what you think… if it rings any bells, jogs any memories. Oh, and Balzac was right."

Sam Wood. Marcus was in shock. At the very moment his world was collapsing around him, one of the most successful writers in Hollywood had sent him a screenplay. Sam was the last person on earth Marcus expected to hear from, let alone receive a script. Twenty years ago, he and Sam had been almost brothers, but on a typhoon-lashed movie set, their bond had been broken by death and violence. They had not spoken since.

He stood stock still for a moment trying to absorb the enormity of that call. A beat, then he rushed down the thinly carpeted hallway to the reception desk.

"You have anything for me?" he panted as he reached the reception desk.

The young girl on duty looked up startled by the tall disheveled Englishman.

"I'm sorry. No manners," Marcus took a deep breath. "Please, did anything come for me by courier today, while I was…out?"

She handed over a manila envelope. "I knocked on your room, but you were…no answer…," she trailed off as Marcus gave her his last twenty dollar bill as a tip and ran back up the corridor.

Shutting the door, Marcus ripped open the envelope. Inside was a screenplay, titled **FALL OUT**, with a handwritten note attached.

Dear Marcus,

THE SECRET OF A GREAT SUCCESS FOR WHICH YOU ARE AT A LOSS TO ACCOUNT IS A CRIME THAT HAS NEVER BEEN FOUND OUT, BECAUSE IT WAS PROPERLY EXECUTED.
—Honoré de Balzac

You've got an eighteen-month free option.

Sam

An hour later and with shaking hands, Marcus put down the screenplay. His body was pumping pure adrenaline. **FALL OUT** was far and away the best thing the Australian had ever written. A gripping plot with box office smash written all over it. It was exactly what Marcus needed.

"Ha-le-goddamn-lujah," he breathed in relief. He didn't care why Sam had sent him the script. He just knew that this was a lifeline, and he was grabbing it with both hands and his teeth, if necessary. He looked at his watch. It was nearly midnight.

"Too bad it's late," he muttered as he punched in the number listed on the note. Nothing.

Despite the hour, he picked up his car keys and headed for Venice Beach.

 # CHAPTER 3

SANTA MONICA, CALIFORNIA

It was raining hard and the worn-out wiper blades on Marcus' car just smeared the screen rather than cleared it as he headed towards Sam's house.

Marcus barely noticed. He was deep in thought, going over and over various permutations of what he could say to show he wasn't desperate, but, of course, he was. In his heart he just hoped Sam had reached out to his former friend in the Englishman's hour of need; willing to build a bridge over the torrent of resentment from the past.

He pulled up across the street from the house he had once visited so often. A dim light came from downstairs. He rang the bell. No reply. He rang it again.

"Sam, it's Marcus," he shouted, banging on the door. He noticed a neighbor's blind twitch. Not deterred he yelled out "A drink, at least?" Nothing. He was about to leave but stopped. He remembered from drunken nights together that Sam liked sitting out on the deck. He went around the back and saw the verandah door open, so he clambered over the balustrade and wandered in.

Marcus froze. The big man was lying on the floor, a crimson ring of half dried blood under his chest. He looked around the silent room. The only light was above the Ken Done painting, which tilted away from the wall revealing a safe.

Marcus's immediate reaction was to call the police, and he reached for his cell phone. But at that moment he saw a piece of paper on the floor beneath the desk with his name on it. Puzzled, he reached down. It was a list of names and addresses in Sam's writing. Along with his name were the names of *Cara Baines, Stefan de Turris, Robert Kelso, and Louis McConnell.* A shudder. Had Sam sent the script to all of them?

Before Marcus could decide what to do next, there was a screech of tires and red, blue, and white lights flickered outside. A knock at the door.

"Mr. Wood? LAPD. Are you OK, sir? We got a call…." Every sense of self-preservation was screaming at Marcus to leave, but he hesitated. He owed his friend and did not want to desert him. However explaining to the cops about why he was here, and the screenplay was going to be messy.

Flashlights waved like light sabers, spearing through a window into the room. A moment later the door crashed open and two policemen ran in.

"Freeze," yelled one. "Hit the deck, now."

As Marcus kneeled down to do exactly as he was told, he slipped the scrunched up scrap of paper into his mouth and swallowed it. Moments later a knee thudded into the small of his back and handcuffs clamped over his wrists.

The next morning, the local news on KTLA 5 ran with the story of the death of a successful writer following what appeared to be a struggle with an intruder during a break-in. A suspect was in custody. Charges seemed imminent.

 # CHAPTER 4

SANTA MONICA POLICE STATION, CALIFORNIA

All Marcus could think about was Sam and his screenplay.

"So, Mr. Riley, let's go over this one more time, shall we?"

As he repeated his version of events, Marcus's mind was working on why Sam had chosen to send him the script. And why had he sent it to the others? Would they say anything to the police or stay quiet? The five of them shared a dark history, and Marcus did not want to be hooked back to a cold case murder enquiry. He needed to speak to the others soon.

He focused on the cop in front of him.

"We were old buddies in the past. He left me a voice message."

"Which you deleted?"

"Yea, why save it, Detective McNeile? He asked me over for a drink …"

"At midnight?"

"Sam was Australian. If you were standing up, it was time to have a drink. Be logical. If I had anything to hide, I would have run," he added.

Marcus had been at the station for over 18 hours. All he wanted was to get out of that interview room and into a shower. He thought about his options; maybe protesting, 'You can't hold me. I know my rights', though in his experience when anyone said that, they invariably didn't. Demanding a lawyer may look good in the movies, but in real life it just pissed cops off and made him look guilty. They had a million ways to make life more uncomfortable. Better to wait.

Eventually a uniformed cop came into the interview room and whispered something to the detective.

"Seems Mr. Wood had been dead for a number of hours before you got there," sighed the Detective. "Your hotel confirmed that at the time of his death you were out cold in your room. Pains me to say it Mr. Riley but you're free to go… but do not leave the city without telling me."

The police were satisfied Sam's death was a result of him surprising a burglar during a break-in. Now they were just tying up loose ends before dumping the case on the pile of unsolved break-ins.

The first thing Marcus did on returning to the hotel was to thank the woman behind the desk for providing the alibi.

"And that package, just another script rejection I'm afraid," he added in case the police dug any deeper.

He needed to contact Sam's widow, Jax. It was going to be a very hard call.

She eventually picked up the phone. The grief. The anger. The recriminations. Eventually the flow subsided.

"Marcus, how did we all lose touch? You know, there was a time when I considered you one of my dearest friends. Then that disaster in the Philippines" she said.

"THE LAST COMPANY left us all with scars, Jax."

"It may have scarred you, but it killed what I loved in Sam. He turned bitter. Why did you let it happen, to him, to us? Oh God, and poor Bill?" her voice drifting off without finishing her thought.

That name hit Marcus hard.

"I was the one who was angry. With Sam…with you. When the marriage collapsed and I left him and came to Seattle, I would have decked you if you had walked through the door in the first year. Deep down, I wanted my old life back…wanted the old Sam back."

"And now?" he asked.

"I'm at peace here, not some coke-crazed hard-ass, living the LA lifestyle. But that won't help Sam, will it? He's gone…a stupid, pointless ending."

There was a beat as she pulled away from the past. "Now you want me to let you try and make this script he sent you…on some whim?? Why, what's the point, Marcus?"

"Because it's damn good. You'll be so proud of him."

"You sure this is what Sam wanted" Jax queried?

"I promise, I'll do what he wanted."

"Let's hope so," she said. "The funeral is next Wednesday. See you there."

Marcus felt at once both elated and guilty. He did, however, have what he wanted. He was going to see it through.

He had managed to track down the address of Cara Baines only to discover she was away on vacation. He had googled Stefan de Turris, who seemed to have retired and still lived in London. That left Robert Kelso and Louis McConnell. They both had good reason to hate him.

 # CHAPTER 5

TOPANGA CANYON, LOS ANGELES

Director Robert Kelso had spent years determinedly navigating his directing career from an 'about to be' to a 'whatever happened to'? An Emmy and a Golden Globe award two decades old gathered dust in an alcove, which was stacked with scripts and treatments long ignored.

Back in the day Kelso had been on the cusp of success. He had followed up a hugely successful TV mini-series with a commercial and hit movie. He was the creator and director of the first in a cycle of teen slasher horror movies called **POLE-AXED**, following trends set by Freddy in *A Nightmare on Elm Street* and Jason with his hockey mask in *Halloween*; but **POLE-AXED** had an eloquent and artistic flourish that put it above the rest of the genre.

He had unleashed a franchise that even now, without his involvement, was in production on movie sequel number 11. Each movie paid him a handsome royalty, in exchange, it seemed, for the sale of his creative soul.

After **POLE-AXED** became a box office smash, he was determined to make high quality drama and pick his way to an Oscar. Instead his career suddenly and spectacularly imploded with a movie called **THE LAST COMPANY**.

THE LAST COMPANY was a simple heist movie, albeit with a twist. Set in April 1975 the script began with the fall of Saigon and the image forever seared into America's collective memory of that last helicopter rising from the US Embassy rooftop. At the same moment, thieves were plundering the Embassy safe in a room below.

The idea was both shocking yet plausible. For years rumors had swirled that in excess of $75 million had gone missing during the final hours and chaos of the evacuation.

In the film the thieves are a stranded bunch of bad-assed US soldiers known as **THE LAST COMPANY**. After the robbery they flee for the Thai border, continually harried along the way by Viet Cong who know what they have stolen. With their numbers dwindling from casualties inflicted by their pursuers, the few survivors decide to bury the cash in a cave and retrieve it later. However, the heat and desperation of their plight starts to wear the men down. They fight among themselves as they dig in the cave. Eventually there is a sole survivor. All alone, he slowly goes mad and runs off screaming and naked to be swallowed up by the jungle. The audience is left with the tantalizing idea that the treasure is still out there awaiting discovery.

It should have been a box office and creative success. However, no audience ever saw the movie. The Executive Producer Louis McConnell was forced to call a halt more than midway through filming and Robert Kelso's career, like nearly all those associated with the movie, became toxic. Flops in Hollywood were common but failing to complete a movie was rarely forgiven.

It wasn't only that no one wanted to hire him, Robert stopped asking. He gave up. He descended into drugs and alcohol and stewed there a long time until he met Christo Murray in rehab. Christo, kind and beautiful, had been a member of the staff and now, he was Robert's companion and partner.

Although off drink and drugs, Robert lingered outside the movie world waiting for his creative flame to reignite. He and Christo retreated to Topanga Canyon in the hills northeast of Hollywood. The canyon suited him; a place rooted in the past, full of people reliving the sixties, most of whom were too young to have been a part of it, but too scared to live in the present.

It was midday. Robert was sitting under the large ceiling fan in his cluttered study, the double doors open to the garden. Barefoot, he had settled into the embrace of his black leather and wood framed chair, feet on the footstool.

Christo, stripped to the waist and squatting on his haunches, was glowering at some garden weeds. He had tended the vast garden for years, always taking it as a personal affront when something sprouted that was not on his green-fingered agenda.

"You want a Diet Coke?" he asked as he stood up. There was no answer.

Christo was used to one-way conversations with his lover, so did not bother to wait for a reply. He walked into the house through the open patio doors to the kitchen where he pulled two cans of soda out of the fridge.

He had occasionally glimpsed the sparkle and energy that had made Kelso a powerhouse director. He had found his vocation; to bring back the bloom in Robert Kelso. All that was needed now was a spark, a catalyst, a perfect script.

As he entered the study with their drinks, he saw the director reading, fully engrossed. Not unusual in itself except it was neither a book nor a newspaper, but a script. That was a first. A new shoot, in every sense of the word.

Without looking up or even acknowledging his partner, Robert lifted his index finger to his lips to signal 'silence' and turned another page. The cover of the screenplay read **FALL OUT**.

An hour later, Christo heard Robert pick up the phone.

"Louis, do you still represent Sam Wood…or should I say the estate…terrible way to die…well, if you don't who does? You need to read his last script. Got it a few days ago. Only just got around to reading it and…"

The voice on the other end cut Robert short.

"Oh…Oh, I see…." And with a slightly trembling hand, Robert hung up.

 # CHAPTER 6

BEL AIR, LOS ANGELES

Roneale, read the sign in elegant wrought iron lettering. The home in Bel Air looked too big for the plot of land it was built on, hemmed in by what was left of the garden. An endless number of extensions and add-ons had turned the mock French chateau into a mishmash, in which only one man and his staff rattled around.

The Asian cyclist was always puzzled by the rejection of land for interior space, for rooms no one would use instead of a garden and sky. The assassin tapped in the series of numbers on the security pad to activate the gates and entered the grounds.

Years ago, a realtor had told the prospective buyer, Louis McConnell, that the rumor was the house had been designed for Gloria Swanson as a gift from her lover Joe Kennedy.

The cachet of class and sophistication this brought had quickly tipped the balance, but the realtor failed to understand that it was not the name of Swanson and all she represented of 'old Hollywood' but the name of Joe Kennedy and his support of Irish heritage that had helped close the deal.

The rotund middle-aged man bought the house that day, deftly signing a check with his solid gold fountain pen. From that moment, agent turned businessman Louis McConnell owned a part of Hollywood history and more importantly in his mind, a connection to a great Irish patriot.

The cyclist dismounted from his bike, wheeled it to the side of the house and then approached the main section well out of the line of vision of the security cameras. He saw Louis McConnell through the conservatory glass. He was talking to someone.

The burly 65-year-old owner of the house looked pensive. A Monte Cristo No. 3 cigar was screwed into the corner of his mouth. McConnell paced the floor of the newly built conservatory, filled with Napoleonic furniture that he had bought in an attempt to gain ancestry. Louis turned to his guest who was sitting languidly on an ornate silk upholstered chair.

"So how about it?" he said with an attempt at a smile.

"Why that part of Asia?" replied his guest.

"It's wide open for us and production is on the up in that part of the world. It's a launch pad for the rest of Asia. Even better there's no competition, just one man, Haribon Guinto. We just need to persuade him to step aside." He paused. "Forcefully," he added. "A minor detail, like we've done elsewhere, Tyler."

"Louis, you were the first guy I met in this zoo of a town who never tried to sell me a script...but still let me fuck a bunch of starlets," said the man with a grin. "I liked that. You were right. Producing is for suckers. We started a real business and now we own just about every type of movie supply company in town, for chrissakes."

"All hidden behind a number of dummy corporations," added Louis to himself.

"Louis. We got it good. We control everything from lighting rigs to catering, crystal generators to transport. Even those mega trailers stars like to hang out in. We have this town locked up, and the Teamsters in our pocket."

"I've never steered you wrong," Louis smiled through a cloud of cigar smoke. "So, trust me on this one. It's a real opportunity. Cigar?"

Tyler shook his head. "Let it go, Louis. Another continent? I just don't see it for my guys, but I'll ask. While on the subject of trust though, a few of my colleagues are asking questions. The numbers seem to be getting light," he paused, "Do we need an audit?"

The emphasis on the last words made it clear what finding a shortfall would mean.

"Studio cutbacks. Movie production revenue will be down for a while," replied Louis reassuringly. "All the money is pouring into TV now and those fucking kids at Amazon, Netflix and Hulu. Even my A-listers are begging to do TV. For no real money."

"I don't see talent accepting austerity for long," said Tyler. "I gotta go. Need to check on a new string of polo ponies."

With that Tyler Gemmell rose from the chair, straightening his jacket and palming his straight brown hair. Although nearly the same age as Louis, physically Tyler was Louis' opposite. Suntanned and handsome, his tall, lean frame still hinted at the Golden Gloves champion boxer he'd once been.

In Louis' opinion Tyler's physique failed to compensate for clothes and shoes that displayed too many designer logos. No class. Louis smiled and shook Tyler's hand, hoping his utter contempt for him and his associates was well hidden. He bade his guest farewell as a formally attired butler escorted Tyler to the front door. Louis followed.

"Thanks Benjamin," smiled Tyler to the butler as he opened the door. "If you ever need a change of scenery....?"

"Trying to poach my staff? You haven't a hope. It's all about loyalty, isn't it, Benjamin?" The butler's face showed no reaction. Tyler shrugged and turned to walk down the drive.

"No car, Tyler?" observed Louis, "It's a long walk. Times must be hard."

"Just my arteries," replied Tyler. "It's called exercise, Louis." He glanced at his host's midriff. "You should try it. Anyway, before polo ponies, the Polo Lounge at the Beverly Hills Hotel and lunch with a hot little actress, beckoning; a client of yours actually," and with that he turned and sauntered down the drive, his casual gait concealing his conviction that Louis was stealing from him.

The cyclist slid quietly into the room.

"Good afternoon, Jonathan," Louis drew on the cigar and turned around exhaling a cloud of smoke. "That job out in Venice Beach. The cops still think it was a break in. The case will just rot on the pile of unsolved homicides." Louis expertly rolled the ash off his cigar. "For us however it is not case closed. Sam Wood's first mistake was to even go back…." He blew smoke at the ceiling as his sentence ended, his thoughts unfinished.

"His fatal one was threatening you on his return," Jonathan added quietly.

"Exactly. However, he even topped that when he scribbled out a screenplay based on what he had found. He sent one to Kelso and to me. That's a problem," he added firmly.

Jonathan gave him a quizzical look.

"And judging from a recent call requesting a meeting, I suspect he sent one to Marcus Riley as well." Louis paused and let that sink in.

"Go back home, do some digging. Discreetly. Just make sure whatever Sam Wood found out stays buried….

"And Haribon" Jonathan asked?

"Keep well clear of our dear, former partner. I am trying to get Tyler Gemmell to deal with that problem."

With a wave of his hand Louis dismissed Jonathan, sitting down at his desk to figure out his next task. How to ensure that a dead man's script would never see the light of day?

 # CHAPTER 7

BEL AIR, LOS ANGELES

Take-off was in three hours. Jonathan slipped on the overalls. Minutes later he left his apartment next to the garage and his personal workshop at *Roneale* en route to the private airport. He'd done this more than a few times. He'd be safe. No one would know he was going back.

As the cargo plane with its sunburst logo on the tail fin swung out across the dark Pacific towards his homeland, Jonathan buckled into the jump-seat and mentally drifted back to the days of his youth, Haribon Guinto, and Manila.

MANILA 1965

As a young scrawny kid, Jonathan had run with a dangerous crowd, all testosterone and hope. Always first with a blade and last with an apology, he became a feared member of the most respected gang in Manila. Their leader was Ferdinand Guinto, but everyone called him Haribon, the name of the huge eagle of the Philippines.

Jonathan was around eight years old when they first met. He had been slinking back home after an evening of petty larceny. A car radio here, a tourist's fat wallet there, whatever he could threaten and get away with.

He was already an expert at balisong, the lethal art of Filipino knife fighting using the fearsome weapon of the same name. Also known as butterfly knives, the handle was in fact made of two halves that folded over each side of the blade like a butterfly's wings yet could be opened in a blink by an expert flick of the wrist. He was thinking about treating himself to a new high-end version from one of the local craftsmen over by the Port.

Jonathan had rounded the corner to his home. At the end of a dusty street in the shanty *Quaipo* district of Manila, he could make out the figures of two disheveled older boys of about 15, sauntering away from his house. When they saw Jonathan approach the door, they grinned at each other. The uglier of the two had a toothpick clenched between his teeth.

"Don't worry, nothing worth stealing," he said, moving the pick to the corner of his mouth. "And that old woman was barely worth fucking," he added as Jonathan passed him.

Jonathan stopped.

"He's joking," said the other. "We never touched her."

"Not the point," murmured Jonathan.

In a flash, he turned on his heel and kicked the first boy square in the groin. Jonathan heard the rush of air sucked into the young man's lungs as the toothpick fell from his mouth. Even before the youth dropped wide-eyed to his knees with both hands cradling his crotch, he felt the sting of the blade slice through his cheek. A foot connected with his jaw, and then merciful blackness.

"Tell your friend I accept his apology," said Jonathan to the shocked accomplice.

It was an introduction the unconscious Torres and cool headed Haribon would never forget.

"Never confuse smallness with lack of guts," said Jonathan as he thrust out his tiny hand to Haribon.

"You wanna be a part of my crew?" the older boy asked, impressed at the little kid's retribution.

And so it had started; the two boys became inseparable. Haribon all ideas, Jonathan a silent enforcer. Torres just glowered.

Jonathan hated weakness. People mistook his small physical stature as a sign of it. Those who made that mistake and managed to live, had regrets as deep as their scars. Jonathan's size was made up for by his ruthless streak and a knife he unsheathed in the name of retribution and respect.

He never revealed his full name nor the names of his parents. He was just Jonathan. His passport said his last name was Reena, though he never used it. The name Reena, however, meant a lot to him.

'Aunty' Juanita Reena had brought him up in a tiny house in Manila. Their only company was a mongrel named Fritas. The dog was small but took no shit from hounds three times his size. He was Jonathan's first real friend and taught the boy all about being the 'bite-you-first' underdog.

Reena was widowed at 30 and unlike her sister who had escaped to Los Angeles with her husband, was barren to boot. Deciding she was on the shelf, she was happy to play mother to this abandoned kid, her "nephew." He wasn't even pure Filipino, but rather mestizo – half Japanese, half Filipino.

The years unwound; Haribon, Torres, and Jonathan running their crew until one day Haribon got a short prison sentence for handling stolen goods. Having no respect for Torres who stepped up in Haribon's absence, Jonathan left and found a job at Manila International Airport in the cargo department near the Villamor Military Airbase.

He learned a lot about cargo and the routine and rules of freight transportation. He earned a good living, selling off the contents of 'damaged' cargo containers, and managed to use the money to provide some comforts for Aunty Reena.

Just as everything seemed to be going Jonathan's way, Reena was diagnosed with ovarian cancer. She refused medical support, rather putting her faith in God and the statue of the Black Nazarene at the church in Quaipo. It was to no avail. Jonathan buried her a week before his 17th birthday along with any trust in religion or salvation.

The young man had connections in the minor underworld that permeated the streets of Manila and once again he crossed paths with Haribon. Freshly released from prison, Haribon had managed to set up a small trucking business. With Jonathan at work in air cargo, it was a match made in heaven.

Haribon delivered shipments from the air cargo terminal to destinations in Manila and further out into the country. The information Jonathan gave him about what was in the shipments was invaluable. Haribon always assured him that no driver was ever hurt when asked to hand over some, if not all of the contents of his truck. Jonathan was amused by this. He did not care whether anyone was hurt or not. If they showed no respect, they took the consequences as far as he was concerned.

In 1976 everything changed. A massive operation was being undertaken by a group of Americans in the Philippines. The amount of equipment they ordered, which arrived on a weekly basis, was simply staggering. Haribon wanted in but did not want to steal any of it. He believed there was more of an opportunity in actually delivering a safe and reliable service than in ripping these people off.

That's when he and Torres finally fell out. Torres wanted to steal as much as he could from the *Kanos*.

On a storm drenched night, Torres and a splinter group decided to hijack a legitimate delivery being made by Haribon. Having eyes and ears everywhere, Haribon got wind of the plot and asked Jonathan to come along for the ride. It was the second and last time Torres would cross Jonathan. The truck was laden with electrical equipment from Los Angeles as well as pasta, cheeses, wine, and even cigarettes from Italy, all of which Torres knew would disappear like spit in the rain in the huge black market of Manila. The delivery was going to the home of the head of the huge operation, who had taken up residence in *Dasmarinas*, the Beverly Hills of Manila.

As they drove along from the airport into town, a brightly decorated *Jeepney*, usually the poor man's bus, swerved past them. It had four scowling men in the back and Torres at the wheel. They forced Haribon's truck into a deserted alley.

"*Hinto...* stop," cried Torres, the scar on his face clearly visible in the moonlight. The air was humid, the rain had stopped. Not even the clouds could maintain much energy in the hot damp air.

Reluctantly Haribon killed the motor. He leaned out the window and watched the men unwind themselves from inside the Jeepney. One carried a crowbar, one a baseball bat, two had knives, and none a friendly face.

"You don't want to do this," Haribon warned Torres.

Two of the men walked through the puddles and, using the crowbar, easily snapped off the padlock securing the shuttered cargo door to the platform at the base of the truck.

Haribon looked up to the sky. He appeared to be checking for rain, but in fact was asking the Divine for forgiveness. Unlike Jonathan, he had a conscience and still believed in God.

"I removed you once before," said Torres, "thought that a spell in prison might toughen you up. The police even gave me a reward for ratting you out. You're a cute businessman, Haribon, the trucking business is clever .... if you exploit it. Fuck these *Kanos*," he sneered. "Out of respect, once we have checked out the delivery, you can take the *Jeepney*. I suggest you keep driving till you are far away in the islands to the west. And never, ever come back," Torres warned menacingly.

With that Torres took a baseball bat from behind his back and swung it down on Haribon's forearm that had been resting on the open window frame. There was a loud crack as the bone broke.

"That is, if you can drive with one arm. Out," whispered Torres, with a flick of the head.

Haribon slowly got down from the truck, staring at the men without flinching. He was aware of the shutter slowly opening at the back of his van. Suddenly, he made a movement as if bunching himself up to run at his attackers. As he intended, their eyes quickly focused on him.

Jonathan was out of the van before the steel-slatted door had rolled even halfway up. With the characteristic *click-clack* the blades of the two balisongs unsheathed like a deadly fan in each of Jonathan's hands.

He spun on his heel extending his left arm while in a crouching position. The first man dropped to his knees watching his intestines fall out through the gash in his stomach. Still spinning like a ballet dancer, Jonathan leapt up and severed the carotid artery of the second man. It happened so fast that Torres had only realized something was wrong as the arterial spray of blood from the second victim pattered onto his face and clothes. Even then Torres looked up thinking it had started to rain, before he noticed that the spots on his shirt were dark.

"Blood in the moonlight," said Haribon. "Black as death."

Torres turned as he saw the third man have his hamstring tendon severed as Jonathan executed a perfect forward roll. Before the stunned victim even felt the pain in his buckling ankle, another blade entered his back and he was dead before his jaw broke on hitting the asphalt.

Jonathan stood up and performed two backhanded 'helicopter' movements, spinning the blades and the two sides of the handle around each hand, like some deadly cheerleader's baton.

The action was so mesmerizing that, rather than run, the fourth man just stared in amazement. Jonathan lunged forward and the thug crumpled to the ground, the knife having pierced his chest just below the sternum, severing his aorta.

He then turned to Torres, beckoning him to try and take him on. Torres roared as he lifted the bat and charged. Jonathan calmly let him make his run. At the last second both of his arms flashed in front of Torres' face and the next moment the man was blind.

"I am the last thing you will ever see," jeered Jonathan barely audible over the blind man's cries of agony. "I hope you live years to remember it."

He picked up the bat as a trophy and memento, handing it to Haribon. Haribon glanced around at the dead bodies and then at the stumbling Torres, still screaming in pain. He gave a single nod to Jonathan.

"We're done here."

The big man heaved himself into the front of the truck, cradling his arm and fashioning a makeshift sling from his shirt. Jonathan walked around to the rear and slowly pulled the shutter down. They set off to make the delivery; Jonathan in his new post as Haribon's permanent enforcer and right-hand man.

They left Torres stumbling in his world of darkness and pain that would end five months later in a pauper's grave.

The memory of Torres always made Jonathan smile. That stupid act of treachery had allowed Haribon to make his delivery and demonstrate his honesty. Sure enough Haribon's legitimate business grew and the deliveries increased until that fateful day when Haribon met Louis McConnell and Stefan de Turris. That's when all of their fortunes changed forever....

The wheels touched down in the Philippines and Jonathan gathered his thoughts to the task at hand, his business for Mr. Louis.

He was glad he didn't have to clear customs through Manila's Ninoy Aquino airport. This way was much better. Mr. Louis had arranged it for him so often in the past.

He checked in his pocket for his balisong. The plane landed. Just like clockwork. In a moment Jonathan was gone.

CHAPTER 8

BEVERLY HILLS, LOS ANGELES

Marcus had been rebuffed on his first call but eventually Louis McConnell had agreed to see him.

"My office is 245 North Beverly Drive, same building as MGM. Be there at 2:30 Wednesday. I can spare twenty minutes."

Marcus had not mentioned Sam, nor the screenplay; neither had McConnell.

The carpet in the McConnell Talent Agency was so thick that footfalls sounded like crushing velvet. A bronze statue of a cowboy on a bucking bronco decorated the foyer, along with photos of Louis' most famous clients. Marcus announced himself at exactly 2:30 to an uptight PA. She pointed at a seat. He had to wait. It was typical Hollywood.

Marcus had left school at 17 with top grades and several universities offering places. He declined them all and to the consternation of his parents declared he had secured a job in a UK advertising production company as a runner, a fancy name for a young person who is required to run and fetch anything. From there he moved into feature film, steadily working his way up.

After a few years he decided he had learned enough about both the physical aspects of production and financing to try to go it alone. He managed to raise enough money to buy the option on a book about a London based gangster. The money was nonrefundable if he couldn't put together the necessary financing for the movie in the agreed upon limited time frame. He was right to have been nervous; none of the UK agents were prepared to risk their client's reputation writing a script for an unknown young producer—especially at the very low fee Marcus was offering.

With time running out and in desperation, he reached out to an agent in Los Angeles whom he had dealt with in the past whilst trying to hire one of his clients.

"I may just have someone, Australian" said the agent, Louis McConnell. I've just taken him on after I read a book he wrote. I understand he also writes scripts. I suggest you get together. If it works, I'm Co-Executive Producer. I'm not putting up cash…but my name will get you money."

That was the beginning of Sam and Marcus' friendship. Authors don't normally make good screenwriters, but Sam was an exception. The script he delivered was fast paced with tight, witty dialogue interspersed with exciting action sequences. It was the real reason Marcus managed to raise the money to make the film. Sam Wood was a rare talent.

The movie did well at the box office, establishing Marcus' credentials as a producer of low-budget action films and Sam as a writer to watch. Marcus and Sam had become close friends during that production, talking late into many nights about movies as well as sharing a love of fast cars and slow meals.

Over the next few years Sam sent Marcus ideas, treatments, even full scripts as well as the manuscript of the book that he had sent to McConnell. Marcus was toiling away financing more low-budget gangster movies in London as Sam's career moved up several gears in Los Angeles. He was thrilled for Sam's success but sadly thought they would never get to work together again. Then one day they both got a call from McConnell.

"I've recommended you and Sam Wood for a job," the agent said. "Vietnam movie based on a story idea I developed. Sam will write the screenplay. Director is Robert Kelso. Shoot in the Philippines. Decent budget and lead this time. Big action. Bill

Baines is stunt coordinator. We need a line producer on location. You interested?"

Marcus was still in his mid-twenties, full of hope for the future. Thanks to Sam and Louis he was now being asked to produce a movie for the US market with a successful director and a great writer. The effect on his career would be electric.

"I'll do it for free," he said impulsively, immediately regretting it. Louis was not a man with a sense of humor.

"Deal," replied McConnell dryly. "Airline ticket and script are on the way," and he hung up.

The package arrived a few days later. Although a note said Marcus drove a hard bargain, he was thankful it included reasonable employment terms and a healthy advance on his fee. Still green and inexperienced, Marcus eagerly signed on as line producer to *THE LAST COMPANY*.

The struggles of making the film would bind a group of them together as close as brothers, Marcus, Sam, Robert Kelso and Bill Baines.

With a tight shooting schedule, every day was a fight to complete the day's set-ups. Working 18-hour days, Marcus gritted his teeth and drove the production through sheer determination. The rain never seemed to stop, and costs kept escalating. Then the air freight company was beset by labor problems and compounded by the bad weather, couldn't ship out the 'dailies' that were the raw cans of film from each day's shooting. Even though McConnell was rumored to be setting up his own airfreight company to solve the problem, the dailies started to stockpile.

It was a dangerous situation. Should those dailies get damaged or lost, the footage had cost hundreds of thousands of dollars in production, which they could never afford to reshoot.

Damage didn't turn out to be the problem.

"He'll see you now," McConnell's PA nodded a coiffured head towards the huge double doors and brought Marcus' mind back to the task in hand.

Louis looked much as Marcus remembered, well-manicured and even better tailored. A hint of a face lift and a hair weave but there was nothing Louis could do about his waistline.

"Enjoying Hollywood, Marcus?" he asked in a tone laced with irony.

"Never had a bad meeting."

"You and every other hopeful," he said. "I'm busy, Marcus. I see that since you let me down, your career back home has risen without a trace."

"Sam Wood's last screenplay," replied Marcus getting straight to the point.

"Sam has not been my client since that fiasco. I'm sorry about his death, but I have no idea what you are talking about."

"It's brilliant. I want to make it."

"It may be, Mr. Riley, but you are a spent force. People don't forget out here. *THE LAST COMPANY* was a huge burden."

"Sam rose above it."

"Well, he had talent. I doubt anyone in this town will have anything to do with you. However, if you think it's that good, I'll read it. I can always buy the rights off the estate. But I'll never make anything with you again. And from what I hear of your struggles over the past months nor will anyone else."

"You can package it, but the rights stay with me. Sam gave me an option before he died. Think it over. Sam Wood's last screenplay. That's a big draw. You have my number."

As Marcus left the room, he knew he needed to see Cara Baines, Robert Kelso and get back to London and call on Stefan de Turris.

Louis understood that it wasn't enough to play hardball, he had to get those rights and ensure that movie never saw the light of day; or *FALL OUT* would be his death sentence.

CHAPTER 9

THÉOULE-SUR-MER, CÔTE D'AZUR, FRANCE

The young man entered her. Melinda 'Mako' de Turris gave a gasp and her blue almond shaped eyes widened. Well, she knew the right reaction was expected, and as her adopted nickname suggested, she was a fearsome man-eater.

She quickly flipped the young man round so she was on top and in control; straddling him with her knees locked on either side of his hips. She looked down. He was brutally handsome and he knew it; young, no more than 25, almost 11 years her junior. He had danced so well at the Caves du Roy nightclub in St Tropez the previous night. It was lust at first sight. She did not even bother to remember his name.

"Oh God," he repeatedly mumbled. Mako bent forward to kiss him, just to shut him up. No man she had ever met was an atheist in bed; they would have no one to talk to.

She pulled away and arched her back and started to rock, moving her hips as if gently riding a horse. A single droplet of sweat slalomed down from her long jet-black hair across the Asian features of her face and cheek. She had chosen well; he was a great lover. She felt the beginning of her climax and threw back her head….

Lying on the bed she watched him, lost in post coital sleep. His body was gleaming with sweat, with the wonderful muscular definition of youth. Just what she had wanted. She liked superficial. He stirred and opened an eye. Go on, surprise me, she thought. Try and avoid just one cliché.

"That was great," he sighed, right on cue. "How was it for you?" he asked, compounding the offence.

She nestled into his ear, licking and biting the lobe.

"Over," she sighed.

His eyes sprung open. With a laugh, she spun round and leapt out of bed, dragging the tumbled mass of silk sheets with her, and ran to the shower. As the water hit her lithe body and she pumped shampoo from the container on the wall, she could not stop herself humming 'So beautiful, but so boring'. Still, he had served his purpose. Now it was time for her to face the world again and go to work.

Her villa was truly beautiful. It was set into the rock face of a small promontory jutting out to sea just outside Théoule-sur-Mer, a few miles along the coast west from Cannes. To her it looked like a foot dipping in the sea, so she had aptly named it *Pied à Mer*.

She even had her own private beach, not normally allowed in France. When the town had constructed the entrance of the marina in the 1960s, they had built a long finger of rocks that stretched into the Mediterranean. This gave protection to the yachts from the Mistral wind and had the added benefit of changing the current around the rocks below her home, creating a small pebble-strewn beach.

Every May three truckloads of sand were duly laid over the rocks. This would last all summer before being washed away in the winter storms, only to be replenished by another delivery the following spring.

It was now the third week in April and her beach had just received a new delivery of sand. The tourist season was about to start again, which meant her own business had two months of craziness before it would taper off. She made her considerable income mostly from October through June.

Freshly showered, Mako sat on the terrace eating a brioche

and sipping an espresso. She looked past the young man seated across from her who was still awkwardly trying to make polite conversation. She gazed out to sea where she could clearly see the outline of the underwater nets of the fish farms, laid out like huge cages full of the local fish, *loup de mer*.

The young man paused and pushed his sunglasses onto his face.

"I can get Garance to call you a cab if you like," Mako smiled into a lull in the conversation.

Everything was the wrong way around, the young man thought to himself. He should be the one aching for the conquest to leave. This woman seemed to treat men as badly as he treated countless wide-eyed female tourists during the mating frenzy that was summer on the Côte d'Azur.

On hearing his name, the well-groomed housekeeper stepped out onto the terrace.

"No need, Madame. I will take Monsieur into town…. with the laundry," suggested Garance. The young man knew when he was beaten. Game over. He got up to leave.

Twenty minutes later Mako was rounding the point in the *Melinda 2*, her glorious teak hulled *Riva Aquarama S* speedboat. She was heading towards Cannes, a few kilometers to her east with the island of l'Île Sainte Marguerite on her right.

Already she could see the outline of the *Palais des Festivals*, the massive convention center that occupied its own pier and faced impassively out to sea. That building and the town behind it had been very good to her.

The Riva purred into the new Cannes harbor. Mako deftly lashed the craft to the pontoon. Picking up her briefcase, she kicked off her blue leather deck shoes, slipping on a pair of Manolo Blahnik mules. She walked towards her office in the *Palais des Festivals*.

Her construction crews were already hard at work building the stands in preparation for the *Cannes Festival du Film* better known as the Cannes Film Festival that took place every May.

Cannes was a glamorous holiday destination in the summer months, but in truth it made its money as a convention town. In addition to the Film Festival there were two conferences for television in April and October, and there were other world class events for music, property, advertising and even a convention for Duty Free goods.

These events dominated the town and injected countless millions into the local economy as well as Mako's bank account.

Each festival attracted up to 25,000 delegates, numerous companies with their most senior executives, the international press, hangers on, the deal hopefuls, and the party lovers. Many of the delegates needed stands to exhibit their wares or just someone to plan extravagant parties.

This was Mako's forte. Her company designed and built the stands and organized the best event parties. Clients included record companies, Hollywood film studios, television stations, construction companies, advertising agencies and perfume manufacturers from all four corners of the world. Each had their Cannes 'bandstand' and the most expensive and lavish were designed by her company.

Yet no matter how good her work was, no matter how creative and at times even beautiful, it lasted only a few days. Transitory, superficial. Those words defined not just her work, but her as well. They were her world.

Back at *Pied à Mer* Garance was signing for the weekly package of forwarded mail originally sent to Mako's father, Stefan de Turris. Since his car accident over a year ago, all of her father's correspondence was forwarded to her.

Among the mail that day was an envelope containing a screenplay and a quote from Balzac. It had been sent by a man Mako had never known, and it would change her life forever.

CHAPTER 10

SANTA BARBARA, CALIFORNIA

Cara Baines was completely unaware of Sam Wood's death. It had made none of the papers in the Land of Lakes of northern Minnesota where she had been vacationing.

Her Ford pick-up exited the freeway for Santa Barbara. Cara loved the laid-back seaside town with its white Spanish Colonial style buildings and terracotta tiled roofs. Having spent all her life in Los Angeles with a billboard every few paces, living in a city where billboards were banned was an added bonus.

Behind the city, the Santa Ynez Mountains rose 4,000 feet into the clear blue sky. She could see them from her house and it was up there, under a star-filled sky that stunt co-ordinator Bill Baines had proposed to her.

When she turned into her driveway, a car was parked there with a driver who seemed to be asleep at the wheel.

As she nervously got out of the truck, her little black pug leapt out and started to bark incessantly at the intruder's vehicle. The sleeping man woke with a start then smiled and unwound himself from the driver's seat. He got out raising his hands over his head in mock surrender to the pint size dog.

"I'm sorry. It's Cato, isn't it?" asked the man.

"Marcus…? Marcus Riley. What on earth are you doing here…," said an incredulous Cara.

It was an awkward moment for them both, and it brought back very painful memories for Cara.

"Cara, lovely to see you. Forgive me for my unannounced visit.

Can we go inside? There's quite a bit to tell and not much I can explain," said Marcus with a grimace.

Cara invited him into the house. She turned off the alarm and activated the air-conditioning as the rooms were hot and stuffy having been empty for nearly a month.

Marcus looked at the artwork and photos on the wall and remembered Cara's family had emigrated from the Philippines to Los Angeles in the early 1950s. She had grown up in the foothills of the San Gabriel Mountains, just north of Pasadena.

Cara walked over next to Marcus and smiled softly "That's a photo of me graduating from the make-up course at the Joe Blasco Cosmetics School,that led to a job at Fox where it all started for me. I met Sam during lunch in the commissary."

Marcus took a breath and told her about the terrible events of the past few days. Cara paused in silence then got up and went to the drinks tray.

"I can't believe Sam is dead," she said handing him a glass of Tupay, the Philippine spirit with an eye-watering kick. "And this script...you say he sent it to me...but why...what is going on? What's in it?"

"It's the best script I think he's ever written. I can't explain why he sent it to me, let alone you. Go on and read it, but... keep quiet about it, for now, for me," he said. "I need to make this movie, Cara."

"Let me see if I even have it," she said getting up to collect the mail that someone had piled up on her hall table.

"My PA comes in once in a while to check on the place when I'm away," she explained

Among the pile she found a note from the courier who had tried to deliver something a few days earlier.

"No script but could be this. I'll chase it down tomorrow. Can we go outside to get some air," she suggested.

They sat out in the cool evening breeze, the Santa Ynez range looming above them in the dusk's fading light. Their talk, unsurprisingly, turned to her late husband.

"You remember when Sam and Jax invited me over for dinner one night as a blind date... all she would say was he was a stuntman called Bill. You were there with some pretty thing."

Marcus smiled "Of course I remember." The now half empty bottle of Tupay had lowered their initial inhibitions and the talk flowed more easily.

"'A pearl of the Orient Sea,' the rascal had whispered to me. I suppose Sam or you had tipped Bill off about the term used to describe Filipina women."

"Well, it worked didn't it," chuckled Marcus.

She nodded, with a wistful smile. At dinner Bill had proved carefree and charming. So many stuntmen were just pent-up balls of testosterone, eager to show off their prowess on set, with hints of equal daring-do in the bedroom. Bill was never a threat.

"I asked him to explain what he did," Cara said. "He went all coy talking about wire work till you put me straight and explained, Marcus."

"He was just playing modest in front of you. Bill was *the man* for falling off tall buildings," smiled Marcus, "But you weren't fooled by the quiet act," he added.

"I found out a while after that dinner, and the danger he had lived with. Once it was helicopters and planes he jumped out of," Cara said as she took a long slow gulp. "Instead of cameras shooting at him, it was snipers. I still have a bunch of his army medals somewhere."

It had been during training with the British Parachute Regiment that Bill had come across a machine that he would later adapt so successfully in later years for movie stunt work. It was a winch-like brake whose long cable was attached via a harness to the chest of new recruits. As they jumped from higher and higher platforms onto the mattresses below, the brake kicked in slowing the landing enough to avoid injury. For the movies, Bill simply swapped the harness for an ankle cuff that allowed him to dive headlong from any number of platforms, buildings, helicopters, or even a mountain.

Marcus knew Bill had left the service and mooched about in security until he got talked into jumping out of a crane using his ankle brake for a TV documentary series on some local cable show.

Marcus had been watching the documentary. He needed the bad guy in his latest film to fall from a helicopter. The film's stunt team had baulked at the budget and the price Marcus was offering. Bill obliged and literally jumped at the chance. Work flooded in. Next thing Bill knew he was packing his bags for Hollywood.

He secured his first break in North America on a 'slasher' horror movie located in the arctic wasteland. Shot in Canada and directed by hot new director, Robert Kelso, **POLE-AXED** was made for next to nothing yet generated a waterfall of cash, thanks in no small part to the spectacular falls and explosions that Bill organized. Once that movie was a hit, it was natural that he would be asked to be stunt coordinator on Robert's next production, **THE LAST COMPANY**.

Marcus raised a glass in a toast. "To Bill and Sam."

Cara raised her glass and continued reminiscing.

"One evening a few months after that first dinner, Bill and I were sitting high up in the shadow of those mountains and he proposed."

She paused and looked directly at Marcus. "It was then he told me everything. How much do you really know about his past?"

"Some," replied Marcus. "But tell me."

"He served two tours in Northern Ireland. During the third

month of the second tour he and seven others were ambushed." This Marcus did not know. Cara went on with Bill's story.

Marcus sat silently, transfixed by the story.

Cara continued. "His brick was out on patrol."

Marcus looked puzzled.

"Sorry, a brick is slang for a section. Eight of them. Bill was in charge, there were two Lance Corporals, four Privates, and a radio operator, Joe Trott. Joe was Bill's best friend. They were all carrying SLR rifles, except Joe who had a side arm. It was late afternoon as they turned down a narrow street. There was an injured dog, whimpering, lying in the road. They stopped to see if there was anything they could do, but he was in a bad way. Looked like a hit and run. In a way it was. But it was Bill's section who were hit and the gunmen who ran. As Bill bent down to look at the animal, the doorways of the terraced houses to their left flew open and the gunmen opened fire.

Bill's unit was caught off guard. Point blank. Five died immediately. Bill went down next, a shoulder wound. Joe drew his pistol as he dove for cover and scrambled behind some trash cans across the other side of the street. The front door behind Joe slowly opened and a little girl appeared. As Joe turned to push her back inside, a sawn-off shotgun snaked out from the darkness behind her. Shot him point blank in the face. Joe flew back out into the street as his service revolver clattered to the ground and into a storm drain. The gunman pushed the girl aside and ran off as the terrified parents tried to console their screaming daughter. Before Bill lost consciousness, Joe's killer pulled off his ski mask just a moment too soon as the gunmen piled into a Land Rover. Bill never forgot a face."

Cara poured herself another two fingers of Tupay and offered Marcus the bottle as she finished her story. Bill had slowly recovered in hospital, and when well enough he had resigned his commission.

"He was done fighting for the army. He had a personal score to settle. He made a pilgrimage to the alley and recovered Joe's gun from the drain." Cara paused and took another drink. "Six weeks passed. Took a lot of digging but he found a family name to match the face," said Cara calmly.

She described a lonely windswept cottage outside Crossmaglen and three hard men, two brothers and a cousin, who were shot dead with Joe's missing revolver. A fourth gunman died as he tried to escape in his Land Rover. It exploded in a fireball as it bounced across the moors, presumably laden with illicit and unstable explosives.

"The gun's owner had been served his revenge, and Bill a measure of closure. That's real danger not make believe," Cara said.

Marcus looked at her for a beat. He thought back to that night when he had last seen Bill alive.

She leaned over and filled Marcus' glass snapping him out of his thoughts from the past.

"Bill understood the danger of taking action, Marcus. He was always going to go after the bad guys in the Philippines. I don't blame you. I just miss him still. Always will."

"We all do. That movie broke so many things. But you suffered the most."

"I know you tried, Marcus. I appreciated the calls and the visit after you got back. But I was so alone. Not a day passed without wishing I could have done more to find out what had really happened to him. But it had been hopeless."

"You know that bastard McConnell even threatened to sue me. Said Bill's disappearance had cost him the movie!" She gave a sarcastic laugh. "The local police shrugged at my pleas for help and without a body, the Consulate suggested Bill might simply have run off. He disappeared thousands of miles from home and no one could help me."

Marcus looked at her as she pulled her shoulders back and sat up straight.

"He's dead. He would have moved heaven and earth to come back to me."

She took a final drink and looked up to the mountains.

"So, after a year I left Hollywood, the bullshit, and sound stages and bought a home here. The Union told me to accept the pittance McConnell was offering to pay me to settle this. I took his money. Started my florist business."

Cara had assumed the grief would subside and that someday another man would fill her days and nights. A few drifted in and out of her embrace, but she now accepted that her future would be without a steady partner. Instead her life centered on her flower business, her friends, and her small black pug.

"So now you are here, Marcus. And Sam sent you a script. And it also seems, to me. Maybe some kind of catharsis?"

"Sam wasn't the sentimental type, Cara… I feel guilty bringing up bad memories, but I want to get this made. In fact, I have to," said Marcus quietly.

"So, he reached out to you… be grateful. I'm sure he had his reasons. But why send it to me?"

"I honestly don't know. Maybe you can tell me. Read the script and call me. Now, I have to get going." As Marcus got up the small pug gave a low growl.

"How did you know his name," she said, nodding to the pug at her feet?

"Cato's famous. He's on your *The Santa Ynez Proposal* website."

Cara smiled. "Promise me I can do the flowers for the Premiere if you pull his off."

"When I pull it off. Sure… or for my grave as I die trying."

Marcus knew the moment the flippant remark came out of his mouth that it had been a mistake and saw a shadow of fear on

Cara's face.

"I will call you, as soon as I've read it. Now be careful," Cara replied

Marcus gently kissed her on the cheek. He was glad he hadn't told her about the others in the group that had received the screenplay. Cara's feelings towards McConnell were clear. She would never help him if she thought he was involved.

CHAPTER 11

SANTA BARBARA, CALIFORNIA

"Don't you dare piss on my azaleas!" Cato's round black face stared back at Cara, his hind leg cocked in midair.

"Now, how's today going?" Cara asked her PA who was shuffling her papers.

"The shipment for the Cheetham's wedding leaves at 11AM. They have now finally paid in full… once I threatened not to deliver," the young girl replied.

"You're learning. You just have to be tough, Bella. Some rich people need to be reminded that we can all bite," Cara said with a smile. With that she turned and went out into the loading yard, Cato snuffling at her heels.

Her dedicated workforce of gardeners, buyers, and floral display team were her real family now. Her business, The Santa Ynez Proposal, had grown from a small shop to five retail outlets and a successful contracting business.

"Oh, the courier re-delivered that package here to the office as I requested," Bella added following Cara as she handed over a manila envelope.

After a long day Cara returned home and listened to a single voice message left on her home phone.

That loathsome man Louis McConnell wanted to know if she had received and read a screenplay from Sam Wood. How the hell had he known about that?

Making a face at the answer machine, she really wanted to go to bed, but the message had upset her and now she wanted to know what was in Sam's script that was bringing all these people back into her life. She started to read. Like Marcus, she was quickly drawn into Sam's fast-paced thriller. However, she grew uneasy as whispers of the past echoed in Sam's story. Is that what had triggered McConnell to contact her? She read through it again focusing on what had happened to her husband and trying to see if Sam was telling her more. There must have been a reason he had sent it to her.

FALL OUT was about the founding and eventual implosion of two criminal empires. The screenplay opens with the suicide of 55-year-old property magnate Frank Kiddo leaping to his death from the window of his eleventh-floor office. The story then flashes back to the mid-1990s and an old flour mill in Panama City and the story that leads to his suicide. Former strong man President Manuel Noriega has been sent to rot in a Miami jail, but his cronies are everywhere. Two men, each representing two criminal organizations, jointly buy the mill and start its demolition, but their secret goal is to strip the business of a hidden fortune buried inside.

Frank Kiddo, a powerful young New York property developer, leads an American syndicate and provides credibility for the project. He is joined by his finance partner, Joe Nisten. The other group is run by a Panamanian local wise-guy Aguinaldo Sosa who owns a demolition and construction company.

The men's secret plan succeeds, and they discreetly melt away to divide the proceeds, their tracks hidden by the banker. Over the years, they continue to work together to build a massive illegal arms business that feeds weapons to criminals and armed conflicts worldwide. But greed ultimately destroys their partnership. The title said it all: **FALL OUT.**

It was 4:30 AM by the time Cara finished reading the script for the third time. Cato had long given up any hope of his mistress going to sleep and was on her lap, the only sound in the house his rhythmic snoring.

Cara kept returning to one scene. The first time she read it, something had snagged her memory. The scene was near the beginning when the two heads of the different crime groups are scouting out the mill where a huge weapons stash had been hidden by the ousted President Noriega, the recovery of which would found their empires.

FALL OUT (cont'd) Page 18

SCENE 6
EXT. CLOUDS. DAY. PANAMA CITY, PANAMA 1990

The grey clouds part revealing a beaten-up pickup truck as it rumbles through the mean streets of the city. All the while in the background, an Irish melody plays incongruously, evocative of all that this place is not. The rain lashes down against the windshield as the vehicle pulls to a halt, the road now almost more river than track.

The two men stare through the windshield, the passenger is FRANK KIDDO - small, overweight, early thirties, American. The driver is a tall local man, same age, AGUINALDO SOSA. We are just able to make out a giant outline towering above them in front of the car. It's an old run-down flour mill. A large sign hangs crookedly on the

building, displaying the word Masa (Flour)
painted below a large tiger logo.

                    AGUINALDO
          In there. The old *Bick* flour mill.
          Buried supplies from the old days.

                    FRANK
          CIA support for Noriega?

                    AGUINALDO
          When you guys still put up with
          his pineapple face. Before Reagan
          changed his mind. Enough for a
          small army. Medical supplies too.
          Morphine.

                    FRANK
(Hopelessly drawing on a cigar, which is
now soaked from the rain slanting through
his open window. He glowers at it)
          Think it will work?

                    AGUINALDO
          We'll get permission so long as we
          look real. (Smiling). Demolition and
          reconstruction work and when it
          stops, they'll be more interested in
          looking for our missing friend in
          the *Masa Bick* rubble than in what
          happened.

                              FRANK
(He flicks the stub out through the side of
the pickup truck).
               You're on.

"Oh my God!"
Cato awoke with a start.
"Marcus you're in danger...."
Cara had suddenly realized why the first time she read that
scene something had caught her subconscious eye. It was obvious
now if she read it in the right way. It was 5.30 AM. She reached for
her phone and typed a text message.
  "I'm driving to LA. Meet me at the Griddle Café on Sunset. 8
o'clock. God, Marcus. It's in the script, you just have to look...."

PART 2
THE RAISING

 **CHAPTER 12**

MANILA, PHILIPPINES

MARCH 1945

"*ICHI, NI, SAN, SHI, (one, two, three, four,)*" the crowd chanted in slow disciplined unison. Although in Manila, the assembled were counting in Japanese and accompanied each number with a single clap.

"*GO, ROKU, SHICHI, HACHI, KYU, JU, (five, six, seven, eight, nine, ten.)*" Perfectly executed.

Tan grinned with pride and stood back. He was drenched in arterial spray and behind him lay ten decapitated bodies. The victims' hands still tied behind their backs; their heads were mired in a lake of blood on the stone courtyard floor. He basked in the spontaneous applause of the assembled VIPs as well as his fellow comrades of the *Kempeitai*, the military police in charge of Manila. Tan posed once again for the press, his bolo by his side. The Fort Santiago cells above which he now stood were crammed with an endless supply of prisoners awaiting the same fate.

Since leaving Major Okobudo to rot in the cave with the other men, Tan had returned to Manila with General Yamashita. Tan's strong right arm silenced any dissent to Japanese rule. Again, and again he proved that no one could compare with the accuracy and consistent strength of the swing of his bolo. The weapon was a fearsome long-curved machete whose blade swelled at the tip making it a heavy and terrifyingly effective weapon. He was the most feared executioner in all the Philippines.

Press photos complete, Tan turned back to the crowd, soaking up the applause. These executions were the highpoint of his life.

He was born a Filipino, in his mind a second-class race compared to the mighty Japanese. But now he was not only one of them but being applauded. He beamed with pride. He thought back on his journey to this supreme moment of joy.

Tan had been plucked from obscurity and probable death by a stroke of luck. More accurately, by the stroke of his bolo when he had helped the occupying Japanese troops a year or so before. He had hated his childhood spent in the village of Kalayaan, south east of Manila on the shores of Laguna de Bay. The other children had teased him mercilessly about his looks and called his beloved mother the village whore; no one knew who his father was. He was never called by his first name but merely by his last, Tan. Tough as his beginnings in life had been, he nevertheless had grown strong, tall, and wide.

His physical bulk and a burgeoning mean streak began to counter the snide comments of the other kids. If only he had been born in Japan, he might have been summoned to become a '*rikishi*' (trainee) at a Sumo wrestling stable. Tan admired the Japanese determination to extend their sphere of influence using the only power that could determine change: military might. International opinion was weak. Japan was imposing its strength and discipline on the rest of Asia, taking control of Korea and great swathes of China.

At age twenty, before the outbreak of war and the Japanese invasion of the Philippines, Tan's mother died. He had left the village and vanished into the jungle. He chopped his way into the wilds using only his bolo to make a path. In a clearing at the foot of a small waterfall, he hacked down several bamboo stalks and constructed his own *Nipa*, the traditional peasant Filipino dwelling. Standing on two-foot tall stilts complete with thatched roof, reed mattress and a few cooking pots, this 25-square-foot home was his refuge from the world.

In this lonely retreat Tan channeled his aggression and frustration in a time-honored manner. He bred a fearsome string of fighting cocks and made a good living from it. His success at least garnered him some grudging admiration, if not friendship, from the locals.

His *Nipa* was his sanctuary, no one was ever invited. When he needed female companionship, he would buy it in the local village with the winnings from the fights his cocks nearly always won.

As well as creating his home, Tan's blade had chopped down branches to make pens to house the birds. He had even dug his own pit where he could train the animals to fight.

Before every contest he would hack down some palm leaves and weave a new *salacot*, the Filipino conical shaped straw woven hat. As the cockerels often looked very similar to one another, the bets placed by the crowd at ringside and taken by the *casador*, were identified by the handler as opposed to the actual bird. Each handler held up the bird to show to the crowd before each fight. One handler wore a hat, one did not. Tan always wore the hat. He had hardly ever left a cockpit with a defeated bird, one that would end up in a *talunan* stew made out of the bloodied remains. Death and defeat were for his opponents.

Following the invasion of the Philippines, the Japanese occupiers left Tan alone. Although they enjoyed coming to the fights, their priority was the never-ending skirmishes with the local resistance.

One late lazy afternoon, after Tan had fed his birds and was tending his meager vegetable patch, he heard shots, a yelp of pain and the sound of running feet crunching the dead leaves of the jungle floor. Into his clearing came three youths from the village. He recognized them immediately. How cruelly they had once teased him, but now they were desperate for help. The smallest, named Teodoro, was bleeding from a gunshot wound to his buttocks. Tan smirked to himself.

"Couldn't even get shot anywhere on the front like a real man, just in the ass running away," he mocked.

"Hide us, Tan" pleaded a panting Teodoro. Tan remained expressionless. "We did nothing. We met up with a Japanese patrol. They said we had to bow down to them. We said screw yourself and ran off."

"The Japanese are our saviors, you should show them respect," Tan said, now glaring defiantly at the young men. "Pathetic".

They saw the anger and hatred in his eyes. They realized the kid they had tortured and bullied had grown into a man who was never going to help them. They turned and started to run into the jungle. Trying to keep up but stumbling along behind, Teodoro quickly collapsed but his light frame was held upright by the vines of the forest.

Moments later the group of Japanese soldiers burst into the clearing. Immediately the first soldier in the group raised his gun, aiming it at Tan.

Tan raised his hands and smiling said clearly "You have nothing to fear from me. I embrace the Emperor and welcome your forces and discipline to our land."

The soldier hesitated. Then making up his mind, his finger started to squeeze the trigger, just as a swagger stick crashed across his knuckles.

The rifle now lowered by the young soldier, the Major who had struck him, coolly lit a cigarette "You can identify the terrorists?" he enquired. "If you can lead us to them, we might spare your life. If not, I need to apologize to this brave soldier I have struck and let him execute you. I hate apologizing."

"This way," Tan replied calmly and confident, seizing his opportunity. "Major….?"

"Okobudo," replied the Major with a cold smile as Tan leaned down to pick up his bolo. Three rifles instantly trained on him.

"Let me cut a path. You will catch them. They will never make headway." With the soldiers behind him, rifles still pointed at his head, Tan soon led them to the unconscious form of Teodoro, spread-eagled on the clinging arms of the jungle. The Major yanked the young man's hair.

"Which way?"

Teodoro's eyes flickered open in a haze of semiconscious pain. He made a valiant attempt to spit but passed out as the phlegm rose in his throat. The Major stepped back and withdrew the long sword at his side.

"Permit me, please Major" said a voice behind him. With a swing of his bolo, Tan severed Teodoro's head from his body. Then for good measure he brought the blade down against each arm, so Teodoro's torso fell forward freed from the embrace of the blood-soaked branches.

Major Okobudo grinned. He was impressed and sheathed his sword. He had found the perfect bodyguard, a Filipino, but seemingly totally loyal to the Japanese cause and willing to execute his countrymen. Okobudo nodded in the direction of the others. True to his word, Tan caught the remaining two and dispatched both with equal ruthlessness.

From that day on, Tan never left the Major's side, fiercely loyal to his new master and the Japanese Emperor. Tan's knowledge of the local landscape and customs, and his contempt for his own people made him indispensable to Major Okobudo.

But Major Okobudo had misjudged the loyalty as being just to him, rather than the Emperor. It was this loyalty to the Emperor that had led Tan eventually to inform General Yamashita, the Major's superior, of Okobudo's treasonous act and thereby to seal his fate. Tan knew there would be no alternative but to silence the Major along with everyone involved in the project.

In the spring of 1945, the Japanese occupiers were desperately trying to subdue the local population, which was growing more rebellious the closer General MacArthur and his U.S. forces got to the Philippines. Yamashita decreed that all males over 14 years old were to be treated as guerrillas and arrested, a pronouncement that was quickly followed by mass executions; most carried out by Tan.

The General needed his executioner to instill fear.

Tan's thoughts were jerked back abruptly to the present as an air raid siren suddenly reverberated around the concrete courtyard. A wave of American bombers was flying in low over the city. He turned to run for cover in the deep dungeons but slipped in the pools of fresh blood around him. He crashed to the ground, his head slamming against the stone floor. A few minutes later as he slowly regained consciousness, the bombs were pounding the Fort. He frantically rose to his feet trying to dash to the door and safety below. He never made it. There was a blinding flash, then a rush of heat.

The next thing he remembered was the hospital. His head was heavily bandaged; his right arm a bloody stump just below the elbow. His days of wielding the bolo were over. He stared at what was left of his arm in utter disbelief.

For weeks he sweated in a half delirious state, tended by a Japanese girl who worked there. He remembered the day he first heard American voices at the hospital. General MacArthur had indeed returned. No one had any idea who Tan was, only that he had been found in the wreckage of the Fort, clothes torn from his body. The nurse told the G.I.'s he was a Filipino prisoner who had escaped execution. A few days later she took him home.

When the bandages came off, Tan looked in the mirror as a tear rolled down his cheek. Not because he had become so thin and disfigured, but in relief that no one would ever recognize him. He was safe from retribution.

He married his nurse and they hid in the wreckage of Manila. No one, except his wife, knew of his past but Tan was dead from the inside, his purpose and vision in life ripped from him. Nearly eight years later after she eventually gave him a son, Tan sank deeper into depression and drunkenness. He never had a chance to get to know his half-Japanese son, because the former executioner died of heart failure soon after he was born. Mother and child simply disappeared into the chaos of post war Philippines.

# CHAPTER 13

BEL AIR, LOS ANGELES

Jonathan had returned from his trip to the Philippines and had fully debriefed his boss the day before. Freshly showered and dressed, he got in the Range Rover. He was off to ensure that the Marcus Riley threat was to be neutralized. He thought back on his recent visit to his homeland and the death and destruction Sam's visit there would now bring.

It hadn't taken him long to uncover what had caused Sam Wood to write that script when he had returned from his trip to the Philippines. No surprise. Rafael Satow had been the problem. He had always been weak.

Born in 1953, Rafael Satow had tried to live a quiet life. He was devoted to his mother who had brought up her only child without a husband. Rafael's father had died shortly after his birth, before the boy was old enough to have any memory of him.

His mother simply told Rafael his father had been a kind and gentle man, a hero from the war, who had swept her off her feet. God had taken him, when their boy was barely twelve months old. When he died, she left the big city and ended up in the village of Pagsanjan. She devoted her life to her son, making a living teaching at the local school.

At thirty Rafael fell in love and realized that he was never going to give his mother the grandchildren she yearned for.

"Mama, I am in love," he started when they sat down for dinner one evening, his eyes focusing on the floor.

"I am so happy for you. Tell me more," his mother replied. There was a long pause.

"Mama. It is so hard for me to tell you…. I am ashamed…."

"Because you are *bakla*?"

Rafael looked up at her, his oval face open mouthed in shock. He was astonished his mother had used the term for a gay man.

"My son, I know you. I raised you. No shock, no surprise, and no shame. I am proud of you. You have *pakikisama*, the Philippine ideal of getting on with your fellow man. Well, in a way that's what you are doing," she said quietly. "What's his name?"

"Zino," said Rafael, his shock turning to relief and an ever-deepening love and respect for his mother.

"Ah yes, the young man from the barber and hair salon. I approve. Just remember, be careful. Discretion," his mother advised.

The conversation Rafael had been dreading for so long, was over. It had not been the nightmare he anticipated. His mother was truly the greatest woman he would ever meet, and he swore nothing, and no one would ever be allowed to harm her.

Lying in bed later that evening, his mother thought she had handled the inevitable as well as could be expected, but she was worried. Although gay men had long been tolerated, even accepted, in Philippine society, banking was a most conservative profession, but Rafael had an air of culture and the arts about him. Her son was vulnerable.

He kept his relationship separate from his work. Or so he thought until one day a slightly built man walked into his life and stomped all over his principles and privacy.

It was a rain-sodden August morning in the mid-1990s, when Jonathan, clutching a leather briefcase, entered the bank. He stood in front of the receptionist apologizing for the pool of water that collected at his feet and asking for Rafael Satow by name.

Already an assistant manager, Rafael was stationed to the side of the cashiers' cages and on his desk, he proudly displayed a gold plaque engraved with his name. Hair neatly combed and dressed in a simple but well pressed suit, he heard his name. He looked up across the faded elegance of the old colonial building that had become the town's only bank. The cheap plastic furniture and solitary ineffective security camera looked out of place against the hand-carved wooden panels. The slowly turning four-blade ceiling fans gave no relief to the heat, simply stirring the humid air. Rafael greeted the man who had been directed to his desk and pointed to a chair.

"I'd like to open an account," said Jonathan getting right to the point.

"We need to fill out some forms, run some checks Mr....?"

"The company is Golden Eagle Trust and is owned by Mr. Haribon Guinto," interrupted Jonathan ignoring the man "and as for checks, here is my check. Let's open with one million Pesos."

Jonathan looked intently at Rafael, daring him to stick with conventional formalities and run the risk of losing what was a $200,000 opening balance, a certain promotion, and a probable raise in salary.

Rafael squirmed in his seat under Jonathan's glare then made his choice and pulled out some paperwork, which he quickly signed himself.

"The account is now open, Mr...."

"Jonathan will do for now. Please deposit the check. Perhaps we might go somewhere quiet for lunch?"

Rafael was only too happy to accept the invitation. He suggested to his new client a small local restaurant that specialized in *leche de lechon*, suckling pig. Jonathan nodded approval.

"A proper meal. I love seeing the whole body of what has been killed, rather than just pieces of nondescript meat," Jonathan said calmly as they left the bank ten minutes later, with all the formalities concluded.

They entered the restaurant, settled into an alcove and awaited their food. Rafael ordered two beers. Normally he would not drink while at work, but this was indeed a special occasion. He lobbed a few innocuous subjects into the air for discussion, but his new client seemed uninterested in small talk.

"You like your job?" asked Jonathan coldly.

Rafael nodded eagerly.

"Is your mother proud?"

Rafael nodded a little hesitantly, not sure of the relevance.

"And your boyfriend?"

Rafael flushed, but held his ground. "Why are you interested? What do you want?"

"Service and loyalty," replied Jonathan calmly.

"And you think you can get this by threats about my private life?" asked Rafael, with more bravery than he thought he could ever muster.

"Maybe the bank might disapprove but your boyfriend is just an extra bonus. No, I want you to understand how badly hurt your mother will be when I let it be known your honorable father, the war hero she worshipped, was the most despised man in Manila. He happily executed over 350 of his countrymen." He paused to let this information sink in. "Even some from around here."

Rafael was in a state of shock and was about to try and respond when the waiter appeared. Jonathan held a finger to his lips. He smiled as the food was ceremoniously loaded onto the Lazy Susan in the center of the table. On a tray lay an entire piglet, its skin glazed the color and sheen of brown glass. Next to it the waiter placed the traditional jar of liver sauce, some sweet potatoes, and *pechay* fried rice.

"Looks delicious," said Jonathan. "Hope you've got a good appetite," he added, turning towards a pale and shaken Rafael.

The restaurant was *kamayan*, meaning diners eat only with their hands. Nevertheless, there was a small traditional mallet resting on the table to be used for cracking the piglet's toffee-like skin.

Ignoring the hammer, Jonathan reached into his breast pocket. A flick of his wrist and the balisong blade was open in his hand. "Where was I…. ah, yes, your traitorous father killed 350 men…. beheaded them to be exact."

He tapped the crisp skin of the meat with the base of his balisong knife, shattering it into brittle shards. He dropped a long splinter of crackling into his mouth. The sharp crunch as Jonathan bit the skin was the only noise at their table. His eyes were half closed in pleasure as he swallowed. He snapped back from the moment of indulgence and glared at Rafael, balisong still in his manicured hand.

"Bet Mummy never told you that. Beheaded them," he repeated loud enough for other diners to turn their heads.

He paused again for effect and then sliced off an oval of meat from the piglet's shoulder. Elegantly skewering it on the end of his blade, Jonathan dipped the meat into the sauce and then lowered the morsel into his rice.

Rafael sat wide-eyed in disbelief.

"That is a lie…ridiculous…my father was a hero….," stammered Rafael.

Jonathan carefully wiped his hands and reached into his faded leather briefcase pulling out old newspaper clippings, several handwritten documents and a faded black and white photo. Each was encased in individual cellophane folders. He slid the documents across the table to Rafael but held back the photograph. Indicating the article at the top of the pile, Jonathan began.

"Here's a newspaper story written during the occupation of Manila. Full of praise for your father's skills, no big surprise as the Japanese controlled the press." Pushing that news article to one side, he pointed to the others, "and these are some less than flattering eye-witness accounts written down by the *Kanos* after liberation as evidence for the war crime trials."

A shaking Rafael started to read. He visibly paled. "How do I know this is my father, let alone even true?" His voice was trembling.

"It's all documented. Officially no one knows what happened to the bastard; the Americans let him go by mistake. He was in their hospital. Lost his chopping arm and half his face in an air raid. Some justice, I suppose. However, I found which rock he had crawled under." Jonathan looked at Satow. The man was shaking in fear.

"It's not true. It can't be…." he pleaded.

"I live to uncover little skeletons like yours. It ensures attention and discretion. A witness from your parents' wedding made the mistake of buying goods on credit from me without having the funds to pay. I paid him a little visit. He saw me looking at some photographs including one of your parents. With admirably quick thinking, he wondered if in exchange for his debt, I might like to know the assumed name of the most hated man in Manila; what had happened to him, his wife, and only son." Jonathan paused.

"He sold out your father's real identity for a packet of American cigarettes and a cheap bottle of brandy," he said with a snap of his fingers. "That's the price of your past, present, and future."

"I don't believe you." Rafael was trying to be defiant, but doubt was breathing coldly at his shoulder.

"I'll make sure people believe it's true. Neither you, your mother, nor Zino will have anywhere to hide."

Jonathan smiled and turned the fingers of the hand that still held the knife and squinted at his cuticles. "Your boyfriend did a nice job on me this morning. Hot-towel shave even cleaned inside my ears with those little cotton buds. Conscientious. I like that."

With a smirk, Jonathan slid over the photo to Rafeal. It clearly showed a man surrounded by soldiers standing in a walled courtyard. The ground was strewn with several headless corpses. In his right hand the man held a bolo, in his left, a head.

Calmly Jonathan took the knife and cleanly sliced off the piglet's head. He gently lifted it from the tray by its crispy burnt ears, turning it to Rafael for a moment, glancing at the grisly photo as if for reference.

"Game over. I think I can even see the family resemblance," smiled Jonathan.

Rafael shakily stood up from the table, clumsily heading to the bathroom as vomit rose in his throat.

"No dessert then?" said Jonathan with a slight smile of triumph.

By the time a pale Rafael had returned, the food had been taken away. A glass of water stood at Rafael's place. Jonathan sipped a coffee and nibbled on a piece of *buko*, the local coconut cake.

Time for business. He was clinical and very clear.

"A movie is coming to town, **THE LAST COMPANY.** Your bank will handle all the various accounts needed; production as well as personal. When the movie ends, you start to earn your keep," Jonathan continued outlining his plans.

"Do what I say, and you get a fee. If not…." Jonathan glanced down at the photo.

Rafael was about to speak, but Jonathan cut him off. "Easy money. Don't even think of disobeying my instructions. If you do, there will be scores to settle. They will hound your mother all the way to hell."

No compromise, no choice. Jonathan got up and walked out of the restaurant, leaving Rafael to his fate. He climbed into the rental white Toyota 4x 4, grateful for its air conditioning and swung the car back towards Manila.

It was fixed, just as he had assured Haribon it would be.

Jonathan brought himself back to the present and the task at hand. He swung the Range Rover into the employee parking lot for Terminal 7 at LAX, looped a security clearance tag over his neck, and with his mop and bucket confidently strode over to Departures.

CHAPTER 14

WEST HOLLYWOOD, CALIFORNIA

Marcus lay in bed half asleep, looking at his phone and trying to understand what Cara had meant. Her instructions were clear, but why? What was she trying to say?

Soon he was up and dressed and was about to leave his room for the breakfast meeting with her when there was a knock at the door. "Open up, L.A.P.D."

"Good morning, Mr. Riley," smiled detective McNeile. He was flanked by a uniformed officer and one in plain clothes. "We meet again. But for the last time".

"Aw, Detective, you missed me? Always lovely to see you. Love to chat but I have a meeting….," Marcus responded, trying to inject a bit of humor to hide his need to meet Cara.

"You are going to have to miss it."

"Give me a couple of hours. I'm not leaving town, as you said."

"No, Mr. Riley. You *are* leaving town. Right now."

Before Marcus had time to react, a set of handcuffs were snapped on his wrists. The officers grabbed his suitcase and flung what they could find into it, mercifully picking up his iPad and briefcase.

"We missed anything; you can call for it when you get back to England."

"England?" started Marcus

"Mr. Riley, may I introduce Sean Donovan. He's from immigration," said the detective tersely, motioning to the other plain clothed officer.

"What are you talking about?"

"Your visa. The ESTA seems to have expired," Donovan said, using the acronym for Electronic System Travel Authorization. It was a computer-based visa system that allowed British citizens into the US without the need for individual trip visas. It lasted two years and as no stamp ever appeared in the passport, it was very easy to forget to renew.

"C'mon guys. Happens all the time. It's a quick renew…."

"You broke the rules, Mr. Riley. You're out of here."

With that, Marcus was frog-marched out to a squad car and taken to LAX.

"Mr. Riley, until we resolve this, you are on the banned list for entry into the United States for at least six months," said Donovan coldly. "And you won't be needing this," he added, confiscating the iPhone from a bewildered Marcus. "No contact with anyone until you're out of the US. Ask nicely and I might give you the chip…."

Jonathan emptied trash cans blending in with other workers and travelers in the background until Marcus had been escorted onto the 9:00AM United Airlines flight to England. Once airborne he returned to his boss to report. McConnell's contact in immigration had done his job.

 # CHAPTER 15

SANTA BARBARA, CALIFORNIA

Cara had dropped Cato off with a surprised and sleepy-eyed Bella, cleared the city limits of Santa Barbara by 6:30AM and was in the haze of Los Angeles by 8:00AM. Marcus was not at the café. She called him a couple of times, but there was no response, each attempt just going to voice mail. She hadn't time to worry about him now. She had established that Louis McConnell was in residence, following a brief call on her phone en route. With or without Marcus, she was going to confront McConnell with what she knew. She pulled up to the gate with its elaborate sign and rang the intercom.

"Tell Mr. McConnell it's Cara Baines," she announced sharply.

The wrought iron gates silently opened, and she nosed her truck up the paved driveway. A butler opened the front door and showed Cara into the large and ornate drawing room.

"Thank you, Benjamin," said Louis from behind a desk. The butler gave a curt nod and exited, silently pulling the double doors shut behind him.

No pleasantries or fake bonhomie. Cara went straight in.

She strode to the desk, the copy of **FALL OUT** in her hands. "Is this why Bill died?" she said shaking the script at Louis.

"Good morning, Cara nice to see you as well. Of course not. Please sit."

Louis came around from behind his desk, motioning to an elegant Hepplewhite chair and sat in its twin. A small table between them held a pot of tea and two cups. His face remained impassive.

"Milk or sugar?" he asked as he poured.

She ignored him.

"Was Bill murdered because he found out about hidden guns?"

Louis took a deep breath.

"Cara, Sam was a writer. He made things up for a living. Maybe in his imagination *FALL OUT* hides some twisted explanation of events from the past that he could not accept or understand? It's a story dripping with his own frustrations. Now he's got you going."

"Don't bullshit me, McConnell. What the hell went on out there?"

"*FALL OUT* is just Sam's private therapeutic fantasy. It just resurrects the past. Do you really want to do that?" He handed her a cup. "Sugar?"

"I don't believe you. Sam sent it to me for a reason," she paused. "And how the hell did you know I even had a copy?"

Louis looked at her impassively and put the rejected cup of tea back on the table. Cara slid her draft of the screenplay over to Louis.

"Scene 6."

Louis slowly took out a pair of delicate horn-rimmed reading glasses and scanned the short scene.

"I'd never have noticed without reading it out loud," explained Cara. "You'll never see it," she continued. "That's because you don't speak *Tagalog*, the language of the Philippines. Growing up I spoke it along with Spanish and English. Sam knew that. See where Sam wrote '*Masa*'? It's Spanish for flour," she said tapping the page. "I had assumed Bick was just some company name made up by Sam. But later, he puts the two words together and it reads *Masabik*. It's Tagalog for 'miss you.'"

"So what" asked Louis coolly? He started idly flipping through her copy, stopping at another section.

"It's how Bill ended all his postcards to me. Sam even signed a few to me from that hellhole you sent them both to. Sam's telling me the character they refer to killed under the rubble in *FALL OUT* is Bill. A man killed to cover up a crime…"

Louis hoped he looked disinterested as he flicked through the pages of Cara's copy of the script.

"No, Cara. You are being ridiculous now. You are reading things into this that just aren't there…."

"Maybe there's enough though for the cops to finally ask a few questions about Sam's death, if not Bill's. I hope this movie gets made, it might shake things up," she snapped, grabbing her copy back from Louis and slapping the script against her other hand.

"Did you know Sam sent the script to Marcus Riley too?" Louis asked calmly. "He wants to make it. I don't," said Louis.

"Atta' boy, Marcus," whispered Cara under her breath.

"It's never going to happen, Cara." Louis looked straight at her. He took off his glasses and hooked the two stems into the corner of his mouth. Cara wasn't buying his protestations that *FALL OUT* was just a product of a writer's imagination. He had to change tack.

"Marcus is not going to reopen old wounds by making this movie. He is putting you and others who got the script in jeopardy."

"You just said it's a fantasy. How does the script put anyone in jeopardy?"

"Ask Sam, Cara." Louis paused for effect, to let the significance sink in.

She stared at him.

"Cara, I didn't want to tell you this, but recently Sam went back to *THE LAST COMPANY'S* location in the Philippines. It was for some mad reason we'll never know," Louis continued, spinning lies as smooth as silk. "Whatever he may have found has probably nothing to do with the movie… but angered someone. They are the ones feeling threatened. I guess they hit back. Let's hope Sam's death has satisfied them."

"Bullshit. We have to go to the police. Get them to reopen either case," she interrupted.

"No cop here is ever going to get to the bottom of it let alone protect you or any of us from some hoods coming here from Manila." Louis paused. "Sam kicked a sleeping dog." The last phrase hung in the air.

"In Manila?" Cara asked.

"Let's just say maybe Sam did discover something. Whatever went on out there on the shoot, the rumors about drugs, guns, maybe it's in his new screenplay, maybe not. But whatever he thought he figured out and put in *FALL OUT* may have got him killed. Do you want to risk it?"

Cara hesitated.

"That screenplay is a death sentence." Louis said with certainty. "You owe it to yourself to make Marcus drop it. Stop imagining he is going to turn it into a movie."

Cara cared little what happened to her but her staff, her business, and, of course, her dog did matter. She wasn't going to put them in jeopardy. Just like when they talked about Bill's death, Cara was in a meeting with Louis McConnell and looking down the barrel of no choice.

"If I can reach Marcus, I'll try," she said eventually.

"For everyone's sake, Cara." Louis was so good, he gave himself the slightest congratulatory smile. Marcus was out of his hair.

Seemingly as an afterthought, Louis wrote down something on a piece of paper and handed it to Cara. "When you get home, check these names out," he calmly told her. "Accidents, fate, who knows? *THE LAST COMPANY* brought death."

"And still does?" she asked.

"Cara, whatever you may think, I was desperately sorry about what happened. The people who killed Bill, destroyed the footage…. there was no choice. We had to shut down. We pulled the insurance bond. You took the money we offered as compensation; case closed. We all moved on. Now years later Sam digs up something, somehow. I don't want them coming after us. You can do no more, nor would Bill expect you to. He cared too much about your safety."

Cara thought back to that ambush in Northern Ireland and the revenge Bill meted out on behalf of his dead friend.

"God help you if you're lying to me," she said and without another word turned and left.

Louis reached for his copy and turned to a specific page. No doubt about it. The two screenplays were different. Only Cara's copy made reference to the mill being called *Masabik*. He flipped through to the other scene he had nonchalantly looked for in Cara's version. He was certain it was different. Sure enough the scene included in his version contained specific references that were omitted from Cara's. Sam had made slight changes to each draft of the script, tailored it for each of them.

Louis let out a sigh, "You devious Australian bastard."

Sam had undoubtedly intended Cara to spot that *Tagalog* phrase, but he had also included other clues she had missed. The tiger had meant nothing to her. As for the reference to the Irish tune playing in the background, that too had gone over her head. But Sam had got it dead right. Louis, the Irishman, had most certainly been ever present in the background and the tiger was behind it all.

Louis wondered if Sam had actually wanted to test everyone by sending them slightly different versions to see how they react. What they notice and what they miss? If Cara had been able to confront Sam, like she had him, it just might have proved her innocence and knocked her off the Australian's list of conspirators. Smart.

Louis extended that thought. Could Sam have been equally unsure about Riley, Kelso and de Turris? That could have led to very dangerous waters.

However, Sam was dead, and Louis had it under control. He doubted Cara would be able to convince Marcus to drop it, but he had a backup plan. He heard the sound of the Range Rover pulling into the drive. The door opened.

"Jonathan," he called out. "I assume Riley for now is out of the loop. From what you said about your trip back home…. We have work to do. Let's go over it again please. Exactly."

CHAPTER 16

PAGSANJAN, PHILIPPINES

Jonathan was apprehensive. Over the years he took care of Mr. Louis's problems without providing him many details, preferring to just tell him when the job was done/completed, but this time, this last trip, he had not tied up every loose end. He was worried.

Rafael Satow was a problem. For twenty years he had followed Jonathan's instructions to the letter, that is until Sam returned to the Philippines and everything changed.

It hadn't taken Jonathan long to piece it all together. There was only one place Sam was going to go; Pagsanjan, where they had shot **THE LAST COMPANY**. Jonathan did some discreet nosing around and found himself talking to a local barman at the town's largest hotel, *The Heart of Darkness Hotel Bar and Grill*. The bartender confirmed that a tall Australian had visited a while ago. Men of Sam's size were rare. He nodded at the photo Jonathan showed him.

"Anything else?" asked Jonathan as he slid over some money, his hand resting on the pile, waiting for more information.

"Double rum and coke," said the barman after a pause.

"I don't drink that," replied Jonathan.

"What he ordered," he explained. "Helps me focus if I remember the drink." He closed his eyes as if picturing the meeting. "Said he was off to visit his fairy godmother. Then went into the bank across the street."

Jonathan said nothing.

"Bank's closing early today. Having a party. Manager's retiring." the barman added.

The bank's offices were garlanded with cheap and glitzy decorations. Staff were all unwinding.

Rafael was wearing a black armband as a mark of respect for his mother who had recently died. He looked up and to his utter shock saw Jonathan snaking his way through the crowd towards him, stopping and talking to other members of staff who pointed in Rafael's direction. It was years since the small man first wormed his way into Rafael's life, but Jonathan looked just the same; a small innocuous man with no expression on his face and ice in his veins.

"I hear the old witch is dead," Jonathan whispered, oozing menace, yet still greeting Rafael in the traditional Philippine way with a lift of his eyebrows.

"Get out," hissed Rafael, his voice shaking. "You can't just barge in here and speak to me like this," he added nervously, looking round the room to see if anyone had overheard their exchange.

"If you hadn't spilled your guts to the Australian, I wouldn't be here," smiled Jonathan as he slipped his arm around Rafael's waist, like they were the closest of friends. "The corners of that rug of respectability you stand on are held by me. Want me to tug?" he asked. "What the fuck happened?"

Rafael decided in that moment he was going to defy Jonathan, let him do his worst.

"My mother is dead. You have no hold over me anymore," he said boldly.

Jonathan turned and smiled as a tray of *carabao* cheese wrapped in banana leaf was offered to him by one of the staff. The young man was dressed in the traditional *barong Tagalog* of a loose-fitting embroidered shirt with a long slit on each side worn over black trousers. A pink paper crown perched askew on his head unfortunately diluted the effect of the formal ensemble.

Jonathan shooed the waiter away and winking at an astonished Rafael jumped with a grin onto a chair. He waved both arms for quiet.

"Ladies and Gentlemen, I have been a client of this bank for many years now and have known about the family of *Ginoong* Rafael Satow even longer." He reached into his pocket and removed a black and white photo.

"I would love to show you all some photos of earlier times, of what made the man we have here with us today, but I think it would be unfair of me to do so without first asking permission from my host."

Rafael's horrified expression was enough. He shook his head.

"No please, today is not only about me. It's about us and how long we have worked together," Rafael said, desperation in his voice despite the best attempt to remain jovial.

"You are too modest, my friend. I am sure some would love to see evidence of high jinx from the past, but I will keep this memento with me for another time. Silence must be the rule for today."

He stepped off the chair and picking up a beer, he looked at Rafael for a moment then turned to those present and raised the drink in a salute.

"To Rafael and the memory of his late mother… may she always be remembered with fondness and her spirit kept alive by her son. *Magalak*, cheers. Happy retirement."

With that Jonathan led the clapping. Rafael nervously acknowledged the applause, declining to make any reply.

"Come, let's just go over to your office for a quiet drink, hmm?" murmured Jonathan. He led Rafael into the room, calmly leaning against the door after closing and locking it.

"I'm listening," Jonathan said, returning to his typically emotionless expression.

Rafael started nervously, "Sam Wood was a client… one of Golden Eagle Trusts' special clients, as you know."

"So why was he here?"

"A simple error had been made, one of the half yearly payments was sent to Mr. Wood's domestic account in LA…."

Jonathan cut in angrily "How did that happen?" He was no longer leaning against the door but walking menacingly towards Rafael.

"The Los Angeles account was still on file. We had some IT issues and that one payment went off to the right person, just the wrong account. When Mr. Wood called after speaking to his L.A. bank. I stalled him; I never discuss these accounts over the phone as you insisted. I did some checking and finally realized the mistake. Before I got back to him though, he appeared in person."

"What did you tell him?" He waved the photo in Rafael's face, the threat clear.

When Rafael spoke, Jonathan understood in that instant Sam's actions.

"Nothing… well strangely he wanted that photo. Harmless request. I had another copy made." Rafael nodded over to the picture of him next to the plane Jonathan himself had used to get into the Philippines.

"The people who own the plane are our clients. They took me out for a ride in the plane once. Mr. Wood said he liked the uniform," whispered Jonathan in fear.

Jonathan pulled out his balisong.

"I should just kill you and that fag Zino and be done with it."

Summoning up every ounce of courage Rafael pulled himself up to his full height. "I don't think that would be a good idea. I know Haribon Guinto sends money here. After Mr. Wood left, I wrote a letter detailing everything I have done over the years. Where the money comes from, where it is sent how much and to whom. It's in a safe deposit box in Manila. If I die unexpectedly,

I've left instructions for it to be sent to Haribon Guinto. If I live, well… then I say no more."

For the first time in his life, Jonathan pulled back from killing a man. Louis McConnell had been very clear *'Just make sure whatever Sam found out stays buried but keep it low-key, and keep well clear of our former partner, Haribon Guinto.'*

Jonathan's only sign of tension was a tightening of his jawline.

"One more word, especially about Golden Eagle Trust, and everyone in this place will know who your father really was," Jonathan said in a flat voice tapping his pocket containing the faded photo of Yono Tan. "Your mother's memory won't be worth dog shit. And you and Zino will be history."

With that he downed the dregs of his beer and left. That was the last time Rafael would see Jonathan.

Jonathan remembered the dying Auntie Reena telling him about his own birth mother; how she abandoned her baby and how Reena had taken him in. Soon after Reena's death, Jonathan had tracked this woman down, a small wizened Japanese woman, bitter and old before her time, living in squalor by the docks. She filled in for Jonathan the parts of his story that Reena had not known about.

In 1945 she was working in Manila, during society's meltdown at the end of the war. She'd been the thirty-year-old daughter of a Japanese officer who had died in the battle for Manila. No beauty and still single, she was a nurse at the hospital where the injured Yono Tan had been brought after the airstrike at Fort Santiago. Despite his injuries she knew instantly who he was.

"Yono Tan was an honored guest in our house. He was a real man. I still keep all the press cuttings on him. I nursed him back to life. After trying for many years I gave birth to you. Small, weak. A Filipino. He hated you. He turned to drink. When he died, I wanted you out of my life," she said slowly.

"I gave you to that young *Matandang Dalaga*, Reena," his birth mother said. Jonathan had flinched at the derogatory term for a spinster. "A beggar. I watched people drop coins into her upturned hand. Convinced her a baby might get her more sympathy and a few more coins. I told her your father's name, gave her the news clippings and sold you to her for a bottle of whiskey. You were of no use to me, a runt not worthy of his father's memory."

His mother looked him up and down.

"Still a runt, aren't you? You'd hardly be able to lift a bolo, let alone use it. Your father... he was a real man." she sniffed.

Jonathan showed no emotion. Not a flicker of filial love. This emaciated bitch had just been an incubator. He spat at her, turned away, and never saw her again.

As if a man like Yono Tan could have a son as weak and flawed as Rafael Satow. Satow's father had been a 'nobody'. His son gullible, willing to believe his father was a hated figure just from a few photos and a story spun by Jonathan.

Yono Tan/Jona-Than. Jonathan knew perfectly well where his own name came from... and his ruthless streak. He was an executioner's son.

CHAPTER 17

MID AIR ACROSS THE ATLANTIC

Marcus was sitting middle center seat in economy with an overweight woman to his left and a student whose snoring could wake the dead on his right. A seven-year-old squirming behind him furiously kicked the seat back.

"Maybe he'd like to play outside?" suggested Marcus with a smile as he turned around to look at the unconcerned parents.

He took a deep breath and went back to his notes. He had already spent time breaking down the script of **FALL OUT**, preparing a budget and timeline for production, as well as listing the creative talent he would need to secure financing. He had looked at locations to shoot the film that might provide tax incentives or grants to supplement the advances from distribution companies and investors.

Once home he was going to have to begin calling casting agents and assembling his preferred list of the main HODs (Heads of Departments) for camera, set design and construction, editing, costume design, hair, and makeup. He was hoping to be in production within six months, but the budget was already climbing to $40 million; a substantial sum for any independent movie. Without direct personal access to the US market and distribution finance due to his travel ban, it was a near impossible one.

However, there was one silver lining to the very dark clouds over Marcus' head, a chance to meet most of the movers and shakers of the film industry in one place outside of the US. In less than a month the Cannes Film Festival, an annual event he had always attended, would provide him the opportunity he sorely needed. He was sure he could set up some meetings. He had a great script and would have finished his financing requirements, but what he really needed was 'talent' or a well-known name attached to the project to give it momentum.

The obvious choice was to get director Robert Kelso on board. Everyone loves a comeback and for Kelso to return behind the camera on Sam Wood's last screenplay would hit the headlines and create a real buzz. He knew Sam had sent him a copy. Maybe getting him involved was part of Sam's plan?

"The best screenplays creep up on you... as one story unfolds suddenly another reveals the real underlying truth." He remembered Sam telling him.

Marcus thought the idea of a cache of arms hidden way out in the remote Philippine jungle was beyond fanciful and was sure had no roots in reality. That was quite unlike the notion that guns were hidden by Noriega in war torn Panama. If Sam was really trying to reach out and say something, clearly it was not that.

"Ladies and Gentlemen welcome to Heathrow airport where the time is 7:00 AM, the temperature is 10 degrees and it's raining...."

Back on the West Coast, Cara Baines left another urgent message on Marcus' voice mail imploring him to call her.

# CHAPTER 18

LONDON, UNITED KINGDOM

Stefan de Turris' company, International Film Bond, had paid out a substantial sum after **THE LAST COMPANY** had abruptly stopped filming. Investing millions of dollars in a feature film was a risky undertaking at the best of times, so most movies were 'bonded' or insured. Should a film fall into difficulty, the bonding company would do its best to complete delivery of the film or repay the investors' money.

Marcus had met Stefan several times at his office during pre-production of **THE LAST COMPANY.** They even exchanged Christmas cards for a few years after the movie, so he had, what he hoped was still de Turris' home address.

Stefan had been a tall, urbane man, with barely a trace of an accent despite his Swiss nationality and upbringing. Like a lot of wealthy people, he had an aura of aloofness about him, a slight superiority that Marcus suspected brooked little dissent from those who worked for him.

Stefan de Turris owned a six-story Georgian house in Belgravia, one of those exclusive buildings that a passer-by assumed was either an embassy or several apartments.

When Marcus had googled him in LA, he read that Stefan had been involved in a car crash a few years ago. There hadn't been much else except he had clearly retired with no more outside directorships. Marcus decided lunchtime was the best time to visit. He had bought a new phone at Heathrow, inserted the chip that had mercifully been given to him, and reconnected and downloaded his messages, but it was 5AM in LA. He would call Cara after he had seen de Turris.

It was raining hard, and he asked the taxi driver to do a U-turn and stepped out on the opposite side of the street to the de Turris house at the Berkeley Hotel. He ducked into The Blue Bar, a great place to gather his thoughts. Despite the deluge outside, Marcus treated himself to a Champagne Bellini as a private salute to English spring.

He sat in a corner. He needed to explain to de Turris the circumstances surrounding the screenplay and why, after so many years, he was coming to see him. He had with him a copy of **FALL OUT** tucked in his jacket.

The bar was quiet, a couple of suited businessmen huddled over a small computer screen on some deal, and two women from the mink and Mercedes set, rattling their jewelry at each other and complaining about their husbands.

The rain eventually subsided. It was time to make a move. As he rose to leave, a nurse bustled into the bar, her starched blue uniform oddly out of place. The barman smiled in recognition.

"Mary, sneaking out for a quick one while you're on duty?" he teased.

"Away with you, John," came back the heavy Irish accent. "You don't be having a split of champagne there in the fridge? For some reason we've run out. You know how much he enjoys a glass at lunch."

The barman leaned down and pulled out the requested bottle. He handed it to her. "Give Mr. de Turris my regards, if you know what I mean," he smiled.

Marcus was somewhat taken aback that Stefan was in need of a nurse more than a year after the accident, but this presented with an opportunity too good to pass up.

"Do let me help you with that," was the best he could think of, as if a 200-pound nurse would be troubled by the effort of carrying a quarter bottle of champagne no bigger than a Coca-Cola.

"I was just coming over to visit Mr. de Turris. I see he hasn't quite started his lunch," he added.

The nurse looked him up and down very suspiciously. Marcus sensed that he needed to be careful.

"Know him well, do you?" she asked.

"Not close friends, but we were business associates for many years. The movies, actually…. hence the script," Marcus said pulling **FALL OUT** from his jacket. He smiled at her hoping the effect was warm charm, not cold desperation. The nurse looked doubtful.

"We both go to Holy Trinity in Sloane Square. Thought I'd pop in, if that's alright," added Marcus remembering they had once met there for a wedding and hoping a religious tack would work. It did.

Deciding Marcus was friend not foe Mary smiled. "Let's be off then," she said. She marched out, quickly crossing over to the house with Marcus following.

"I often go and listen to Father Bradley on Sundays myself. I'll look out for you. Nice man, although he likes a drink."

Swiping an electronic card against a pad, Mary led him in. Marcus stopped in his tracks.

"Never been here? It's quite a sight."

The oval shaped hall was spectacular. The floor was an ancient black and white mosaic of extremely intricate Asian design. The walls were covered with glass display cases. Those on the left contained a vast array of small seashells and next to them were cases filled with round coins of copper and bronze, each with a square hole cut into them. Inside the cases both shells and coins were hanging from slender silk ribbons which were in turn suspended from ancient leather belts. The cabinets to the right contained what looked like four-inch miniature scimitar shaped knives. Made from bronze with a circular hole at the handle end, they too were attached to belts by silk ribbons. Lastly there was a display of small bars the size of a man's thumb, made from what appeared to be gold, silver and bronze.

"They're all apparently various types of money," said Mary.

"And those tub things," she said pointing, "I'm told are the sign of an emperor's residence." Circling the room stood nine three-legged oval-shaped bronze cauldrons. Each was about waist high and large enough for a man to hide inside. Marcus guessed each must weigh at least 1,000 pounds. The meaning to anyone entering that house was clear. Here resided money and power.

Mary beckoned Marcus to follow her up the wide spiral staircase. As he climbed, he noticed the curved wall to his left was pocketed with small alcoves, each discreetly lit from above by a halogen spot bulb.

Under each light was a single delicate work of art. An elegant long-stemmed jade wine goblet, an intricately patterned porcelain plate depicting the piercing blues and reds of a dragon and a peacock. On and on the treasures stood lining the staircase like soldiers in their sentry boxes. Everything was museum quality. It was a stunning display of cultured wealth.

In the last alcove crouched two small winged lions. Nestled between them was a small photo of a young girl grinning between two life-sized stone versions of the same animals. A child's writing on the photo read '*Tianlu and Bixie*'.

"It's his daughter," the nurse informed Marcus. "She liked the lions. He keeps her picture there to remind him of her, I'm told."

"Is she here?"

"No. Never visits. She's grown up now, Miss Melinda. She has a business in cans."

Marcus looked at her perplexed.

"In the South of France," Mary added helpfully.

He then understood and smiled. She'd meant the town, not the container.

"I know it well. I go to the Cannes Film Festival there every year," said Marcus.

"I understand she's a builder," said Mary.

Marcus again looked puzzled.

"Of stands and such. For those conferences."

He was intrigued now and continued up the stairs. He became aware of the light hum of machinery and the aroma of disinfectant. On reaching the top, they turned left and walked to the end of a parquet-floored corridor.

Up to that point Marcus had seen no one apart from the nurse and had been surprised at the apparent lack of staff in such a big house. Now he understood. They were all here in the one room at the end of the hall. There were three more nurses, two female, one male and a middle-aged man in a dark suit sitting quietly in the corner behind a desk.

Noticing Marcus looking at the man Mary said "That's Giles, the chauffeur. Miss Melinda asked we keep him on, he being so fond of her father. He felt so guilty he hadn't been driving that day. Do you know Miss Melinda, you being in films and Cannes?"

Giles looked up, scowling at Mary.

"Mr. de Turris had mentioned her," Marcus lied. Depending on Stefan's reaction to seeing him again, Marcus wanted to be as vague as possible. He need not have worried. A shadow of the man Marcus remembered as Stefan de Turris was being spoon-fed lunch. Looking like a small shrunken doll, he was sunken into the bed, as if he was lying in quicksand. Various wires were attached to him and oxygen was being gently administered via a clear tube that forked into two small vents under his nose.

Mary handed over the champagne bottle and a nurse dribbled a few drops into some water inside a small baby's bottle, complete with teat. Stefan's eyes stared vacantly into the room.

"Mr. Vallings, the lawyer who looks after things here, told us Mr. de Turris had a heart bypass about ten years ago. The surgeon said that a little champagne every day was good for him, and right up to the accident Mr. de Turris insisted he had a drop at lunch. We keep up the tradition. Poor man, it's his only treat nowadays," sighed Mary with sympathy.

Stefan's eyes turned to Marcus, but he gave no outward sign of recognition. There was a pause and a glance from Mary to Marcus.

"Father Bradley asked me to send you his best regards. I'll tell him you're surrounded by women and still drinking champagne," Marcus said, smiling gently.

No reaction from Stefan, but thankfully a smile from the nurses. Mary had noticed Marcus' expression.

"You look a little shocked. Did not Father Bradley tell you?" she asked?

Marcus shook his head, "Yes... but I didn't quite understand...."

"Was there anything else" she asked him, nodding at the script Marcus was still holding?

"No, probably not in the circumstances," said Marcus turning to leave. "Poor Stefan, how serious...?"

"It's not good. Let's just say I don't think you'll be asking him about scripts and movies for a while."

"Exactly what I told the other gentleman," said the chauffeur.

Marcus stopped and looked at Giles, still sitting at his desk. "Other gentleman? Who?" he asked trying to sound casual.

"Don't remember his name. We got a call a few weeks ago. A man asking if we had received a script. I told him that all mail sent here goes directly on to Mr. de Turris' daughter. If there was one, she'd have it. I mentioned the call to the family lawyer, Mr. Vallings."

"Giles," admonished Mary. "We don't discuss such things in front of strangers."

"You brought him in, so I assumed he wasn't," said Giles, the implication that she had been less than discreet herself hanging in the air. Marcus sensed tension between the two.

"Seems even if you're at death's door, people still expect you to answer the mail," Mary said ignoring the chauffeur.

"I'd like to write to his daughter. This must be very hard. Could I trouble you for her address?" It was a gamble but after a moment's hesitation Mary made up her mind.

"They're not that close but…." and she went over to a writing desk by the window and looking in an address book wrote the details down on a sheet of paper. Marcus thanked her as she handed it to him.

"She calls herself Mako now for some reason. I also added her phone number. I doubt you will reach her on it though. According to Mr. Vallings when she's not building things, she spends all her time at sea in a *Rover Aquatic S* or some such."

Marcus turned to look at Stefan de Turris, at the same time trying to decipher what possible craft Mary was describing.

"Bye, Stefan. I'll pop in again soon." He turned to the nurse.

"Thank you, Mary. I'll see myself out," he said quietly.

Stefan de Turris' mind was all he had left and it was working overtime. Why had this man, whom he recognized as the callow youth from **THE LAST COMPANY**, suddenly decided to visit him? How dare that foolhardy nurse give him the contact details of his daughter! What was this script about? Who rang? Telling Riley and the caller that his daughter had a copy could only mean one thing. She was in danger.

Locked in his motionless body, Stefan's mind seethed with frustration.

As Marcus walked down the stairs and out onto street, he had to assume the caller was asking about **FALL OUT**. So, who rang? But the real question was why?

If Marcus couldn't speak to Stefan about it, he wanted to speak to his daughter. Maybe she could help. He had heard of the famously abrasive Cannes designer called Mako but had no idea until now she was Stefan's daughter. He needed an introduction that would get her attention and generate an offer to meet at the Cannes Film Festival.

He translated in his mind what he imagined Mary to mean as the *Rover Aquamatic S* and went in search of a very specific kind of shop.

In the taxi home he got an email that gave him a glimmer of hope, news that possibly changed everything.

Dear Marcus,

Sorry not to have responded earlier. I understand you have optioned **FALL OUT**.

I have decided to come to the Cannes Film Festival. Have only one slot available.

First week. Wednesday 11:30AM. Penthouse, 67 La Croisette.

Do not be late.

Best,

Robert Kelso

The flood of relief that swept over Marcus quickly dried up when he read the next message.

Marcus. Where the hell are you? Call me. Drop it. **FALL OUT** *kills.*

Cara

There was an attachment with three names on it. Idly he looked them up on the movie and television data base *www.IMDB.com* and sure enough he had worked with them on *THE LAST COMPANY*. On seeing their photos, he remembered they had something else in common; a shocking event that bound them together.

In addition, all three of them were dead.

CHAPTER 19

MANILA, PHILIPPINES

Haribon Guinto needed to deal with the bound body downstairs.

He drew slowly on his cigar and then gently blew on the tip until it glowed. His jet-black hair was swept back in a widow's peak over his forehead and the heavy black framed tinted glasses framed his face. It was early evening now and he stood looking out over the Makati district of Manila. His large frame was clothed in a dark blue silk suit, a handmade ivory colored shirt with large 24 carat gold eagle head cufflinks.

The office furniture of black leather, glass, and chrome was the same as in any other corporate office; modern, sleek, and expensive. Apart from an oil painting of an eagle there were no other personal touches, no clues as to where this well-groomed man had sprung from.

To most Filipinos, Haribon Guinto had just appeared, like a modern-day Count of Monte Cristo, complete with his own seemingly bottomless access to capital, which he had used to create a property and entertainment empire.

Not far from his office he could see his company's newest development of two massive buildings, one a hotel, the other luxury apartments. Both clawed their way into the humid sky. He had bought himself the largest penthouse suite – at a suitably discounted rate of course. The hotel was completed, the apartments would be finished in just under a year. At least it would save him from hours of sitting in Manila's notorious traffic when he headed towards his current home between the Polo Club and the

American War Memorial Cemetery. And the apartment would be closer to the action.

Well over sixty, he still enjoyed the company of beautiful women. Having no desire to marry or have children was rare in a Filipino man, but his own childhood brought back unhappy memories and his real family was his business empire. In any case, he could not have survived with only the traditional single *querida* or mistress, much preferring the string of girlfriends his wealth and bachelor status provided him.

There was only one person he considered true family. An older woman from his past who lived with him in his large house in the city. He would never sell it. She could remain there when he moved to the penthouse.

As he stared into the twilight settling on the city, he could make out the lights of the port and the large tankers out at sea. It was no more than seven miles northeast, but the traffic was so bad at that time of day had he wanted to drive there, it might as well have been in a different time zone.

He turned, looked down the length of his vast office to the window at the far end and picked out the landing lights of the jets coming into the international airport ten miles to the south. He held a special affection for both the harbor and airport. They were where his career as a petty criminal had started and ended.

His youth had been tough, but at first, not underprivileged. His father, Jorge, had been a cog in the Marcos' machinery, slavishly lapping up the stories and hype about the President and his wife, Imelda.

Haribon's mother, Conchita, had grown up with Imelda. She was always quick to defend her classmate's 'little excesses'. She would remind her only son and his pretty doting nanny, or *ya-ya*, that Imelda had spent her youth living in a garage.

Imelda's father, Vincente Orestes Romueldez, had been a lawyer, whose wealthy first wife died leaving him with a large house and five children. When he remarried, his original children from the first marriage looked down on his second wife and her first child Imelda, eventually banishing this second family to the rooms over the garage.

It was here that Imelda would play with a neighbor's child Conchita, identifying different types of birds while hidden in the lush undergrowth of the garden, out of sight of the hated stepbrothers and stepsisters. Their favorite bird was the haribon, the huge Philippine eagle. Whenever they spotted one, they thought it an omen of good luck.

It was only natural that years later when Conchita had her first and only child, she would nickname him after the lucky omen. Haribon's father however, had christened him "Ferdinand" in homage to the President.

Jorge Guinto owed his position as a local planner to his wife's closeness to Imelda. The two young women had kept in touch and when Imelda married Congressman and future President Ferdinand Marcos, Conchita's connection transformed Jorge's career.

Over a few short years, Jorge managed to accumulate a degree of wealth from the bribes he took from local contractors. However, what he most craved was recognition for his own talent rather than forever riding on his wife's well-connected coattails.

Conchita had been admitted to the 'Blue Ladies', the group of sycophants and aides that swarmed like worker bees around the regal Imelda. Being close to the inner circle, Conchita was aware of the greed and the capricious nature of the President and those close to him. Gossip, scandal, jealousy, and fear were woven into the fabric of Manila society under Marcos' regime.

Life was good for Haribon, but in a matter of days, his happy childhood would unravel. First there was a furious argument between his mother and father about his beloved *ya-ya*. He didn't understand what it was about, only catching snatches of the heated exchange. All he could gather was his father had discovered something about his *ya-ya's* past he felt the President would find of value and duly reward him. Haribon's mother feared Marcos and warned him of sharing any valuable information.

"He will take that knowledge, destroy you... all of us, don't tell him," she had implored.

But her pleas were ignored with disastrous consequences. Haribon's *ya-ya* disappeared the next day. Less than a week later Jorge was arrested at their home on a trumped-up charge of corruption. Haribon hated him and shed no tears as he was dragged away. His father was venal and hid a string of mistresses from his trusting wife. Still blindly in love with her husband, Conchita tried to rescue him, but to no avail. Despite her son protesting her husband was not the man she believed in, Conchita made the fatal mistake of protesting too strongly to the First Lady, implying the President was behind all this. She suddenly found herself alone and ostracized. Their money dried up as fast as their friends.

Conchita was devastated at the betrayal of her friendship to Imelda. She just gave up on life. Haribon came home from school one day barely two months after his father's arrest and found her body lying on the bathroom floor, having succumbed to an overdose of barbiturates.

There was no sympathy for the teenage Haribon, suddenly without any parents or money to protect him. The house was seized by the government and the teenage boy was out on the street. Once a member of President Marcos' inner circle, he was now an outcast and alone. The young man took to the streets and started to fight back. He never allowed anyone to call him Ferdinand again. Haribon was his only name.

He fell in with a bunch of other disaffected youths whose parents had either fallen foul of the regime, or simply never had a chance to benefit from it. Torres was one of them. A few months later Haribon and Torres had their fateful first encounter with the young and skinny kid, Jonathan.

Before being disowned by the Marcos regime, Haribon had been well educated and had a natural eye for business. He could spot a new trend or an opportunity a mile away. In that corrupt society there were always those who refused to wait when there was a shortage of hard-to-get goods. Haribon always seemed able to procure them, charging a decent fee in the process.

Although his former friends shunned him, they knew where to go if they needed a color TV, Gucci jacket, or a few grams of coke. But they all paid Haribon's price. No favors given or expected from this outcast. However, in his late teens he was caught in a sting operation handling stolen goods and served a short time behind bars.

Haribon had managed to save enough money, so that when he was released from prison, he was able to buy a truck and start a small business. He established a reputation for delivering on time, to the most inaccessible places on the tightest of schedules.

He seemed to possess an uncanny instinct of knowing when cargoes of value were left unguarded and could be relieved of 'surpluses'. That 'instinct' was, of course, Jonathan, with whom he had reconnected after his release.

It was because of Jonathan that Haribon's life had begun to recapture the wealth of his youth. It was Jonathan who had supplied him with the details of shipments vulnerable to a lighting fast hijack. And throughout Jonathan had his back. It was Jonathan who had warned him of the treachery of Torres, and it had been Jonathan's ruthless intervention that had saved the day.

But it was via McConnell and de Turris that Haribon Guinto had become one of the richest men in Manila. It was also how his relationship with Jonathan had broken beyond repair.

"We ready," said a discreet and accented voice, interrupting Haribon's thoughts.

Haribon looked at the formally attired chauffeur, complete with polished boots, black leather gloves, and a peaked cap held under his arm. The ensemble looked somewhat incongruous as the man was built more like a sumo wrestler than a driver. He was standing at the entrance to the private elevator that opened into Haribon's office. There was a fleck of blood on his cheek, along with a faint smirk.

"Wipe that off," said Haribon pointing to the driver's pock-marked face. The driver pulled out a white handkerchief from the breast pocket of his jacket to dab the blood and, to make sure he understood every nuance of what his boss said, he also dropped the smile.

"Tell me again, Datu," commanded Haribon to the chauffeur as he strode into the elevator and the doors closed with a hiss behind them.

"He turn up today. He make scene, sir, demand to see you. Say he found marriage certificate in mother things," said Datu. "He shout about father's thumbprint on marriage certificate and about *LAST COMPANY*. Say been redirecting millions of dollars. Orders from Jonathan... I take him out of building... somewhere... quiet..."

The doors opened into the underground car park. In front of them Haribon's stretch limousine stood purring, sitting low on its suspension caused by the extra weight of the bullet proof windows and panels. The engine was running to crank up the air conditioning, ensuring it was cool when the owner got in.

When Datu opened the door, Haribon glanced in and saw the edge of the clear plastic sheeting that covered the limo's thick pile carpet. A naked hog-tied man lay on it—the bank manager from Pagsanjan. Rafael Satow looked up at Haribon with a split lip and pleading bloodshot eyes. Haribon ignored Rafael and stepping over the man, settled into his seat. Datu silently closed the door and positioned himself in the driver's seat, ready for his next command. Haribon pulled a ticket from his breast pocket.

"The game, will we get there in time, Datu" he asked though it was more of a command than a question.

"It start at 10:00 PM. We be fine sir," he replied as he slowly exited the garage and entered the flow of traffic.

Haribon pushed the button that activated the soundproof glass divider and turned to the terrified man.

"After I get out at the Jai Alai stadium, my driver can either drop you at the train station, or in the harbor. Up to you." He leaned forward and ripped the duct tape from the petrified man's mouth. "So tell me, what's so big that you thought you could march into my office and tell my associates I've been duped by a man called Jonathan?"

"The monster… he told me was my father had no right hand. Yet when I found my late mother's marriage certificate it was signed using his right thumb. We have all been deceived…."

Of course, Haribon knew that part of the story but it always helped when questioning someone to start with facts he already knew.

"And the money you have been sending all these years, it appears that at least one of them, Sam Wood, barely got a penny," said the terrified banker.

That fact Haribon most certainly did not know but his face remained calm.

"And the others; Baines, Kelso, Riley, McConnell, and de

Turris?" asked Haribon.

"I have no idea… I sent the money as directed to accounts in their names…. but maybe not…."

Haribon leaned back in his seat. McConnell and de Turris had convinced Haribon they needed to pay a very specified few to keep the lid on what had happened during **THE LAST COMPANY** more than twenty years ago.

There was enough to share. Now it looked as if his own partners may, in fact, have swindled him. A relatively small amount compared to what they had all made. However, no one made a fool of him, or even worse, abused his trust. He lowered the window divider.

"Datu, give this man his clothes back." Haribon looked down at Satow. "This goes no further, or Datu will find you again… and he won't bother to bring you to me."

Rafael nodded vigorously, bursting to try and show this man he could be trusted. He prayed that Jonathan had indeed double-crossed Haribon Guinto and that retribution would find his life-long blackmailer as surely as a heat-seeking missile.

 # CHAPTER 20

HOLLYWOOD, LOS ANGELES

Louis hunkered down in his favorite booth, a cocoon of mahogany, with a deep red leather buttoned banquette. 1940s Hollywood. A restaurant with class. He sat at the prime table facing the door, so he could see and be seen by all those who entered. The usual Jameson Irish Malt Whiskey sat neatly on the table.

His guest walked in. Robert Kelso made his way straight to the booth. There was a time when he would have commanded all the attention in the room, but not now. He was no longer a force. Louis did not get up to greet his guest, instead motioning with his hand for Robert to sit down. A waiter, who had been hovering in the background came to the booth as soon as the important agent had been joined by his guest.

Triple Absolut on the rocks, thought Robert to himself. "Perrier with a twist," he said out loud to the waiter instead. Christo would have been proud of him.

Louis thought Kelso was pathetic. But the screenplay was a minefield, and he needed Kelso to help defuse it. Skipping any pleasantries, the agent got straight to the point.

"Let's make sure we are singing from the same hymn sheet. *FALL OUT* is for you and me, OK? We'll do it right; do it justice."

Kelso gave a hesitant nod.

"Good. Marcus contacted me as I told you, certain he had a hit on his hands and was in control. In fact, he's out of his depth. Wanted me to package it. Told him I wasn't interested in working with him, raising money, or putting any of the talent from my agency into it," Louis swirled the whiskey in his glass, then emptied it in one gulp.

"However, it's a great script. I want us to have those rights, so we need to cut him out. That's where you come in." He raised a finger and the waiter appeared. Louis just pointed to the glass. The man whisked it away and went to fetch another.

"No way will Marcus sell the rights to me, due to our past history, but he'll listen to you. He sees you as a fellow artist."

Kelso bridled a fraction. Louis knew that was a hot button. No Director ever wanted to have his creativity compared to a mere Producer.

"Riley has zero credibility in this town. No idea what Sam was thinking. So, let's get Riley to face the hard cold truth. His confidence needs wearing down. I've made a few calls to some mutual associates, encouraged rumors about incompetence and dishonesty at his old company. No one will touch him. You sent him the note to meet as I suggested?"

Robert nodded again, this time confidently.

"As we both agreed," he corrected trying to assert his position as an equal.

Louis let it pass. "By the time you see Riley in Cannes he will be desperate, even doubting his own judgment. And I suspect he's tight for cash. You'll easily get the rights from him."

Louis knew Marcus was dancing on the edge and would have no choice but to eventually drop the project into someone else's hands; maybe not a hard-nosed packager like Louis but Louis needed it to be someone whose strings he could pull. Who better than someone Marcus respected, someone creative, with an affinity to the story? Robert Kelso.

"And then in return for me transferring the rights to you, you will finance it. Get it made?" Robert asked. "Unlike that clusterfuck you last had me do?"

"Robert, **THE LAST COMPANY** ended badly for everyone. It was years ago," soothed Louis. "I had only the best intentions for the production. I appreciated your help keeping a hothead like Marcus on track. It would have been a great movie. Once those people stole the film though...."

"It cost a man his life, Louis. That place was a hell-hole, those locals were ruthless, one of them even threatened me...."

Louis stared back impassively.

"At least you managed to move on," said Kelso.

"The world has moved on," said Louis dryly. "We all deal with setbacks in our own way. I just plowed my energy into business," Louis continued, leaving unsaid how Robert had dealt with his.

"The important thing is for Marcus to see you're back," he said with encouragement. "I can make it work. You did the right thing when you called me. It will pay off," said Louis.

"I hope so... And we haven't even discussed my fees yet," Kelso deadpanned.

Poor Kelso, always the greedy patsy, thought McConnell. He hadn't *needed* to make **THE LAST COMPANY.** He could have turned down Louis' contract, lost a few bucks but kept his precious credibility. But Kelso was just plain greedy. McConnell knew he could exploit that weakness and had offered him the then unheard-of fee of $7 million to direct the film. Once Kelso had signed on the dotted line, his integrity was screwed. Robert simply became Louis' bitch, jumping through hoops, not allowed to ask questions himself, reciting Louis' answers to anyone who started querying decisions. He had certainly used his age and experience to beat down Marcus' doubts.

Louis knew if what really happened out in the jungle ever came to light, Kelso could never claim innocence. That fee would shine like a beacon of his complicity and guilt. Louis had covered all the bases.

"You are the key here, Robert. Money isn't the problem, Marcus is," cajoled Louis. "This is the plan…"

"Good morning gentleman, my name is Justin. No, you have had your aperitif may I tell you the specials…."

Louis ignored the waiter, angry at the interruption. Old timers and heavy hitters never read menus and certainly weren't interested in the specials of the day, let alone a waiter's name. *Louis* was the special of the day. He just ordered what he wanted and either got it or never came back, denuding a restaurant of a sprinkling of stardust and star power. Louis unceremoniously interrupted the waiter.

"I'll have a large pot of beluga caviar with melba toast, no diced onions, egg, or other needless crap. I'll follow that with a 16 oz. New York strip, medium rare, spinach, and onion rings. And a bottle of Opus 1, 1991."

Picking up his whiskey and addressing Robert he added, "And in case you think I'm getting carried away with my order it's because *FALL OUT* is gonna pay off." Robert quietly ordered a salad and grilled sole. Louis dismissed the waiter with a wave of his hand.

"What did you think of Scene 15?" Louis asked Robert casually. The Director looked blankly at him.

"The references to you?" Louis continued calmly, looking for any reaction. Louis clearly remembered the chill he himself felt on reading the scene.

FALL OUT page 25

SCENE 15

INT.NEW YORK.OFFICE. LATE AT NIGHT.

CLOSE ON man early thirties bent over architect board. KENNY JENKINS feverishly

scrubs out numbers scrawled on pad of
paper, scrunches it up and tosses it on the
floor in frustration. Floor littered with
discarded earlier ones. Clipped to top of
architect board is photograph of old flour
mill, with a large 2-D plan of the new
building below it. On other desk to the
left glows a large computer screen with new
3-D cad cam design of same building plan.
He opens desk. Pulls out bottle of vodka.
He pours it into an empty bottle of mineral
water on desk. Puts vodka back in drawer.

                KENNY (To self)
        It can't be done like this, guys.

                FRANK (OFF SCREEN)
        It can, you have a special gift.

FRANK KIDDO appears.

                    KENNY
        (Startled. Recovers. Looks uneasy)
            Right. The heart attack you just
            gave me.
            You don't knock?

                    FRANK
            (Looking at wristwatch)
        Maybe you could use some of that
        fat advance to pay for
        a cute P.A.

                    (a beat)
          Oh, that's right. I forgot.
          Lone wolf. Very attractive part of
          your resume.

                         KENNY
     (Turning to computer screen on smaller
     desk. Taps key. See breakdown of schedule
     and materials)
               I'm busy. Using *my talent* to
               gut this design so that it'll
               fall over if a rat farts.

                         FRANK
          Not before we flip it back to
          the locals though. Take pride in
          your work. That last piss-ant job
          out at Staten Island, the
          Grandview playground development.
          Made a ton of change for us both.

                         KENNY
          God help the kids

     FRANK walks around desk leans over KENNY'S
     shoulder, examining the screen then paper
     on floor.

                         FRANK
                    (Whispers in ear)
          You just work your magic on those
          specs.

       (Picks up bottled water)
Aqua Regia.
          (Reading label)
Guarantee of purity.
 (He smells it, takes a swig)
Does it cleanse your soul?

          KENNY
Yeah. Helps me cut more corners,
shave safety margins while
you smooth the paperwork and
certificates. It's a Jerry-rigged
shack.

          FRANK
It's fucking Panama.
Jerry-rigged is a design
triumph down there.
Don't get all moral on me.
You take the money.
Every time.

          KENNY
Which is why this is the last one.

          FRANK
I'll pull some strings, get
you some of that new building
work up by Gracie Mansion.
You can flex your true
artistic muscle.

                    KENNY
The demolition process seems fine
but the construction schedule makes
no sense. It's impossible to work
around. These criteria are...

                    FRANK
Written in stone, shall we
say? Schedule stays. Kenny.
We go back in five weeks.
You can make it work. You always
have. Those revised plans,
budgeted, on my desk,
as agreed, a week today.
                    (Pause)
And I said off the booze.
Here's something to keep you going.
        (Reaches into pocket).

                    KENNY
I don't need your money.

Frank tosses him a bag of coke.

                    FRANK
        (turns and leaves)
Nor I your delays. This will stop
any down times

SCENE 16 EXT. STREET-CONTINUOUS.

FRANK reaches for cell phone. Hits

speed-dial, JOE NISTEN'S name comes up.

<pre>
                    FRANK
        He hasn't a clue.
                 (Pause).
        He's a fuckin' drug addict with
        delusions of the scope of his
        talent. No one'll hire him 'cept me.
        But he knows how to dress this up
                 (listens)
        Says this is the last time.
        He's right. When this job is over,
        Pffft he just disappears.
</pre>

When Kelso had sent McConnell a copy of his script with handwritten notes in the margin, the Agent had noticed right away that scenes were different. Just like with Cara. Louis knew exactly why Sam had inserted references Kelso might understand and wanted to see his reaction.

There were some heavy pointers. Kenny was obviously Kelso. The screenplay pointed out the architect's schedule difficulties that were a mirror of the shooting schedule issues of **THE LAST COMPANY**. There was Kenny's/Robert's drug abuse. When mentioning the park in New York, Sam was referencing a studio, nicknamed The Playground in Vancouver where Kelso shot interiors for **POLE-AXED**; a piss-ant job for Louis that had indeed turned into a 'ton of change'. The reference to **POLE-AXE**D was underscored by quoting the strap line from the movie, '*God help the kids*'.

Most surprising to Louis had been Sam's understanding about the significance of *Aqua Regia*.

What Sam was saying was blindingly obvious, certainly to Louis.

"*Kelso, you were being used,*" the pages shouted. "*Louis duped you, made a lot of money from you and then wanted you out of the way. Be afraid.*"

The waiter returned with the salad and caviar.

"You mean in the architect scene?" Robert said after a long pause.

Here it comes, Louis thought to himself.

"Sam being funny, I suppose."

Louis checked himself.

"The strap-line from **POLE-AXED**.... '*God help the kids*'. I thought maybe it was a coincidence, or Sam having a joke. We can take it out. It's hardly a big deal."

Louis felt a sense of relief. Perhaps Kelso really hadn't noticed, but he still needed to be on guard.

"You're right. Minor stuff. It's a great script, but like I said, we need to make it, not Riley. You must direct it, it'll be a hell of a comeback, but we have to squeeze him out. Quietly."

"I want that movie" said Robert.

"Riley doesn't have the clout to pull it off. We do. And I don't want him interfering with you creatively." Louis spooned nearly half the caviar onto one piece of Melba toast and wolfed it down. "He's not going to be part of our movie. Forget him." Another mouthful and the caviar was gone.

"Play it cool. You've agreed to see him in Cannes next month at the festival. I got you an apartment. 'Til then he can sweat."

"But how did you get him to leave and stop bashing my door in, like he did with Sam?"

"I have friends in low places. Now let's eat."

When the meal ended, the two men shook hands on an agreement neither had any intention of honoring.

 # CHAPTER 21

BELGRAVIA, LONDON

At least Stefan de Turris' mind was still free, floating. He looked down on the pitiful scene, his own limp body being attended to by a small army of starched white worker bees.

More like parasites, he thought to himself. All this cost and money for what? Now reduced to this helpless, paralyzed state, his physical presence was just an outer shell that was broken, lying motionless on the bed.

A prisoner confined to a room thrumming with machinery, an eternal annoyance that only perpetuated the purgatory that was now his world. This was not the image he had created for himself or his home to project. He would never have allowed this state to continue had he been able to pull those plugs and end it all. All he could do now was watch and think.

There was a problem. His daughter Melinda; he would never address her by that nickname the staff used. The olive branch that he had held out before the accident was as broken and twisted as the wreckage of his car. He would never have the chance to perform one more sleight of hand, one more mental acrobatic pirouette and bring her back into the fold that was his way of life.

Melinda's mother had rejected it and left him. It all started with that damned Buddha head. The bust had been in the house for years, seemingly just another of his prized possessions until one day his wife had been examining it and its significance had dawned on her. She wanted to know where it had come from.

By her revealing its secret, it had forced Stefan to the truth; what really bound him to McConnell and Haribon Guinto. He told her the whole story, what the three of them had done and why. He had got the pitch badly wrong. When he finished, he had expected her to understand the significance of the legacy he had so carefully built. Instead she was horrified. His wife looked at him like he was a stranger. She left him. Instantly. Stefan had to call Louis. Meanwhile his wife sent a brief note to their daughter who was traveling in the wilds of Hunan Province. Her father had betrayed them. She would explain, but Melinda was to come home immediately. It took more than a week for Melinda to make the journey from the wilds of China to London. She never had a chance to find out exactly what her mother meant as the woman died of an embolism a day before she landed at Heathrow. The doctors believed it was a fatal mix of stress and her high blood pressure. To Mako it was a broken heart.

After a brief and furious exchange with her father where she would not let him try to explain, she turned her back on him too; but for all the wrong reasons.

His daughter had got it all wrong. Melinda was under the illusion her mother had turned on her heels and stormed out over another woman, for chrissakes! That wasn't it at all.

In the years since she had stopped all contact with her father, Stefan had practiced what he needed to say to his daughter, every nuance, each quip—if he ever got a second chance.

He wanted to explain to her that what her mother had discovered and why the Buddha head protected their future. The Buddha head was the ultimate get-out-of–jail-free card, an insurance policy against all that he'd done. All that mattered was his daughter inherit his legacy of power and wealth. He needed her to buy into that; he burned with hope that Melinda would see and understand what his wife had not.

Just in case he never got that chance to explain, his last hope was that someday his daughter might decipher the clues he had hidden in the house in their family home in the mountains; left there for her to discover. He wanted to shake her. There was danger. Certainly, he was the root cause, but she was going to reap the whirlwind. People were coming after her, dangerous people. He had to see her, warn her, prepare her… the beeping from the heart rate monitor suddenly became a monotone note. It grew louder. It cocooned him. Then, nothing.

The people in the room crowded around his figure.

"I'm sorry. It's probably for the best, at least his pain is over," said the doctor who had rushed over from the nearby Lister Hospital.

Her eyes moist, Mary crossed herself then as agreed went off to inform the family lawyer, Mr. Robin Vallings of the death of Stefan de Turris.

An hour later Mako whispered a thank you to Robin and turned off her cell phone. The noise of the nightclub she'd left still rocked in her ears. Her father was gone and now they would never be able to confront their demons. Damn him.

# CHAPTER 22

SOHO, LONDON

".... Let it go, Marcus. For me... screw Immigration. That's bullshit." Cara wasn't budging an inch. "I think you know the story Sam is telling, why he sent it to us," she continued in a softer tone. "He wanted you to read it. I don't think he wanted to make it as a movie. Maybe he just wanted to see everyone's reaction... if it's a fantasy, let it stay that."

"No. If he is right, he wants us to expose everyone... and make the movie."

"If he was right, it killed him. Don't stir it up. Some of us want to live." She paused. Her tone hardened. "You looked up those names? The 'best boy'?"

Marcus was impressed she still remembered such arcane movie terminology. The best boy wasn't a boy at all, but the nickname given to the first assistant to the chief electrician, or gaffer.

"Mike Garland," said Marcus

"Drowned in a boating accident. Then Rory Carmichael and Don Wallis." These were the names from Louis' list.

"Rory suddenly keels over with a suspected heart attack at his local Starbucks, Don killed by a hit and run. "They were all on that movie.... They all died prematurely," she said gravely.

Marcus had really been very disturbed by those names and the group they represented. That was fuel to Cara's fire, and he decided not to tell her.

"Cara, 130 people were in the crew. It was twenty years ago. People die. Sam sent that screenplay to me because he wanted me to make it," Marcus said trying to push those names to the back of his mind and concentrate on his more immediate problem of impending financial ruin.

"Marcus, please. No one wants to dig this up. Can you even raise the money anyway?"

"It'll be tough, but I've been working the phones. McConnell's not interested, told me to forget it. Said I was damaged goods. No one would do a deal with me."

No surprise there, thought Cara to herself. Old friends from her LA days heard that McConnell had been discreetly badmouthing her English friend.

"A chink of light. I sent Kelso a couple of emails to see if this could tempt him out of retirement. I have to believe that's why Sam sent it to him. To help him and get the old team together. I eventually got a reply asking for a meeting in Cannes. I really need to get him on board…. So far, he's my only meeting. I seem to be toxic."

"Let it go, Marcus. Is it really worth it," Cara pleaded?

"To me it is. And I think it was to Sam."

Despite initially being sure she could get him to drop it, Cara knew she wasn't getting through. "Just be careful," she said resignedly and hung up.

She immediately called McConnell. "You were right. He's in London. Some visa issues. I tried to put him off. Maybe he just needs the money or just has something to prove. My guess is he won't budge. He's on a mission," Cara said flatly. "As far as I can tell his hopes rest on a meeting with Kelso in Cannes."

Louis smiled to himself and hung up.

"Riley is history," he grinned to himself.

# CHAPTER 23

SOHO, LONDON

Marcus collapsed on the sofa and stared into the fire. On a nearby table was the framed photo of himself with the crew on the set of **THE LAST COMPANY.** It was taken the first week, about fifty miles southeast of Manila. Yet it took hours of hard driving to get there. The whole crew was based in a lush valley under the gaze of a large rock, with a slow-moving river snaking its way along the valley floor and out into the jungle.

It did not surprise Marcus that this wild and beautiful location had been used more than once for the setting of a film. They were effectively on a huge open back lot, their own private outdoor studio. The day of the photo the production company had thrown a party outside under the stars.

Marcus picked up from the sofa his copy of **FALL OUT** and re-read a familiar scene; one Sam had taken from real life and twisted. The main protagonists, Frank the American and the local Panamanian Aguinaldo are throwing a party in a bar, having successfully set up a distribution pipeline via Joe Nisten for the sale of the weapons. Everything looks set to go and the two crews meet and throw a few back, before starting their work in earnest.

The real-life party on the set of **THE LAST COMPANY** had been replaced by a party in a Central American city. The names had changed but what Sam had his characters go through mirrored what had happened in the jungle outside Pagsanjan.

SCENE 20

NIGHT. PANAMA CITY. INT. BAR.

Both crews present. Over in one corner is
FRANK KIDDO, holding court to a circle
of admiring young women. Frank's gang
are whooping it up, exulting in the free
alcohol. Relaxed... getting looser by the
second...

In another corner is AGUINALDO SOSA,
surrounded by his small entourage of tough
men, looking out of place, even though this
is their home turf. TENSION. AGUINALDO rubs
his forearm, an old wound and a sign he is
uneasy.

> FRANK
> (Calling over to AGUINALDO,
> hinting at fake camaraderie)
> C'mon, join the party. Grab a drink.
> We pulled it off, got the permit to
> start work.

One of Frank's crew, JONAS, tall, thickset,
approaches one of AGUINALDO's men, TIKO,
short, thin, offering him a shot glass of
Tequila. JONAS deliberately drops it as the
man reaches out.

                    JONAS
          Whoops. Butterfingers.

In response to the laughter directed at
him TIKO pulls out a balisong knife and
performs a meticulous number of hand moves,
the blade whirling in his hands.

                  AGUINALDO
          (Yells to Frank on other side)
          Tell that Mr. Jonas to be careful.
          Tiko kills for less.

Nearby stands FRANK's burly enforcer STAN.
He is enjoying the booze and watches the
macho display. He looks over at AGUINALDO,
then at his own boss. He smiles as an
idea hits him and he picks up a discarded
champagne cork that had rolled across the
floor and stopped at his boot heel.

He pulls a few large coins from his pocket
and forces them under the metal cap at the
top of the cork, twisting the wire still
attached around it to secure them in place.
Reaches into his shirt pocket... pulls
out a small detonator, about the size and
length of a cigarette. He rams that down
into the other end of the cork...

Into the eye at the top of the detonator
cap he knots a piece of nylon fishing line.

Grinning to himself, he drops the cork,
coins and detonator into the top of a full
barrel of Tequila on the bar next to him,
so it's barely floating on the surface, the
weight of the coins pulling the cork into
the liquid. The top of the string he winds
around the plug on top of the barrel.

Once the keg's lid is closed only the
detonator top is floating in the clear
spirit, its detonator pin attached by the
string to the top of the barrel...

                    STAN
          Okay, guys, fuck that, you
          want to see something' that
          can REALLY screw people up?

Everyone stops and looks at him. STAN
theatrically shoots his cuffs like a
magician to show nothing is up his sleeve.

                    STAN
          You ever want to know how
          to fuck somebody without
          them even knowing they've
          been fucked? Used to do
          this all the time
          Very simple.... All you have to do
          is drink....
          C'mon, drink, you don't need me
          to show you how to do that, do you?

Do you??

He opens the tap, letting out a stream
of Tequila -AGUINALDO's men hesitate.
AGUINALDO, watching STAN intently for a
moment then nods. His men are soon helping
themselves to generous shots of the free-
flowing alcohol...

                    STAN
          (quietly singing to himself)

     If you drive over the bogs today,
     You're sure of a big surprise,
     If you flee over the border today,
     You can kiss your ass goodbye.

SCENE 21 INT.TEQUILA BARREL

As the level of tequila goes down the
detonator inside slowly stops floating and
is instead suspended above it. The string
is tightened and the detonator hangs like a
pendulum, the weight of the cork and coins
straining against the pin in the alcohol
fumes...

SCENE 22. INT. MARQUEE.NIGHT

Stan now in his stride....

                    STAN
        When we wanted to off somebody
        but walk away totally clean....
        you know how you do that? Let
        your Daddy show you... We used
        to surprise those dumb Provos
        when they were making some secret
        delivery, 'Our day will come'
        my ass. We'd chase them across
        the moors, all the way to Muckno
        Lake in Crossmaglen.... Left this
        little gift. We'd be sure they
        always start off with a full tank
        of gas - go on, you rabble, keep
        drinking! - The tank empties nice
        and s-l-o-w-l-y.... just like this
        little beauty is emptying -

He glances over at JONAS and TIKO -

                    STAN
        Tank fills up with those
        l-o-v-e-l-y fumes - bounce
        bounce, bounce over that terrain.

He pulls back his arm -

                    STAN
        One big bounce….Then that little
        cocksucker detonator and fumes say
        hi and fuck you very much to each
        other….

STAN WHACKS the keg

SCENE 23.INT. BEER KEG. NIGHT.

The pin PULLS out of the detonator -

SCENE 24 INT. BAR. NIGHT.

- The keg EXPLODES, showering STAN's
impromptu audience with Tequila, much to
Stan's amusement

                    JONAS
          You sonofabitch!!!

                    STAN
          Perfect way to blow up a
          runaway car....Patented by
          Stan Barnes Esq. and Her
          Majesty's Armed Forces.
          Yours to use if you so desire...
               (Takes a bow)

                    TIKO
          (Calm despite being drenched)
          War is based on deception.

                    STAN
          Very good. Sun-Tzu's Art of War?

                    (a beat as he surveys the room)

                Here's another
                You cannot stop innovation.

TIKO expressionless. AGUINALDO stares in
cold fury at the soaked chaos. A beat, then
throws back head in laughter.

Marcus had witnessed Bill Baines going through the exact same routine in front of the crew of **THE LAST COMPANY** all those years before. Nevertheless there was something about that scene that didn't gel with Marcus' memory. It wasn't Sam's snappy dialogue, who could remember exactly what was said? Just something added or out of place. Maybe he just couldn't separate truth from Sam's creative license? He tried harder to recall the real events.

At the actual party for **THE LAST COMPANY**, it had been the locals, the set construction gang that had been soaked. No one had said a word. Their leader had slowly taken off his drenched leather jacket.

Marcus remembered tensing up ready for the big man to leap at Bill. Instead he had raised the jacket over his head and slowly twisted the garment until the booze ran down into his upturned mouth.

"Mustn't waste," the big man said. They all burst out laughing. Bill had made his point though. He was not a man to be crossed and earned the big man's respect.

Amid the mud and the rain of the shoot were whispers of illicit deals and suspect finance; but movie sets were always a hotbed of rumor and scandal especially when referring to the 'suits' back home.

McConnell had made things very clear. Marcus was the man on the spot, this was his big break. If there were problems, he had to sort it or be replaced. However unbeknownst to Marcus, at McConnell's request, Kelso had been quietly undermining the young producer's schedule and budget.

THE LAST COMPANY'S largest set had been inside a big rock. It was where the renegade unit was to have made their last stand and hide the money looted from the American Embassy at the fall of Saigon.

On McConnell's instructions the set designer had been kept in LA and simply sent his designs to Kelso and the construction gang on how to dig out this last resting place from a cave in the rock face. No one was allowed to visit during the complicated excavation and set dressing process. Only Kelso checked on progress with the head of construction who visited the director occasionally on the sets in the valley. To Marcus it had seemed one of a number of puzzling decisions, as normally the cave scenes would have been shot in a studio; a controlled environment which would have cost a fraction of what they spent on excavation and build.

"Screw a studio if we can use the real thing. It will look fantastic! No one's allowed on that cave set till it's ready to be dressed. It's bloody dangerous in there," Kelso enthused when Marcus confronted him.

"Just handle my schedule or I'll get McConnell to replace you with someone who can," he said with a grin but with enough of a concealed threat to make Marcus comply.

Kelso was also trapped by Louis' demands but was aware the size of his fee made real confrontation difficult. He just hoped Louis' strange requests were founded in some sort of logic.

It didn't all make sense to Marcus, but he didn't have the time to argue.

Sitting in the production office of *THE LAST COMPANY*, one

afternoon Marcus was wrestling with a ransom note.

"We have your dailies. $250,000 in 48 hours or we start burning a can every four hours. Instructions to follow. You have no friends here." Marcus had called an emergency meeting. Kelso and Wood were there, Bill was on his way.

"Can we raise the money," asked Robert?

"In 48 hours…" replied Marcus?

"We're screwed," Sam cut in. "You gotta call McConnell. Even if it is the middle of the night. Fuck him. Make *him* sweat for once."

Bill burst in joining Robert and Sam.

"Some local leaning outside the door saw me coming in. Instructed me about how to deliver $250,000. I asked the little bastard what the fuck is he talking about and he hooked his thumb over his shoulder towards you lot and walked away a few feet. You can see him".

Marcus quickly explained and showed Bill the note.

"But why you?" asked Marcus.

"Who knows or cares?" Bill quipped. "It's just overambitious locals out for a buck. The amount is bullshit. They need some sense knocked into them. Lemme go negotiate."

"You're nuts," said Sam.

"I've dealt with tougher people than these guys. Believe me, I can sort this. I'll put a little team together, we'll go have a pow-wow."

"Seems like an easy answer to me. Just do it," Kelso said. "I've got to get back to the set."

When Kelso left, Marcus was wavering. Sam, however, was adamantly against this idea.

"If this goes tits-up and we lose those dailies 'cos you let Bill play G.I. Joe, this movie and our careers are screwed. And I am gonna blame you, Marcus. Swallow your pride and ring McConnell. We need help," Sam said, storming out.

But it had been hard for Marcus to refuse Bill. He had an easy charm. He balanced danger with fun, but behind it all was a serious streak. Every time Marcus had watched Bill handle a weapon or choreograph and block an action sequence, he knew Bill's world of make-believe was based on stone cold reality. If you wanted rescuing, he was your man. If he was chasing you down, God help you.

"OK, no heroics. We just need that film back. I'll man the phones and try and raise the money."

"I guarantee you won't need it. At worst it will be only a tenth of what they're demanding. Just stay cool Marcus. We can find $25,000 in the budget."

It proved to be a monumentally reckless decision. Marcus let his ambition and Bill's enthusiasm overrule common sense and seek help from the outside. Marcus let Bill go. With three sidekicks by his side, Bill turned to give Marcus a thumbs up and a broad smile as he headed out. It was the last time Marcus saw his friend.

A few hours later only Bill's three back-up men came back, white with fear and with only one day's rushes. The kidnappers were holding the remaining film and now Bill as well, until the ransom of $250,000 was paid in full. If not, neither would ever be seen again.

Marcus never had a chance to even try to get the money. The next day the local crew vanished. The kidnappers were not heard from again. Bill never re-appeared. The three men who had been with Bill swore they had not seen the faces of the kidnappers nor had any idea who they were. With no one to pay the money to, even if Marcus could raise it, everything ended. The movie, friendships, careers and almost certainly Bill's life.

Marcus poured himself another drink. The three men who returned without Bill were the same three from Cara's list. All dead.

# CHAPTER 24

PRIVATE JET TO CANNES, FRANCE

'Kelso is '*Back in the Saddle*', announced the banner headline on a pre-festival interview he had given *The Hollywood Reporter*. Robert was news again. Louis was right. He didn't need Marcus. He also didn't need Louis. The Citation Bravo jet accelerated down the runway gently pushing the director back into his plush leather seat.

He and Christo had spent the weekend in Paris and were taking off from Le Bourget heading to the private airstrip at Mandelieu just north of Cannes. It was here where nearly all the major celebrities touched down during the Film Festival, unless they arrived on some leviathan of a yacht adorning one of the two harbors in Cannes itself. As the light of day dimmed on the horizon, the light inside Kelso was beginning to glow again.

Of course, he'd seen Sam's finger pointing at him in veiled references to **THE LAST COMPANY**. Admittedly, not at first and, unfortunately, well after the initial euphoria of reading the screenplay and the mistake of ringing Louis and sending him his notes.

Robert knew he had to tread very carefully. His playing dumb with Louis over lunch seemed to have worked for now; had at least bought him time to see if he could go it alone. Louis was easy to handle if you didn't come over as a threat. Even better if you appeared less intelligent than he was. Robert thought his matinee performance at lunch had given just the right balance of enthusiasm and deference. Pompous ass.

Sam wasn't the only one who was going to cleanse his creative soul by opening up the past. So was he. The self-imposed exile was over. He was going to put it up there on the screen. Make the film on his own terms. Just as soon as he could get Marcus to sign over the rights.

Thinking about premieres and his rekindled career was getting ahead of himself. There were more immediate dangers he needed to focus on; the inexorably intertwined angels and demons that were pulling him toward the camera and boosting his self-confidence were also trailing the drink and the drugs behind them. He hoped to God that Christo would see this blossoming confidence as being brought about by this wonderful screenplay and not from falling off the wagon. He could keep it under control. He just needed the occasional line; just enough to give him the boost to take the project out of Marcus' hands and the courage to defy Louis.

"Screw him," Robert said out loud, quite by mistake.

"Who?" Christo asked looking up.

"Louis," he replied quickly but knowing he had really meant his old self.

"So, what should I really expect? Help me not look like a Cannes virgin," Christo asked.

"You need to remember three things. One, never lose or forget to hang round your neck the white accreditation badge, or *carte blanche* as it's called, which is exactly what it gives you," Robert said, counting off each point with a raised finger. "Two, never stop people walking in the street to chit chat; they're on their way somewhere and everyone is always late. Talk is to be done over a drink or a meal. Three, and most important of all, never believe that the greeting '*J'arrive Monsieur*' from a waiter in a crowded bar means 'I'm coming sir'. It means 'Fuck off, you foreign jerk, I'll get to you when I've served all the French first, and that young starlet in the corner."

"That it?" asked Christo.

"Just that he'll still expect a big tip."

An hour later Robert and Christo descended the steps of the plane onto the tarmac and into a waiting limousine, the rear door held open by a short and immaculately attired driver.

They settled into the back seat. Soon they were driving up *La Croisette*, the famous stretch of road that ran along the shoreline. On the sea facing north-side stood many well-known landmarks and hotels. Movie billboards were displayed at regular intervals along the palm-lined central boulevard and already the town was overflowing with crowds who looked like they were permanently dressed to party.

"Before this all kicks off, Bob," said Christo taking Robert's hand, "I want you to know how much this means to me to see you so re-engaged with what you do best. I'm proud of you." He looked him straight in the eyes. "Don't let yourself down."

Kelso took a deep breath then calmly replied, "Thanks. I'm glad you are here with me. I'm going to get those rights, Christo. When I do, I'm not assigning them to anyone, least of all Louis. This time I'm going to call all the shots."

The car pulled up to a marble clad apartment building and they entered. The vast penthouse had over 3,000 square feet of living space, with a roof garden above it the same size. The apartment had panoramic views not only of the bay in front of it, but of the hills behind it too. The outdoor space had a barbecue area, a shaded grove of olive trees, a hammock, sun deck, multi-colored plants, flowers, and a blue tiled swimming pool.

Beautiful as the garden was, it was the pool itself that drew the biggest gasp from Christo. Sunk into the deck, one whole side of the pool had a glass wall like an aquarium, so that those in the room below had a grandstand view of people cavorting in it. The effect was to bathe the vast reception room in an aquamarine glow.

The chauffeur, who had collected the bags from the trunk of the car, set them down discreetly in two separate piles just inside the penthouse silently awaiting instruction as to which bedroom he should deliver them to. There were five in all.

"Bonsoir."

A petite lady of about 55, dressed in a formal maid's outfit, appeared from the kitchen with a trolley laden with a bottle of Crystal Champagne, canapés, hot coffee, and, as a nod to her American clients, two cans of Diet Coke.

"Yvette," she smiled, second guessing the question, her body almost at attention and her salt and pepper hair neatly tied in a bun.

In one move she gestured to the driver, provided by the apartment's owner, that she would now take over and surreptitiously handed him a €50 gratuity. She turned back to her new charges.

"Leave your bags. I will unpack them, if that is acceptable to you?" The twinkle in her gentle grey eyes betrayed nothing. A devout Protestant, nearly everything about Cannes shocked her. As a professional she held it all back and was resigned to the fact that the good Lord would still probably forgive all these sinners, so who was she to judge?

"Bedrooms?" asked Robert, as he picked a can of Diet Coke from the cart and snapped back the tab.

"May I suggest this," she said, leading them to a large double door off the hallway to her left. "They all have wonderful views, but the decoration in this one is, ah….," she struggled to find the most appropriate words in English, "most pleasing."

With that she theatrically pushed open both doors. Unlike the living room, which was decorated with modern red Italian leather furniture, and a Hockney painting of a pool, the contents of the bedroom were antique, regal and decidedly authentic.

The furniture was French Empire. The escritoire was mahogany with exquisitely turned legs decorated with carved honeysuckle leaves. On the desk top stood brass and ormolu mounts of Roman Eagles and a Sphinx. Next to the desk were two Egyptian style chairs.

"*Denon*, a favorite of Napoléon," said Yvette. A sleigh bed faced out towards a large private balcony with an uninterrupted view of the sea. The lights were glittering on l'Île Sainte-Marguerite in the distance.

Robert admired an enormous portrait of a fair-haired young man in a white military jacket framed by an ornate gold frame. Engraved on a gold plaque at the base was the name '*L'Aiglon*'.

"*L'Aiglon* was Duc de Reichstadt," Yvette added helpfully. "The soubriquet of *L'Aiglon* or baby eagle is the nickname for Napoléon's son," she explained to Christo.

"Are these real?" Christo asked a little wide eyed

Yvette smiled and gave a nod.

"McConnell would have a fit. He's a Napoleon freak," murmured Robert.

As she turned, she saw the chauffeur had come to the door of the room with the bags and was looking in. Yvette clapped her hands and made a shooing motion, slightly irritated that this man was still here after being dismissed.

The driver nodded and went into the elevator. As he got back into the Mercedes, Jonathan removed his driver's peaked cap, sunglasses, neatly trimmed mustache and beard. He had heard all he needed. Clearly Kelso's comment about his boss loving Napoleon showed he had no idea he actually owned it. In fact, as the small tiger carved over the portico subtly denoted, the entire apartment block belonged to one of McConnell's companies. He recalled Kelso's indiscreet outburst.

Mr. Louis was right. Talent means treachery, Jonathan thought to himself as he drove away.

 # CHAPTER 25

CAR EN ROUTE TO CANNES

Marcus travelled light. He slung into the trunk the soft bag containing his clothes and tossed a *Guide Michelin* on the passenger seat of his beloved Maserati Mistral convertible. The cost to retrieve it from storage had been covered by a good chunk of his savings and to give him some extra cash he had sold off some of the few valuable items he still had left. He knew that image was all and the more you look like you don't need money, the easier it sticks to you.

He headed via the 'Chunnel' towards Cannes and the *Festival du Film*. The car meant a lot to him. He had proudly bought it for a pittance twenty years earlier with the advance on his fee from **THE LAST COMPANY**. It was the epitome of *La Dolce Vita* and everyone's idea of a classic 60s Italian drophead.

Returning to London after **THE LAST COMPANY** had been shut down, he had wanted to sell it, to rid himself of any reminder of that disastrous shoot in the Philippines. But he came to see the car not as an indulgence, but as a warning not to let his own desire to get things done blind him to danger. The car kept him grounded. It was a stark reminder that no matter how much he achieved; tragedy often walked hand-in-hand with success. It was one of the only things outside of the royalty payment generated from his movies that Marcus still truly owned; and the last thing he would sell.

Despite all the glitz, glamour and awards, including the coveted *Palme d'Or* prize for the best movie in competition, the true business of the Cannes Film Festival was business; the financing and distribution of new movies.

Marcus drove down the mountain, the bark of the exhaust note bouncing off the cliff walls. Below him he could see the glittering Mediterranean as he descended into the small, fortified coastal town of Antibes, about five miles east of Cannes. It had become a ritual for him to always park his car during the Festival at a favorite fish restaurant, *Le Bacon*. His reasons were practical. Leaving valuable cars for days on end in car parks in Cannes or in busy hotels, however well-guarded, invited the attention of wandering fingers. It was also impractical to try to drive during the Festival. There was never anywhere to park and the traffic moved at a snail's pace. Here the car was safe and as an added bonus he could enjoy a quiet lunch before heading into the craziness of the Festival.

It was nearly 4:00pm when a taxi arrived for the short ride around the Cap, past the lighthouse to the magnificent *Hôtel du Cap*. Set in 22 acres of pine forest right on the water's edge, it was a bastion of extravagance and elegance. Although searingly expensive, Marcus always justified the cost. He had made as many deals in the hotel's bar in the small hours of the morning as he had at meetings during the working day in the Palais des Festivals. He really hoped this year would be no different, but he was worried. A large number of people had declined a meeting or had initially agreed, and then cancelled. He checked in.

"Only one night this year Mr. Riley?" said the well coiffured receptionist with a hint of surprise.

"Only need one deal," he smiled, trying to keep up the appearance of the successful producer.

"Here are your messages and accreditation badge."

The sun shone, the sky was blue, and the sea glittered.

"May I take you to your room?" asked the porter.

Among the large stack of messages were two more cancellations and a blizzard of pointless PR events. He stopped at the last one, reading it twice. It was short and to the point.

'*Drop it or join Bill Baines.*'

# CHAPTER 26

BEL AIR, LOS ANGELES

Louis glanced around the magnificent room filled with the treasures he had acquired over the years. Not bad for a second-generation Irish immigrant. He forever rankled at the cruel and soul-crushing treatment of his people that had gone on for centuries. Well, now he was just as cruel, just as rich and just as powerful as those who had looked down on him and his heritage. Looking at the bounty he had stolen from unsuspecting dupes made his soul soar. Revenge takes many forms. No one was going to take all this away from him.

His first name hinted at a French background although he disliked the association with monarchy. He was a republican through and through. The last name was closer to his dirt-poor roots. Many years ago, Louis' grandfather Ronan had set sail from Dublin, leaving behind the country's troubles, but bringing his anger and violent nature with him. The boomtimes of the early1920s had just begun and Ronan had arrived at Ellis Island accompanied by his young daughter Rosaleen, who would become Louis' mother.

After the hardest of starts in the new world, Ronan made a way in the tough underbelly of the Irish immigrant's world ending up in Boston and Rosaleen eventually married a third generation Irishman, James McConnell, a career sailor. Sadly she died when Louis was only five, leaving James alone to bring up his son. Louis, an only child, grew up a Navy brat and, hand on heart, could claim no state in the union as his own. Whenever his father was deployed that meant home was the lilting voice of his grandfather, whom he'd stay with in Boston. It was where the old man had settled after a lucrative career in whiskey smuggling during prohibition and other kinds of borderline activity ever since. From the stories heard at his grandfather's knee, Louis became infatuated with history, especially the overthrow of monarchies. He had no real friends or heroes, except for his grandfather... and Napoleon Bonaparte.

Although Louis knew Sam's script could unravel his little empire, Louis was confident he had a well-planned defense. Marcus had to be feeling uneasy by now. Louis had instructed Jonathan to make his presence known to those poor fools on Marcus' appointment list that had not yet heeded Louis' request to cancel their meetings.

He had Kelso all primed to appear as the shining knight, Marcus' last hope. Marcus must have sold his soul to raise the development money for *FALL OUT*. The lawyers' and accountants' fees would already be in the tens of thousands of dollars. Marcus was rolling the dice but the odds were stacked high in the McConnell house's favor this time.

Louis had expected a more compliant and grateful Kelso at their lunch; after all, he was offering to finance his comeback. The interest from the damn press had apparently given him balls. Talent, you could never completely read them.

When *THE LAST COMPANY* had folded, Kelso's coke induced paranoia had made him believe the collapse was somehow his fault. Instead of licking the wounds from his damaged career and lying low, he had started jabbering to McConnell. "What have I done.... how did we let it get so out of control... is Bill my fault...?"

At that point Louis had seriously thought about silencing Kelso. He started making plans for an accident or overdose, but before Jonathan could get to him, Robert had checked into rehab.

Nevertheless, Louis had nearly pushed him over the edge when he had Jonathan slip a bouquet of evil smelling purple flowers into his room. Kelso knew exactly what those blooms from the jungle signified.

Louis had not bargained on Christo. Luckily, the young man's calming presence unwittingly solved McConnell's 'Kelso problem'. Christo convinced his lover that his guilt was simply the drugs speaking and that what happened in Pagsanjan had been outside anyone's control. When Robert was clean, Christo insisted he needed a break from the career that was killing him before he could rebuild it. The director became a busted flush. A recluse, not a threat.

All Louis needed to do now was relax, sit back, and wait for the rights to **FALL OUT** to drop into his lap.

A rush of fire flowed through Louis' body, bringing his thoughts back to the here and now, as he looked down to his groin and the blond-haired girl bobbing her head backwards and forwards. An old guy like him, getting blown by a babe like that. Only in this town. That was power.

The girl got up to leave, trying to make herself believe that the powerful man would give her a break with a decent role and that the $400 was just taxi fare, not payment for services rendered.

Louis watched her leave. Youth trading favors for hope.

Precisely on time the phone rang. It was Jonathan. He was brief.

"Repeat it again word for word," instructed Louis.

"I'm going to get those rights, Christo. When I do, no way I'm assigning them to anyone, least of all Louis. This time I call all the shots."

A fan churned the humid air as Jonathan lay back on the thin mattress. This faded hotel suited him, reminded him of his simple beginnings and values. He disliked overt luxury, although he never minded that it seemed so important to his employer. Mr. Louis had other virtues.

"Well," said Louis, "Kelso's made his bed, so let him lie in it—and die in it. What about Riley? And that de Turris girl?

"Riley's Film Festival is only going one way…" replied Jonathan.

Louis gave a clipped response.

To which Jonathan calmly replied, "It's under control."

There was a click in Jonathan's ear as Louis hung up. Jonathan knew his boss had utter faith in him. He snapped the 'burner' phone in pieces, dropping it in the bin. He pulled out another from the dozen or so he had purchased. He then gently lifted the old Bakelite receiver from the cradle of the 1950s rotary phone and asked for a beer.

Tomorrow they'd all be dead.

CHAPTER 27

THÉOULE-SUR-MER, FRANCE

Mako spent the day basking in thanks for work done well or dousing the odd complaint with her easy charm. Her team had met every challenge head on; her reputation as a CEO whose company delivered creatively and on time had continued to grow, along with her bank account.

And the nights? The nights had been full. Despite the death of her father, her anger at him still burned brightly. His funeral was in a few days, and she hadn't yet decided if she would go.

Returning to her villa to dress for the evening, she pulled back her shoulder-length black hair with a ribbon to apply her makeup. Standing in front of the mirror she squinted, her tongue licking her top lip in studied concentration as she applied mascara. She was willowy and unusually tall, her almond shaped eyes bright blue and piercing above her high cheek bones. A true mix of her Chinese mother and Swiss father.

Tonight's extravaganza was taking place at the Carlton Hotel's private beach to promote a new 3-D animation movie '*PARKOUR NIGHTS*'. The entire area had been decorated to look like a scene from the movie. A gang of cats host their own parkour championship on a huge construction site in New York.

There were going to be real parkour athletes dressed as the lead characters jumping around girders, ladders, concrete blocks, pick-up trucks, a cement mixer, and even a small crane. The waiters and waitresses would be dressed as construction workers complete with hard hats and tool belts.

There were workmen's huts for drinks and barbecues of lobster and steak hidden among the random piles of bricks. The cost had already made it into six figures; the set a light show with lasers topped with a firework display that would light up the sky for miles around. A couple of dozen parties would all be competing tonight for media attention and, ultimately, cash at the box office. Mako was confident that hers would be the best event tonight and would attract the most press coverage.

A few days earlier she had added a name to the guest list; Marcus Riley. She could see the model of the Aquarama Riva S he had sent reflected in the bathroom mirror. That was a novel way of introduction. Quite cool. A note inside the box had simply read,

"Dear Miss de Turris,
I'm told your real version of the enclosed model is far more beautiful.
Apart from a shared love of fine machinery, we also have mutual acquaintances. Love to chat in Cannes.
Best,
Marcus Riley"

She was intrigued. She had googled him. Not bad looking. An up and down career but not a quitter. She liked that. What on earth did he want? In view of her hard and fast rule of not mixing business with pleasure, she genuinely hoped it was about mutual friends, but she doubted it. That model was a very expensive calling card. He wanted her attention, and it had worked. The right button had been pushed.

Mako pulled the ribbon that held back her hair and shook it loose. She put on a short black evening dress and picked up a matching clutch bag. She slipped on a white gold ring with a four carat tanzanite stone, supported on each side by smaller two carat diamonds. Never wore a watch and this time no necklace, the deep cleavage on the dress held all the attention needed there. She wore a Tahitian black pearl in each earlobe and two white gold rings on her pedicured toes.

This was a beach party, so she had decided on a pair of black Emma Hope slippers, embroidered with black and silver sequins. She wondered how many stilettos would be discarded once their owners realized the dance floor tonight was sand.

She gave herself a final check in the full-length mirror and judiciously sprayed a three mist clouds of perfume. She re-checked the contents of her handbag and skipped out the patio doors and down the stone stairway to the boat tethered below at her private pier.

She looked up a moment at the naked bronze statue of herself. She had commissioned it a few years earlier to sit perched on the rock guarding her private harbor. The figure was seated with her arms locked around knees drawn up to her chest, head buried as if not daring to watch who came into the house.

She turned the key, hit the starter for the twin V8s, and gripping the turquoise and white leather rimmed wheel, pulled back the throttles and gunned the boat out into the inky black sea, steering around the point towards Cannes.

Ten minutes after she left, the phone rang at the villa.

"M'sieur, as I have told you before Madame does not take meetings during Festival week, *comprenez- vous*? From her private line, never, *jamais*." Garance impatiently listened to a question.

"*Oui*. She read it, but no interest to her. She does not finance films. I threw it out today. Please *téléphonez son bureau demain* call her office for an appointment. She is at an event now. *Au revoir*," said Garance.

Jonathan hung up. That was all he needed to know.

CHAPTER 28

CANNES, FRANCE

Marcus wanted this year's Cannes Festival to begin all over again; put another coin in the slot and reboot what should have been the frantic pinball game of ricocheting from meeting to meeting. Depressingly so far, all attempts at setting them up only flashed '*tilt*'.

He was running out of money and hoped he could remain pokerfaced at the meeting with Kelso the next day. With Robert on board he could be shooting within a year. Without the director things were looking pretty bleak.

With some effort, he turned his mind to more pleasurable prospects, perhaps a ray of sunshine in an otherwise shitty day? He was dressed for a party organized by Stefan de Turris' daughter and was looking forward to meeting her. He was pleased with himself that he had managed to translate the nurse's garbled description of the boat into the fabled teak-hulled speedboat *The Riva Aquarama S*; the *sine qua non* of the jet set in the 1960s. Mako had received his gift and sure enough, it had got a response and an invitation to one of her events.

She was clearly successful…. that apple did not fall far from the tree. A few calls to some of her clients had revealed that in business she was utterly focused, smart and when needed to be, ruthless. She never mixed her day job with her apparently prodigious appetite for pleasure at night.

Twenty minutes later he could see the flashing camera lights as he stepped out of a taxi and approached the Carlton Hotel's stretch of beach. The event was in full swing, with security on every entrance and reckless abandon on the dance floor.

Over the beat of the music, he heard the distinctive deep-chested throb of a pair of V8s. Looking across the beach, Marcus saw the familiar silhouette of Carlo Riva's most celebrated creation glide up to the Carlton's private pier.

Marcus just hoped that she would know something about the past that was locked in her father's mind.

Mako handled her craft with expertise as she approached the dock. She was standing, the driver's bench seat pulled up behind her. She eased both levers into reverse and gave a blip of throttle, before turning the engine off to let it glide to a halt at the dock.

"Here," she said throwing a rope to the two security men, whose walkie talkie aerials and power packs could be seen bulging in the small of their backs. They bent to catch the line and then assisted the glamorous woman onto the wooden deck of the pier. She ran her fingers through her hair and adjusted her dress.

"Thanks boys," she said as she slipped the two guards €50 each and walked down the jetty to the party. The Riva had drawn more than a few envious glances. She was pretty sure she had seen Marcus watching as she sauntered towards the revelers, but he could wait.

He had indeed seen Mako. The little girl from the photo between the lions had grown into a truly beautiful woman. He smiled at how she had arrived, guess there's no point in making an entrance if no one is watching.

As Marcus turned back to the party, he saw a familiar face, though now more lined. Robert Kelso. The director was standing next to a lean suntanned man of about forty with a crown of dark curly hair, broad shouldered and dressed in black right down to his pointed Prada patent leather shoes. The man was looking from one face to the next, presumably to spot anyone famous. A first timer thought Marcus.

"Robert, good to see you made it," Marcus said striding over to the director. "It's been far, far too long. You look great. I wish to God Sam was here with us."

Kelso nodded. "A great loss," Robert held out his hand in greeting but held in any emotion. Not a hint of warmth. "Marcus, this is Christo," said Robert.

"Hi. Welcome to the mad house," Marcus said. Christo smiled in acknowledgement.

"We on for tomorrow? 11:30?" Marcus asked, turning to shake Christo's hand.

Kelso seemed distracted looking at someone in the crowd. After a moment he turned back to Marcus saying without much enthusiasm.

"You know where it is? On time please. The code on the lift is 1234. So much for French security," he added with a shrug. "Look I'm sorry I was slow getting back to you. The whole Sam thing shook me up. My first reading was probably too emotional. I'm less sure now. What I have decided is it's time to come back and direct. I have had a huge number of offers, more than I could have hoped for; so, *FALL OUT* is on a long list of options."

Cannes was doing its best to grind away all of Marcus' optimism in just one day. "First impressions are usually right, let's do this together," Marcus countered.

Kelso shrugged. "We'll see. Till tomorrow," he said. The director turned away and walked over to one of the stars that had provided the voice-over for the movie.

Kelso guessed from his lunch with Louis and the expression on Marcus' face that he was desperate. But once *he* had the rights, Louis and Marcus could both go jump in a lake.

Mako glowed. Men made passes at her, while insecure women who saw her glamour as a challenge, threw dart-like bitchy remarks behind her back. She glided over the sand in her flat shoes, plucking a tequila shot glass from the tray of a passing construction worker. The director of the 3-D animation movie came over to her with a slightly fidgety PR girl at his side.

"Ms. de Turris. Great event. Best party so far," he complimented her, the PR agent nodding in agreement. "The studio is thrilled. Must have taken you ages to design this."

"It takes you guys up to 13 hours to do a single animation frame," smiled Mako. The director raised an eyebrow in surprise at the depth of her knowledge.

"So this is a piece of cake," she grinned.

"Expensive cake from what I hear; the suits squawk about your bill," he shot back with a grin. The PR girl flinched and a smiling Mako bowed and then moved back into the crowd to mingle with more guests.

Marcus was mesmerized by her. Men's stares trailed in her wake, yet when she stopped to talk, you could see her utter commitment to what she was saying mixing with the fire in her eyes, reflecting from the burning braziers. This woman was all about passion, and nearly everyone she talked to seemed drawn into what she was saying and how she said it.

"I hear she's a terrific root," said a strong Australian accent who had sidled up to Marcus and saw where his eyes were looking. "So long as you aren't in business with her, that is. We bloody hire her company every year, so she's off limits, more's the pity." He took another long draw on his drink.

Marcus gave a polite smile to this uninvited commentary.

"On the other hand, I wouldn't say no to that either," he said waiving the glass in his hand.

Marcus followed his leering glance. An Uma Thurman look-alike was gliding elegantly across the sand.

"Hi kiddo," the Australian whispered under his breath as she walked by "or should I say Mrs. Kiddo," he said a little louder the moment she passed.

"*Mrs. Kiddo*?" Marcus asked, the name leaping from Sam's screenplay.

"You know, from the Tarantino movie. She plays The Bride. Her name was Kiddo."

"Which movie?"

"*Kill Bill*. Tarantino at his bloodiest! Kiddo was the one who killed Bill."

Marcus was in shock as he ran the man's last sentence through his mind again and again. He could not believe he hadn't made the connection himself. Sam was very deliberate when choosing names and what he was saying was very clear. *Kiddo killed Bill.*

Mako caught a glimpse of Marcus talking to that oaf of an Australian who had spent every meeting she had ever had with him talking to her breasts. To be fair, Marcus didn't look as if he was enjoying himself.

Marcus walked over and stood patiently while Mako finished her conversation with a teenage actor. She knew he was there and extended her discussion for a minute longer in an attempt to show she was in control. Eventually she finished and turned to Marcus.

"Great party. I hope you liked the gift," Marcus held out his hand. She looked blankly at him then reached for the badge around his neck to get the name. Cute, thought Marcus.

Mako had seen him coming. He had a genuine, open face, almost innocent, with an endearing smile, which he gave with his head cocked on one side.

"Ah, Marcus Riley. Yes. Thanks. I looked inside the box after I took the model out but couldn't find it."

Marcus gave a quizzical frown.

"The catch," she explained.

Easy does it, Marcus thought to himself. Try not to come off as a jerk. "No catch, except the invitation to the best party in Cannes."

He looked around, noticing the care her company had expended. Even the assembled tools and girders when lit by a spotlight above, threw a shadow onto the sand of the studio's instantly recognizable logo. Clever and fantastic attention to detail.

"Your work is really special. It must hurt like hell that it only lasts a moment or two."

"I like to think it's appreciated during its short life... as well as being original," she countered. "And you?"

"Original in my business means no one worked out where you stole your idea from."

She looked at Marcus as if waiting for an explanation.

"Glad you liked the model, but I do need your help."

Then Marcus blew it. "I remember hearing when visiting your father a while back that the Riva was a passion and I thought...."

Mako's whole expression turned cold.

"I don't know when you had this little *tête-à-tête* with my father as he was in a coma for some time, but he knows nothing about me. Too late now anyway. He died a couple of days ago. So whatever you came to find out, forget it." She turned and quickly strode away.

The vehemence of what she said took Marcus totally by surprise. He had no idea the rift between them was so deep, let alone that Stefan had just died. Marcus actually felt for her, all that pent-up anger and frustration. What had caused such a catastrophic breakdown between father and daughter?

He turned and followed her down the dock. She heard his

footsteps on the wooden boards and turned as the guards untied the ropes.

"Just fuck right off. At least you won't have to report back on your failure to get to me." She turned her back on him and strode off.

He kept right on walking behind her. Mako glared. The security guards drew up to full height, all buzz cuts and muscle, blocking Marcus' way.

She twisted the key, fired the engines and then felt a judder. Marcus had neatly sidestepped the security guards and jumped into the stern of the boat onto the large white sunbathing mattress that sat like a saddle over the stern of the boat covering both massive engines.

"We have to talk. Throw me into the sea later but give me a chance."

Mako turned and glowered at him. "Chances aren't given, they're taken." She gave a nod to the security guards that it was OK, then punched both throttles forward. Marcus tumbled over backwards onto the large built-in white cushion.

From his vantage point in the shadows on the beach, Jonathan watched them go, the music replaced by the sounds and sight of the fireworks lighting up the sky.

# CHAPTER 29

ON BOARD *MELINDA 2*, MEDITERRANEAN

Mako deliberately aimed the prow of her boat diagonally at each crest rather than let it run in the cradle between the waves. The resulting crash of hull against water threw curtains of sea spray over the cockpit, which was protected by the windshield yet drenching Marcus at the stern. He shouted something at her, the wind whipping his words away and his accreditation badge fluttering round his face.

He was beginning to wonder if some of what that Australian had said was true. Mad bad bitch. He had just wanted to find out what she might know about the past. He had chosen an introduction with no ulterior motive other than to give her something he knew she would appreciate. In return he was being soaked and ignored just because he mentioned her father.

He drew himself up and gripped his way up the boat using the seats to cling on to. Once behind her, he reached forward and firmly pushed the throttles to stop. He flicked on the internal lights. For good measure he yanked the keys from the ignition.

"I'm sorry," Marcus said, panting lightly from the effort.

"Don't be. I hated him."

"No, I'm sorry you are so angry with him, and he died before you could resolve it," Marcus replied.

"You have no idea... and your parents?" Her voice trailed off for a second. Then she looked at him directly. "Perfect like their errand boy son, I suppose?"

"Loved 'em up to 12 years old, questioned them on every

decision up to 15, then didn't even listen until I was 22. At that point I guess we just forgave each other, or more likely they forgave me." He took a breath, flipped the seat bottom on his side of the front bench and sat down. She hesitated, trying to figure out if he was friend or foe.

"I need to speak to you. For myself," he said after a long pause.

"My father. He didn't send you….?" She lowered herself onto her side of the bench.

"In a way he did." He looked her in the eyes and continued. "The last time I saw your father was only a few days ago. He couldn't help me, but I learned about you. The last time I actually spoke to him was many years ago…. after a man died," Marcus said as calmly as possible.

Mako was silent for a moment, the boat swaying in the choppy water. "Who died… and why did you want to see him again" she asked?

"A few months ago, a screenplay called *FALL OUT* was sent to him… and to me and at least three other people. Our only common link is a movie. A disaster out in the Philippines that stopped shooting due to the death of the movie's stunt coordinator, Bill Baines. Your father's company had issued the completion bond…."

Under a sky brimming with fireworks, the craft slowly drifted out towards Morocco, and Marcus told Mako about *THE LAST COMPANY*, Robert Kelso, Louis McConnell, Cara and Bill Baines, Sam Wood, his last script, the break-in, and Marcus' own promise to Jax. He explained the plot of *FALL OUT* and his worry as to why the others had received a copy.

"Like all great stories, *FALL OUT* is based on a nugget of truth. Trouble is, I think that nugget may be bigger than I had bargained for. I was hoping your father might help; if he could see references to our shared past in Sam's script. Obviously he never read it. It was, however, sent to you."

"Well I never read it, why would I?" She thought for a moment looking out to sea. "You think there's some truth in what this Sam person was saying… **THE LAST COMPANY** was a front for dealing in guns?"

Marcus hesitated, weighing up the implications.

"Don't worry. I wouldn't put it past my father to be involved in shit like that. Right up to his neck," she added curtly.

"No, I don't think so. We were in the middle of nowhere. There was no major civil war going on or any need to have a huge arms stash."

"So you say," Mako replied.

"Sam just had an uncanny ability to ruffle people's feathers. **FALL OUT** is fiction, pure and simple," said Marcus more trying to convince himself than Mako.

"He did more than ruffle feathers. Marcus, you are just avoiding the obvious. Something in that script got him killed….?"

Marcus shook his head. "No, can't be. It was a simple break-in. Bad luck."

"If you believe that, why come here on your white horse to warn me?"

"I didn't come to rescue you. To be honest, it was purely selfish. I really need this movie. I wanted your father, or maybe you, to tell me that it was nothing other than a great screenplay, to stop worrying about ghosts and make the film."

Mako was impressed at his brutally honest approach.

"I told you, we never speak… I mean spoke."

"And the screenplay?"

"Been lying around my house for weeks. Garance, my housekeeper, even picked it up and asked me about it. Each time I got curious I stopped. It reminded me of my father. I think Garance did mention a couple of calls about it though. Why?"

"Calls?" Marcus asked nervously, "Do you remember from whom?"

"No. I told you. My father's world is not mine," she said firmly.

He wanted to change the subject. He didn't want to alarm her.

"Decision time. Do you want to talk about your father...? or push me overboard?"

"Both," she replied with a laugh, beginning to relax at last.

She had never discussed her father with anyone; yet here was someone she had known barely an hour and she was opening up to him. She leaned down under the wheel and flipped open a small fridge, pulling out a bottle of champagne.

"Not that we have a lot to celebrate," she said as she unwrapped the foil, expertly twisting off the wire. There was a hiss as she turned the bottle and removed the cork, which she dropped still wrapped in its wire cage onto the Riva's wooden floor. "No glasses," she added as she took a slug, the champagne frothing at her lips. She handed him the bottle. "My father destroyed the only two people I loved. My mother and my younger self."

Marcus sensed she trusted him now and relaxed a bit on the bench.

"My mother's parents fled from China and settled in the US. She was everything I wanted to be. Clever, brimming with style, full of love and life. It's from her I got my passion for art and beauty. The love of Asian art was the one thing she showed my father that stuck. They collected quite a bit together over the years."

Marcus took that as a modest understatement in view of what he had seen at her father's house in London.

"My father wasn't around much. I really only saw them together at Christmas at our holiday home in Switzerland. I couldn't really judge their relationship. But whatever it was, he threw it all away."

"He was successful and traveled. Never makes for a great family man," observed Marcus.

"Ha. That old excuse," she replied bitterly.

She fingered the delicate antique Chinese hair pin in her hair.

The ivory and gold piece of jewelry had been one of the presents her father had hidden for her in the special game of hide and seek they used to play on Christmas morning. It seemed so long ago. The holidays in the snowy retreat were one of the few times during her childhood that she had spent time with him.

"I grew up in boarding schools in Europe but went to Colombia… to study architecture, believe it or not." She paused. "Unlike many of the girls there, I thought beauty was not synonymous with youth. I looked at everything from a long-term perspective, and I guess I came across as aloof. Their endless superficial pursuits went against everything my mother instilled in me."

Marcus leaned forward and helped himself to a mouthful of champagne. He handed her the bottle.

"After I graduated, I took an extended break to travel around China. To see firsthand some of the treasures and craftsmanship my mother had lovingly described to me and find myself, a bit. A cliché but true." She took a sip.

"I'd been on a trek in the middle of nowhere for two weeks. Came back to my hotel to find two messages, each barely a few days apart. The first from my mother. Cryptic. Made no sense. 'Your father has betrayed us, call me. He has misjudged me.'" Mako took a second slug of champagne.

"The second from my father was equally short. Just to come home immediately, my mother had got something so wrong. No way back then could I make a call in the wilds of China. I was frantic. It took me many days to reach an airport. At last on the way home the plane stopped in Moscow. I was able to call the family lawyer, Robin Vallings. He broke it to me as gently as he could that my mother had died of an embolism. The last leg of that flight back to London was the loneliest of my life. I was sad, hurt, angry, and confused."

"I'm so sorry," said Marcus.

"Don't be. When I landed, I became a different woman. Nothing and no one can be relied on for permanence. Life can end in a beat. Love can be deceived and betrayed. The here and now and myself are all I have. I returned to the house to confront my father. He always had an eye for a pretty girl. Must have been screwing someone behind my mother's back, but he tried to deny it. That made me even angrier. His betrayal killed her. After the funeral service, I never wanted to see him again. The only thing left to explain is how my mother never saw through him….

Did you know my real name is Melinda?" She half grinned, half grimaced. "Well, that girl died at the funeral."

"Was that the last time you spoke," Marcus said with a heavy sigh.

"Last time we met," corrected Mako as she took another mouthful of champagne. "He tried to call, even wrote to me at my flat in London. I wanted out." She looked out towards the lights of the Riviera.

"I left London, set up shop here in Cannes. Then a year ago, a plea came from Robin Vallings," she said after a pause. "Desperately wanted me to take a call from my father. I caved. When we eventually spoke, he sounded contrite, so I agreed to see him, but only if he came himself to pick me up from the airport instead of sending his chauffeur." She stopped and made a small grimace.

"He was side swiped by a truck. Never found the driver. You know the rest. If there isn't a God, there is at least Karma." She raised the bottle in salute and finished the last mouthful.

Marcus found himself connecting with Mako in that moment of extremes of emotion. A strong woman who had bared her soul to a stranger. Vulnerable yet at the same time so strong… and beautiful. He was trying his best to stay focused, but Mako had a sexual allure he could not ignore. He was programmed by nature as much as the next man, but she needed to talk, not be gawked at with teenage-like longing, he chided himself. Instead hoping to change topics and bring her back to the present he cocked his head to one side and asked,

"And life here? Are you happy?"

"It's great," she said, a little too quickly. "The money, the weather, the beauty. I live every day in the present."

Another bottle appeared from the fridge, the boat and the conversation rocking gently on the current.

"And you?" she asked as the cork eased out with a hiss.

Marcus gave her a brief resume of his ups and downs and how he had now rolled the dice with FALL OUT.

"A few big hits checkered by defeat," summed up Marcus, shrugging his shoulders.

"Are we checkered at the moment?" Mako asked with genuine concern.

"Game is still in play," he smiled.

Mako laughed and gently punched him. They continued exchanging confidences, the champagne making each revelation more intimate but less threatening as they sat side by side. The night and Marcus and Mako were at peace now.

The pyrotechnic display long faded, the sky was velvet black pinpricked with the ghostly white and silver of the stars and moon. Mako was relaxed, vaguely aware of the gentle lapping of the waves on the boat's polished hull.

She leaned forward and put both her arms around his shoulders. He just couldn't help closing his eyes and puckering his lips only to hear her laugh. He blushed. The moment cracked like glass. However instead of moving away she gently lifted the badge and its ribbon over his head as it fluttered in the breeze.

"No use taking that off" he laughed, "push me over and they can still identify the body."

Without responding she flicked off the main forward beam, leaving only the glow of the port and starboard lights, and ambled down to the stainless chrome flagpole jutting out at the end of the boat.

"You have *carte blanche*, I see" she murmured, tying the accreditation badge to the flagpole by its ribbon with a neat bow. With that she stepped up onto the sun mattress on the rear deck, unhooked her dress, let it fall from her shoulders, and in the glow of the moonlight, she beckoned.

A fabulous paradox.

CHAPTER 30

BEL AIR, LOS ANGELES

It was a beautiful morning. Pulling on his silk dressing gown and shuffling his feet into velvet monogrammed slippers, Louis walked out to the patio for breakfast *al fresco*. Benjamin dealt with most of the mail, but always handed him the important envelopes as well as the entertainment industry magazines and *The Wall Street Journal*. Louis insisted the latter should be ironed to rid it of creases.

Benjamin knew that butlers only ironed newspapers back in the 1920s to help set the ink used at that time, as it tended to come off on the reader's hands unless heated. The butler kept that nugget of information to himself. He never made the mistake of making his boss look a fool, even if his pretentiousness made him one.

Louis finished eating then shook the small silver bell that rested on the table. Reading his paper and not bothering to look up he said, "Benjamin, draw me a bath."

The man's affectations knew no bounds. "Fifteen grand a month in my pocket," Benjamin muttered as he turned on the bath taps justifying to himself why he put up with this crap.

Ten minutes later Louis turned on the jets to the Jacuzzi and sank into the churning water.

The water pummeled his back and thighs, where the cellulite riddled skin quivered like pink jelly.

Stefan's death was a relief. Despite all their success, Louis had become increasingly concerned with Stefan and his obsession about family and the reach of his achievements.

"My success should stretch forward into the future. My art collection a legacy," he had told Louis during his only visit to Stefan's Swiss mountain-side retreat.

"Who cares?" Louis had replied. "Once you're dead that's it. Being alive is what counts."

Over dinner that night Stefan rambled on about bringing Melinda back into the fold, to make her see sense.

"I owe her an explanation as to why her mother and I really argued. She needs to know what her mother discovered, what's in that Buddha head and what it means," Stefan said.

"So why don't I hang onto it?" soothed McConnell. "Just in case."

"Trust is not my strong suit, McConnell. The head stays with me. Don't worry. It's safely tucked away," he added coolly. "I've reached out to her again. This time I got my lawyer to help. She's agreed to meet me in London. She has to know what we did, accept it…." Stefan said determinedly.

Louis was certain Stefan's daughter would reject those overtures but said nothing. He preferred the rift unhealed, with Mako angry at her father, locked into moral free-fall in the south of France.

Later that night alone in his room in Stefan's chalet, he rang Jonathan in Los Angeles. He briefly recounted the evening's discussion and then pondered aloud to Jonathan, "I wonder if it's such a good idea for Stefan to seek rapprochement with that daughter of his to tell her the whole story."

A few weeks later a large curtain-sided truck carrying steel girders violently smashed into Stefan's car, while he drove to the airport to collect his daughter. The short Asian driver seen leaving the scene made sure he was never found.

With Stefan dead, Louis was free to retrieve the head which he assumed Stefan had hidden in plain sight among his art collection.

He heaved himself out of the bath and lay on a thick towel

placed on the black and white marble tiled bathroom floor. He commenced doing his idea of Pilates. Benjamin was standing at the door and imagined his boss more like a beached whale. Satisfied he had done enough to keep the grim reaper at bay and prevent others reading about him in the obituary column, he wandered into his bedroom, followed by Benjamin to get dressed.

The doorbell rang, and after a few moments Louis heard the clipped footfall of Benjamin's Oxford brogues as he walked across the marble hallway. A moment later there was a knock at Louis' dressing room door.

"Enter," Louis commanded. Benjamin was preceded by a huge black funnel shaped package with a clear water-filled cellophane bag at its base, finished off with an elaborate purple ribbon.

"These were at the gate, sir." He handed Louis the card and began to unwrap the bouquet.

Benjamin stared open-mouthed at the content. The ugly black and purple flowers were twisted around each other, like a bouquet of barbed wire, exuding an aroma of rot and decay. Louis recognized them immediately. Death Flowers. He opened the small envelope. Inside was a small card embossed with a golden eagle.

In neat blue fountain pen ink was a note. "You have thirty days to repay me. Haribon."

Louis let the card drop to the floor.

# CHAPTER 31

THÉOULE-SUR-MER, FRANCE

The next day was to prove full of surprises. Mako woke up in her bedroom and slowly reached out, but Marcus was not there.

Garance watched with admiration as Marcus, still stark naked, prepared a breakfast tray, over which he had just sprinkled some lavender freshly plucked from a bush in the garden. With the tray balanced on the points of his upturned fingers, Marcus smiled a thank you to Garance as he held the kitchen door open.

Mako was sitting in bed, her knees drawn tight against her chest, her forehead resting on her knees, the same pose as the figure in bronze outside. The sheets were still tangled around her and she was lost in thought, depressed at waking in an empty room.

"As beautiful as your statue," murmured Marcus as he snapped a napkin from the tray to put on her lap. "Room service, Ma'moiselle."

Surprise.

She was so happy to see he was still at the house, and just as glad he'd noticed the bronze figure as they had scrambled up the stairs barely three hours earlier. Her expression now radiated joy, edged with a wry smile at the effect his naked torso must have had on Garance.

The moment was ruined, however, as Marcus tripped and a wave of coffee, fruit, freshly squeezed oranges, yogurt, and croissant fell onto the bed. Through a curtain of juice Mako glared up at him, but only for a moment. Breaking into a wide smile she reached up and grabbed him, pulling him down onto the bed. Laughing they made love again with passion, and for Mako, something unexpected, with affection.

Another surprise.

A few miles down the coast, Robert and Christo's breakfast was far more conventional. They were sitting at a lavishly appointed table in the roof garden, Robert engrossed in the trade magazines, Christo snapping the pages of *USA Today* as he speed-read the articles.

"*Bonjour Messieurs*," said a voice coming up the wide spiral staircase.

Yvette appeared with a dazzling array of French pastries, juice, even bacon and eggs. Smiling at her charges, she swiftly laid out everything on the white cloth covering the glass topped table. Looking up as she smoothed the linen, she took in the view of the sea, glinting in the fresh morning sunlight. Cannes was slowly waking up. The shutters in front of shops could be heard clattering as they opened and the previous evening's carousers were either gulping down aspirins or jogging along the shore.

After laying out the breakfast to her satisfaction she sighed "*Comme il fait beau ce matin,*" more to herself than to Robert and Christo. "Perhaps Monsieur would like to see the flower market" Yvette asked having noticed Christo peering with a semi-professional air at some of the plants in the garden?

"Yes, very much," said Christo brightening at the suggestion.

"Maybe something in purple for your room," smiled Yvette.

"No" said Robert, so firmly that it made Yvette jump.

Christo gently took Yvette's hand and whispered to her.

"I'm sorry. Purple flowers…. they bring back bad memories. In the jungle, Robert came across evil smelling purple flowers. Death flowers they called them. They grow by graves. We never have purple flowers in the house."

Yvette nodded her understanding.

Christo turned back to Robert. "Ok, Robert. Can we get you anything in town, a box of apologies to keep by your chair to regularly offer to Yvette….?"

"Yvette, I'm sorry. Now will you two leave me in peace to wait for Marcus to beg me to help him?" smiled the director.

"Never push a man too far, he might bite back," scolded Christo.

Robert waved his hand asking for quiet and dismissing the advice.

Exhausted, Mako lay looking up at the ceiling. "Garance always has the sheets laundered in town, but these may raise a few eyebrows," she smiled tracing her finger of the small crescent shaped scar over his left eyebrow. "Someone get jealous," she teased him?

"Forgot to duck… when a boom swung across the deck of a sailboat. Hence I prefer speedboats."

"Me too. I never trust the wind."

"I think I need a shower," said Marcus as he picked off a sliver of croissant that had somehow attached itself to his butt. As he rolled out of bed, he grabbed Mako's arm and in one swift move, hoisted her in a fireman's lift onto his shoulder.

"And from a long habit formed by boarding school," he said, "I always have a cold one."

Garance looked up from his work in the kitchen and smiled as he heard the joyful shriek from Mako, not realizing it was simply caused by the cold water from the shower.

Ten minutes later as Marcus toweled them both dry, he looked at the crumpled pile of clothes on the floor.

"I need to get back to the hotel and change… and pack I suppose. Know anywhere I can get a bed for the next few days?"

Mako pushed him playfully in the chest. "If you want to come with me, we leave now. I have a client to see this morning."

She opened the bedroom door and called, "Garance, do we have clothes that will fit this gentleman in the stash we keep for such situations?" Glancing over her shoulder she saw the look on Marcus' face.

"What, you don't keep spare panties for the girl who might drop by?" she said with an exaggerated batting of her eyelids.

Sure enough Garance found some clothes, expensive and neatly pressed. He also produced a small grip bag for Marcus' creased ones. Garance looked at the breakfast spread in pieces all over the bed and then at his mistress.

"You going grocery shopping? I will be back at midday. We are heading out soon. I am taking Mr. Riley with me into town…. what do you think? Do we let him back in tonight after such a mess?" she asked teasingly.

"If it pleases Madame." Garance replied with just a hint of a smile. As they left the room Mako blew Garance a kiss. She seemed genuinely happy.

More surprises.

CHAPTER 32

CANNES, FRANCE

Despite the bright start to the day, the gusts of an incoming storm blew away the effects of lack of sleep as Marcus rested his arm on Mako's shoulder and the boat headed to Cannes. Regardless of the shared passion of the previous night, he had been given a firm rebuff when he asked if he could pilot the Riva.

"You stick to your cars.... this is my domain. Anyway, you'll probably just bang another part of your body" she told him.

As they pulled into the harbor Marcus patted his pockets to check for phone and wallet as well as instinctively reaching up for the accreditation badge. He turned as he remembered what Mako had done with it, but it was no longer attached to the pole. She saw his look of concern.

"If it fell in the sea, forget it. Garance may have untied it, he usually checks the boat each morning. I'll call him when he gets back from town."

Marcus gestured towards his cell. "Can we call him now?"

"Garance doesn't have one. He believes a phone should only be attached to a cord. However, *I* do have one." She smiled. "Good luck with the director. Call me when you're finished." She leaned forward and gave him a quick kiss. "And don't worry about your badge. I'm sure Garance has it."

She reached into her handbag and holding a small business card between the fingers and thumb of both hands, bowed slightly and handed it to Marcus in the respectful manner used throughout Asia.

"*Gănxiè nǐ*, thank you," Marcus said remembering one of the few phrases he knew in Chinese. He bowed back.

"*Nǐ huānyíng*," she replied. "You're welcome!" With that she jumped onto the dock and was gone, completely focused now on another day of work.

Marcus took a stroll back past the mega yachts and got into a cab at the taxi rank in front of the *Palais*. Once back at the *Hôtel du Cap* he packed his bag and checked out. Before he headed to meet Kelso, Marcus directed the taxi the short distance towards the restaurant *Le Bacon*, where he asked the driver to wait while he put his bag into his car and paid the restaurant his usual fee for being allowed to park there. After his meeting with Robert, he would return to collect the Maserati and drive down to Mako's lair. His phone vibrated and there was a text message from Mako.

"*Garance sez badge must have fallen in2 Med. C U later. xx. Mako. p.s. another call re script last nite, Garance gave my message, read it then threw out with the trash!!*"

Marcus spent the short taxi ride going over the pitch he had prepared to entice Robert to direct **FALL OUT.** He was precisely on time as he punched in the security code Kelso had given him and entered the elevator to the apartment. A few moments later he opened the doors into the Penthouse.

"Robert, it's Marcus," he called out. No response. He was a little surprised there was no staff there nor could he hear a response from the director.

Kelso's copy of **FALL OUT** lay on a table in the small entrance hallway. There were notes in the margin and Marcus picked it up, idly flicking through the pages and walking towards the main room. He figured they would refer to it in their meeting and was encouraged by the work Kelso had done. He felt relieved. Kelso was taking it seriously.

He stopped dead in his tracks. The director was standing in front of him, but behind the glass wall of the swimming pool, an arm outstretched as if in greeting. A thin wisp of red was curling away in the water from his forehead as his vacant eyes stared back at Marcus.

Marcus ran to the glass banging it with his fists as if trying to wake the director up. Kelso's left leg was securely fastened to the concrete base of a sun parasol sunk at the bottom of the deep end. He stared at the corpse floating in its limpid blue world as an accreditation badge whose ribbon was clenched in Robert's hand slowly twisted in the water. The picture grinned back at him. It was Marcus' face, Marcus' badge.

The sound of the elevator snapped him back to action. He had to get out, not for him, but for Mako. What had she said in the text to him? *"p.s. another call re script, Garance gave my message, read it then threw out with the trash!!"*

He had to get to her, and fast. He pulled open the door to the fire exit stairwell, still clutching Kelso's copy of **FALL OU**T and ran.

The taxi rank for the Martinez Hotel was steps away from the entrance to the apartment. "Here's €200 if you get me to Théoule in under 30 minutes," he said to the driver.

He dialed Mako's cell. It just rang once and went to voice mail. He sent her a text to call him urgently. As the taxi driver honked his horn and swerved towards *Pied à Mer* Marcus tried the house phone. Garance answered.

"Madame has gone for a swim. Oh, and your *carte blanche*, it was not on *Melinda 2*, but maybe stolen? Last night, we had problems with *les ivrognes* …. drunks, *ou peut-être un renard*…. maybe fox…. rubbish from the trash cans everywhere…"

"Please go get her. Now. It's urgent." He held the phone tightly as he heard Garance call Mako's name. There was a pause.

"I'm afraid Monsieur the wind carries my shout, she cannot hear. She will be back in half an hour. I will get her to call you then. I must prepare lunch." Before Marcus could explain there was a sharp click as Garance hung up.

Marcus tried to collect his thoughts and stop the panic that was rising inside him. His right hand was still clutching Robert's copy of *FALL OUT*. He doubted very much if it had been foxes scavenging in the rubbish. The taxi suddenly pulled up and Marcus was flung forward in his seat. A large garbage truck that was collecting the trash bags from the homes on the steep incline approaching Théoule, had suddenly stopped for a collection, blocking the road. Marcus slapped the money onto the passenger seat, flung open the door and ran the last half mile to the villa.

Garance buzzed him in and he burst into the house. Mako was rubbing her hair with a towel in one hand and had the phone in the other.

"Just ringing you…." she started to say.

"Get a passport, a bag, your wallet and any cash," he interrupted. She stared at him.

In staccato bursts, still trying to get his breath, he told her what had just happened.

"Robert's dead, I'm in the frame and my bet is you're next."

"Marcus, we need to go to the police…"

"That's exactly what someone wants. Me out of the way. You left vulnerable and Sam's message unheard."

Mako hesitated.

He grabbed her by both shoulders and shook her hard.

"Sam and Kelso are dead. We could be next. Pack. Do it now."

She ran into her room and threw a few things into a light hold-all, grabbed her handbag and pushed her passport and a roll of banknotes into the back pocket of her jeans.

"We've gone, you don't know where. We left last night." Marcus said to Garance. He looked quizzically at Mako who nodded in agreement. They ran down the stairs and onto the boat. The wind was getting stronger now; the tops of the waves curling with white crests.

"Where?"

"Out of France and quickly. East, to Italy," said Marcus firmly.

They pulled out into the sea, speeding past Cannes, spearing towards the Cap d'Antibes and the lighthouse near the *Hôtel du Cap.*

CHAPTER 33

CANNES, FRANCE

Jonathan finished the last of his beer. He was seated at one of the beachfront brasseries, huddled against the wind, alone under a parasol designed to give protection from the sun but now giving shelter from the stuttering rain. Nearly all the other patrons had run for real cover and the waitress was anxious to do the same. She waited awkwardly for Jonathan to leave and pay the bill she had given him. He remained seated and waived her off.

As he had predicted, Mako's Riva rounded the point, heading east. That was all he needed to see. Leaving no tip, he paid for the beer, picked up his bag from under the table and took a taxi to the airport. He had one more stop before he could return to LA; a loose-end, which Mr. Louis needed him to tie up and neatly snip into a dead one. He was going to London.

Mako was tapping the fuel gauge, a quizzical expression on her face. She saw Marcus looking at her.

"Maybe the gauge is stuck. Garance must have filled it earlier but he usually fills it up. We were practically empty this morning, now it's half full. Can you check the spare jerry cans?" She pointed over her shoulder. "Under the seats. In the back. We will need them to make Genoa."

Marcus grabbed at the handrails and chair backs as he hauled himself down the boat, which bucked and rolled like a bull in a rodeo. He bent down and lifted the seat covers and saw the cans. He reached down to lift one, then the other. They were empty.

"He must have used these."

"No, he would have used the pump in the shed at the jetty." she yelled over her shoulder, her voice nearly lost over the bellow of the engines.

One of the previous night's champagne corks rolled at his feet and it triggered a faint memory of Bill and a hot steamy night in the Philippine jungle.

Had the howl of the wind and roar of the twin V8s not been so loud, Marcus might have just heard the faint chink chink chink of the weighted cork as it bobbed inside the three-hundred-liter tank.

He saw the small neat knot of wire poking out of a hole drilled in the top of the gas tank just as the boat rushed towards the wake left by a large ferry. The bow bucked into the air. In one movement he lunged at Mako as the boat arced skywards and they rolled over the side into the swirling water. Less than a dozen yards away the hull crashed back down into the choppy foam-flecked sea and with a roar, the boat erupted into flames as the percussion cap exploded and ignited the fumes in the gas tank.

PART 3
Sun-Tzu

CHAPTER 34

CAP D'ANTIBES, FRANCE

Marcus and Mako stumbled up the beach of the secluded bay of *La Garoupe*, tucked into the southern tip of the Cap d'Antibes. Exhausted, both of them collapsed on the sand. To their right the lighthouse stretched out its arms of light into the storm filled sky. Above the roar of the waves they could hear the air-sea rescue helicopters flying out to the wreckage, their lights sweeping the waves for survivors.

"We have to stay dead," Marcus gasped, "And disappear." He slowly pulled himself up and extended a hand. "Let me help you."

Mako slowly turned her face towards him. No tears, not even fear, but anger. "You brought this to me," she breathed, ignoring his hand. "I want whoever did this. I'm not hiding from anyone." She was up, marching shoeless towards the road, patting her pockets to see what had survived the plunge into the sea.

"Mako, self-preservation isn't hiding," pleaded Marcus running to catch up with her. "My car's not far, at *Le Bacon*." A quick pocket check had revealed passport, keys, and wallet. His cell phone, however, had not survived.

Without turning back, she hurdled the low stone wall with ease that split the beach from the road and continued at a brisk walk.

"I hope you've got cash; my money has gone. Dead people can't use credit cards," said Mako finally.

"Some. Why?"

"Because we're going to The Nest."

Marcus looked at her quizzically.

"In Habkern, above Interlaken. My father's retreat. The place is actually called *Nisten*."

Marcus stopped walking.

"How on earth did Sam know about that?" said Marcus.

"What do you mean?"

"You remember what I told you about Uma Thurman and Kiddo? Sam littered his screenplay with names that referenced something or someone else. The banker is called Joe Nisten," he said looking at her.

Mako's jawline tightened. "This thing stinks. And that rotten father of mine is the reason."

After a long walk, cold and wet, they reached the car. Marcus opened the passenger door, grabbed his small leather hold-all that was on the seat, helped Mako in, and handed her the bag. He had only put it there a few hours earlier, but it seemed like a lifetime ago.

"See if you can find something dry to put on for now."

The rain had stopped, the squall blowing and blustering further down the coast. The mid-afternoon air warmed and so Marcus flipped the chromed levers holding down the mohair top and lowered the convertible's roof. The wind and warm muggy air filled the car as he headed northeast.

Marcus had no idea if the Coast Guard thought they had drowned or if the police were still searching for them. They could be on TV or Interpol's most wanted list for all he knew. As a precaution they stayed off the faster and well paved conveyor belt of the auto-route keeping instead to smaller roads. With open borders they were soon in Italy, hugging the coast road towards Genoa before turning across the flat fertile planes of the Po Valley. In a few hours they were past Milan and speeding north towards Switzerland.

Marcus drove in near silence. He was still shaken up, trying to work out if he had caused this, or events had simply found him. More upsetting, he had put Mako in danger. They needed to confide in each other rather than pull away or try to deal with this alone. Before he could say anything, Mako broke the silence.

"Marcus, I'm sorry. That was unfair back there… the boat… how on earth did you know….?"

He told her about Bill Baines and the tequila stunt.

"Jesus. Why target us both? I don't understand."

Marcus looked straight ahead without answering.

"It's that script isn't it? My father, you, Robert Kelso, Cara, and me…." Mako said.

"It's more than just that script. It's what binds us all. The past. Someone is pissed. Cara tried to warn me. I should have faced up to her fears and the past"

"We both have to face up to things from our past." Mako paused and turned to him. "A lot of things sank along with that boat. No more burying my head in the sand. Whatever my father was, did or didn't do, I can't run from it now. If we are going to survive, I want answers."

"You and me both," Marcus said approaching a crossroads.

"Other side!" she shouted as a car horn blared at them. Marcus had drifted over to the wrong side of the road. "We're not in England."

He swerved back, feeling the adrenalin pump into his surprised body as Mako sank back into her seat.

"Let's try and live long enough to work it all out, huh?" she suggested, trying to lighten the moment.

"Nice wheels by the way. I thought you were broke?"

"When I bought this, classic cars were worth nothing, automotive shrapnel. What it reminds me of is priceless," he said, then explaining to Mako the car's significance.

They were now on the western shores of Lake Como, northeast of Milan. The 28-mile-long body of water was bordered by hills on both sides and was home to some of the most beautiful villas and palaces in Europe. The lake's shoreline was carved with numerous inlets and coves where picture-postcard villages and hamlets had nestled for centuries. Tiny local shops with white-washed walls and terracotta roofs stood side by side all the way down to the water's edge, where the major palazzos with their magnificent gardens hugged the shoreline.

They stopped in the small village of *Cernobbio* and pulled into a gas station to fill up the tank as well as top up the oil and water. They drove over the rubber tube on the tarmac that rang a bell advising the elderly patron of their arrival. The old man hobbled out, pointing at them and waving his arms, as he reached for his cell phone.

"Move it," said Mako urgently. "We've been recognized. He's calling the cops."

Marcus' muscles tensed as he put the car into first gear prepared to drive straight out, but then, he paused. He let out a sigh of relief.

"I don't think we are on a 'most wanted list' yet. We're in Italy. Birthplace of the car fanatic," he said with his first smile in a while.

She gave him a sideways glance and then looked back at the garage owner. He gave a whoop and was obviously telling friends nearby to come and check out the rare car that had meandered out of the late afternoon haze and into his establishment.

"*Mi faccia il pieno per favorita* Fill her up, please," said Marcus.

The garage owner checked the oil, lovingly cleaned the screen and generally clucked around the classic Maserati like a mother hen. He shooed the two of them down to *Harry's Bar* for a drink. Satisfied that the car was in good hands they entered the bar. It was situated at the water's edge of the small stone cobbled harbor where the river boats and taxis collected and deposited both tourists and locals.

They both had a coffee and Mako a Cointreau on the rocks. Behind them, the lights from the white stuccoed *Hotel Villa d'Este* reflected into the black water. A little further up the lakeshore George Clooney's villa was bathed in the sun's late afternoon rays as the orange disc gently slipped behind the mountain peaks on the western side of the lake.

Mako had changed into Marcus' French-cuffed white shirt and some dark blue shorts. Both ridiculously big on her but with the sleeves rolled just below her elbow, the shirt tied in a knot at her midriff and one of Marcus' ties woven through the belt loops to bunch the shorts around her small waist, she somehow managed to look chic. Her hair was tangled from the sea salt and wind, and they were both barefoot.

"I'm not driving any more. I need a decent drink… and food" said Marcus.

"I need a shower, and some proper clothes," said Mako.

"We could always throw caution to the wind and spend the night up the road," he nodded towards the well-known hotel that dominated the town.

"Looks expensive. You have enough cash for that? I am pretty sure there will be some in the house when we get there."

"Let's risk it," he said.

Marcus paid the bill and they wandered back over to the car, still being wiped and polished.

He opened the trunk.

Inside was a small compartment that housed a toolkit roll and a healthy reserve of cash

"In case I break down. Emergency stash" Marcus said. The wad contained €10,000, the last of his cash.

"I've seen how you drive. You mean more like speeding tickets than breaking down," Mako replied with a grin.

"After the past few days, probably a totally different kind of breakdown," Marcus replied deadpanning, then bursting into a laugh.

Peeling off some bills, he turned to the garage owner,

"When you have finished, I suggest you take it for a brief test drive to check it's all working. Then, if you don't mind please deliver it to the *Villa d'Este* if that's OK?"

The wide grin on the old man's face said it all.

Grabbing Marcus' bag from the car, they wandered up the narrow lane that ran through the town. They stopped to buy some shoes and Mako a change of clothes which she kept in the bag.

"No way I'm wearing anything till I'm showered and shampooed."

Looking barely more presentable than a couple of tramps, they turned right through the wrought iron gates that guard the manicured acres of the *Villa d'Este*.

"Ever been here? The most romantic hotel in the world," said Marcus.

"Hmmm," she murmured looking around the grounds. "So who did you come with? Was she beautiful? I am not sure I should be going with you to old haunts."

"Come on, we all have a past, Mako. And yes, she was. But it was the car. They have a classic car concourse event here each spring, and I brought the Maserati here one year."

"Shame, looks exactly like the right place for a sex-fueled weekend," Mako replied.

They entered the high porticoed front door and went straight to the reception desk. Their disheveled look didn't seem to faze the elegantly attired woman behind the desk. She looked up and smiled straight past Marcus to Mako who was standing just behind him.

"Signorina de Turris, how lovely to see you again. Your normal room is, I'm afraid, occupied but I'm sure we can find you a lakeside view."

"We all have a past," Mako winked at Marcus.

CHAPTER 35

CANNES, FRANCE

"We have to be very careful M'sieur. *Le Festival du Film* is also a victim," Detective Inspector Pierre Groelet said. The balding officer with an unkempt mustache wore a crumpled black leather jacket and seemed permanently to be pinching a cigarette between his nicotine-stained forefinger and thumb.

Christo sat staring at the floor in the dingy interrogation room. One bright light, a mirror that was obviously two way and a plastic chair with a wobbly back. He was in a living nightmare. The only man he had ever cared for was dead, he knew practically no one in Cannes, and now the police were worried about bad publicity.

"And your relationship with Monsieur Kelso was…." continued the detective?

"Very happy," replied Christo with a mixture of exhaustion and frustration.

This was the hundredth time he had been asked the same question. The first time he had been frightened, the next indignant. Now he was just pissed off.

It must have been almost 24 hours since Christo had discovered the body. After a wonderful couple of hours wandering amongst the explosion of color at the flower market, he had left Yvette to continue her shopping. With a fabulous bouquet in his arms, he had been eager to return to see how Robert's meeting with Marcus was going.

He went straight to the kitchen with the flowers he had bought, to arrange them in several vases. He heard no voices, so assumed

Marcus had left and Robert was alone upstairs working on the balcony. It was at least ten minutes before he wandered into the main room. Then he saw him. The two vases he had been holding had smashed to the ground. Flower petals crystal shards and water covered the ground as Christo remained standing motionless.

He had actually laughed. His initial reaction was that it was a trick, a mad gag using some stunt model. It was only a moment, but it would haunt him forever that the first time he saw Robert's dead body, he thought it was a joke. Then he let out a scream as reality hit him like a thunderbolt.

No joke now. His French was non-existent, but at least Groelet spoke English. At last, someone arrived from the American Consulate in Nice, but he too, seemed more concerned with the impact and ramifications of Robert's death vis-à-vis the press and the Festival than the minor matter of apprehending who did it.

"Do you know this man?" Groelet slid two photos towards Christo. He glanced down. Neither was very clear but enough to suggest a man from the Pacific region or Asia.

"Should I?"

"We believe this man may have information on the death of M'sieur...."

"Murder, not death."

"Oui, d'accord...." Groelet said impatiently. "Do you recognize this man?"

"Then call it murder." Christo peered at the image. "This doesn't look like Riley."

"We suspect M'sieur Riley is not responsible."

Inspector Groelet took a gulp of coffee. "We believe this man may have killed M'sieur Riley as well. *Eh bien.* Again, do you know him?"

Christo was not sure he had heard right. He looked up and was about to dismiss this change of suspect, but the stare of the hooded dark eyes told him this was serious. Christo studied the photos again, this time more closely.

"It's difficult to tell. I don't think so. Please… who is he? What do you mean he killed Riley?"

Detective Groelet was brief, information at a minimum. A camera in the building opposite had recorded the first blurred image of this Asian man leaving just as Riley was arriving. Following the subsequent explosion of a speedboat of an acquaintance of Marcus Riley and with Riley on board, enquiries revealed someone matching the description of the suspect had been spotted by a road sweeper near the garbage bins and the boat very early that morning. The police suspect foul play in the boat explosion as well as the death of Monsieur Kelso. Though no bodies had as yet been recovered, they believed both passengers to have perished. Logic would dictate Riley was also a victim, not the culprit. For now though that news was just being played out as a local boating accident, victims as yet unknown. Nothing that unusual and certainly not going to hit the international papers.

The police had spent hours going through all the photos of attendees and no accreditation badge matched the Asian man's features.

"Because of the sensitive nature of the enquiry and the potential negative effect on the town and *Le Festival du Film*, I was able to obtain all security camera footage both public and private," explained Groelet as he sucked hard on the tiny stub of his cigarette. "Grâce à Dieu, thank God, the second photograph placed the same man at Nice airport leaving for London. We alerted Interpol but, *malheureusement*, sadly by then the plane had landed. The suspect…. *Disparu*, disappeared."

The relief in his voice was not lost on Christo. It was enough for Cannes to carry on, everyone relieved to know the culprit was not one of their own, certainly not a delegate, and far from Cannes.

He had flown out soon after the murder. Unfortunately, too late to alert London to meet the plane, the man had vanished.

"Look again, are you sure you don't recognize him?" Groelet repeated pointing at the photo.

"No, I told you. Did you get a name from the airline?"

"The passport and ticket was a Dr. Meeling, most likely fake. Keep the photos in case they jog a memory. This is a matter for Interpol now. The case here is closed."

Groelet turned to the man from the consulate. "I strongly advise you to get this gentleman out of France."

Three hours later, and still with depressingly few details, Christo was packed and on his way home. He flew to Paris and changed planes to fly to San Francisco rather than LA in an effort to avoid the press. He could drive home from the airport as he wanted to make a stop on the journey south.

Sinking into his leather airline seat ready for the long flight home, he popped a couple of sleeping pills and started to drift off. He was worrying where life without Robert would take him, with faces and places of the past few days dropping in and out of his heavy dreaming. At 35,000 feet over Newfoundland he awoke with a jolt and sat up from the first-class bed, knocking the remains of a cranberry juice into his lap.

A flight attendant appeared with a warm napkin to dab away the spilled drink. Christo ignored the fuss. He now knew that he had seen the face in the security photo before.

The man had been wearing a hard hat and carrying a tray of drinks.

CHAPTER 36

BELGRAVIA, LONDON

Mary's palm flashed out and smacked Giles firmly on the wrist as the rusty shears moved to perform the beheading.

"Have you no respect for the dead, Giles?"

The chauffeur rubbed his reddening hand.

"I just wanted one for my buttonhole. There are so many flowers and no one to appreciate them."

Mary gave him a scowl of disapproval and turned to attend to a bouquet of white lilies that was heaped on the antique pine table. She thoroughly disapproved of the chauffeur. He drank, he smoked and in addition, failed to realize she was in charge in this world and The Almighty in the next. They had disliked each other from the day she had arrived at the de Turris mansion.

As the late afternoon sun's rays burst through the window, the air was bathed in the scent of flowers. She and Giles were seated in the pantry next to the large, rather old-fashioned kitchen, in the garden entry basement of Stefan de Turris' home. Unlike the elegance upstairs, the room was all mismatched cupboards of aged pine and worn Formica surfaces, harking back to the time when the cooking took place in a room seldom visited by the owner of the house.

In a vase, shaped like the open bud of a giant iris, stood two dozen long stemmed white roses, sent by Hollywood Producer Louis McConnell. One of those buds had been the target of the chauffeur's attention.

There were a couple of other equally beautiful bouquets and

one hideous display of foul-smelling flowers that had arrived with a note that simply read, '*Haribon Guinto.*' Mary had immediately consigned both note and flowers to the trash.

Mary was puzzled that for a man of such obvious wealth and power more flowers and cards had not arrived. She knew his parents and wife had died and being an only child there was no family other than his daughter, from whom he seemed estranged. But so few friends. Then again, she had only known him since the accident.

Giles knew the answer. His employer had been a self-centered workaholic who, apart from his daughter and wife, only seemed to relate to a few rich business acquaintances. Any social friends had been through Mrs. de Turris and after her death, he had seen none of them. His real passion was his art collection, although Giles suspected Mr. de Turris also had a roving eye; no doubt the reason for the heated exchange between Melinda and her father after her mother's death. After her mother's funeral, he had never seen Melinda again. Giles reckoned that his employer's private funeral service at Holy Trinity Sloane Square would be attended by only himself, Mary, and Mr. Vallings.

"You think Miss Melinda will come?" asked Mary as if reading his mind.

"Doubt it. There's bad history there," Giles said, thinking it was none of her business.

Before Mary could reply, the buzzer from the intercom broke her train of thought. Giles got up and walked over to the white entry monitor attached to the wall by the sink.

"Delivery," said a voice. Giles could see in the screen a large wreath and a man struggling to hold it. He was trying to talk into the intercom and offer a clipboard for signature all at the same time.

"Coming," said Mary into the speaker, as she wiped her hands on the apron. "You take these upstairs," she said to Giles nodding towards the flowers she had neatly arranged in the vases on a large tray. "In the lift, please, so you don't spill or drop them."

With that she walked crisply through the door towards the main staircase that led up to the antique-lined reception hall. Giles thought about sneaking a cigarette but decided it would not be worth the lecture he would undoubtedly get from Mary, so instead took a last swig of his tea and wandered over to the service elevator.

He pulled it open then carefully carried the tray inside. As there was to be no wake, Mary had decreed that all the flowers were to go in Mr. de Turris' bedroom as a mark of respect. Giles, put the tray down, closed the metal grill and began to ascend.

As he passed the ground floor, he caught a glimpse through the elevator grill of Mary opening the door, no doubt asking the man either to stay outside while she signed or wipe his feet if he had to come in. Giles saw her cloud of dyed-blond hair bob in conversation as he continued his ride up to the next floor.

A moment longer and he would have seen her left leg twitch then buckle at the knee as she fell slowly backwards onto the mosaic floor. One hand of the delivery man was holding the bib of her apron, the other still holding the wreath. Embedded in the center of her forehead, like a unicorn's horn, was the steel point of a small architect's pick hammer.

As she crumpled onto the tiles, Jonathan leaned down, tossing the oval of leaves and flowers onto the body. A pool of blood started to spread like a scarlet halo under the dead nurse's head, slowly seeping across the ancient stone.

"You need a hand?" called a voice from upstairs.

Jonathan was in no mood to play hide and seek. He pulled the small hammer out of the nurse's forehead and swung it at the nearest cabinet of treasures, loudly shattering the glass. He calmly hid behind the large pillar at the foot of the main stairway. The noise had the desired effect. Giles came down the stairs and into the entrance hallway. At first, he was puzzled by Mary's prone figure on the floor. Maybe she'd had a stroke or fallen, he thought. As he approached her, he noticed the blood, but his self-preservation mechanism was too slow. The last thing he was aware of was light footsteps behind him, a gentle rush of air above his head from the descending hammer, and then a flash of pain.

Jonathan stood silently over the two bodies, but no one else came running. He looked down at Giles, then to the pick-hammer in his own blood-spattered hand. He walked over to the full-length curtains, held in place by gilded ties, and casually wiped his hands and weapon on the material.

Jonathan now looked slowly round the room. In the corner he saw sitting in its own alcove, what he hoped he was searching for. It was the life-size sculpture of a placid Chinese head, eyes closed in meditation under a canopy of snail shell–shaped hair curls. A plaque underneath read Buddha Shakyamuni, 17th century, Late Ming Dynasty.

He reached over and ran his fingers over the face, his eyes closed, rather like a blind man trying to assimilate the features but in fact trying to ascertain the weakest point to strike. In a replay of his earlier attack on Mary and the chauffeur, he brought the hammer point down on the crown of the head of the Buddha. Stone chips rained on to the floor. After another couple of blows, he had opened up a jagged hole. He looked inside. Nothing.

He systematically ransacked the house looking for another Buddha head. There was none. After two hours he stood in the hall breathing heavily, stone, glass, and debris littering the mosaic floor down around the two bloodied corpses.

The head he wanted wasn't there.

CHAPTER 37

LAKE COMO, ITALY

"Don't…close…your…eyes." Mako's dark red nails clamped into Marcus' shoulder as they both hurtled towards another orgasm.

They were in a large room at the corner of the fourth floor of the *Villa d'Este*, looking out across the lake. It was furnished with a gilt mirror that took up the entire wall and, in whose reflection, they had both watched their passionate embraces. The bed itself was king size, but all the other fixtures and furnishings, including an 18th century portrait of a smiling young girl with peonies in her hair, were small and delicate. Both French windows were flung open onto the narrow balcony to help them gulp down the night air.

They both knew they were making love not just because of the strong physical attraction but because they had managed to survive a day of unreal tension and stress. The passion was heightened by the danger that was binding them ever tighter together.

Marcus slowly rose from the bed, picking his way through discarded clothing that littered the carpet. He caught a glimpse of his naked six-foot frame and was happy to note that he still looked lean.

He sauntered out onto the balcony and peered over the waist-high solid balustrade at the last of the hotel's guests who were drinking out on the white-graveled terrace below.

"*Salute*," said an elderly gentleman, raising a glass to Marcus. He nodded in reply.

"My mother warned me about women like you," Marcus said over his shoulder as he leaned back into a cool wrought iron chair.

"And after all that time looking, was I the first you found?" teased Mako as she strolled naked onto the balcony to join him, her slim body shimmering with sweat in the moonlight?

She had the remains of a bottle of *Prosecco* in her hand. She took a swig and collapsed into the chair opposite, gently lifting the bottle above her head. Chilled water from the ice bucket dripped onto her upturned face.

"Beautiful," she sighed. "I feel much better. All this danger makes for great sex, huh?" Despite her bravado, she was glad he was with her. There was a knock at the door.

"Room service," said a discreet voice.

Throwing on a robe and grabbing his wallet from the bedside table, Marcus opened the door. He smiled, gave the waiter a healthy tip and theatrically rolled in a trolley himself. A simple salad, some *lavarello* fish from the lake and a *tiramisu*.

"If you're not going to put on any clothes, can you at least dress the salad" asked Marcus as he uncorked another bottle of *Prosecco*? "It'll be a novel experience. You have Garance to do things like that," added Marcus with a little dig.

"Ah, but he doesn't prepare breakfast in the nude," she replied with a grin.

As they ate, Mako started asking him more about his business.

"So if you're an Executive Producer, who the hell is the Producer, Line Producer, Associate Producer, Assistant producer, etc, etc, etc?" she said in mock frustration.

"Well at least you read the credits."

"I can't help it, they run across the screen forever!" she laughed as she took a mouthful of fish.

"Why don't you ever ask your high paying clients?"

"And look uninformed? Never. Anyway, I suspect half of them don't know," Mako grinned back.

"OK. A Producer usually works alone for himself or runs his

own Production Company. He initiates the project, raises the money, and hires key personnel."

"Like he reads a book or comes up with an idea and he hires the people needed to make something," Mako queried, a forkful of fish in front of her lips?

"You got it. He is the 'Chief of Staff' in all matters, save creative, which is the Director's role. The Director is responsible for overseeing all the creative aspects of the film, including casting and performance, script, location, soundtrack, editing, and camera positioning," said Marcus both happy to talk about things he genuinely loved as well as deflecting their thoughts from the day's events.

"Got it. Next," she said as she ate her food in big bites realising how hungry she was.

"An Executive Producer was originally just a title to allow senior people at major Hollywood studios to get a credit. Nowadays it's often the guy who raises the cash. He can mirror much of a Producer's role, but rarely goes onto a set. Probably been a Producer once. That's me... or should be. Know-how of actual film making, but now I tend to spend more of my time financing and deal making."

"You mean you're a suit?!"

"I'm allergic to wool so don't own one, but yes. The good news is I can be involved in several projects at a time," replied Marcus between mouthfuls. He was also very hungry.

"If anyone will still touch you," Mako smirked taking another mouthful of *Prosecco* as she finished her meal.

"*Touché*. A Line Producer, which was my role on **THE LAST COMPANY**, is on the set and responsible for the daily running of a shoot. He only works on one project at a time. A Co-Producer performs either a substantial creative or fund-raising function but is less responsible than a Producer for the completion of a project.

An Associate Producer has a role in either the production or post-production process, which would otherwise have been done by the Producer or Executive Producer. That's it. Easy." Marcus stood up and pushed the remains of their meal and the trolley back into the corridor.

"You forgot Assistant Producer," she called after a beat as she lay on the sofa.

"An Assistant Producer is occasionally hired because she has a great body or he is very handsome," Marcus replied matter-of-factly as he joined her on the sofa with two glasses.

"What a business! So tell me why are all movies the same" she teased him, poking the toes of her left foot into his groin?

He looked up at her and lifted the now empty green *Prosecco* bottle at his feet.

"Want another?"

She nodded her head and reached over, pulling on the cord of his robe. With a grin on her face she led him back to bed, her interpretation of his question very clear.

"A wise man once said there are only seven stories anyway," Marcus said as they fell into bed.

"That's six more than I ever see."

Leaning on his elbows Marcus gazed down at her upturned face.

"Overcoming the monster, rags to riches, the quest...." he whispered kissing her after each one on the list, "the voyage and return. ...."

"Ya-di-ya-di-ya. It's all one movie," she teased, looking away from him, pretending to be bored. He quietly reached down into the ice bucket still at the side of the bed and popped a cube into the side of his mouth.

"You know what the most common line in a movie is?" he slowly licked her throat, pushing the ice cube against her hot skin.

Mako looked down at him. There was a glint in his eye. He moved down her body and started to kiss her firm breasts, her nipples responding quickly to the ice.

"I'm too old for this shit?" she sighed, repeating an overused movie cliché.

Without stopping he shook his head, intensifying the sensation.

"Th-Th-That's all folks?" she asked, a slight tremor in her voice.

He turned for a moment before his head dropped between her legs, "Try and get some rest….," he whispered.

She gasped as the cold of the ice melted into her warmth and wetness.

An hour later Marcus turned to Mako, her black hair matted with sweat, her long legs still intertwined with his. He kissed her.

"You know, I really need to call Garance," she sighed. "It's not fair, he must be beside himself."

"You trust him?"

"With my life. He treats me like his ward."

"Your call," Marcus replied.

Mako reached over for the phone and started to dial.

"And I need the copy of your screenplay as well as Kelso's, which I left at your place. Can he forward them?" Marcus added.

Mako nodded.

"I should have read it, but no one has sent me a script before" she said, waiting for Garance to answer, "But when I looked at it and saw how long it was, I just couldn't bring myself to plough through over two hundred pages that had no relevance to me. And at the end of the day it's my father's world. Not mine."

Marcus gave a small start, his finger quickly pushing down on the phone cradle, halting the call.

"You sure?"

"Sure about what? What's wrong? Mako asked.

"The number of pages," Marcus responded, worry in his voice.

It struck me, stuck in the memory. Two hundred and two pages It's…. was, my father's pet number. His peg from prep school. His car registration was SDT 202."

"Get Garance to scan it and send it as an email."

"Garance can't work computers…."

"Then express courier them to your house in Switzerland. Mako, my screenplay only had 199 pages."

"Maybe it was done on a different printer, so what?"

"No Sam was a seasoned professional. He would have typed **FALL OUT** encoded on *FINALDRAFT*, the industry standard for screenplays. To avoid confusion, it always prints the same numbers of pages. Your father's copy has a couple of extra pages. Just the odd line perhaps, but it's definitely different."

"Why would Sam do that?" quizzed Mako.

"We'll know when we find out what the hell those extra lines say. Now call Garance."

CHAPTER 38

MARINA DEL REY, LOS ANGELES

The sign read "Please wait here to be seated."

"Ignore it," Dalinda whispered in Cara's ear, walking straight in.

Cara followed her friend out onto the patio and chose a table not far from the large circular open fire pit. The flames from the gas below licked at a pile of imitation logs adding warmth to the mid-morning air. Seagulls cried overhead telling their friends that brunch was now being served.

The Cheesecake Factory in Marina Del Rey had panoramic views of the beach as well as the marina and was already crowded. Cara flipped through the lengthy menu and wondered how so many slim people could possibly be regulars.

Having walked in with the two women, Cato was lying at Cara's feet, his eyes half shut and his hind legs stretched out behind him. The dog was delicately sniffing, as if trying to filter out the smells of the beach and concentrate on the plates of food being served to the assembled customers. Dalinda and Cara ordered, with Cara adding a couple strips of crispy bacon to her whites-only omelet as a treat for Cato.

Despite having turned her back on the film and television industry, Cara still had clients who worked in it. It had been a few weeks since she had been in LA to see McConnell. She had been so happy to return to Santa Barbara, hoping never to see him again. His pragmatism disgusted her. Today she was in LA to follow up on wedding plans for the daughter of a wealthy actor. His PA wanted to go over the final floral design details and lock the budget.

"Mad money," explained Cara to her old friend who had agreed to join her for brunch before the meeting. "I should be grateful that it filters down to me, but it's obscene what some of these people get paid."

"You saw the news this morning? Not everything goes the way they plan," replied Dalinda.

"No, I was up early to get here in time. What happened?" asked Cara, taking a small bite of her breakfast omelet and slipping a piece of bacon to Cato.

"Some director drowned in a pool in Cannes. Trying to make a comeback.... probably all too much."

Cara suddenly stopped eating and looked up.

Before Cara could say anything Dalinda pointed her fork at a silent tv screen over the bar running the story with subtitles to the assembled patrons, "There you go."

A picture of Robert Kelso flashed across the screen. "Ever come across him?" Dalinda asked.

The look on Cara's face gave her friend the answer.

Cara was no longer hungry. "I'm sorry Dalinda," said Cara, dropping her fork and pushing back from the table. "Got to see someone. Excuse me." As she got up to leave, she turned to her shocked friend. "Please. Can you keep Cato for the day?"

Louis blinked as he held the phone to his ear and looked up from his waiting room chair at the starched white-uniformed nurse beckoning him.

"No, not later. I need to see you *now,*" Cara was saying emphatically on the other end of the line.

"Cara. I will not discuss this now." He paused as the nurse gestured towards a sign displaying a cell phone with a red line through it. He squirmed inwardly at the thought that this young girl knew perfectly well why he was here and the discomfort, let alone humiliation, the examination was about to cause him. He held up his index finger to signal just one more minute.

"You are in no position to argue. I am running into a meeting and cannot keep these good people waiting. Meet me at the Polo Lounge at 1:30." The nurse was not impressed. "Ask Emilio to take you to my regular booth," he added abruptly ending the conversation with Cara.

The mention of a regular booth got a glimmer of respect from the nurse. Louis was sure she'd fuck him in a heartbeat if she realized he could get her a job in a movie, rather than waste her time looking into other people's assholes. He'd wipe that superior look off her face given half the chance. He walked towards the consulting room for his examination, prepared for an embarrassing and painful half hour.

"It's partly your age and partly your lifestyle," said the smug young doctor as he snapped off the rubber gloves and handed the endoscope to the nurse.

"You can avoid surgery if you take my advice, change your diet, cut out alcohol, clean up your lifestyle…."

"Work less and exercise more," sing-songed Louis, finishing off the standard litany of do's and don'ts that seemed to accompany all his visits to doctors. The specialist handed over a leaflet full of useful lifestyle information and with a smiling middle-aged man on a bicycle on the cover.

Louis scoffed at it and got dressed, seemingly oblivious to the nurse. He checked himself in the mirror then pulled a huge cigar from his jacket breast pocket.

"Let me explain how this works. I pay you. But if I want to smoke I will, eat good red meat I shall, and when I want your advice, I'll ask for it. You diagnose then give me the options that I can choose from. You do as *I* suggest. I'll take the surgery, get it over with. I'll let you know when I'm ready."

With a perfunctory nod, Louis walked out stopping to tuck a $100 bill into the breast pocket of the astonished nurse. "Nice hands," said Louis, "but next time make sure they're warmer."

Cara was already waiting in the booth by the time Louis' Bentley Continental swooped up to the entrance of the Beverly Hills Hotel. A doorman snapped to attention and opened the car door.

"I'll be an hour max," Louis barked at Benjamin who had tried to rush around to open the car door for him.

The doorman smiled and saluted. "Good day, Mr. McConnell."

Ignoring the doorman, Louis marched into the famous bar of the Polo Lounge, the scene of legendary fights and trysts of Hollywood royalty. He entered the room and walked past the assembled groups of well-healed rubberneckers and industry big shots who had gathered for lunch.

"Don't even think of screwing with me, Louis," was the greeting from Cara. "What the hell is going on? What happened to Robert?"

"Good afternoon to you too, Cara," he replied coldly, taking his seat. He looked around the room, waving at a famous actor's alcoholic son. Not that Louis knew him that well, but to show he knew who he was. The small gesture distracted Cara and enabled Louis to ignore her question and take back control.

"May I remind you we are in a public place, where bad language is frowned upon, and indiscreet remarks are picked up to be reported in the trade papers and posted on the internet before you even get the check."

She took a breath, then a mouthful of the Tequila on the rocks she was holding with both hands. Louis noticed they were trembling slightly.

"Cara, I know as much as you do. The director was there to meet our producer friend to try and buy the rights for *FALL OUT*. Next thing I know Robert is dead and no one is giving any information. Police are very tight lipped. Who knows? Something may have gone wrong, they might have argued. What I do know is we all need to stay quiet."

She looked at him, then, checking over her shoulder to make sure that no one was listening, said in a hushed tone,

"Oh come on… Marcus? That's bullshit. He was desperate to do a deal with Robert. Killing him serves no purpose."

There was a faint buzz. The Polo Lounge frowned on calls, so Louis' phone was on vibrate for calls but was still active for text and email. He saw a text from an unfamiliar number but from a country code he wanted to hear from.

"I need to take this," Louis said rudely. He got up and walked to the bathroom, entered a cubicle and locked the door.

'Head not here. What next? Will wait ten minutes for answer' read the short message.

Louis was torn. On the one hand he had a growing problem seated in a booth not 50 feet away, as well as an increasingly dangerous Haribon Guinto in Manila; something made clear by those flowers. He wanted Jonathan back. On the other hand he needed the secret of that Buddha head. There was only one other place Stefan would have stored it.

He texted back Jonathan details from his address book and a curt order before hitting send.

Louis turned back to deal with Cara.

In two hours, Jonathan was back on a plane in a different disguise and with another false passport. He had been in London for less than a day.

 # CHAPTER 39

LUGANO, SWITZERLAND

Marcus and Mako left the hotel early the next morning, both wishing they could stay there forever but knowing burying their heads in the *Villa D'Este* sand would solve nothing. Instead they crossed the border into Switzerland and stopped at a small gas station to refuel. Marcus paid the forty Swiss Francs for the annual 'vignette' that everyone needed to use the country's motorway system and attached the small square sticker to the windshield.

Mako went to use a payphone to contact the family lawyer Robin Vallings. A shocked Garance, so relieved to hear they had survived had told her on the call the previous evening that Vallings had rung earlier, frantic to speak to her. Garance had been unsure what to tell him. Despite his denials, Mako suspected Garance had told him everything. Marcus' words about trust had echoed in her head that night as she had tried to fall asleep.

She slowly walked back from her call, head down as she climbed back into the car.

"Didn't you get through" he asked, seeing she was upset?

"To his secretary, but Robin was out. He's never out on a Friday unless it's shooting season and he's on the moors killing grouse," she said slowly.

"With a client?" Marcus suggested as he started the car and pulled back out onto the road, trying to find out what was troubling her so.

"No. But I left him a message to say I was alive, to say nothing to anyone, and to call the house in Switzerland…. Oh Marcus. After everything that has happened. I just forgot…. He's at my father's funeral…."

Marcus knew nothing he could say would take away her guilt or make her feel better. All he could do was stop the car for a moment and put his arms around her.

They soon drove on in silence, Marcus letting Mako think things through. A few hours later, after crossing over the *Lukmanie*r then *Susten* passes, they drove with the top down towards Interlaken, the sky crisp with late spring air and filled with the scent of mountain flowers.

Mako again broke the silence. "It's done, Marcus. I wasn't sure if I was going to go to the funeral anyway. Seems fate made up my mind for me. Time to focus on the present. At least this place has happy memories for me," she said giving a faint smile.

Literally meaning 'Between the Lakes,' the famous resort lay in the folds of the Swiss Alps, cradled between the two large lakes of Brienz and Thun. The ancient and picturesque town offered majestic views of three of the highest peaks of the Alps; the *Moench*, the *Jungfrau* and the *Eiger*. Their destination was seven kilometers above Interlaken in the tiny town of Habkern.

Before taking the narrow winding road to *Nisten*, they stopped in Interlaken to fill up the car again. Mako went to the small stalls and shops of her youth to buy some provisions for dinner. Marcus wandered down Interlaken's main street until it opened out to a vast expanse of green. He sat down opposite the huge lawn at the café outside the 19th century *Victoria Jungfrau Grand Hotel*.

He drank an espresso in silence, looking towards the majestic mountains. To his left stood a row of gingerbread-style houses. One displayed a plaque stating that Lord Byron had stayed there during the early 1800s, no doubt during one of his sex, drug, and alcohol-fueled tours of Europe. Judging by the happy faces parading past Marcus on their way out for an evening's fun, nothing much had changed. He looked up and a cluster of hang gliders gently descended onto the grass in front of him. Everything was bathed in the early evening's golden glow.

Peaceful. Normal. No danger.

Jonathan's cab pulled up at the small *Eiger Gasthaus* thirty yards from the imposing *Victoria Jungfrau Grand Hotel*. He was barely out of the car when he saw a dead man quietly sipping an espresso on the grand hotel's terrace.

# CHAPTER 40

BEL AIR, LOS ANGELES

Louis took a mouthful of the brandy he had been gently swirling in the balloon glass. He glanced at the gilt clock ticking on its marble mount, feeling no guilt at drinking what others considered an after dinner '*digestif*' at three in the afternoon. Benjamin had prepared an excellent lunch.

He was in a reflective mood. That damned script was shining a hot light into some very dark corners. At least Wood, Kelso, Riley, de Turris, the man's staff, and his daughter Melinda, were out of the way. With deaths on two continents and three different countries, he was satisfied no law enforcement agency would be able to join up those dots. Anyway, it wasn't him causing all this, he rationalized to himself. It was Sam. It was his fault.

However, Louis knew there were still a few others that could cause problems. He never needed to know the specifics, he just needed someone to make them disappear as well.

Cara. Ungrateful bitch. The truth had been buried out in the jungle. She took the money. Now she was getting all moral on him? He really didn't see why he had even bothered to come up with stories of innocence each time they met.

Now Christo. He had left some garbled message from San Francisco airport about recognizing a blurred photo the police in Cannes had shoved in front of him. He thought Louis could help.

But the smoldering fire that could engulf him was Haribon. He was not a man to double-cross. Jonathan said he had dealt with it all when he had gone back to the Philippines last Christmas.

With the arrival of those flowers though, Louis knew Jonathan had failed him.

His only real solution now was Tyler Gemmell, without the man really understanding he was being used. Louis was certain that Gemmell's colleagues would act decisively if Tyler's group felt threatened with exposure by Haribon. Others would see them for what they really were, just a bunch of hoods. So that's what he needed to concentrate on. That was their hot button. Crack that veneer of respectability.

He remembered what a famous British film and TV impresario had once said to him when his TV series had come to an abrupt halt due to a union dispute.

"Jam donuts. That's the secret. The man who has a steady supply of jam donuts can take care of business coz everyone loves 'em. And I have a very big bag of them." The local union representative went to a number of premieres on the arm of several beautiful and compliant young starlets…. jam donuts, indeed, Louis had thought at the time. Sure enough the dispute was settled quickly, the union got back to work. But Louis had learned a valuable lesson.

He called Sean Donovan at U.S. Immigration Office, a man who had a prodigious appetite for Louis' own brand of jam donuts.

"Thank you for Riley… and I am glad you were able to 'audition' those two little actresses I sent over." There was a chortle, then he got right down to business.

"Now I need another small favor. Details aren't important but I need a little heat on Mr. Tyler Gemmell. Those illegal immigrants you have turned a blind eye to. This time, how about one or two being suspects in something. Nudge Homeland Security or the IRS? Rattle Gemmell's cage a bit. So long as it's never tied back to me."

 # CHAPTER 41

INTERLAKEN, SWITZERLAND

This was the first time in his life Jonathan had failed. How and why Marcus had survived was not important. He assumed Mako would be close by. He was thankful that at least Marcus had only fleetingly met him years ago on the Pagsanjan set. He would make sure the next time they met would be final.

First, a change of plan. He needed to rent a motorbike.

Mako had collected the basics as well as a large baguette and some grated vacherin and gruyère cheese to make a traditional moitié moitié cheese fondue. Comfort food, Swiss style. Memories from her youth assailed her from every corner as she walked through town and she had wanted to enjoy them alone. The chocolate and patisserie store where her mother would let her buy something after the grocery shopping was finished, the shop where she had bought her father a special limited edition Swiss Army Knife for his fortieth, even the clopping of the horses' hooves as they drew tourist carriages over the cobblestones; all heartwarming images and comforting sensations.

She purposely sought out the bookstore she and her mother had visited so often, fueling her mother's passion for Asian works of art as well as igniting her own. She wanted to go in, but it was already closed. This place reminded her of happier and less complicated times.

Now she was with a man she barely knew who was somehow connected to at least one death, probably more. Someone had tried to kill them both. She had missed her father's funeral and she was going back to a house that she hadn't called home for a number of years. She would return to the bookstore later. She went back to meet Marcus at the cafe.

The car edged its way towards her former home. Nisten was situated at the end of the long road up from Interlaken at the very north end of the village of Habkern. The lane petered out at the entrance to the house's gravel driveway. After that the only way out of town was by foot or 4x4 SUV or return the way you came.

The car crunched to a halt outside the Hof-designed house that had been her father's winter home. It was a glorious ultra-modern construction of glass, steel and wood that allowed fantastic views both down the valley and up towards the permanently snow-capped peaks. In the moonlight the house appeared to be asleep, with steel shutters covering the huge windows like corrugated eyelids.

"Can you give me a minute and stay here?" she asked. "It's been a long time."

Marcus nodded as Mako opened the car door and approached the house. Standing guard at the entrance were two large Chinese stone lions, the same as those in the photo from Stefan's house. She hoped the alarm code was the same and that the spare front door key and alarm fob were safely guarded by her old friends, each with their nine rolls of mane that signified they had come from an Imperial Palace.

"Hello boys," she whispered.

Mako approached the one on the left, squatting down in front of him. She put her arms around his neck, locking her fingers over the ringlets of his stone mane and pulled. To her surprise, there was no movement. She tried again. Nothing. She looked into the wide-open eyes and gaping jaws of the stone beast and began to worry. She examined the statue more closely.

"You got a flashlight?" she called to Marcus, without turning around.

Marcus leaned over to the glove box and pulled out a small blue Maglite. "Here. You need help?"

Mako ran back to the car and took it and gave Marcus a concerned look. "Maybe we need a hotel. How much cash have we got left?"

Marcus reached into his pocket and held out a small number of notes. "Enough for a tent."

She ran back to the two lions. She looked at the bases where, as a child, she had scratched the names of her two beloved friends; 'Tianlu' on one and 'Bixie' on the other. Her father had spanked her when she had proudly showed him the scratches she made on the valuable lions. Yet it was because they had been defaced that her mother had decided to get a stone mason to cut a recess into one of them to create a secret hiding place. In doing so she turned a damaged item into something unique and special to them.

Mako took a second to look at the names. "He switched them around," she sighed. This time, she knelt before the lion on the right, and hugging its neck, pulled. The head eased forward and revealed a grooved recess at the back of the neck. She pointed the flashlight beam inside and sighed with relief. What she needed was glinting under the Maglite's beam.

"Got 'em," she said to herself. "Marcus, can you bring everything in?" she called back as she headed towards the house.

She approached the massive front door. Marcus watched as she unlocked it and it swung open. The lights came on and with a whir all the shutters began to rise; the eyes of the sleeping giant now slowly opening.

"Gimme a hand will you?" Marcus asked as he tried to balance his small bag, groceries, and the wine. There was no answer.

He walked in dumping everything at the elegant entrance, devoid of any decoration other than a large photograph of a teenage Mako and a smiling beautiful Chinese woman. The two had the same delicate features, high cheekbones and jet-black hair and he was sure the elder woman was Mako's mother. The two women were outside an old timber-framed building holding a certificate in their hands. An elderly gentleman with a wondrous jet-black walrus mustache was standing opposite them, applauding.

"Mako?"

No reply. He went into the main drawing room. She was sitting motionless, her slim body almost entirely hidden from him, slumped in a wing-back leather chair. Her eyes were open and staring in shock.

"My God look at this," she whispered. He followed her gaze and saw row upon row of cabinets filled with Asian art.

"So? It's just like London," he said.

Mako slowly turned to Marcus.

"What do you mean? London's like this? I haven't been there for years. Marcus, this stuff is priceless. I mean serious, serious money."

"So, he was a wealthy man," he said, still confused by Mako's reaction.

"He was wealthy, sure, but these... these?" She said sweeping her hand out to indicate everything in front of her. "The collection has changed out of all proportion. This is all museum quality. Rare....so rare. A Qing Dynasty porcelain... those bronze Tings, the jade carvings. And the coins. Marcus this is worth millions...."

Jonathan crouched behind a small rock formation not far away. A pair of powerful binoculars had been focused on the couple ever since their arrival and was now locked through the open front door into the hallway and drawing room. He had seen enough and crept back to the black motor bike. He silently free wheeled it down the hillside, only starting the engine after a few hundred yards. He was formulating a plan for Marcus and Mako. This time there would only be one outcome.

CHAPTER 42

SANTA BARBARA, CALIFORNIA

"We need to talk," whispered a voice.

Cara dropped her front door keys in shock and Cato erupted in a barking frenzy as a slim figure stepped out of the shadows.

The meeting with Louis and the deaths of Sam and Robert had Cara's warning sirens wailing at full volume. On his return to the booth that day he had abruptly dismissed her. Told her he would contact her once he had any real news. She was already worried having tried to raise Marcus on his cell phone while driving back from Los Angeles. Ominously it just kept diverting to his voice mail. He never picked up; never rang back. Grabbing Cato, she shrank back, not sure what to expect, except that it would be bad.

"I'm sorry I didn't mean to scare you," said the man stepping out of the shadows his arms raised above his head. "I'm Christo. I am ... was... Robert Kelso's partner. It's Cara, right? "

Cara relaxed back a couple of notches from panic to controlled fear. Cato was less convinced and kept up the incessant barking bravado.

"Please... Can I come in?" He looked exhausted, dark rings under his eyes and his hands trembling.

Cara could see he was not a threat, just afraid.

"Oh, do be quiet," she admonished, her voice hard and firm.

Christo hesitated, thinking she might be addressing him.

"I'm sorry.... Christopher Murray." He held out his hand. It was still shaking as she clasped it and caught a glimpse of his bloodshot eyes.

"I flew into San Francisco from Cannes. Press would have been all over me at LAX. And I wanted to drive down here to see you before going home...."

She made a judgment call and bent to pick up her keys. Christo was there before her, scooping them up.

"Allow me."

Ten minutes later Cato had slowed his barking and Cara her heart rate. She poured Christo a Diet Coke and herself a Tupay. As soon as they were seated, she went straight in; no pleasantries.

"So, tell me what happened?" she asked gently

"All these deaths...."

"We've both lost partners," she said. "You start. From the beginning."

"I met Robert a few months after he got back from the Philippines.... Well not really met, more like watched."

Cara frowned.

"He was in rehab in Malibu. Cold turkey. A mess. I was part of the program. Gave seminars on horticulture."

"Gardening for addicts?"

"You know, health, nature, back to basics."

"You can bury a lot of troubles digging in the dirt," she replied. "Believe me I know." She paused and smiled sympathetically. "We were all in a mess then."

"Right," Christo nodded. "Well at first he didn't want to talk to anyone, let alone participate in anything. Just sat in his room alone, in silence. So I started to pop in each day and leave a plant. Told the staff not to remove them, just water them.

After a week the place looked like a garden nursery. A month, you could barely move without knocking one over. But it got to him and he opened up. We talked a little bit more every day. In the beginning it was simply small talk, my showing him how to trim some of the plants, where to put them, in the light or shade, basic stuff. Three months later he was nearly recovered, tackling subjects on just about anything and everything…. except what had driven him to such despair…. but at least he started to live with himself again."

"Bill said he could be …difficult," Cara volunteered with a genuine smile. She wanted to keep this as honest as possible.

"Don't get me wrong. He had his downsides. Bull-headed, naïve about the world's underbelly; always thought he could put on an act to fool people. But at least he was communicating. I grew to love him. The center was even discussing his departure.

Then one day he came back to his room and someone had delivered some ugly purple flowers. It triggered a massive panic attack. I didn't understand or know how to help. I never left his side from then on. It took a while, but he eventually recovered and was discharged. I agreed to move in with him, just to be sure. We found a place in Topanga, with a wonderful garden. We've been…. were…. there ever since."

"Did he stay clean?" asked Cara.

"I made it clear if he got back on his brand of snow or ice…. coke or vodka on the rocks, I'd see him through another session of rehab, then I'd be off. For years he stayed on that wagon. Drink and drugs were part of the life he was adamant he had left behind. The prostituting of talent, the compromises, the ass-kissing, the deals within deals- the whole shebang." Christo looked over to Cara.

"And recently?" said Cara.

Christo sighed not looking her in the eye. "He guessed I wouldn't notice. As I said he wasn't as good an actor as he thought he was. He stayed clean until **FALL OUT** arrived or rather until Louis McConnell got involved."

"That damn script, and that damn man," said Cara quietly.

"I should have stopped him, confronted him. But the prospect of making a movie again…. he was so alive…. a new man I wanted to see grow. I was frightened he'd go back into his shell. Against all my training and better instincts, I fooled myself that he could keep the odd line of coke under control until he got the rights, then I was going to step in."

"Did he ever mention the shoot in Pagsanjan?"

"He hated talking about it. Only twice. Most recently in Cannes but the first time was at the clinic. Sam Wood had come to see Robert one day when I was not initially in his room. I heard raised voices and came in at the end of their meeting. It hadn't been friendly. Sam then accused Robert of ruining his career. Said the whole thing stank. Robert should have known better than to let that hothead Baines…." He stopped talking and raised his hand to his lips, as if trying to put back the words he had spoken. "Oh, I'm sorry Cara."

She nodded forgiveness "It's OK, go on."

"Sam said Marcus had been too wet behind the ears to take on this project, let alone Robert and McConnell. Said it was a disaster waiting to happen and stormed out. At first shocked, Robert eventually told me not to worry, Sam ran hot and cold. It had shaken me up though. Then Robert opened up a little. Somehow, he felt he'd sold his soul to Louis and the price had been to obey, rather than create. As he had descended into drug hell at the end of the shoot, he started to blame himself for Bill's death, though would not say why. 'Everyone got screwed up by it', was all he'd say…." Christo hesitated realizing once again he had come across as insensitive. "I'm so sorry about Bill."

Cara sighed. "It's the past, Christo. Over. Please continue."

"I tried to rationalize, to make Robert see that they had all done what they thought was right, struggling through so much. Everyone was young and headstrong. Marcus, Bill, Sam. I could see Robert wrestling with his conscience, going over all that had happened. And then suddenly he asked me, 'Do you know what you use nitro-hydrochloric acid for?'"

Cara looked at him blankly.

"It was something Sam had asked him once on the set. He'd seen a shipment sent to the site construction manager. He thought it might be dangerous and wondered what it was doing on the set. Bottles labeled by its street name; *Aqua Regia*. Robert had no idea." Christo grimaced, "I should never have told him."

"What?" asked Cara?

"I told him the only thing I knew hydrochloric acid is used for is to refine heroin from opium paste," he sighed. "Sam obviously figured that out later."

Cara gave a sharp intake of breath.

"A day or so later those purple flowers showed up and Robert went into relapse. We never spoke of it again until the afternoon before he died. He was on the balcony in Cannes reading that script for the umpteenth time when he suddenly said, '*Aqua Regia*'. That's it!"

Christo paused for an effect that was obviously lost on Cara. She just shrugged.

"The screenplay," he replied by way of an explanation.

"I still don't understand."

"You have your copy?"

Cara went to a drawer and returned with it, handing it to Christo.

He found the scene. Then fell silent, a look of confusion on his face, "It's not here," he said slowly.

"Christo. You're not making sense."

"In Robert's copy, it's the scene with the architect, Kenny. In your version there are some lines missing. In Robert's version of the scene, Kenny is drinking from this bottle. Frank says to Kenny something about *Aqua Regia. Guarantee of purity. Does it cleanse your soul?*"

Cara sat motionless.

"For each of us a script with our own clues….," she finally said slowly.

"You think so? Robert had picked up little hints in Sam's screenplay about connections with the past, but this was what he'd been looking for. Robert became convinced Sam was telling him it was drugs they took out of the Philippine jungle. That's what killed Bill… and now Robert."

"And probably Sam. My God, you think they used that shoot as a cover up for a drug deal?" Cara said grimly, replenishing her glass then emptying it just as quickly. The alcohol wasn't helping.

"That first day in Cannes, Robert insisted we go over exactly what Sam had said to him in the clinic as well as on the set. He spent the rest of the day thinking back to the shoot. I sat with him as he went over everything he could remember. The people, the places, trying to extract every ounce of memory.

That night we were at a party on the beach. As Robert and Marcus were talking, I noticed Robert staring at someone in the crowd. I followed his gaze and saw a small guy dressed as a builder/waiter slip out past security. Just a glimpse. I thought nothing more of it. Robert snapped out of it. But…"

"But what…?" Cara's mouth was so dry she could hardly speak.

Christo took the folded pieces of paper from his breast pocket and handed Cara the pictures the police had given him in Cannes. "It was him. He's what jogged Robert's memory at the party the night before. He was there at the apartment when Robert was killed; the police got this photo of him leaving around the time of his murder. The more I have been thinking about that face, the more I'm damn sure he also disguised himself as the limousine driver who picked us up at the airstrip and drove us to the apartment in Cannes. I rang Louis. Left him a message. He had made all the arrangements for the trip, I thought maybe he could find out where the guy came from."

Cara stared at the photos in disbelief.

"My God, what was Jonathan doing there?"

"You know this man?" Christo looked at her in shock.

"He's my cousin, or at least he was raised by my mother's younger sister."

"Your cousin!"

"And Louis knows *exactly* who he is," she said angrily.

She got up and walked over to a photo of a group of men. All smiles, with their arms on each other's shoulders, and a young fresh-faced Cara sitting cross-legged below them. She picked it up, looked at the faces and pointed at one. "Jonathan worked on that movie. He seemed to be the right-hand man of the construction manager. He told me they'd grown up together."

She explained to Christo that she had gone with Bill to the Philippines to visit relatives.

"You went to the shoot?" asked Christo surprised.

"I spent only the first few days on the set …. but at least I got to meet my cousin, Jonathan. He was very quiet, a good listener. While Bill was stuck in a meeting with Robert, I spent a day and the following evening with him, telling him all about my life and Bill's. Getting to know each other's past and present. How Bill and I met and our stories before that," she continued. "The next day I offered to stay on, help in the production office or make-up. I spoke some Tagalog and had worked in movies all my life. And I liked the idea of not being separated from Bill for a couple of months. Marcus seemed happy for an extra pair of hands, especially someone he knew. The bosses said it would be a problem though; even Jonathan said I'd be better off back at home. All the time, they were plotting."

Now it was Christo who was silent.

"I guess I didn't think much more about it. I went back to LA.

As usual Bill sent me his postcards, sometimes with a note and joke added from Sam. Then nothing. I started to worry. Could not get through to the set, not that unusual though. Then I got a call from McConnell, telling me that Bill was 'missing.' No more explanation. Next thing I know the movie folds its tents. Everyone leaves. Friends never talk to each other again. A wall of silence is built. I didn't even get a body. I was frantic." She paused as her fingers gently massaged the jowls of the small black pug now asleep on her lap.

"Slowly hope faded. It started to sink in that Bill wasn't coming home and that I was never going to find out what happened. Then I got angry. Demanded to see McConnell, threatened to raise a stink. Get the Union involved. Louis contacted me with a not so gentle warning to back off. Next I get a battery of lawyers coming after me. I was so mad at them."

Christo sensed Cara's inner strength and yet the utter hopelessness of her position.

"I was alone," she said evenly. "They offered me a bunch of cash. I couldn't collect insurance for years unless a body appeared. I just wanted it all to go away. I took the money and never really knew what happened."

"Cara, you had no choice. And this Jonathan?" asked Christo breaking his silence.

"There must have been a rift between him and his construction friend. After the movie stopped shooting, he quietly appeared in LA, but I never asked him why. Jonathan keeps things to himself. Has a business in Santa Monica. Rents and sells bikes. He also seems to do the odd job for Louis. In return Louis has let him live above the garage at his mansion like a shadow. When we did occasionally talk or meet, he always asked me to keep it quiet. I just assumed Louis got him in illegally or has a friend at Immigration. Hardly anyone ever sees him. He likes Cato. Would you believe he likes small dogs? My God, what did I turn a blind eye to all those years ago? Robert must have wondered what the hell Jonathan was doing in Cannes."

"We still don't know for sure what happened, or even if it was Jonathan."

"I'm sure," she said firmly looking at the picture. "Sam was equally sure about something. Christo, whatever burned away at Robert was the same thing that got Sam all riled up. Sam found out something. It's there in **FALL OUT.**" She leaned over and took her script from him. She turned to the scene she had shown Louis.

"Is that the same as yours? The bit about the name of the flour mill *Masa Bick*? Can you remember?"

"Cara, I went through that screenplay numerous times with Robert." Christo read the scene. He looked up. "They're different. Robert's copy had no name for the mill, but both reference a tiger."

Cara wondered. "What the hell does the tiger signify? We have to contact Marcus," she said.

Christo drew a sharp breath. "Cara… I'm sorry. I didn't realize you hadn't heard about Marcus…."

CHAPTER 43

HABKERN, SWITZERLAND

Nisten was arranged over three stories with a basement used as a wine cellar and a parking garage. Bright and modern in design, there were not many rooms, but each was enormous.

To the left of the front door was a chef's dream kitchen, brushed aluminum and steel with every conceivable electrical gadget and accessory. Many of these were hidden, sunk into the work surfaces, to be summoned by a flick from a bank of toggles to the right of the eight-ringed gas stove. Each switch was marked with the corresponding appliance. When summoned, the specified item would gracefully appear as an entrance hatch as the worktop slid from view and a silent lift from below brought the gadget to the surface.

Behind the kitchen and looking out over the valley was a beautifully decorated dining room, with sixteen straight, high back rosewood chairs, each decorated with carved symmetrical trellis work. These *taishiyi* or grandfather chairs also had arm rests at right angles to the backs, but the traditional hard flat seats were now covered with plum red silk cushions.

"The extra padding is something the originals would never have had, but no doubt improved the comfort at the dinner parties my parents gave," explained Mako. In each corner of the room, standing silently to attention were four full-size Chinese warriors.

"Meet John, Paul, George, and Ringo," said Mako. "My mother bought three at an auction in London when I was a teenager. My father went ballistic as they were not cheap, but they formed the beginning of their serious Asian art collection. Before then most of the pieces were smaller and less valuable. My father later added one more and my mother nicknamed them after the Fab Four."

Mako explained that the earliest suit of armor was simply a breastplate made from a tortoise shell tied together with leather cords and dating from about 1200 BC; the Shang Dynasty. She turned to the other three. One was a warrior in chain mail, complete with a large helmet and a fearsome black face mask.

"Now I know where *Darth Vader's* look came from," Marcus said. The resemblance was remarkable.

"Well, he didn't come from a galaxy far far away. Tang Dynasty, 65 AD. And that dao he's holding," she said pointing to a spear with a large flat curved blade, "is still razor sharp."

She turned to the next soldier. "This one's a ceremonial suit from around 1600. Those intricate swirling patterns are actually painted on cloth and leather. Lift up the hem of the jacket."

Marcus reached behind the beautifully engraved sword and raised the edge of the jacket. It was surprisingly heavy.

"It's got metal plates concealed inside for protection." The uniform was topped off with a pointed golden helmet complete with a magnificent black plume and held in place with a leather chinstrap. She turned to the final one. "He was the last one my father added. Came from a burial site," she said. "One of the soldier's arms has been broken, that club he is holding in the other is a *shu*, a weapon to guard an Emperor," she added.

The terracotta soldier also had a quiver and bow slung across his shoulder. The figure was similar to ones from the huge Terracotta Army, some of which Marcus had seen exhibited at the British Museum.

They headed back to the entrance. Opposite the front door was the picture Marcus had noticed earlier and a small doorway to the basement. To the right, opening to the living room stood a floor to ceiling door. It was decorated with gold plated studs, each about the size of a tennis ball.

"There will be eighty-one," said Mako as she saw Marcus admire it. "Number nine signified an emperor, so nine rows of nine studs. Eighty- one. Eight plus one, nine."

"How do you know all this stuff?" It was obvious to Marcus that she had been surrounded by works of art her whole life, but her knowledge was encyclopedic.

"*Nu-wa*," she replied quietly. He looked at her not understanding what she meant.

"It was my mother's name. Funny, I never really like it when kids call their parents by their first name. Dad was always Dad…. at least until we stopped talking, but my mother's name was Nu-wa. It means *Mother Goddess* in Chinese. It was so appropriate. I was a tiny girl when she told me. From that day I called her nothing else….," she paused for a moment. "Today was the first time I've said her name out loud since she died."

"You OK here?" asked a concerned Marcus.

"I'm fine, really. Right now, I feel happier than I have for days. I know that must sound crazy, but this place… so many wonderful memories."

Enjoy the moment, Marcus thought. He somehow doubted it would last.

"Asian art was Nu-wa's passion. While I was growing up, she would devote evenings to showing me pictures in books, explaining the stories behind the art. It was like fairytales. Dragons and princesses, witchcraft and magic. I lived on a diet of practically nothing else. The original works of art from my childhood…. I know their provenance by heart. This new stuff though…. It's unbelievable quality."

"I feel like there's a village missing an idiot, standing listening to you. Educate me!" It got the laugh he wanted and on they went.

She gave detailed explanations of types of calligraphy, methods of firing pottery, carving quartz or jade, and the history behind religious artefacts.

"See that?" She pointed at a delicate globe-shaped vase whose white surface covered the original green below like a gossamer slip and had been delicately hand cut with patterns of peony, lotus, and fish. "That work is Korean. Called *Choson*. Most examples disappeared after the 1930s. Discover how my father could afford this, and we'll start to find some answers," she said.

"Do you really want to?" he asked her.

"I have to," she answered calmly. "So do you."

The drawing room took up the rest of the first floor. Marcus reckoned it was nearly the size of a tennis court. A set of sliding glass doors led out to a large balcony at the rear of the house. The platform was suspended by solid stainless-steel guy ropes above and below, giving a fabulous vista over the dramatic sweep of the moonlit valley.

The cherry-wood flooring in the house was a masterpiece of carpentry as it swept in fluid lines like a wooden wave. With a gentle continuous gradient rising to the floors above rather than actual steps, this wooden pathway spiralled upwards accompanied by a balustrade of matching wood, suspended by chrome poles from the ceiling above.

"It's beautiful but try walking down it in high heels. My mother wanted him to put a rubber strip down the middle, but he wouldn't hear of it. We used to have to carry our shoes each time we clambered up or down 'the wooden hill'!"

The vast master bedroom occupied most of the second floor. At first glance Marcus thought its floor and walls were covered entirely in terracotta tiles but they were in fact rectangles of dark oxblood leather, imbuing the room with a rich and warm aroma of expensive hide.

The bathroom was partially in view, with only a shoulder-high dividing wall of beaten copper between it and the sleeping and dressing areas. The bath and two sinks were also beaten copper and shaped like shells. Only the actual toilet was hidden behind a solid antique wooden door, with a small one-foot square metal grill cut into it at head height.

"It's an actual prison door," Mako grinned. "My mother's idea of a joke as my father spent so much time reading in there. She said she should lock him in."

"This place is astonishing," he said giving a low whistle.

"Yeah, well, just a handful of the new works downstairs could easily pay for the construction of three or four whole houses," Mako said matter of factly.

They carried on with their tour. In addition to the master bedroom, the second floor boasted a well-equipped gym and a screening room with half a dozen black leather Lazy-boy reclining armchairs. The wooden path rose again to the top floor, where there were another three bedrooms, all with shower and sauna ensuite.

"This used to be mine." Mako hesitated for a moment before twisting the handle and gently pushing the door open. The room was completely empty. Not a stick of furniture, not one single work of art. Any human presence had been erased. As she turned and sharply pulled the door shut, she heard a faint rattle on the other side. She opened the door again and peered round to look.

"Well, what do you know?" She reached up and unhooked something. It was a framed diploma, all fake parchment, swirly writing and a large wax seal and ribbon. She read it again, the first time in years.

"He was so proud of that. My first real academic competition and I'd come first," she said in a sing-song voice tinged with cynicism.

"Still, he hung on to it. It meant something," Marcus said gently.

"But for all the wrong reasons. He was celebrating my victory against others, not excellence in something I cared about. For him, it was all about beating someone else." She tossed it to Marcus.

"Here. You keep it."

They didn't even stop to eat; she kept on opening drawers, cupboards, desks, everything in her quest for an answer as to how her father had acquired this extraordinary treasure trove.

She scoured the house from top to bottom, searching for a credible and legal explanation. In her heart she knew there wouldn't be one. Everything seemed to be pointing towards her father being more than just fallible in terms of his relationship with her mother; he was also part of something murky, deceitful, and ultimately deadly.

Marcus eventually got her to bed at three in the morning, and for the first time they fell asleep without making love.

CHAPTER 44

INTERLAKEN, SWITZERLAND

The razor made a barely audible scrape as it arced over the dome of Jonathan's head. He stared intently into the mirror as the blade swept away the last remnant of shaving foam. His small rough hands lowered to the sink. He leaned closer gazing into his own dark eyes as if to reassure himself of who he was, never to forget where he had come from, and to be crystal clear where he was going. A beat, then he splashed ice cold water from the basin over his face, neck, and head, breaking the spell.

Having completed his morning run, he folded his trainers, sweatshirt and running shorts onto the chair behind him. He believed in himself. You wanted exercise, just go for a run. Diet, just don't eat so much. Got a problem, deal with it head on. Simple. Trying to justify actions just stopped a man from actually achieving anything. Self-analysis never produced results.

When Jonathan had been jogging in town, he instantly recognized the building he had glimpsed in the family photo just inside the doorway at the de Turris' house. He stopped a moment to think, fine tuning a plan.

He had three very clear tasks today and was going to be utterly ruthless in the pursuit of them. Retrieve the head, once and for all take care of Marcus and Mako and destroy any evidence of Mr. Louis' involvement.

As he started to dress, he went over the plan. It would be far too risky to try and simply break into the house. He was certain Mako and Marcus would be looking for answers. Their knowledge would save him a lot of time. She would have no idea how the treasures had materialized. Somehow Jonathan had to appear as if he could provide them with the answers they wanted. He needed an invitation.

The suit he had bought that morning looked reassuringly ill fitting. The brown lace up shoes and wire-rim glasses gave him the faded aura of academia. A slight hunch of the shoulders and he looked about as threatening and dangerous as Mr. Magoo. He was certain where Mako would return to. All he had to do was wait.

CHAPTER 45

HABKERN, SWITZERLAND

Mako was exhausted but could not sleep past dawn. She needed her own space and time to think, to analyses everything she had seen. She was sitting on the sofa in the vast drawing room, hugging her knees, going over in her mind the treasures she had inspected so closely the night before.

There were far more items than when she had last been in the house, but she also had a nagging sensation that a number of the old as well as the new pieces were somehow not quite right. To start with, the lions were there to greet her, but for no logical reason she could think of, her father had swapped them around. It looked the same. But wasn't.

The feeling of things being slightly off kilter grew when she had entered the dining room last night and glanced over at the four suits of armor. Again, something was not quite right. She could not put her finger on it at first, but the answer had come to her in a flash as she had been lying awake. She had quietly gone downstairs to check, leaving Marcus asleep in the bed. She had been right, but why had her father done that?

This game playing was typical of her father. It used to be an annual ritual. Every Christmas, rather than unwrapping a stocking full of presents hanging by the fireplace, Mako would awaken early to begin the treasure hunt for presents hidden all over the house. Excitedly she would leap out of bed and proceed to peer into, hunt through, and crawl over every inch of the home to find them. The number of presents was the same as her age that year. When Mako was very young, her mother would help her by whispering "hotter" when she approached a hiding place or "colder" as she moved away.

The search started with relatively simple tests of observation such as the tops of a nearly identical pair of pots being swapped over, inside each, nestled a brightly wrapped toy.

As Mako grew older and her understanding of Asian art improved, the clues became more complex. One year her father's prized Chinese abacus had three beads on one of the rods on the upper deck and six on the lower deck, instead of the correct number of two and five.

Adding the beads together had given her a number. In that particular hunt the number was written in Chinese as a piece of calligraphy hanging on a wall. As Mako gently lifted the work, she could see something hidden in a silk cloth in a long thin recess in the brickwork. She unwrapped it, her face beaming.

"You know what it is?" her mother asked.

"It's a *ruyi* or an '*As you wish*'" Mako cried out, using the rough translation by which a backscratcher was more commonly known.

Small and exquisitely carved from ivory and with a gold handle with inlay of jade, the delicately curved backscratcher once belonged to a princess. It was still one of her most prized possessions from her childhood and lay on her dressing table at *Pied à Mer*. The hairpin she nearly always wore was another present from the same princess's collection.

And so the treasure hunts evolved over the years, ever more cryptic, ever more fun. Then bang. Nu-wa left and days later was dead. Mako had never returned to *Nisten*, the Christmas tradition over....

Now she was back and her father had hidden things not for a bright-eyed child on Christmas morning, but to help her or lead her in some way to an answer. Perhaps he knew she would someday be in danger. With all this wealth on display, it could not have been the items themselves, but rather their provenance that he had been so careful to cover up. At first, she wondered if he had simply obliterated all trace of where these precious things had come from let alone how he had managed to acquire them. However, she knew her father well. He had been a cautious and clever man. He had undoubtedly had accomplices; others must have been involved. Evidence of that was his protection.

She unhooked her arms from around her knees and leaned back into the soft curve of the sofa....

Her eyes slowly opened. It was after eight o'clock, and she had dozed off three hours ago. She crept back upstairs. Marcus was blissfully asleep, hugging one of the pillows.

The day was bright and sunny, so she decided to hike down into Interlaken to the shop where her mother had taken her so many times in the past. She would ride back on one of the narrow-gauge railway trains that crisscrossed the valley.

Such was the popularity of hiking that there were several well-signposted footpaths that cut and zigzagged down the mountainside. The gravel-strewn trails crunched underfoot as she breathed in the heady aromas of wildflowers and newly mown grass. She was lost in thought, trying to understand the contents of the house and any clues they might reveal. She needed help and was hoping that the old man from her past would still have his shop in town.

It was nearly 11 AM when she approached the four-storied timbered building that housed the bookstore. She wondered if she should call *Nisten* from the shop and tell Marcus she would not be back for a couple of hours. She was sure he would still be asleep and decided to leave him be. However, her real worry was whether the shop would have the same owner. She took a deep breath and pushed open the door. The small cowbell hanging above it announced the arrival of a new customer.

The smell of books and leather brought into sharp focus the images that swirled around in her mind. Little had changed. The shop itself had no ceiling between the first two levels. Floor-to-ceiling mahogany shelves packed with old, leather-bound books clung like ivy to the bowed walls. Against them, stepladders hung silently at attention from brass rails. One alcove housed a diverse collection of china, jade and porcelain. Clusters of creased leather armchairs stood on threadbare Persian rugs and beckoned visitors to sit and thumb through one of the volumes stacked in the shelves.

Opposite the entrance on the far wall was a huge open fireplace with a wrought iron grate that was shaped like a rowing boat. Hanging above was a large black frame encasing a crimson cloth on which two items where mounted. The first was a photo, a copy of the one at the entrance to the house and the second was a duplicate of the certificate Mako had thrown at Marcus the day before. She read the small inscription written at the base:

'To Xavier, Thank you for all that I took from here as well as all that you gave me. I could not have done it without you. Première Place: Prix National Suisse des Arts et des Lettres. Le 20 mai 1998." All My Love, Melinda.'

This is where those two items truly belonged. Yet again, something wasn't quite right… Her thoughts were interrupted when the curtain covering the entrance to the stairs up to the living quarters above was pulled back and in walked an elderly man.

"Madame?" He was smaller than she remembered, the luxuriant mustache now quite white. "May I help you?"

"Xavier!" Mako said with a broad smile.

For a moment the man was puzzled how this woman knew his name, but as she turned from him and looked back at the photo above the fireplace, he remembered.

"*Mélinda, Viens ici que je t'embrasse!* Let me hug you!" He came down the stairs at a near stumble.

Mako wrapped her arms around the old man.

"So lovely to have you here. Are you two speaking?"

Xavier was obviously unaware of her father's death. She dryly broke the news to him.

"I'm so sorry," he said.

She stared back showing no emotion.

"He was still your father, no matter what" he said quietly holding her gaze. "So tell me about you. You have turned into a woman even more beautiful than your mother. Such beauty must have countless joys."

Mako passed an hour telling Xavier what had happened since her mother's death. She then started to probe him about what he knew of her father and the contents of the house.

"Those were happy days when you and your mother came to look and learn. But your father, he only wanted to buy things or know their value. I was of no real help to him. After you and your mother... well, we hardly spoke. I really saw very little of him."

"Did you ever meet anyone with him," she asked?

"Once. An American I believe? Can't remember his name. He came in here looking for books about Napoleon, designs, furniture and such. He said your father recommended that he stop by."

There was a brief pause, then Mako looked at the cuckoo clock on the wall and stood up. "I must be going, Xavier. If you can think of anything about my father or the things he bought, please call me. We are at the house."

"We?"

"Another time. I'll explain," she said with a shy smile.

She kissed him once on each cheek and left the shop that contained so many memories of the happy days of her youth.

"Miss de Turris?" said a voice as she stepped outside. "Melinda de Turris?" She turned to see a slightly built gentleman remove his spectacles and begin to rub the lenses as if he could not believe what he was seeing.

"Your father. I was so sorry to hear... I just did not expect to see you." The look of utter shock and surprise on Mako's face made him start again. "Please forgive me. My name is Masanobu, Professor Yoshio Masanobu." He held out his hand.

"I bought and sold several works of art on behalf of your father. I live in Lugano but have a small house up the valley in Wengen. I recognized you from that photo in the hall I saw a few years ago when I last visited." And as meticulous as a spider spinning his web, Jonathan lied to her about how he had met her father and what he had done for him.

"I'm sorry," Mako said slowly. "I... my father and I have not been close over the past few years. However maybe you can help me. I have so much to find out about his collection. Why not come up to the house... for a late lunch. My boyfriend thinks he can cook and you may be able to fill in some of the blanks." She gave a little smile.

"That would be most kind but perhaps another day. I really must...." He turned to go.

"Please," said Mako. "I insist." She reached out to touch his forearm quickly doing a small curtsy as if in mock supplication.

Jonathan inwardly congratulated himself on how easy it had been.

"How can I resist such a pretty invitation? Of course."

Mako knew from the outset that he could not possibly have been telling the truth, but this strange little man knew something, and she needed answers. He looked harmless enough and she was confident she and Marcus could take care of him if needed.

"So.... let's catch the next train back up," she smiled. "There is so much I want to ask you...."

CHAPTER 46

HABKERN, SWITZERLAND

Marcus awoke late to an empty bed and a room full of light.

"Mako?"

He pushed back the duvet and pulled on a robe she had laid out at the foot of the bed. He wandered into the bathroom.

"Back later," was written with her lipstick on the bathroom mirror.

Frustrating, as he had so many things still to ask her but there was little he could do about it. He again cursed the loss of their cell phones at sea. Worried about not being able to reach Mako whenever he wanted, he made a mental note to pick up some disposable phones the next time they went to town. At least the substantial amount of Euros, Swiss Francs, and U.S. dollars Mako pulled from one of the wall safes was more than enough to keep them afloat for a while.

He logged into his email via a small laptop Mako had dug out and found a reply to some research he had done while Mako had been asleep at the *Villa d'Este*. He needed to talk to Garance alone and now with Mako out of the way, he had his chance. He quickly called the villa and went through his confidential request.

"....If I find it, I tell you. M'sieur," concluded Garance. "I will say nothing to Madame."

Marcus went back to his email. As he scrolled through his messages, one in particular leapt out at him. It had been sent the day Marcus had hurriedly left Cannes. It was from *jumpingjax@comsusa.net*.

Dear Marcus,

Thank you for your kind words. I was so surprised you weren't at the funeral. McConnell explained your visa issue. Ridiculous but what can you do? No doubt will get sorted. I hope all is well, good luck at festival.

FYI, after an eternity IRS still not granted probate on Sam's estate. They have frozen a payment of $300,000 and keep asking what it relates to. It came from the Philippines but they keep hitting a brick wall of silence and are driving me crazy, muttering about bringing in DEA. I've no idea what it was for. They found an entry in Sam's calendar on the day the money hit saying, 'GET PAYMENT'.

From who? Does this mean anything to you? Let me know. Take care. I am relying on you to make that film. Don't let it be a bad decision.

Best Jax

It was of course possible there was a logical explanation. Royalties due to Sam, a fee for a screenplay that never happened, even investments of some sort. However, Marcus didn't buy it for a second; that would be clutching at very thin straws. Someone had paid Sam out of the Philippines. Why?

The doorbell sounded and he went downstairs. It was the courier with Kelso and Mako's versions of the script. He decided to wait for her to return as it would be easier for them to compare the two scripts together.

Marcus went into the large kitchen, found the coffee beans and flicked the appropriate switch. With a gentle hum, like an electronic fanfare, the chrome espresso machine rose to greet the morning from its hiding place below the work counter.

As he stood waiting for the steam pressure to build, he turned

Jax's message over and over in his mind. He looked out of the kitchen at the huge wooden door with its rows of studs that led into the drawing room, idly examining it. He stopped, looked again, then walked over and bent down to check his hunch.

The phone rang, making him jump. He hoped it was Mako, telling him where she was and when she would be back. Before he could find a handset though, the answering machine briskly kicked in.

"Melinda, this is Robin. My dear, we need to talk. Firstly, I was so relieved to hear from you. I had feared the worst and quite understand why you could not be at the funeral. You are in danger. There have been tragic developments. Giles and Mary.... they've been murdered. I have been in touch with the police both in London and Cannes. They believe there is a connection, one man. Call me... and please do not allow yourself to be approached by strangers, least of all a small Asian man. I'll explain."

A high-pitched alarm went off. The coffee machine was well past the safety pressure point and was sounding a warning that it needed to be turned off. Marcus ran back to the kitchen to switch it off. A moment later he heard the front door open and in walked Mako with Professor Masanobu in tow.

# CHAPTER 47

HABKERN, SWITZERLAND

Jonathan estimated he had no more than a few seconds to act. While studiously wiping his feet, he slipped his right hand deep into his coat pocket, his gloved index finger scooping out the contents of the small pot nestling there. He then passed his briefcase to that hand, surreptitiously smearing the paste against the underside of the handle.

"Marcus," Mako called out, "I met this gentleman in town. He knows both my father and his art collection. He kindly agreed to come up to the house for lunch, despite your cooking, and may be able to provide us with some answers."

As Marcus stepped from the kitchen doorway towards the entrance, Mako arched her eyebrows in mock surprise, conveying to him her disbelief at such a coincidence.

"Marcus Riley, Yoshio Masanobu," she said with a formal flourish. Mako's initial expression of amusement changed to concern when she saw the look of fear on Marcus' face.

"How long is it since you were last here?" queried Mako. "I'm not too sure about all this new lighting and electrical stuff my father installed. Alarms, cameras…," continued Mako but with a look of puzzlement at Marcus' tense body language.

"*You cannot stop innovation,*" he said answering Mako's question but looking straight at Marcus.

Marcus' expression was clear; he recognized the quote. He had last read it at the end of the exploding tequila keg scene.

"So, you know your Sun-Tzu, Mr. Riley?"

"No, my Sam Wood," said Marcus flatly.

Jonathan passed Mako his briefcase to her, then turned to Marcus and executed a slow bow.

There was a thud as Mako flinched, dropping the case on the floor and looking at her hand.

Marcus' head snapped round. "Are you OK, what happened?" he asked Mako who was looking down at her hand.

Suddenly Jonathan swung round and smacked his glove across Mako's cheek, as if challenging her to a duel. It was so totally unexpected Mako's eyes snapped open in shock. The brown paste which had transferred from the underside of the case's handle to her hand was now also smeared across her face, leaving a rancid-smelling brown streak. Mako instinctively lifted her fingertips to her cheek, rubbing them across the smarting skin. Blood now seeped from both fingers and face.

"You have fifteen minutes, I would guess, before she goes into convulsions, then maybe another hour before she is dead. Where is the Buddha head?" said Jonathan flatly.

Making the poison had been remarkably easy. The six large tins of pipe tobacco Jonathan had purchased from the newspaper shop had spent the previous night soaking in a jug of water. Before going for his run, he simply strained the mixture through the washcloth provided by the inn, then wrung out the remaining liquid in the damp mound into a mess tin. Next he flushed away the mush of soggy tobacco and threw the cloth in the trash can.

After he had shaved and showered, he slowly heated the mixture in the mess tin over a small gas camping stove, both of which he had purchased in town along with the suit. Reducing the mixture over the heat, he stirred it as if he were preparing a sauce. Finally, he poured the sticky syrup into a small ceramic jar that had once contained skin balm.

The paste was pure nicotine, three times more powerful than arsenic, nearly twice as deadly as strychnine, but a hundred times easier to get hold of. A few drops mixed with a cup of coffee would kill a man. Indeed, Jonathan had added a couple of drops to the coffee of the trusting steady cam operator Rory Carmichael at a Starbucks outside Encino. The effect was fatal. The other two men from Bill Baines' rescue party had been dispatched by a hit and run and a boat explosion; the latter thanks to Bill Baines' special fume bomb.

There were two advantages to nicotine poison. First, it was quickly and easily absorbed through the skin (as it was in the much less virulent form in nicotine patches) and secondly, it was just about undetectable, even in a serum toxicology screen. For extra effectiveness Jonathan had shattered a water glass, sprinkling shards into the paste, ensuring the tiny cuts they would create would speed the poison into the bloodstream. He had been careful to wear the thickest of leather gloves to protect his skin from any contact.

Incredibly for such a lethal poison, Jonathan knew the antidote was just as easy to get hold of. All that was needed was an atropine sulphate solution, which was often sold over the counter in Europe as eye drops. In cases of nicotine poisoning it would need to be injected and taking the common muscle relaxant diazepam would stop the convulsions.

Marcus moved forward, unsure what to do.

"What the hell are you talking about? Mako, are you OK…?"

"Don't make the mistake of others who questioned me and are now dead. Violence is my job." The vicious blade fanned open in his hand, the point kissing Mako's neck. Marcus hesitated.

"By the time you work out what the poison is, let alone get an antidote, it will be over for her. Now give me the Buddha head."

His eyes locked onto Marcus.

Marcus held the gaze for a second. He knew this man was dead serious. Mako was starting to sway.

"I have an antidote I could give her," said Jonathan holding out a sliver of hope. He had left a small package outside by the rock where he had watched the pair on their arrival the night before. He had no real intention of administering it as he planned to leave both Marcus and Mako dead. It was there just in case they became obstinate, instead of just obstacles. And, you never knew, accidents can happen. He might need it for himself.

Marcus saw a glimmer of hope. If he could take it from this man…. Once again Jonathan read his mind and was way ahead of him.

"It's not on me, so don't even bother trying. I came up here last night to check on you two lovebirds and hid it. My own game of hide and seek shall we say? Carrot and stick." Jonathan had heard from Louis about the games that Stefan had played with his daughter. He neither had the time nor the inclination to ransack a house full of hiding places. He was sure the fastest and most certain way to retrieve what he wanted was to put one of them in mortal danger. They would crack. No problem.

Jonathan turned to Mako, resting the blade against her cheek.

"So, you show me your treasure and I'll show you mine," he whispered.

Mako was already starting to perspire, feeling dizzy and sick. The blade still at her face, she was helpless; all she wanted was to lie down and wipe away the tar like substance from her cheek and hands that she knew was now slowly killing her.

Marcus felt the dull fear of losing Mako threatening to overwhelm him. He was way out of his depth. He looked at her.

"OK, OK. I know where it is," she said in a voice growing weaker by the minute, "It's upstairs. In jail."

Jonathan snapped the balisong away from her face, grabbing her wrist and scored a deep cut in her hand, allowing more of the sticky paste to enter her bloodstream. He then threw her roughly into a chair.

"I said no more games, Melinda." He glowered at her.

"Don't. I know what she means," Marcus said forcefully, hoping to keep the desperation out of his voice.

Jonathan looked up. "Then... go fetch, boy," he hissed.

Marcus turned towards the stairs.

"Run," Jonathan ordered after him. He reached down to his case, flipped the locks and took out a stack of bricks, tossing them to the side. "Ballast," he said matter-of-factly smiling at the weakening Mako, "to drive in those shards." He pulled out a cloth and carefully removed any trace of the poison left on the handle along with a few glass splinters. Finally, he pulled at two clasps on the side of the leather case and it expanded into a large cube, deep enough to receive the precious cargo.

Looking at the blood mixing with the deadly paste he shouted after Marcus. "My ETA for death has moved up. Hurry." He turned to Mako, "Hope he loves you."

Marcus pounded up the wooden gradient, questions bouncing around in his head as insistent as the beat of his footfalls on the polished surface. He had no idea what this man was talking about. There was no reference in Sam's story about a head. He'd never even heard anyone discuss such a thing.

However, he did know what was in the 'prison'. He'd seen it when in there that morning. God, she scared him.... nearly as much as that cold-blooded bastard downstairs. She was gambling her life on his bravery.

He pulled back the rough-hewn wooden door and ran in. He turned and looked at the alcove above the entrance. There, nestled under a framed old Monopoly game card which read 'Get out of jail free,' stood an old short-handled fire axe, a wide blade at the front, a sharp pick like point at the back. It was Stefan's lighthearted response to his wife's threat of locking him in.

Just to be certain it was what Mako had wanted him to retrieve, Marcus ran his fingertips over the wall and floorboards, desperately hoping he had misread her intentions and that there was indeed a Buddha head of some description hidden in a concealed space. He even stood on the toilet bowl and peered into the antique cistern, praying there was something inside.... nothing. Mako's decision was absolutely clear. Save ourselves. Attack this intruder.

He wrenched the weapon from the wall and tucked it into the waistband of his trousers, at the small of his back. He pulled down his sweatshirt and quickly checked in the bathroom mirror to see if there was a discernible bulge.

"Man up and take him," he could almost hear her say. Jesus, Mako he thought. No time for self-doubt, no turning back. She had rolled the dice for both of them.

"Hurry, my friend. She doesn't look good." Marcus heard the little bastard shout.

Rushing past the bed Marcus yanked a pillow from the mattress, peeled away the pillowcase and ran into the gym. He lifted a heavy leather medicine ball into the pillowcase and staggered back to the head of the staircase.

"Here," he stood straining and with both hands lifted the bulging pillowcase. "Now you show me yours."

"Bring it," ordered Jonathan.

"Screw you," answered Marcus with as much defiance as he could muster. Mako smiled weakly at him.

"Show me," the man shouted.

Mako had drawn Marcus into playing hardball; there was no going back now. He turned, opened the veranda to the second-floor balcony and lifted the pillowcase over the balustrade.

"Without this, whoever sent you will no doubt see you die too. I reckon they want this very badly…. certainly more than her dead. Now antidote…. or Buddha flies."

Marcus started to swing the pillowcase back and forth, high over the steep incline of the valley that ran down to the lakes below. Marcus' hands were shaking and his heart was pounding, hoping he looked as if he meant what he said.

Jonathan made a split-second decision and started up the incline. Slowly at first, his determined pace picking up with surprising feline agility until he was sprinting fast, balisong in his hand. The look and determination on his face made it clear what action he would take when he caught Marcus.

With a massive heave Marcus lifted the pillowcase back over the balcony railing, turned and ran down the incline towards the assailant, swinging the pillowcase then letting it go.

The missile landed on the stairway, rolling fast down the slope. It knocked Jonathan over as if he was the last remaining ninepin on an inclined bowling alley. The force of the ball and the slippery flooring sent Jonathan sliding back down and out through the open doors onto the main veranda.

An insane mixture of machismo and shame at being shit scared made Marcus half roll, half run after him, and he collided into the body of his attacker. The sheer force of the impact had them both skidding over the veranda floor out towards the edge of the balcony.

Marcus reached for the small axe as he saw the man fumble, then drop, his own wicked looking blade. Marcus wanted to hurt this man, force him to save Mako. Nothing else mattered. The relief at seeing him drop his knife lasted a fleeting moment as Marcus found his weapon had become entangled in his trouser belt loop. He couldn't get it out, so instead he just lunged at his attacker.

No finesse, no well-judged blows, just frantic kicking, punching and gouging. If Marcus could have, he would have bitten him. The two men rolled to the edge of the balcony, a wheel of fists and feet. Between the bottom edge of the balcony's glass wall and the floor was a gap of about 18 inches. They were both lying sprawled on the ground, the small man with his back to the glass wall. Marcus saw his only chance.

Lying on his side, Marcus shot his right leg into his opponent's solar plexus. Instinctively Jonathan bent in half and his slight torso slid under the lip of the glass wall. With another almighty kick, Marcus forced the small body through the gap. Jonathan desperately tried to haul himself back, only his arms, legs, and head still on solid ground, the rest hanging out over the void.

"Where is the antidote?" Marcus yelled, managing to free the axe stuck in his belt. He hesitated, threatening to hack at his attacker's arm.

Through gritted teeth Jonathan flashed a grotesque grin. The next instant he corkscrewed himself away and slipped through the gap into the void. Twisting in midair he just managed to grasp one of the guy ropes that was attached to the base of the balcony. He hung for a moment then staring at Marcus with a look of sheer hate…. let go.

He fell about thirty feet, tucking himself into a neat ball as he hit the rock-strewn grassy incline with a thud. He rolled down the steep hill, tossing and cartwheeling like a rag doll. He tumbled down the incline for well over 250 yards where he eventually came to a halt against a tree.

Marcus did not give a damn about the fate of his attacker. He hoped he was badly hurt, maybe even dead. He was terrified he had failed Mako. He had no idea how to save her. As he got up to rush to Mako's aid, he glanced back down the hill at the pathetic little bundle. In utter amazement he watched as the assailant's body twitched as he began to regain consciousness. Christ, Marcus thought, he's indestructible.

Mako had managed to drag herself to the kitchen sink where she'd grabbed the chrome vegetable cleaner hose from the sink faucet. She was slumped on the floor, holding the showerhead over her face and hand, at the same time as desperately rubbing both with a cloth, trying to remove the paste. Blood, vomit and water swirled over the stone tiles.

"He saw the photo," she said weakly, "The one of Nu-wa and me outside the shop." She indicated to the hallway where it was hanging.

"He went there. He knew I'd go." Her breathing was now shallow, her skin damp. "If he really brought an antidote the other night, he hid it somewhere outside…. that has a direct view to the picture."

"Mako. Let me get you to hospital," he pleaded.

"I won't make it. Marcus, look for it…. Go." She nodded her head towards the open front door.

Her body contorted as she heaved again, dry vomiting, nothing left in her stomach.

Marcus hoped to God their assailant had done as he had said.

He ran outside. The only possible line of sight that would have allowed Jonathan to look through the door and clearly see the photo of Mako and her mother would have been from a small grassy bank to the right of the road.

As Marcus ran towards it, he noticed a single set of tire marks tracking through loose soil and veering off to the right. There was no view to the house from the first rock, but a little further up a small outcrop of four or five boulders gave a clear view of the entrance and there were more tire marks in the soil just below.

He ran to the base of the rocks. Some earth looked disturbed. He frantically scraped at the topsoil and quickly came across a smooth flat surface. It was a small oblong tin box. Inside was a small syringe, pills and a plastic bottle of eye-drops.

He ran back to the house.

"Mako I found something. The pills are diazepam, I know they stop convulsions, but eye drops and a syringe?"

She looked at him, her hair damp and matted, her complexion grey, beads of sweat on her forehead.

"Fill the syringe. He put it there for a reason. Do it." she said weakly.

Marcus hesitated for a moment, but her hand snaked out to grab his leg.

"Now," she pleaded.

Marcus filled the syringe with the liquid from the eye drops bottle, squirting it to ensure there were no air bubbles, then plunged it into her arm. He quickly filled a glass of water and helped her take four of the diazepam.

"Get the certificate," she mumbled. "The one from my room." Marcus looked at her with amazement.

"Why the hell do we need that? That psychopath is on his way back up to the house. We need to get the hell out of here," he replied.

"Trust me," she said as calmly as possible.

Marcus ran upstairs and pulled the certificate out of its frame. He quickly threw some things in a bag, grabbing the laptop, passports and money. As he raced back downstairs sweeping up the screenplays on his way, he glanced out over the balcony. Slowly but surely the man had managed to inch his way back up the hill and was over halfway back to the house.

Marcus threw the items in the car, stuck the keys in the ignition and ran back inside.

He knelt down in front of the huge gold studded door that had caught his attention just before the phone call from Vallings. He started twisting the bottom corner stud.

Mako stared at him.

"It's not 'nine by nine', it's 'ten by ten'. These lines look new. They've been added and this corner one is askew," Marcus said. He feverishly turned and pried the stud.

"Come on, come on," Marcus muttered in frustration, aware that every second counted. Eventually it gave. He twisted the stud and it finally turned in his hand. A bright red USB memory stick fell to the floor. Marcus shoved it in his pocket and ran to the kitchen. Bending down he lifted Mako to her feet as gently as he could.

There was a sharp shatter of breaking glass from the cellar below as Marcus half-dragged, half-carried Mako towards the front door. The convertible's top was still down and with time running out Marcus simply dropped her into the passenger seat and ran around to the driver's side.

"Wait. I know where it is," she said gulping down air and looking up at Marcus.

He frowned "Where what is…?"

"The head," she whispered as if their attacker might somehow hear her.

"Who cares? We have to get out of here now."

"If I survive, I care, if I don't, you should." There was a thud from the basement.

"He's trying to get in the house. We have to go."

She looked at Marcus and smiled weakly. "Ringo's got the wrong weapon, look under the headgear."

Shit, she's impossible, thought Marcus as he ran back to the dining room. In his haste he had forgotten to ask her which one was Ringo, so he just smacked at each helmet in turn and they rolled to the floor. No Buddha head. But the last one didn't move. It was the terracotta soldier. Marcus grabbed the axe he had replaced in his belt and smashed it into the top of the soldier's head. It shattered. Underneath was a serene calm face.

Marcus manhandled the Buddha head into Darth Vader's upturned helmet, but he had to heave to move it. He heard a crack as the locked cellar door at the bottom of the stairs started to give way. He had an idea.

Moments later Mako saw him stumbling to the car, with the helmet cradled in his arms. "Move your feet. This is damned heavy," Marcus shouted loudly as he dropped it on her side of the foot well. He jumped into the car and punched the starter button just as a bloodied Jonathan burst out of the front door. The engine fired into life and in a spray of gravel the car shot off down the road to safety, leaving Jonathan cursing and vainly hobbling in their wake.

Mako was slowly beginning to feel better. The diazepam had started to kick in and reduce the spasms while the atropine sulphate tackled the nicotine. She gave a quiet clap and bent down to tip over the helmet at her feet. She barely touched it as it rolled over. It was empty.

Marcus shot her a glance.

As Jonathan had burst from the house in his vain attempt to stop Marcus driving away, the kitchen echoed to the faint hum of the Kenwood chef mixer returning to its recess below the work counter, a Buddha head staring up from the deep stainless steel mixing bowl.

PART 4

THE EAGLE AND THE TIGER

 **CHAPTER 48**

THE CAVE, PAGSANJAN, PHILIPPINES

NOVEMBER 1944

As his life slowly ebbed away, Major Okobudo's fingertips searched in the darkness for the items he had risked his life to take with him; the map and the Buddha head in one box and artillery shells in the other. Both were by his feet.

The original cave had been four times larger. The first clue to its existence came nine months earlier when a young soldier had ducked away by some rocks for a sneaky cigarette break while meant to be on patrol. As the momentary flare of his match struck the cliff face, he had caught a glimpse of an enormous cavern.

Troops were on constant alert to find well concealed areas for storage. The soldier who had found this one had been well rewarded. He was permitted first pick from the new delivery of 'comfort women' supplied to the Fourteenth Area Army for their enjoyment. The virtual enslavement of women was viewed by Military Command as a useful by-product from the various nations they had subdued.

The soldier had also been promoted to corporal and given a minor medal, but death was awaiting him. He too would become entombed within his discovery.

Major Okobudo who commanded the local garrison at Pagsanjan had advised General Yamashita back in Manila, of their find. The order had been brief and to the point. Prepare the cavern for an ultra-secret consignment directly from the General himself. The Major must assemble a large work gang to assist the POWs and Japanese engineers General Yamashita was sending down with secret military assets.

The General insisted that Major Okobudo leave the comfort of his local headquarters and personally oversee the elaborate and painstaking camouflaging of the storage of this precious cargo.

"What we are doing here will forever ensure the survival of the Imperial Family and of Japan itself. The whereabouts are never to be divulged; the contents seen by no one. Any attempt to inspect the consignment or copy the coded map carries a death penalty." the General had told Major Okobudo, with the ever-present Tan standing silently behind him. The big man was in awe of the famous General.

When the Major had enquired as to the nature of what was being stored, the General had been furious at his impudence.

"The ultimate weapons of war!" he shouted, making it clear that was all anyone needed to know.

The Major, stinging from the General's rebuke, hoped that whatever destructive force he was so keen to hide would have the desired effect when the Imperial Army had to retaliate against the advancing Americans. Major Okobudo's trust in General Yamashita was absolute.

Under the Major's direction, local troops quickly blasted a large hole in the cracked rock-face at the side of the cliff. It was large enough to drive trucks through. Next they cut through the roof of the cavern, creating a hole to provide sunlight to help them in their work. One by one the mass of assembled vehicles that had been arriving in a constant stream over the previous ten days was driven inside.

Not quite everything had gone to plan. As instructed, Major Okobudo duly supervised the storing of the vehicles and their cargo. Every day he stood on a small rock in the cave that served as a stone rostrum. Waving two long white batons, he pointed to each driver in turn and directed them to their designated space.

One afternoon a driver misjudged the distance from the rear of his flatbed truck to the neighboring half-track. There was a crack as the five and a half thousand-pound truck slammed into the six-and-a-half-ton half-track.

A crate fell out onto the rocky floor where the Major was standing, its contents spewing out. At the sound of the crash, the work force immediately stopped, all eyes instantly fixed on the roof of the cave. No one would dare glance at the Major or the contents at his feet. Each knew it was instant execution to even peek under the heavy tarpaulins secured to the trucks, let alone see the actual contents.

"Guard," the Major shouted. The soldier at the entrance snapped to attention. "Execute that fool of a driver." The Major's gaze swept over the upturned faces, still desperate not to be accused of looking at what had fallen to the ground.

"I need one volunteer," barked Okobudo.

Silence. No one was that crazy.

"Thank you, I accept," he said to one hapless Filipino conscript who, of course, had not offered it.

"Everyone else. Out!" Major Okobudo commanded in sharp clipped tones.

It was not until they had all left that Major Okobudo himself looked down at the contents strewn at his feet. When he saw what was inside the crate, it filled him with shock and anger; a tidal wave of utter betrayal engulfed him. He immediately understood the significance of the 16 petal chrysanthemum stenciled on the side of the broken crate. It was the symbol of the Imperial Family.

His loyalties changed in an instant. The values he had cherished and honored simply evaporated. He cursed his own naivety. Pragmatism won. Especially if you had power. And right now,

Major Okobudo had the power. He just needed to cover his tracks and hide the evidence.

He looked around and saw some artillery shells stacked in wooden crates. They had been brought up to the cave to supply the Type 11 37 mm infantry gun that had been positioned outside to deter prying eyes.

The Major briskly made his way to the parked vehicles and removed several gas caps. Then he walked over to the box of artillery shells, grabbing one. "Fetch those wrenches," he ordered. The conscript ran to collect the tools. Kneeling at the box the Major locked the teeth of his wrench onto the body of a shell.

"Now grip the casing," he barked.

Together they pulled the shell apart.

"Pour the explosive powder and charges into the gas tanks. Replace the caps and bring the empty shells back to me," he commanded.

One by one they exchanged the explosive cores inside each brass shell casing with the contents strewn on the floor from the packing case.

Within an hour all the shells were back in their original wooden box. The Major then placed his shell box the furthest away from the gun, confident that the other cases would be chosen first in the unlikely event of the gun being needed. His own stash should be untouched until he could recover it.

Okobudo then broke up the wooden case that had fallen from the truck and shoved the pieces into the duffle bag containing his personal supply of food and drink that Tan brought to the cave each day.

He was certain the contents of each Imperial container were well documented. If there was an audit, it would be far better to lose an entire crate and say it was never delivered, than be left with any evidence of its existence. He could claim it must have fallen out on the journey and simply have another driver shot. No one would doubt the Major.

All that was left was the head, which was still lying on the dusty floor. He needed to get rid of the thing. It had no value to him. "Bring that to me," Major Okobudo hissed at the man.

The scraggy man bent down to pick it up. There was a pause. "I can't," said the meek voice.

The Major looked over and saw the half-starved Filipino squatting down on his haunches. He was heaving, trying to lift the face, which was staring up at him. The serene calm features and tightly curled ringlets of hair made it instantly recognizable as Buddha. Life size, the bust was made from a pale stone and delicately carved. Only the base of the neck seemed worn, badly scratched with a myriad lines and markings.

The Major looked around and found an empty square tin box with handles at each side. It had contained some of the flares his troops had used when they had originally entered the cave. He brought it over and placed it on the ground close to the head.

"Together," he said. Slowly they raised the head and turned to lower it into the open box.

Suddenly the Major lost his balance on the uneven floor and the smooth stone figure slipped from his grasp, dropping back to the rocky ground. A splinter of stone came away from the back of the head with a loud crack.

The young conscript's eyes widened at what he saw. There followed another even louder crack as the bullet from the Major's Nambu service pistol closed those eyes for good. Okobudo would explain it away with ease. Local conscripts could never be trusted. The fool had started to look into the vehicles.

The Major bent down and examined the Buddha head. He understood now why it weighed so much. He rolled the head into the overturned container, righting it again with an almighty shove.

He dropped in the chip that had come away from the head and snapped the top shut.

"Tan," he shouted. His personal bodyguard's vast frame filled the entrance way. Behind him the anxious looking faces of soldiers peered into the cave, rifles at their shoulder in response to the gunshot.

"Throw this corpse in the river and take this box and my duffle bag to my office. The rest of you, back to work."

The glare on the Major's face made it clear he would brook no further questions. He strode back to his stone rostrum. The huge bodyguard managed to lift the metal container onto his broad shoulder, sling the duffle bag over the other and dragged the dead soldier by his leg out of the cave.

The work force silently filed back in.

"Begin," the Major ordered, as the men nervously clambered back into their cabs. One at a time the engines coughed back into life and the drivers nervously edged their vehicles where instructed.

After a few days the entire cavern floor resembled a car park, filled with trucks and wagons of every size; each vehicle crouched low on its axles, the weight of their canvass-covered loads compressing nearly all travel out of the springs in the suspension.

Once all the vehicles were in place, the Japanese engineers began fashioning a three-foot-thick fake ceiling above them. The base was made from steel girders that formed a honeycombed roof. This was filled in with rock, which the workers smeared with a mixture of porcelain and concrete, like icing a giant cake. When it had hardened, they painted the 'floor' to match the surroundings, strewing the new surface with large jagged stones.

Next, with boulders hauled in from the surrounding area, the men constructed fake walls to reduce the width, leaving the chamber a fraction of its true volume. Finally, the entrance way was filled up with rubble and painted with more porcelain cement, with the last of the workforce exiting via the hole in the ceiling via the winched platform. Once the giant boulder was heaved back over the airshaft like a giant stopper, the cave itself would be nearly impossible to find. If it was, no evidence of the vehicles entombed beneath would be visible. Even if someone got inside, there were booby-traps to contend with. The only safe way back in was by using the sole copy of the coded and heavily waxed map, which had been updated daily by the Japanese engineers. The place was impregnable. It's secret safe for eternity.

On the evening of the completion of the works the Major commanded the three senior engineers to come to his office with the map. He glared at the men as they came in, each saluting the superior officer with fear in their eyes.

The Major walked right up to the men, his face inches from their own.

"Information I have received tells me there is a traitor amongst you," he barked at them. He pulled out his pistol. "I am not sure who this man is… so I simply choose you!" he said to an astonished engineer, shooting the innocent man before he was able to utter a single word of protest. "Is there anyone else?" he added.

The shock and terror on the other men's faces assured the Major of total cooperation.

"No one is to be trusted. I alone will guard this document on behalf of the Emperor. Leave. Remember, we are on parade in two days for the ceremony. And take that body with you."

Tan's silent presence ensured there would be no argument. They all respectfully bowed to the Major and exited, carrying the body of their dead comrade.

This is my chance, the Major thought to himself. Among the

stick-thin British prisoners working on the cave was an expert draughtsman. That night Tan hauled the man from his insect infested straw mattress and dragged him before the Major.

Okobudo pulled out the map that he had taken earlier from the terrified engineers. His heart thumped as he remembered General Yamashita's precise orders. Any copies would result in instant execution.

The Major took out his gun and held it to the prisoner's head. He leaned forward to whisper in the man's ear. "Copy it exactly and I will ensure you and your men receive some extra rations. I might even be prepared to allow you to relocate to a less strenuous place." He then pointed to the Buddha and the shard that had broken away. "And repair that. You have till morning. Tan, stand guard outside. Get him whatever he needs. No one comes in, no one goes out." The Filipino saluted and did as ordered.

The exhausted draughtsman had no fight left in him. All through the night, he painstakingly replicated the intricate designs of the coded map. Finally, he managed to reaffix the broken stone chip to the sculpture's neck as the sun was rising. Throughout Tan stood guard, displaying no emotion; but he was a conflicted man. His sense of loyalty to his superior officer was wavering.

Tan never even opened the box he had carried back on the day the trucks had crashed, nor when he returned it to the cave on the final parade. However, he had been at the Major's side when General Yamashita had made it clear no one was to make a copy of the map. The Major had disobeyed a General of the Imperial Army. His mind was made up. It would be Tan's duty to report it.

"Take this prisoner back to his quarters," the Major snapped when he returned in the early morning and inspected the engineer's work.

"And Tan, all this never happened," he added, arrogantly sure of the Filipino's loyalty. "Now leave."

Once alone, the Major eagerly poured over the duplicate document. It was unlike anything he had ever seen before. A myriad of symbols and signs, flags pointing to the left, flags to the right. There were clock faces with different numbers of hands and with the numerals on some faces going clockwise, some counterclockwise. Each icon had a different and precise meaning. Symbols for bombs, symbols for poison and symbols for the fulcrum point that would allow a man to dig through to the right depth.... yes, Okobudo was coming back. All he had to do was survive the inevitable Allied victory. The Emperor had betrayed his loyalty, and in return the Major would betray the General.

In a way Major Okobudo kept his promise to the draughtsman about relocation to a better place. The poison in the meagre extra portion of rice given to him at breakfast that morning had eventually sent the man, jack-knifed over in agony, into the next world.

But it was Tan, who sealed the Major's fate. Terrified, he had managed to obtain a brief interview with the fearsome General during a snap inspection ahead of the Major's closing ceremony. The General listened expressionless to Tan's tale, undecided whether to have him shot for his own disloyalty to his superior officer. However the General had heard about Tan's skill with his bolo and had a use for him.

As the last breath of life choked out of him, the Major found what he had been looking for. One hand clasped the handle of the metal box, which tipped to its side as he pulled it towards him, the other gripped the wooden box full of artillery shells. The items he clung to were the ones he had hoped would ensure his future, but his future was over. The last thing he saw as the cave returned to darkness was the smile of the Buddha's face from where it had rolled out of the box toward him.

 **CHAPTER 49**

WILL ROGERS POLO GROUNDS
PACIFIC PALISADES, CALIFORNIA

The only thing 'polo' in Los Angeles that Louis really liked was the Polo Lounge at the Beverly Hills Hotel.

Nevertheless there had been an association between talent and the game of polo for years. This morning Louis was at the Will Rogers Polo Ground in Pacific Palisades basking in the spring sunshine that was spearing down from a cloudless sky. The air was heavy with the scent of designer perfume as he watched Tyler Gemmell's polo ponies in action.

The grounds were overlooked by the deceased film star's white ranch house and set in 186 acres of lush parkland. It was all preserved exactly as it had been when the famous silver screen cowboy had lived there.

Every Sunday in the early 1930s, Will Rogers played polo on his own pitch with David Niven, Errol Flynn, Hal Roach, Spencer Tracy, Clark Gable, and Walt Disney. There had been over 25 polo fields in those heady days, now this was the only one left.

God, I wish I'd been around then, Louis thought to himself. He got a real kick out of the idea of studio heads and big shots of the day playing a game whose origin was using the severed heads of their enemies instead of a ball.

"They need to score from this 'bowl in'", the actress seated next to Louis said with an air of superior knowledge. The umpire resumed play by rolling the ball down a line-up of polo players. She was Tyler's current girlfriend. She took a sip of champagne as she watched a lithe Argentinean check, turn his pony, and then chase after the white wooden ball.

The young man's wiry piebald pony darted expertly between the others. The lean rider, clutching the flying mane and reins in one hand, swooped down and making a well-judged 'neck shot', struck the ball as it rolled in front of his mount's chest, rocketing the sphere between the two posts.

"Wow," said the actress exhaling with a slight sigh that betrayed her admiration for the horse was also directed at the tanned rider. "That is one hell of a 'made' pony."

Louis found the term used for a well-trained polo pony ironic considering Tyler Gemmell owned it. Hoods buying respectability. It now even extended to owning polo teams. This particular team owner had better not catch his actress girlfriend with the handsome '10 handicap' rider, or the rider's handicap would just be busted knees, mused Louis.

Originally a bit part actress, she was kept on the books at Louis' agency with an annual retainer. In reality she was a hooker whose starring role was to help smooth deals. A fully co-operative player in the power game who no doubt now was adding to the chorus of #MeToo outrage that Louis thought was blighting his industry. She, of course, had seen herself more as a star-in-waiting. Her working name when Louis had hired her had been Lucy Aurore but not anymore.

She had gone to an open audition a couple of years ago and surprised everyone by winning a small returning part in a legal drama show. It had become a major hit, with the main characters on the covers of every magazine, even though in private the stars seemed to be at loggerheads.

Lucy had become a minor celebrity too, basking in the reflected glory of the show's success. She had changed her name in a vain attempt to distance herself from her past, but no one forgot a face and body like hers. Her previous 'starring role' was an open secret to all those involved in film and television. Nevertheless, members of the public who knew nothing of her earlier life now stopped to chat, or covertly pointed at her as she walked by. This agreeing to and acceptance of visibility was a novel experience for her as she was more used to creeping away from hotel rooms or lying down in the back of stars' limos, eager not to be noticed.

The whistle blew for the end of the final seven and a half minute period of play. "End of the chukka and this game," said the girl, eager to continue showing off her knowledge of the arcane terminology of the sport. "Time to tread in the divots," she added a little too loudly.

A riot of women in wide-brim hats and body-hugging dresses walked onto the pitch. Louis could not help but smile at the irony of all these overpriced high heels tottering over the turf to stamp back down the gouged sods of grass cut up by the flying horses' hooves.

Louis was counting on Jonathan stamping down right now on some sods of his own. The fact that he had twice let Marcus and Melinda slip through his hands made dealing with other matters even more important.

"There's Tyler," said the girl, waving madly at the broad figure lumbering towards them.

"Louis, I hope you are making a pass at my girlfriend," greeted the big man extending a hand the size of a baseball mitt.

"It means you think she still has something special."

Tyler had singled the actress out months ago at a discreet party thrown by Louis. He had no real interest in her but she had been easily seduced by his wealth and charm. It was not long before she was happily gossiping to him about the excesses on the set, tantrums about billing, the squabbles about wardrobe, and jealousy about the size of the trailers. After Tyler asked her to snoop around the studio a bit, she'd found the back lot was littered with the 'mega-trailers' he had asked her about.

"You aren't a star without one. Louis is so smart. They're nearly all his," she had told him.

Tyler's hunch was right. Louis was ripping him off.

"Good afternoon, Tyler," said Louis shaking the big man's hand. "She turned me down. She knows where her best interest lies. I've just been watching over her," he added wondering if Tyler knew she'd bang his whole team of polo players at the drop of a hat. No surprise there. Old habits die hard, Louis mused to himself.

"Honey, if you two are going to discuss my career, I'll hang right here." She looked at them both. Their faces were expressionless.

"Fine, then I'll be over at Sarah's Point," she said referring to the pasture named after Will Roger's pet Brahma bull. "Need to check out our 'string.'"

With that she flounced off towards the team of bronzed riders, the spring breeze rippling the polo shirts against the riders' muscular torsos. Tyler couldn't have cared less. She'd been much cheaper and more effective than an auditor. Studio cutbacks! Where else was this bastard stealing from him? He would no doubt eventually find out, but bigger issues had arisen that needed to be dealt with immediately.

"Whatever dispute you may or may not be having with your ex-partner Haribon Guinto has *nothing* to do with my associates," Tyler spoke in a flat but dangerous tone, as he bit the end of a *Cohiba Esplendidos*.

Louis feigned shock. His contact at Immigration Services had caused trouble. If there was one thing sure to rile Tyler and his associates it would be inspection by any government agency.

"We've had U.S. Citizenship and Immigration Services on our back," continued Tyler, "saying we're employing a number of illegals. Then what? Those clowns are gonna throw in a coupla' criminals on our books next? They are rumbling about going over our books, threatening subpoenas. Next thing you know it'll be Homeland Security shouting terrorists. This has to do with you and Haribon Guinto. We don't appreciate being implicated." Louis could hardly miss the clear threat in Tyler's voice.

"I'm sorry Tyler, Haribon Guinto's dripping poison into someone's ear at Immigration. He has a long reach. He's obviously pulling you in to get to me. We have to stop him."

"Louis, I passed on Guinto's business. He's your problem," he said clearly. "This ends now."

Louis shrugged. "If Guinto thinks the immigration card and those guys at USCIS can bring me down, he'll make it difficult for everyone, including you," he said. There was a pause. Tyler turned to leave but Louis quickly added, "Just hear me out."

Tyler hesitated and gave a sigh.

"OK. Give it your best shot, Louis."

"Haribon is a big player, but weak. For you and your friends, it's too good an opportunity. Real estate, leisure, casinos, movie theaters, cable TV. No shareholders. Just one man. There is no competition if he is taken out. Once done, you move in and I'll fade away. Retirement beckons," Louis said. "This new market and Haribon Guinto's empire is my gift to you. It's the doorway into the rest of Asia." Louis sensed a slight change in Tyler, a flicker of doubt. Louis had him.

"Let me make a few calls. Perhaps I could send someone over… for a look-see," said Tyler.

"It has to be quick, Tyler, before anything else heats up," replied a confident Louis. "I have all the details."

As the Polo teams returned to battle on the green expanse of the playing field, Louis agreed to email Tyler the necessary information, hoping he was elegantly nailing down the lid on Haribon's coffin once and for all.

All Louis needed to complete a perfect day was confirmation that Jonathan had been successful with today's assignments. Then everything would be back on track.

CHAPTER 50

TOPANGA CANYON, LOS ANGELES

Christo slowly stepped down out of his battered Land Rover and started to unload the small trailer. There were over half a dozen bags of fertilizer and a collection of small cacti. It was early morning; the sun was just coming up.

The cacti were to have been an anniversary present for Robert later that month; one for each year he'd been clean and sober.

A few years earlier Christo had arranged with the American Rose Society to name a rose after Robert's elderly mother, who was slipping away with Parkinson's disease.

The gesture had been greatly appreciated by the old lady and she filled the small garden outside her room at the San Clemente nursing home with 'Hannah Kelso Blush.' A floribunda, the bushes were bursting with bi-color blooms of luscious white, with deep pink borders. The aroma was light and with the doors opened to her patio, the evening onshore breeze had filled her room with its perfume. She died a short time later, her small bedroom filled with the scent of the flowers named after her.

"Don't even think of naming a flower after me," Robert warned on the drive back after the quiet funeral.

Christo looked at him.

"I'm sorry that was thoughtless…" Robert said quietly, "You remember rehab…. flowers can bring back bad memories…."

"Ungrateful prick," Christo muttered.

"Now there's a name for a rose," Robert countered.

It had taken Christo over six months to persuade the Southern Cactus Growers Association to allow him the privilege of naming a strand of organ pipe cacti after the once-famous movie director.

He had received notification they were ready to be picked up when he arrived back from France. The press interest in him had started to wane after days of 'no comment' along with the willingness of other people to crawl out of the woodwork to talk about 'the late great Robert Kelso'.

The only other message was from the local police. A few questions, but it seemed that Detective Inspector Groelet of the Cannes Police had done a good job of handing over all responsibility for the case to others; it was now a matter for Interpol. Of course, Christo could have let fly with stories about Sam's script but he had decided not to. That meeting with Cara had helped him make up his mind.

He was genuinely scared, being pretty certain that bringing up anything related to Sam's script or what could be pieced together would come to the attention of the wrong kind of powerful people. Long before the local cops got even halfway round to figuring out what was going on, he and Cara would be dead in a ditch somewhere. The fact that someone might eventually piece it all together would be no consolation.

Christo was getting out. He had put the house on the market and was expecting his first viewing that afternoon. The cacti would be planted right down at the end of the garden as a memorial to the man who had once lived here.

As he reached into the back of the truck, he felt a sting on his arm. Cursing, he started to pull back to look at the puncture mark he assumed one of the cactus spines had made. As he did so he felt another sharp sting, then another.

He heard the tell-tale rattle and saw the three sets of bite marks in his arm. The diamond-back rattlesnakes slithered out from behind the plants in the trailer. The loading area was alive with them sliding their way over the plants and tools.

His earlier experiences had taught him what he needed to do.

After escaping Allentown and before settling in southern California he had first worked in the desert on an illicit marijuana farm in the Devil Ridge Mountains south of El Paso. If you were bitten out there and didn't know what to do, you were dead.

It was his time at 'the farm' that had turned him to working in rehab. It wasn't the drugs themselves, but the ruthless bastards who ran the place. They mercilessly picked on the shy young man from the north and jeered at him for his sexuality. The idea of preventing lowlife scum like them from becoming any richer had become a crusade for him.

Christo knew the most important thing was to remain calm and not to panic or run. A fast-beating heart would speed up the poison coursing through his bloodstream and kill him before he could do anything. He needed the antivenin, which he always kept up at the house as a precaution. The serum needed to be drip fed into a bite victim for thirty minutes at least. On his own it would take him some time to set up, so he had to act now and try to remove at least some of the poison.

He reached into the cab and grabbed his water canteen and a handful of tissues. He quickly undid the top of the container. He took the Kleenex and scrunched them into the tin drinking cup and quickly placed it over the first set of puncture wounds. He pulled a lighter from his jeans and, lifting the edge of the cup, lit the tissues. As the paper burst into flames, he pushed the container back over the wound, the heat creating an airtight vacuum between his arm and the cup, which gradually began to suck the poison out of the bite. He began walking back to the house, his wounded arm held out in front of him. As he walked, he poured the water from the canteen over the other two bite marks. Nevertheless the swelling was already very pronounced.

Clap. Clap. Clap.

Christo looked up to see Jonathan staring at him with a smirk on his lips. His heartbeat quickened, recognizing Jonathan at once.

"Desert survival for snakebite. Who'd have thought a simple gay gardener knew such things?"

Christo at first froze to the spot. As Jonathan slowly picked his way down the hillside towards him like a cat approaching his prey, Christo knew that to stand still was also a death sentence.

He made a decision and went for it, hoping to slip between Jonathan and the open veranda doors, locking Jonathan out. It was uphill and the sun was hot. Within a short distance the poison began to take effect; breathing became difficult and he began to drool. As paralysis started to set in, Jonathan pounced. He knelt over Christo, who was lying on the ground slowly losing consciousness.

"Let me help," whispered Jonathan.

He reached into his pocket and pulled out a small hypodermic, injecting pure adrenalin mixed with snake venom into one of the bite marks.

With his heart now racing and his body racked with pain, the last thing Christo saw was Jonathan reaching down with heavily gloved hands to gather up the snakes slithering around the trailer. Jonathan smacked at them then dropped them hissing on Christo's bare forearms.

The dust on Christo's shoes and his footprints in the soil would show he had made the fatal mistake of panicking after being bitten.

Jonathan walked back once again to Christo's 4x4, casually reached into the back of the trailer and picked out a rake. He carefully covered over his own footsteps as he walked up the path to the drive and out onto the main road where he had parked the car.

The realtor who showed up three hours later had not found her client waiting as agreed nor anybody answering the doorbell, so she wandered into the back garden, looking for him. She had spoken to the prospective purchaser over the phone and Jonathan was pretty sure she would not remember much about him; certainly, the name he had given her was false. The only time she ever met the seller was when she threw up over him after discovering his twisted body lying in the dust.

# CHAPTER 51

GENEVA, SWITZERLAND

"I just don't understand. What's the significance of the head?" Mako's voice was still weak, but the grayness in her skin was slowly disappearing. Remarkably, her skin was not damaged, only off color. Since leaving *Nisten* two hours ago, Mako had drifted in and out of sleep, drowsy from the drugs and the effort her body was putting into fighting the poison.

"It was enough to kill for," Marcus said over the drone of the engine. "Your dad never mentioned it?"

"I don't think so… no, never. You notice anything special about the head?" Mako asked.

"A large Buddha head. Made from stone. Some kind of markings that covered the base and unbelievably heavy. When did you work out it was Ringo?"

"When you were sleeping last night. Something was nagging me; didn't look right. Then I remembered he was an archer, had a quiver on his back, so why carry the weapon of the select bodyguard of the emperor? A bodyguard, not an archer. He was protecting something special. Seemed a typical clue from my father," she shrugged.

"In future can we share little things like that?" He asked dryly.

"At the time I wasn't aware it carried a death sentence." She looked over and gave a wan smile. "Probably just as well I don't tell you everything or you'd never have gone for the axe."

She leant over and planted the softest of kisses on his cheek, more like the beat of a butterfly's wings.

"Proud of you. Thank you. That's twice you've saved my life."

"Can we at least try to keep it to two times rather than go for the more traditional fairy tale three times?"

She smiled and gave a yawn. She was recovering fast. "So, where are we headed?"

"Geneva. Lots of people. Easy to leave. Safe to think. We both know we have two options. Run and hide or…,"

"…. face the demons," Mako finished. She looked out into the valley below bathed in the late afternoon glow.

Marcus paused hoping she would pick up the logic in his train of thought. "The airport, we can fly out…."

"You mean go to where this started?" said Mako at last getting his drift.

He knew it was their only choice.

"Yup. Back to the heart of all this, back to the Philippines and Pagsanjan."

Mako looked at him for a beat.

"Agreed. Geneva airport it is," she said. An easy decision for her.

"You sure? You still look like shit," he asked, wanting to be certain.

"A date with you is a riot of compliments." She paused and her tone changed. "I don't run," she said emphatically. And despite your smart-ass comments covering up your fears, you don't either, Marcus, she thought to herself. She gave him a friendly little punch, wincing slightly as her injured hand made contact. "We fight."

She was the toughest person he had ever met.

A few hours later he swung the car into the long-term car park on the Swiss side of Geneva Airport. He parked the Maserati, pulled out their bags and gently helped Mako out of her seat. As a security measure and with no idea when he would be back, he flipped the battery 'kill switch' hidden above the passenger foot well.

"Steal it now and you'd have to tow it," he explained.

They went into the airport and headed to the information desk. They needed to track down two tickets to Manila.

There was an Etihad Airways flight leaving at the end of the following day to Manila via Dubai. They needed a rest so that worked perfectly. Marcus was worried about Mako, and he had a few ideas he wanted to check out in peace. They stood at the desk surreptitiously unrolling some bank notes from the substantial bundle they had found in Stefan de Turris' house.

"We'll take the tickets please. Where's the best place to stay near the airport?" Marcus asked after handing over the wad of notes.

The woman at the counter recommended a hotel.

"We have a special rate with them, shall I call?"

"Thank you. Tell 'em we're on the way," Marcus said and turning to Mako added, "You need to lie down."

"Madame is unwell?" enquired the woman at the counter barely looking up counting the bills, as the tickets spewed out of the machine on her desk.

"A little hung-over. We're on honeymoon," Marcus explained with a sheepish grin as he grabbed the tickets and headed towards the exit and a taxi ride to the hotel.

Mako's shocked expression said it all.

"It's an explanation for how we look, buys us sympathy, and gets us privacy," he whispered in Mako's ear.

Marcus was not even close.

 **CHAPTER 52**

SANTA BARBARA, CALIFORNIA

It was 8:00 AM and Cara was packed. She wasn't running, she tried to reason to herself, just needed time to get away and think. She needed somewhere safe and out of the country, so she had picked a retreat in the Andes. She wasn't sure which event had hit her hardest: Sam's death, the revelations in **FALL OUT**, the truth about Jonathan, or the murders of Marcus and Robert. She'd told Christo he needed to get away and lie low as well.

"I have one last thing to do in Robert's memory, then I'm gone," he'd said.

For so long she had wanted to believe that the disastrous final moments of **THE LAST COMPANY** were all down to Bill's bravery, his belief in himself. If he hadn't been so insistent on going after the dailics, maybe none of this would have happened. Now she had let go of that explanation, yielding to what she had always suspected. It was a lie. His death was part of a bigger plan, a small yet crucial role in a different story.

She looked up at the kitchen clock as the doorbell rang and Cato scoffed up the last of his breakfast.

"C'mon Cato," she said over her shoulder as she reached to unhook his lead that hung by the kitchen door.

"That will be Bella. She's early. Momma's off for a few days of R&R. Be good," she said as she slipped the harness around the little dog's barrel like chest. "Coming," she said as she crossed the hall.

She pulled open the door and locked eyes with a Filipino standing impassively in her doorway, a gun in his hand.

CHAPTER 53

GENEVA, SWITZERLAND

All Marcus and Mako wanted was to check in discreetly at the hotel. However, having been tipped off by the airport ticket agent who had assumed their look of exhaustion was down to enthusiastic lovemaking from the first few nights of being married, the reception desk staff made a great fuss on their arrival. They were greeted by a round of applause from the staff, offered a suite at a special rate, flowers, and champagne - all compliments of the management.

"Christ, so much for anonymity," Mako muttered as they headed down the corridor.

"All I want to do is get you into bed," Marcus replied to Mako.

The bell hop leered at this remark as he slid the plastic key card into the lock.

The suite was luxurious, complete with a vast bed, a gigantic flat screen television and a Jacuzzi the size of a small swimming pool. However all they could do was tend to Mako's face and hand, and then collapse fully clothed on the bed falling asleep almost instantly. Another night without making love.

The next morning, they woke early, ordered room service, and started to undress.

"First time I've undressed after sleeping," Marcus muttered pulling on a bath robe.

"Try being a woman. Stockings, lingerie, bustier. We do it all the time," yawned Mako.

After they showered and had breakfast, Marcus took the tray

outside. "We need total privacy," he said as he hung the *do not disturb* sign on the door.

"Newlyweds with that sign on our door? They will give us a wide berth," said Mako nonchalantly. "Now what's the plan?" she asked as she hunted for something in their bag.

Marco had the laptop from *Nisten* under his arm, peered into the small business alcove with a printer that came with the suite and put his computer on the desk.

"I need to print out my version of **FALL OUT** to compare alongside your father's and Robert's copies. I kept a copy in my online files along with a budget that I can access. We also need to see what's on this," he added, holding up the USB stick he had found in the door stud at Nisten. He inserted the red USB into the laptop. "That's odd," he said as he tried to access the content.

"So is this," said Mako. She had pulled out of their bag the certificate she had been so insistent Marcus take from the house. "OK, you first. What's your odd?"

"This USB…. it's partly protected," Marcus said looking at the screen.

"What do you mean…. partly," she said only half interested and intently looking at the certificate.

He spun the laptop round so it faced her. "See?"

Mako turned from her seat without getting up.

"Access is security protected…. except it isn't quite."

The screen flashed a collection of random jumbled symbols that morphed into a tiger and then back again. Above it was one sentence, which kept on appearing no matter what he typed.

HER SECRET FRESH FOOTWEAR_ _ _ _ _

"OK let me think…." Mako said from her seat, but she really was only half paying attention. "Now you come look at this."

He went over to the table by the window where she had laid out the certificate.

"What's the big deal?" asked Marcus.

"The one in the bookshop in Habkern…" she started.

"Where you met that lunatic?" he interrupted to be sure.

"Outside… right. This certificate is supposed to be the same, but it's not. The lettering is the same, but the date and the seal are…well, wrong."

"You sure?"

"This date next to the seal is August, but the one in Xavier's shop is May. And I know it was May. I remember. So why did my father change it? And the seal itself is completely different. The one I got was red with a star shape cut into the wax with a red ribbon underneath. This is gold with what looks like a Minotaur with wings at the center and a blue ribbon."

Marcus leaned over and stared at the seal as the significance dawned on him.

"It's a Taurus," he said slowly.

"You mean a bull?"

"Yes… well… no… it's an award… in fact the Taurus is *the* annual movie world award for stuntmen. Bill won a few," Marcus stopped talking.

"What's wrong?"

"The date. It is usually in May. This is August 15th. That was the day Bill disappeared. This document…. It has to be about Baines."

Marcus lifted the thick vellum paper up to the light. There was something inside. What he held in his hands wasn't a single sheet but rather two identical sheets glued together.

"How do we separate the two sides?" she asked.

Marcus thought for a moment, then snapped his fingers. He walked over to the closet.

"Every good hotel room has one… and just what we need," he said pulling out the steam iron.

After a few moments he carefully applied blasts of steam to the edges of the vellum document and started to peel the two sides of the certificate apart. Inside was a pair of nearly identical typed sheets of paper.

"It's part of an insurance document," Marcus said after his first read through. "And maybe Bill's death sentence."

"How? What do you mean?"

"It's part of the bond taken out with your father's company. It's an 'Essential Element' clause."

Mako shrugged. "What's that?"

"An 'Essential Element' is usually a rider to the policy taken out on a star or director who's critical to funding. If during the shoot that person becomes hurt or somehow incapacitated and is unable to complete the film and withdraws, the bond would trigger." He looked up at her.

Mako nodded that she understood.

"OK. So, this 'Essential Element' clause states quite clearly that should the director or the named star of **THE LAST COMPANY** be unable to fulfill their services, the bond could be called," he said holding up the first sheet. "However next to the standard clause is a hand-written note that adds Bill Baines as the named stunt double and stunt coordinator with the words 'insert this, L.M.' under it. The other page," Marcus said now lifting the second sheet, "is the same but now with the handwritten clause about Bill inserted as typewritten text."

Mako saw where this was going.

"Bill was the *named* stunt double and coordinator. That means he specifically had to be the stunt double for our star," added Marcus.

"So Bill not being available was the same as if the star himself or the director wasn't available. The death of Bill Baines breached the 'Essential Element' clause," said Mako understanding his logic.

"Ba-da-boom," he said dryly.

"But why write it in? It looks like an afterthought. I assume L.M. is Louis McConnell. Didn't you know about it?"

Marcus took a deep breath. "No, well, not really. We all just assumed the production couldn't go on after Bill's disappearance or the loss of the rushes... not to mention the whole local crew just left. The star quit. I had meetings with your father, told him what had happened. But the exact nature of how the bond was triggered, that would have been between the Executive Producer, Louis McConnell and your father. Remember, I was just a kid... and damned frightened at what had happened."

"But why?" she asked. "It doesn't make any sense. Paying back the money didn't make anyone rich. It just reimbursed what had been expended. The movie would have closed down anyway, even without his death. So why do it? Why kill him?"

Marcus thought for a moment, "...Suppose it was an added bonus to someone to have Bill dead? What if that was all just a side show?"

"That's murder and fraud... and needed my father's compliance, Marcus," she said resignedly. "And for what? And why did my father keep these two copies?"

"As protection... and maybe salvation? He knew you'd find it."

Marcus saw the doubt on her face, and he couldn't blame her.

"OK let's leave that for now. Help me with this, Mako," he asked trying to take her thoughts away from the repercussions raised by the documents. "What the hell is *HER SECRET FRESH FOOTWEAR?*"

She sat in front of the ever-changing image, thought for a moment, then a faint smile came over her face.

"A new shoe. Nü-shu. N-U-S-H-U," she spelled out. "God, he knew I would find all this."

"And what the hell is Nü-shu?" Marcus asked as he typed in the letters.

"It's practically extinct now. It came from southeast Hunan. It was a secret script, a complete system of writing known to very few and only used by women."

Again, he was astonished at the depth of her knowledge. "What, you mean as in letters of the alphabet?"

"Sort of. Chinese is logographic, a character represents a word. Nü-shu is phonetic with about 1,500 characters representing a symbol. It's virtually unknown outside the province."

"And you know this because…?"

"My mother. Her family was from that region of Hunan. She taught me their history and how to decipher it. I can read it. My father knew that." That sunk in for both of them. This was all deliberate and leading somewhere.

"What was it used for?" he asked her.

"Telling secrets. In the days of arranged marriages, and subservient females with bound feet, women were just chattels. They certainly weren't allowed to receive an education or learn how to read or write.

So many years ago, and in great secret, the women from the Yongjiang Province developed their own script. They wrote about their fears and hopes and criticized their lords and masters in secret letters to other women. I suppose they became the earliest voices for women's rights. The writing was a symbol of rebellion against domineering men. Nu-Wa and I used to tease my father that we would only write to each other in Nü-shu."

As Marcus hit enter, the words *Tiger of Malaya Corporation* appeared with an arrow key in the bottom right hand corner.

"So now we have our Tiger," he said clicking on it.

What followed were page after page of dates and numbers. They started a month after the collapse of **THE LAST COMPANY** and ran for years afterwards. Each entry was prefixed by the small outline of a rising sun followed by a date, and two sets of figures in

US dollars; *reported* and *actual*.

The *reported* sums were paid into something called *Golden Eagle Trust*, an account in the Philippines. The difference between *actual* and *reported* was paid into *Tiger of Malaya Corporation's* Swiss bank account.

"So, what does *reported* as opposed to *actual* mean?" asked Mako.

"At a guess Tiger of Malaya is either taking a commission or skimming. The difference between actual and reported on this first page looks about 5%," started Marcus.

"So how much…."

"We'll get to the totals. Let's try and make sense of it all first. It looks like of the total *reported* money deposited to *Golden Eagle Trust* in the Philippines, it kept 30% and 70% was paid via the same bank to six numbered accounts, although not in equal amounts," said Marcus with Mako now leaning over his shoulder following the numbers on the screen.

"So of that 70%, I can see two accounts got 30% each, 60% in all, and the other four each received 2.5% making 10% to get to the 70%. But it's crazy as the funds from all six then bounced back via a series of offshore accounts to the *Tiger of Malaya Corporation* in Switzerland. Why bother to do that and not send from *Golden Eagle Trust* all 70% back to the Tiger account in Switzerland?" asked Mako.

"No idea but now we know the journey the money took. Let's add up the amounts involved. Time for some math."

"I'm good at that," brightened Mako as she turned on the calculator on her mobile. "Right let's go."

It took the better part of the rest of the morning to do the calculations. Marcus read out page after page of numbers as Mako punched them into the calculator, checking, and rechecking as they went along.

"What's the answer?" he asked her after they had finally gone through all the spreadsheets on the computer. He got up and walked to the fridge. "Soda or there's a coffee, tea whatever." But Mako was not listening.

"Jesus, Marcus. The total here is just under $500 million. The skim at 5% is around $25 million. The 30% kept by Golden Eagle Trust is around $140 million with $330 million going to accounts in the Philippines."

"And the six individual accounts from the Philippines?"

"No idea, just numbers. But it looks like all went back to the *Tiger of Malay Corporation's* Swiss account." Mako looked up at Marcus. She looked dog-tired, the effects of her near-death experience etched in lines in her face and dark rings around her eyes.

"Clearly the dates and the insignia mean something. The big question is, where's all the money coming from?" he wondered aloud.

"*FALL OUT* is pretty clear on what. Guns, weapons, and shit like that," said Mako. "It stinks. Damn him. My father knew I'd chase this down. The clues in the house, on that USB... no one else would get the Nü-shu clue. My worst fears and what does he do... points me towards finding out the truth? What for? Just to crush any traces of affection I might have had for him? Suppose I couldn't have a real drink? I'm all in."

"Sure. They even have your favorite. Cointreau on the rocks coming up." He poured the drink along with a double vodka for himself.

He sat down beside her, handing her the drink. "Cheers." Mako raised her glass in salute.

"You know maybe he wasn't asking for forgiveness or absolution. Maybe in his mind what he did was right? He thought he could convince you. He *wanted* you to know. He left a clear path for you to follow in case he couldn't tell you himself," reasoned Marcus.

"That's seriously screwed up logic. If true I'm not sure I want to know," Mako sighed heavily.

"Yes, you do," he replied firmly.

He put his hands on her shoulders and looked her in the eyes. "Anger, disappointment, disapproval. He knew you could live with that. It's not knowing the truth that would eat at you for the rest of your life…. 'Here I am', is what he is saying. 'Take it or leave it… but face it.' That's why he asked you to come to London… you sensed there was something he wanted to tell you and you wanted to know."

"And you….?"

"Mako, I have lived with the guilt that someone died because of a spur of the moment decision I made," he said, the weight still heavy on his conscience.

"Albeit for the best intentions," she added, trying to lighten the load.

"I'd like to think so… I really wanted that movie to get made, wanted to climb a peg or two up the career ladder. Was letting Bill try and play '*Rambo*' one of the rungs?" He tilted his head and raised his eyebrows with a sigh.

"You said Bill was jumping at getting out there and dealing with the bad guys, and he had real experience, for chrissakes. You were young. No one is cautious in life till they screw up. You were on a roll; this was your break… Bill was the only one of you who knew about the ugly side of life, about death," Mako said, still trying to divert the guilt.

"Maybe that's why we were chosen? Callow youth, eager and gullible. These papers hidden in the certificate; your father kept them for a reason… Bill was killed. Maybe he wanted you to find out why, how, and by whom?" He emptied his vodka glass.

"That's your journey…." She leaned over and put her arms around him.

"Both our journeys. I need to read those screenplays. You take a rest. You look beat," said Marcus leaning to give her a gentle kiss.

Mako quickly faded and fell into a deep sleep giving Marcus the privacy he needed. Before picking up the scripts, however, he rang the number in France.

"Hi Garance, It's me. Any progress?" Marcus whispered when the line was answered.

"*Un peu*, a little," the voice replied continuing with an update.

"OK, thanks. She's asleep. She knows nothing. Let's keep it that way," looking over his shoulder all the while to make sure she was asleep.

He spent the remaining hours before they had to leave for their flight reading the three versions of the scripts; his, Robert's, and Stefan's. By the time they returned to the airport and were settled in their seats, and with Mako still half asleep, he knew what Sam was pointing his finger at.

And it wasn't arms dealing.

# CHAPTER 54

BEL AIR, LOS ANGELES

"Not there, what do you mean not there?" said Louis trying to control his anger.

"I went out to Kelso's place in Topanga first... as you instructed. Problem dealt with. I came back for Cara, but she was gone."

Jonathan was standing in front of the ornate desk in Louis' office. A shaft of sunlight cut through a gap in the long red velvet curtains that remained drawn. A delicate cup of espresso sat untouched on the leather topped desk.

Jonathan had not been offered a seat; his mantle of reliability was slipping. He registered the flick of frustration in his boss' voice.

"She left before I got there. Without the dog."

Louis barely resisted hissing back 'screw the dog'. He loathed small animals and was always unnerved that a man, who easily inflicted pain and even death, was so concerned about the welfare of small canines. He looked back at Jonathan, waiting for more details.

"Neighbor saw someone pick the dog up around 8:30."

"Well, that's a relief," Louis sighed with undisguised sarcasm. "Did the same neighbor see Cara leave?" he inquired.

"The gardener next door saw her getting into a car."

"That's it?" Louis clenched his teeth. "Why am I having to drag out everything one phrase at a time Jonathan?"

Jonathan did not react. "He said the man was well built, tall... and that his facial features were... like mine." Jonathan stopped as he saw the implication of what he had said dawn on Mr. Louis. They both knew who had Cara.

"I'll go," Jonathan said firmly.

"Jonathan, I can no longer be sure of your success. You would never get near Haribon. I've got someone else on it."

Jonathan remained impassive. Louis reached over for the phone and pushed one of the intercom buttons.

"This coffee's cold. Bring me another," he ordered tersely and turning to Jonathan in the same tone added, "Why are you still here?"

He waved him away. The meeting was over. He was being dismissed like a schoolboy. As he stepped out of the office, his future now in doubt, Jonathan made a decision. He would go after Haribon himself.

The next morning Benjamin gently slid a rosewood tray onto the table beside Louis' bed. Balanced on it was a fine bone china tea set, a freshly brewed pot of leaf tea and an envelope lying next to an ivory letter opener.

"It would appear Jonathan neither slept in his bed last night nor is his bike in the garage. I took the liberty of making sure nothing valuable was missing," Benjamin said. The butler briskly pulled back the curtains, adding, "All he took was that airline overall. This letter was on the bed." He pointed to the small vellum envelope addressed simply to 'Mr. Louis'. Louis looked at it, half wondering if Benjamin had already steamed it open earlier.

"There is no passport in the drawer where he usually keeps it, he did at least leave behind the cell phone you pay for," the butler added as he noted his employer's hesitation in opening the note. He realigned a picture.

Louis marveled at the degree to which Benjamin noted every minutia in the house. All the better that his own secrets were locked in the vaults of his own memory. Paper trails led only to danger and Louis left no traces for anyone; least of all his manservant.

Benjamin picked up Louis' dressing gown and laid it on the bed, turning to leave the room to prepare breakfast. Louis slid the flat ivory blade under the lip of the envelope.

The note was brief. *'I must deal with Haribon. If Cara is there, she will not return'.*

Louis put down his glasses and pinched the bridge of his nose.

"Jonathan will not be returning, Benjamin. Under any circumstances," he said to the retreating figure. "Dispose of his things. Give them to someone or just burn them."

He thought for a moment and added as Benjamin reached the door, "and get me Mr. Gemmell on the phone."

A moment later the light on the handset by his bed flashed. Louis picked it up.

"Tyler, is your man on the way…? Good. Jonathan will be in the background. Just for cover." Close enough to the truth, he thought.

"I want these guys off our backs, Louis," Tyler said angrily. "But I blame you for them being there in the first place. Immigration inquiry or not, you somehow started this, but now we have to finish it. We will need to review our options and relationship when this is settled," he snapped.

Louis ignored the not-so-veiled threat. He was set. Problem solved.

Ever since Benjamin had brought in Haribon's floral 'gift', Louis had beefed up security in the house. The butler had hired two uniformed security guards to pace the grounds. Security cameras now covered every angle of the house and there were motion sensors in the garden, on the rooftops, as well as inside the building itself.

Even with Tyler Gemmell sending someone to deal with

Haribon, Louis was concerned for his own security. He needed to become even less accessible. It would be advisable to get away from his normal haunts to a place where security was the priority. He was never the kind to hide out in some lonely lakeshore shack in the Greenhorn Mountains. He knew the perfect refuge, somewhere that would keep him locked in and others out.

Picking up the phone and dialing the familiar number, he resignedly said into the phone, "This is Louis McConnell. I'm afraid my bad habits have caught up with me again. I'm surrendering. You can get out the large file you have on me... Yes, today. I know the drill." He pulled the silken green cord hanging next to his bed. Benjamin reappeared.

"I'm turning myself in. I need to report to jail."

Benjamin nodded and waited. "Prepare a small bag," continued Louis. "Nothing much. All casual. Prepare a decent farewell breakfast first though."

Within a few hours, the Bentley was purring south towards Fiji Way in Marina Del Rey. It pulled up at a jetty where two uniformed men were waiting to take Louis away.

Benjamin got and then opened the door for Louis, who strode down to the jetty where he boarded the launch. He settled down for the two-hour journey south to an isolated island forty miles out to sea.

The Arrow Point Clinic, better known by its select group of regulars as *The Catalina Jail*, was one of the most exclusive and expensive health resorts and addiction treatment clinics in America.

Its cosmetic surgery clinic enjoyed visits from the select few in Hollywood who could afford it. Due to rigorous secrecy, its clientele frequently swore publicly they had never been under the surgeon's scalpel but that their startlingly youthful appearance was down to good genes… and of course the diet and exercise book they were currently promoting.

Louis felt safer. He knew the owner was an associate of Gemmel's. Certainly no thug hunkered down several thousand miles away across the Pacific could threaten him here. He pondered over his two other strands of unfinished business; Marcus and Mako and how to find that Buddha head. The head was the key, and he was sure no one else understood why.

From what Jonathan had told him, Mako and Marcus either had it or knew where it was. Since they had escaped Jonathan twice, Louis knew he could no longer underestimate them. They may have gone to ground, but they would resurface eventually. And when they did, he knew they would have only two places to go for the answers they must surely want. Himself or Haribon. Right now though, he was lying low. If Marcus and Mako somehow decided to track down Haribon first, it could prove awkward, though not terminal. By the time they tracked down Haribon, Gemmell's man would have dealt with him. So they would have to come to Louis, and there was no way they could travel with the head. He would just need to persuade them to tell him where it was, or they were going nowhere. Easy.

Jonathan was of no value now that he had started to act without his employer's express wishes and instructions. To Louis independence was the ultimate betrayal.

It was not all bad news, though. He was confident Tyler's 'envoy' would take care of everything.

Louis walked to the prow and looked out to sea. At least he was going to be able to try a few of the dietary changes recommended by that smug doctor before he went for surgery. A gentle feeling of sated lust rippled through his body when he remembered the nurse. He'd been right, of course. A discreet word in her ear from another client as to who Louis McConnell really was and the next visit she had been all over him.

He smiled at the throbbing she must have felt the next morning after the way he had turned her over and ravished her after the perfunctory dinner at The Palm. It must have been similar to his own discomfort following the rectal examination at the doctor's office. He never returned her calls.

The spray from the sea thrown up by the prow of the magnificent motor launch pattered across Louis' jowly face and droplets formed on his heavy-set features.

At that precise moment Jonathan was hunkered down in the plane trying to doze, despite the incessant drone of the engines. He was on a mission. The irony was that even though he was acting out of a feeling of loyalty to Mr. Louis, he knew he had lost all of the man's respect.

His boss had made clear he was sending someone else to clear things up. Jonathan had to make amends. As for Mako and Marcus, he'd pick up their trail and deal with them later. A few moments alone with either of them and he'd get back that head.

Right now he had to deal with Haribon. Haribon had sent those flowers, clearly threatening his employer. Haribon had sent his people to take Cara. Jonathan would kill him, end it now to prove his worth to Mr. Louis and rid him of his nemesis….

 **CHAPTER 55**

MID AIR
EN-ROUTE SWITZERLAND TO PHILIPPINES

Marcus and Mako had been airborne for several hours. At first they both slept heavily but were now reading. Marcus held his copy of the screenplay. Mako looked up deep in thought, Kelso's version in her hands.

"Finished?" he enquired.

She nodded. "Are you sure? I just don't see it," she replied.

"OK. Now read my version. This part." He handed it to her, the manuscript already turned to the first scene of the movie."

```
EXT.NEW YORK.DAY.
                FADE IN:
PRESENT DAY
WHITENESS....Nothingness....which reveals
itself to be clouds full of snow....A bird
SWOOPS down....through the cloud....towards
the snow-covered peaks of Manhattan....The
Chrysler Building....the Empire State....
the Flatiron...past them all, down towards
the white expanse of Central Park...

EXT.CENTRAL PARK.DAY.
A lone JOGGER leaves a trail of footprints
behind him in the virgin, china white snow,
his breath visible in the chill morning
air....
```

EXT.EAST 54TH STREET.DAY.
A silver Mercedes Maybach limousine idles
outside an elegant apartment building....
The CHAUFFEUR, in black coat and gloves,
shivering in the cold, opens the door
for FRANK KIDDO, a Big Man, mid-fifties,
thickset....

                    FRANK
     (To himself, seeing the jogger down the
                    street)
          God gives you a finite number of
          heartbeats, why would you waste
          them running through snow?

The chauffeur smiles, shrugs his shoulders.
As he turns to get into the car the passing
jogger drops something.

                    CHAUFFEUR
          Hey, buddy
The JOGGER continues, ignoring the call and
disappears into the snow. CHAUFFEUR picks
it up. It is an envelope addressed simply
FRANK KIDDO. It bears the logo of a small
eagle.

INT. LIMOUSINE. DAY.
Plush, silent. FRANK activates a switch
to darken the side windows and panoramic
glass roof, turning the back of the car
into a private cocoon. He picks up the pile

of mail on the seat next to him as well as
THE NEW YORK TIMES and THE NEW YORK POST.
A headline. PANAMA BUSINESSMAN KILLED IN
ATF SHOOT OUT. He notices the car has not
started and taps impatiently on the screen
divider.

>   CHAUFFEUR
>   (Lowering the divider)
>   I'm sorry sir.
>   This was just....
>   delivered.

The driver passes the envelope to FRANK. He
takes it, hesitates then closes the screen
divider.
He tears it open....

Ext. Manhattan street. Day.

The limo pulls up outside an old-style New
York office block, GIRO HOUSE Above the
doors - a sign A FRANK KIDDO DEVELOPMENT
A doorman hurries out, opening an umbrella
for FRANK....

>   DOORMAN
>   Morning sir
A moment - and then a grim FRANK emerges
and walks straight into the building,
ignoring the surprised doorman and his
umbrella...

INT. ELEVATOR.DAY.

Frank pushes 51.... The elevator rises. He closes his eyes....

INT. OUTER OFFICE. DAY.

FRANK enters his outer office. His PA, BONNIE - 30s, efficient, elegantly groomed within an inch of her life - rises -

>   BONNIE
>   Good morning
>   Mr. Kiddo, what
>   would you -

Without pausing he strides past her and into his office, shutting the door behind him....Bonnie stops, taken aback. Puzzled, she sits back down at her desk.

CLICK.... Bonnie looks up in surprise - FRANK locks his door from the inside....

INT.FRANK'S OFFICE. DAY

FRANK stands motionless, staring out at the New York skyline....

INT.OUTER OFFICE. DAY.

Frank's perplexed chauffeur stands in

front of Bonnie's desk, holding his boss's briefcase and almost all his mail.

                    CHAUFFEUR
          Everything okay?

Concerned, Bonnie gets up, walks over to the door.... Taps on it...No answer....

EXT. FRANK'S OFFICE. DAY.

Close up. FRANK'S face.... Dead-eyed.... Snowflakes appear on his cheeks.... He's standing outside his window, on the narrow ledge of the balcony.... He looks down, at the distant traffic below and sees squad cars, sirens blaring and lights flashing pull up at his building - He steps forward into space.

CRASH CUT TO OPENING CREDIT

FALL OUT

"But why do that?" she looked at Marcus, puzzled. "Why the differences?"

"You tell me."

"Same beginning… but the other script is set in the rain whereas yours is...."

"In the snow...."

"Did you see the other smaller changes to the scene?"

She looked down and opened Robert's copy. "*Giro* Towers

instead of *Gatlin…Frank pushes 51*, instead of *the elevator operator nods as Frank gets in and presses the 50th floor*?"

"And the inclusion of *BIG MAN* to describe Frank. In capitals. Think. What's the connection?" Mako was smart. Marcus knew she'd get there.

"They're drug terms.… *Big Man* is a drug dealer.… *Pushes 51*, fifty-one is crack and marijuana. He's pushing drugs. God, china white in the snow is heroin…"

"And *Giro House* is a street name for where drug money is laundered. My screenplay is littered with that kind of reference and drug slang. Mako, Sam is telling me it was drugs. That's what he's pointing at."

He pulled out the notes he'd made the night before.

"OK. Here goes my list so far. There's an extra section in Robert's screenplay in the scene in Kenny's office that talks about a playground, but I just can't work out what it means. I mean Kenny is obviously meant to be Robert. All three scripts mention *Aqua Regia*. What's that about? Must have meant something to Sam, though."

He showed her the section.

"No idea. I'm sorry, Marcus." She hesitated a moment. "You think it's possible Sam might have left clues in each version?"

"Maybe. We won't know unless we get all five versions."

"That's not happening any time soon."

"There are two bits added to your father's copy. Literally just the odd line, but enough to push up the page count. The biggest insert is at the beginning of a scene about how Frank Kiddo started the double cross.

The money laundering team is dividing income from the gun-running cartel. The finance guy, Joe Nisten, is working on a hacked computer terminal from a bank sending proceeds to key personnel.

In my version Joe manipulates the amounts so that the New York guys get more than their fair share. In your father's version, they send funds to various accounts, former partners they have told Aguinaldo need to be paid off and whom they use as a cover. The funds are then routed back to Kiddo and Nisten," Marcus finished.

"Funds going in a circle, that sounds familiar," Mako said opening her father's copy.

"There are also a couple of lines added from a frustrated Frank needing money and giving Nisten instructions on wiring it to him."

```
                    FRANK
               (v.o. ON PHONE)
        Do I have to spell
        it out to you?
        G...E... T CASH


                    NISTEN
        O.K. message
        understood


                    FRANK
        Good.
                 (Phone goes dead)
```

"There's another difference in the scene where Bill, I mean, Stan performs his party piece," said Marcus.

"You mean how to blow up my boat and us along with it? Show me," she said.

He leaned over.

                    STAN
    When we wanted to off somebody but
    walk away totally clean.... you know
    how to do that? Let your Daddy show
    you.... We used to surprise those
    dumb Provos when they were making
    some secret delivery, 'Our day
    will come' my ass. We'd chase them
    across the moors, all the way to
    Muckno Lake in Crossmaglen.... Left
    this little gift. We'd be sure they
    always start off with a full tank
    of gas - go on, you rabble, keep
    drinking! - the tank empties nice
    and s-l-o-w-l-y....just like this
    little beauty is emptying -

"It's also in mine. But this is what Robert's says."

                    STAN
    We used to get those dumb Provos
    to chase us across the moors,
    but we'd been at their vehicles
    before they set off.

"Make any sense to you?" he asked her. "Our day will come....
I've seen that somewhere...." Marcus said. "When I read that
scene, something didn't seem right to me. I can see it now though.
That little bastard who tried to kill us, he was just a spectator in
the background at *THE LAST COMPANY* party, not the one who
got soaked. Sam was warning us, pushing him to the foreground.
What does Aguinaldo say?"

Mako flipped the page.

```
                AGUINALDO
                (To Frank)
        Tell that Jonas to be careful.
        Tiko kills for less
```

She shook her head. "Too late for some," she said with resignation in her voice, staring out of the airplane window.

He reached out to her with his thumb and forefinger gently holding her chin and turned her face towards his. He kissed her forehead.

"We have a while before we land... try and get some rest," he said with a smile.

 # CHAPTER 56

ABOVE MANILA, PHILIPPINES

Several hours had passed as the plane started its descent through the soft humid air of a Philippine dawn.

"Twenty minutes to landing," came the announcement as all the lights in the cabin came on.

The flight attendant came over with immigration and customs' forms. With Marcus still flipping through the scripts, Mako pulled out both their tickets and passports to get the required information.

As she looked through his passport and travel documents, she noticed something, "So your *Esta* expired. No wonder they kicked you out." Marcus was lost in thought.

"ESTA you know Electronic System for Travel Authorisation," she added.

He blinked then turned to her suddenly, giving her a huge kiss.

"Mako, you're a genius. That's it!"

"What are you talking about?" she said as papers fell from the travel pullout desk as Marcus excitedly punched the keyboard.

He quickly opened the laptop, pulled up his email and showed her the one from Jax that concluded.

FYI, after an eternity IRS still not granted probate on Sam's estate. They have frozen a payment of $300,000 and keep asking what it relates to. It came from the Philippines but they keep hitting a brick wall of silence and are driving me crazy, muttering *about bringing in DEA. I've no idea what it was for. They found an entry in Sam's calendar on the day the money hit saying, 'GET PAYMENT'.*

From who? Does this mean anything to you?

Best Jax

"I'm so stupid," he said. "In your father's script. Remember what Frank says? It's not *get cash* but G.E.T cash. Sam's note in his diary wasn't to get payment, it was G.E.T payment. *Golden Eagle Trust.* When he was in Pagsanjan, he must've gotten through to someone at the bank.

"But, that makes no sense. Why would they talk to him? " asked Mako.

Marcus picked up a script. "Here, in your father's version. These people who fronted for the payments. What if somehow Sam was unwittingly fronting for a share of the money that goes to The Tiger of Malaya Corporation and the $300,000 alerted him?" said Marcus.

"We're landing now. You have to turn that off please," said the flight attendant. Marcus slammed the laptop shut and flipped through the pages on the script.

"The quotation …." continued Marcus, "***THE SECRET OF A GREAT SUCCESS FOR WHICH YOU ARE AT A LOSS TO ACCOUNT IS A CRIME THAT HAS NEVER BEEN FOUND OUT, BECAUSE IT WAS PROPERLY EXECUTED***'. The $300,000 is part of the secret of a great success that was never found out."

"Why now? His account in LA? Makes no sense," said Mako as she shook her head. "We know from the spreadsheets that payments were made regularly ever since the film ended. This is just one."

"But to the wrong place. What if it's not one payment, but one of many?" Marcus' mind was in full flow.

"How could it have been going on for all that time? He'd have noticed it," argued Mako logically.

"Pagsanjan," he said slowly. "We all had accounts there. We all put our domestic details on the forms we filled out. Standard practice so any surplus can be remitted home. We closed all the accounts when we left, but who knows? Maybe the bank kept them open to receive funds but just changed where the money was eventually sent. Money could have been going there for 15 years, then bang, a screw up, an accident, and one payment goes to Sam's account in LA. Mako, this makes sense."

She was doing her best to follow his train of thought as she buckled her seatbelt. " So keep going."

He paused for a moment, gathering his thoughts. "So Sam finds he has this one payment, traces it to Pagsanjan, decides to check things out. They'd talk to Sam, probably thought he'd been in on the scam and they'd told him it was a *Golden Eagle Trust* payment. What's 20 years multiplied by two bi-annual payments of $300,000...," asked Marcus.

"$12 million," said Mako in a flash.

"Jesus, Mako. No wonder Sam was so angry," he said. "We all had accounts there. Sam, myself, Kelso, McConnell, Bill, and your father."

"My father and McConnell?"

"When the movie got into trouble, your father was to have come down to the set. He needed an account. As for McConnell, we held an account for him to pay fees.

Six. Money from *Golden Eagle Trust* went to six numbered accounts that eventually found their way back to the *Tiger of Malaya Corporation*," said Marcus.

"Sam's script was telling my father he knew about the accounts. But why doesn't your version mention them?" Mako asked.

"I just hope it's because he believed I had been used too," said Marcus.

"And it has all been funded by a massive drug smuggling operation started on *THE LAST COMPANY*?" whispered Mako.

"It still doesn't completely explain what we found on the USB. I'm not sure what the hell was going on. If the $500 million was from drugs, what was the first set of figures? Why did they show a $25 million difference between reported and actual? Why take so long to sell?"

The planes' tires gave a 'chirrup' as they touched the tarmac.

 # CHAPTER 57

MANILA, PHILIPPINES

"Can we take a break for a moment?" pleaded Mako as she waited in the immigration queue. Marcus had been standing next to her, quietly talking to himself as he kept re-running the scenario, going over the conclusions he had reached, testing and probing to see if they really held water.

He did not answer so she pulled his face towards hers. "It's still early in the morning. Let's just get to the hotel, relax. Gather our thoughts."

He blinked as if being pulled out of a dream.

"Ok sure. Sorry. But this is beginning to fit."

They eventually cleared immigration and headed to customs to collect their luggage.

Marcus had reserved a room at a newly built hotel and apartment complex in Makati. The hotel offered a car hire service, and he had also booked one to drive them to Pagsanjan.

The limousine sent by the hotel was waiting, the chauffeur standing patiently at the arrival's exit with a placard reading 'Mr. and Mrs. Ry Lee'.

"Very funny," said Mako with mock sarcasm as she climbed into the back of the Mercedes.

"Welcome to Manila," said the driver. "Honeymoon?" he ventured as he pulled out into the early morning traffic.

Mako kicked Marcus before he could answer.

An hour later they pulled up in front of the imposing glass and steel entrance of the new hotel, which occupied one of two towers. The other would house luxury apartments but was still under construction.

"All rooms sound-proofed," said the driver obviously used to the immediate reaction of visitors when they drove up and realized the hotel was next to a large construction site.

They were courteously greeted and quickly taken up to a room on the 23rd floor with a magnificent panorama of the city, hazy and blurred by the humid air and smog. As they started to unpack Marcus rang reception to confirm the rental car for the next day.

"A cash deposit will be fine," said the concierge.

Just as Marcus was about to hang up, he paused. "Do you have a portable printer I could use? Thanks, yes, please send it up. No hurry."

Mako looked at him quizzically.

"I want to print a spare copy of my script. I don't want the originals with my numbers and notes on them with us," he explained.

"We'll put those in the hotel's main safe, not the room one. I never trust 'em," added Mako as she started to undress.

She peeled off her clothes, giving him a slow look and with a barely perceptible grin, turned and walked towards the huge shower cubicle. The multi-headed shower system pumped water from every angle over her entire body, and she closed her eyes and luxuriated under the spray that pounded her like hot rain.

There was a gentle gust of air as the glass door opened. Eyes still closed Mako smiled to herself. She gently splayed her legs and leaned her forearms against the marble wall as she felt Marcus' hand cup her breast, his lips on her neck as he slowly entered her. A moment later he had to stop. There was a feeble, barely audible knock at the door. Then the doorbell sounded.

"Stay right there," he whispered as he got out of the shower and pulled on a robe, checking to ensure there was not too much evidence of the effect Mako's naked body had on him.

"You sure know how to give a girl a good time," she cooed with an exaggerated sigh, crossing her arms as she leaned against the shower wall.

Marcus opened the door to an elderly man who staggered in, weighted down by a large printer.

"Here let me help you," Marcus said, but the man shooed him away and plonked the machine on the desk.

"*El placer es todo mío, señor.*" The old man paused. "Anything else, *Algo más?*"

Marcus caught his meaning and picked up his hastily discarded trousers lying on the floor. All he had were Euros, Dollars and Swiss Francs.

"Let me," said Mako as she stepped into the room, a robe covering her body and a towel majestically wrapped around her long dark hair. The old man could not help but stare at this beautiful woman. She reached into her handbag and pushed 50 Euros into the old man's palm.

"If they don't change it for you, let me know," Marcus said eager to be alone again.

"Don't let them rip you off; it's worth a bit more than 3000 Pesos," added Mako.

The old man's eyes lit up with gratitude.

"That is too much, *es demasiado dinero,*" the elderly bellhop stammered as he made a half-hearted effort to find some change from his own pocket to give back to Mako.

"You earned it," Marcus smiled, bowing slightly and gesturing towards the open door hoping the generous tip would speed the bellhop's exit.

The old man shuffled towards the door, shaking his head and looking at the €50 note in disbelief.

"More money than the Tiger of Malaya, *rico como el Tigre de Malaya*" he muttered closing the door behind him, unaware of the shocked expressions on Mako and Marcus' faces.

CHAPTER 58

MANILA, PHILIPPINES

"Sir, the *Tiger of Malaya* is a name every Filipino knows. Part of a myth, a fairy tale we all took comfort in during the bad times of poverty after the war," said the concierge as he peered at Marcus over a pair of half-moon spectacles.

Marcus had quickly collected what he wanted to put in the safe and was now downstairs talking to the concierge. The man exuded efficient calm in his pale grey trousers, black waistcoat, and elegant long-tailed morning suit jacket. Marcus was still dressed only in a robe and was starting to attract the stares of several well-heeled guests.

"Listen, there is someone... claims to be an expert... rarely sees foreigners. I'll see what I can do, *señor*." The concierge reached over for a phone and cradled the receiver under his neck. "Now please, may I suggest you return to your room? Your attire is maybe not suitable?"

"OK. Sure. Thanks. Apologies. One more thing. Could you please lock these in the hotel safe?" asked Marcus handing over the scripts, his budget, notes, and the USB. Already dialing the phone, the concierge nodded, and Marcus went back to the room and his unfinished business with Mako.

The concierge was as good as his word and later that morning Mako and Marcus were sitting in the back of a limousine. The driver introduced himself as Datu and looked as if he could drive in masonry nails with his bare hands.

"And where are we going, exactly?" asked Mako as she knotted her long black hair into a ponytail.

"Up by South Harbor, Ma'am. Entrance Pasig River," said the driver, glancing into the rearview mirror. "Fort Santiago. Ramon meet there you," added the hulk without even turning around.

"Are you also our interpreter?" she inquired trying to keep a straight face.

"Ramon English good. I here to serve and protect."

This time Datu turned and flashed a smile, showing off two gold teeth as well as his knowledge of the Los Angeles police motto, no doubt gleaned from watching endless cop shows on multi-channel Philippine television.

"Is the Fort dangerous," asked Mako

"No, many tourists. Sometimes a pocket-pick," he added, "so leave valuables in car."

"OK, but we would like to talk to this Ramon alone," added Marcus.

"Talk with Ramon is the danger. I be in background," grinned the big man, his head half swiveling to his guests for a moment.

With that he turned back to look at the traffic and the blinking brake lights as the car stopped-started its way up Taft Avenue.

The heat and humidity were fierce. Mako looked out of the window as they passed a ticket booth whose guard waved them through with a salute.

"Seems our friend has juice with the locals," muttered Mako.

The car continued up a red brick pathway lined with a lush garden. In front of them was a moat and stone gateway that led to the ancient fort. The car halted and was immediately set upon by local vendors with everything from tacky souvenirs to offers of guided tours. The big man got out and his sheer bulk had the desired effect; nearly everyone melted away.

A stooped figure dressed in dark trousers, a white short-sleeved shirt, a *salacot* hat and clutching a bamboo walking stick was the only one who remained. The figure approached the car, removed the hat, and peered in. Marcus opened the window and looked up at the deeply lined face of an old woman.

"*Magadang umaga*. Good morning. Welcome to Fort Santiago. My name is Consuela Imee Ramon… and you have some very powerful friends," she said in a calm voice.

Mako gave Marcus a puzzled look as they climbed out of the car.

"Who?" she asked.

The woman neither offered her hand to shake nor answered Mako's question. Datu followed a respectful few paces behind them.

"I have not given a private tour here for many, many years. Please follow me," she said. With that she turned and with her cane tap- tap- tapping over the cobblestones, she headed over to the ruins marked 'Spanish Barracks'.

Mako could not help noticing Consuela's gnarled misshapen hand, which held her cane. She discreetly pointed this out to Marcus as she mouthed "What happened to her?"

"Do you know our story of the origin of man?" the old woman asked, not turning around. Without waiting for an answer, she continued, "According to myth, long, long ago, there was a giant eagle that was continually flying between the earth and the sky, unable to find any land to rest upon. Crying out as to why this should be so, the eagle told the sky that the sea had designs of rising up and drowning it.

The sky was so angered by this that it told the bird it would throw down rocks and islands to pin the sea down should it try such a thing. The eagle relayed this message to the sea, who immediately retaliated by sending waves lashing into the sky.

The sky however proved too powerful and rained boulders

onto the water's surface until it was so weighted down it was no longer a threat. The eagle then alighted on a rock, here, in what is now Luzon Island. A bamboo shoot," she continued, lifting up her cane, "much like this, washed ashore and tapped at the bird's feet."

She did exactly that, rapping with her stick on the warm stone floor at the entrance to the ruins. Then at last, she turned to them. "The eagle pecked at the shoot and out popped a man, followed by a woman. Our Adam and Eve."

"So, is that why in your fairytales and culture bamboo is so important?" Marcus asked, vaguely recalling some tales told round a film-location campfire long ago.

She nodded, adding, "And that's why we also have a healthy regard for the guile and cunning of our great eagle, the Haribon." There was a pause as she looked at them both in turn. She took a deep breath as if summoning up her strength and pointed to the building.

"This site was once the palace of *Rajah Sulayman*, a chief during the pre-Spanish era. It was destroyed by the conquistadors and around 1571 this Fort was erected in its place. Ever since then it has been the strategic stronghold for whoever has wanted to control and occupy Manila… of which there have been far too many."

She walked slowly over to a nearby wooden bench and sat down. Mako looked at Marcus and they joined her, offering her some water they had brought from the car.

"No thank you, I have my own," she said, pulling a small silver vial from her hip pocket. She took a nip. "During the closing stages of World War II, the Japanese invaders, under the command of a fearsome General, converted the barracks into dungeons. The lucky ones were dragged up here to be beheaded. Those in the lower cells drowned each time the tide came in, like so many rats in a hole. Every day the dead bodies were hauled out and thrown into the river, the cells then replenished by newly captured men and women." She paused taking a nip of the contents of her flask.

She pointed to small knots of young couples as they strolled along the promenade, oblivious to the horrors that had occurred so close by. "In a way I hope they never really know what happened here." She turned her attention back to Mako and Marcus. She could see the shock on their faces. "My father died here. Had I been older I would probably have died as well, raped to death. Instead I was beaten, my hands and legs smashed with hammers for trying to escape. I finally managed to scramble out after an air raid."

"Why were you here?" whispered Mako in shock.

"My grandfather had been a stone mason. So was my father, originally. He was very skilled at cutting stones… but precious ones. He is buried right here along with many others," she said stamping her foot on the heavy paving stone. "You will never see the tomb, or those like it. There were 172 by the end. Many people say they never existed. I know different. You know why?"

They both shook their heads, totally focused on the frail woman.

"Because I managed to sneak in one day and saw my father at work. That was why he wanted me to escape, to tell what I had seen, what he knew."

"Which was?" asked Mako.

She looked up at the sky and the seagulls hovering above the river, targeting scraps of food for their evening meal.

"The largest collection of booty the world had ever seen."

"You mean treasure?" Marcus asked. "Not drugs?" the thoughts of the past two days still rolling around in his head.

"Oh, I'm sure there were drugs. The Japanese Army had controlled the flow of opium for years and used the product and the money it generated very effectively. But much more important was looting valuables and bullion. The Japanese Army had been on a rampage throughout Asia for much of the first half of the twentieth century; Korea, China, looting and pillaging wherever they went. The Rape of Nanking was the tip of the iceberg. Then came the outbreak of World War II and the invasion of Burma. Quickly the Japanese systematically sucked up everything they could find. Diamonds, rubies, sapphires, all manner of precious stones, artwork and treasures, along with bars of precious metal in every shape and size. Pyramid-shaped gold statuettes weighing several pounds, bricks of silver and platinum all the way down to little slabs of a few ounces; hundreds and thousands of them."

"Biscuits. Every Chinese family had them," said Mako quietly, an understanding now spreading over her face. "Back then, the Chinese didn't trust banks, they hoarded the gold at home."

Consuela gave a nod.

"You know your culture's history. Tell me, with two thousand years of hiding family wealth under the bed and seventy percent of the world's population in Asia at the beginning of the last century, do you seriously believe the West's official figures at the outbreak of war with Japan? They somehow calculated that the whole of Asia had less than five percent of the world's mined gold? My father would always smile at such naivety."

Marcus stared at Mako, his theories of the last few days being ripped to shreds by this old woman.

"But the Japanese had a problem. Once America entered the war nearly all their homeports were blockaded. So the Imperial Army systematically shipped what was left of 25 years of plunder to this set of Japanese controlled islands, especially Manila's harbor with this Fort. The Japanese hid tons of booty here waiting for a time when either the war was won, or as became increasingly apparent, if they were to lose, enable a chosen few with the right maps to recover it in the aftermath."

"You mean they planned to come back, no matter what," asked

Marcus incredulously?

"Most certainly. They didn't worry too much that anyone else would steal it. The workers who built the hiding places were always buried in them. Without the maps the sites were virtually undetectable… and if you were unlucky enough to stumble onto one, the booby-traps would kill you long before you could remove anything."

"This is unreal," said Mako, her forehead wrinkled and her whole face a frown of denial.

"No, it is very real. The Japanese High Command named it operation 'Golden Lily'. It has since become better known by the man who buried much of it. He was the General in charge of all the Philippines and built the tomb under your feet. General Tomoyuki Yamashita. Yamashita's Gold. He also had a nickname of course…."

"The Tiger of Malaya?" Marcus said slowly.

"So you've heard of him? He's quite a legend here."

"The bell-hop introduced me. Exactly how much are we talking about," asked Marcus as casually as he could?

Consuela paused, "The estimated value in 1945 was over $100 billion, say over $1.25 trillion in today's value."

Marcus let out a laugh. "Oh come on… that's, that's insane. Surely this would have been huge news. You can't keep something this big a secret," he said bursting with incredulity. "You had me going for a while there but… c'mon Mako. Let's go. This will lead to some sucker punch."

As they rose to leave, Consuela's tone became cold, hard edged.

"Money of that size controls nations. The victors and the defeated were always going to sit down and make a deal. And Communism, or the threat of it, was the argument they used. The Allies secretly dispersed most of the money. There were whispers that the CIA funded the Black Eagle Trust with it; their secret slush fund that fought communism for fifty years in Asia. President Marcos of course got his cut, even Japan benefitted."

"Oh, that's the most ridiculous conspiracy theory I've ever heard," snapped Mako." Japan was on its knees after the war."

"Think. Japan, unlike Germany, was never forced to pay war reparations. In their view they already had, at least to the Western Allies. To the victors the spoils. The losers weren't the rulers of Japan but rather those from whom Japan had stolen. China never got one piece of treasure back and the Allies denied its very existence. China has been desperate for proof of the looting and offers indemnity to anyone who can prove it."

"This is bullshit," Marcus replied.

"The man I live with, who gives me shelter. He knows my background. He is a powerful man now. He even owns the hotel where you are staying. He will be waiting for you tomorrow in Pagsanjan," said the old woman. "Listen to him. Then decide."

Marcus shook his head.

"I think the concierge just set us up." He moved to leave and lent towards Mako's ear. "Next thing you know she's going to try and sell us a map to take with us," he whispered a little too loud, but his conviction was wavering.

Consuela allowed herself a smile. She knew she still had enough of their attention. "Only 151 of the 172 maps were recovered by the Americans. General Yamashita was hanged, but his driver Major Kojima was tortured. Kojima led the US forces to many of the other locations and even a hiding place for some of the maps and codes."

"Oh yes, sure about that are you?" Marcus said sarcastically.

"The number is correct. I should know. While here," she said tapping the stone floor, "I made a number of them. Later Marcos forced me to decipher the remaining maps that eventually came to light after the Americans had left."

Her reply hit Marcus like a blow to the solar plexus.

Consuela got up to leave. Marcus made a move to follow her, but the burly bodyguard stepped forward and held him back, an arm locked around his chest.

"Now you know why he's here," said Mako. "C'mon, we have to leave… please let my boyfriend go."

Datu's vice-like grip relaxed. Mako curled her arm around Marcus and they slowly headed to the car. A sudden thought struck him and he turned back to the departing woman. "Your father. Did he ever mention *Aqua Regia*?" he called out.

She stopped and turned to face him. "It's a mixture of hydrochloric and nitric acids. You rarely see it now. It was used to test the purity of gold."

Marcus didn't move a muscle as her answer sank in. Sam had got it all wrong. It wasn't drugs; *THE LAST COMPANY* was all about Yamashita's Gold.

PART 5

THE CAVE

 # CHAPTER 59

PAGSANJAN, PHILIPPINES

MARCH 1977

"Last Looks."
 "Quiet on the set."
 "Turnover."
 "Speed."
 "Tag it."
 "Action."

It was March 1977 and the first time Louis had ever been near a movie set. At just over nineteen years old, he was mesmerized by the number of people scurrying around with clipboards and walkie-talkies strapped to their belts. Craning his neck from his hiding place, Louis and his friends could see an oasis of light in the distance where a scene was being filmed. Louis was astonished at the amount of money and logistics needed to mount such a massive operation. Pagsanjan was a small village just outside Manila, but it was now populated by people from every corner of the globe, who had been working nonstop on the movie ***APOCALYPSE NOW.***

The movie would turn out to be one of the most critically acclaimed ever made, as well as being a substantial financial success. Unbeknownst to those involved though, it also created a river of cash for a lowly lorry driver named Haribon Guinto, a gate crasher with dreams, Louis McConnell, and a recently fired banker, Stefan de Turris.

In 1977 Louis McConnell's father was stationed at the huge base in Subic Bay just outside Manila, the largest U.S. Naval installation in the Pacific as well as the single largest overseas military installation of the U.S. Armed Forces.

Louis was bored and ventured further and further from the base to taste the delights of Manila's night life in Quezon City. He was pleasantly shocked at the expertise and willingness of the beautiful hostesses; paying for sexual encounters was a justifiable expense he would keep up throughout his adult life. He also noted that for a deeply Catholic country where bars with nudity should be fined, paying off the right person was the most effective method of getting things done.

While visiting a regular haunt, he bumped into a young, tall blond-haired Swiss banker with an aquiline nose and noble profile called Stefan de Turris. They started talking and Stefan explained he had been out to the set of the famous movie. His boss from New York had lapped up the stories and rumors of the difficulties on the shoot. Two days earlier they had flown in uninvited to try to offer short-term finance for the production.

"No luck, they weren't interested. I made the mistake of telling my boss he had not handled the meeting well. He fired me on the spot, so I'm here in town spending my severance pay before going home."

"What will you do next?" asked Louis.

"Short-term lending is a fool's game. Do you know what a film bond is?"

Louis shook his head.

Stefan explained the business of insuring the delivery of a film.

"I just have to find some cash to start a business on my own.... I know how to pull it together and really compete."

Louis wanted to know more about this world of film and finance. He had become fascinated by the events taking place just south of the city; the stories about **APOCALYPSE NOW** had been national and international gossip for over a year.

"Tell me about what's going on in Pagsanjan," asked Louis.

"It's one hell of an undertaking. I hope to God the movie works. It's costing a fortune," said Stefan. "But Francis Ford Coppola is a genius. I suspect it will be a massive success."

"Maybe I should go check it out, might learn something?" said Louis.

"Forget it," said Stefan. "Stay here in Manila. It's much more fun," he said turning to a young cocktail waitress. However Louis was interested in this strange new world and wanted to know more.

"Come on. Show me," he pleaded, his hands raised in mock supplication.

"We won't get near the place," said Stefan.

Louis took out a roll of cash, money his grandfather had sent him.

"Two thousand bucks to add to your new business fund if you get me there. A bit of look and learn."

You're naive… but money talks, the banker thought to himself.

"Deal," he said. "Meet me at the bus station tomorrow at 6:00am. Be ready for a long journey." He then turned and smiled at a cocktail waitress, waiving Louis' bankroll.

The more Louis talked to Stefan during the bus ride, the more he learned. What really attracted him, what fascinated him, what he wanted, was the power of so much money being spent and controlled by so few.

He himself had neither the skill nor talent to write or direct. He was not blessed with the looks or presence required to act. But he was determined and resourceful. Somehow he would control that talent and become the power behind movie making.

father was one of our president's lapdogs, but one day he pissed off someone other than just me …. the police hauled him away. My mother killed herself and *WHAM!* I went from a life of privilege to a street urchin in a week. I was just a kid," he said lighting a hand rolled cigarette.

He continued with his story, the fall from grace of his family and his own subsequent rise from the streets. As Louis listened, Haribon passed him the sweet-smelling joint. It was actually the first time Louis had ever smoked grass. He took a tentative draw, passing it to Stefan who took a quick sharp toke.

"You ever meet Marcos; I mean before they hauled your father away?" Stefan asked between coughs.

"I'm pretty sure my mother fucked him," said Haribon speaking in short staccato bursts, trying not to breathe out the smoke. "Yin and Yang… I am sure it was Imelda who fucked my family," he exhaled immediately following it with another deep drag, passing the joint back to Louis.

"And we thought 'Tricky Dicky Nixon' was bad," said Louis as he took a lungful of air and weed, held his breath then exhaled. His mind started to fuzz over.

"Now you are being rude, *Kano*. No way would my mother have fucked Nixon…" Haribon flashed a fierce look at Louis, who was scared he had somehow insulted him and dropped the reefer. "He's so ugly".

Haribon collapsed into laughter, tears streaming down his face at his own joke. Even Stefan started to laugh. Not Louis. Haribon lit another joint and offered it to him. However Louis declined any more drags. He liked being in control and the fog in his brain from the joint prevented that. He also had no sense of humor, so the laughter that usually came with getting high passed him by. It would be the one and only time he ever took drugs.

"What's your background, Mr. Clean?" teased Haribon. Louis

hesitated. He turned to Stefan.

"You first," Louis said realizing he had never asked anything about Stefan's past while pumping him about movies.

"My story is pretty simple. My father runs a successful fancy antique and furniture import business with a discreet but high-priced showroom in Zurich. Benches for bankers I call it. A strict childhood, I learned a lot about what my father does, but my real gift is numbers. School followed by a scholarship to university in the United States studying law and specializing in film finance. First class degree snapped up by a bank. Fast track to partner but my boss… is not so smart. As Louis knows, I made the mistake of telling him that. Now I seem to be a delivery man," he joked looking at Haribon. "I'm back to square one unpacking and carrying heavy crates like I did as a boy for my father. Great career path," he chuckled and turned to Louis.

Louis thought for a moment. He wanted, in fact needed, to have a more glorious background than this Filipino truck driver or Swiss shopkeeper's son.

"My grandfather was Irish. A freedom fighter. Imprisoned by the British. He escaped with his daughter, my mother and fled to the U.S. He built up a number of businesses, but we are still fundraisers for the cause."

Haribon looked blank, the marijuana clouding his thought process.

"If you want to smuggle something out of the Philippines, I'm your man," he grinned.

Stefan thought for a moment. "As you know, we Swiss are neutral in all things… so long as we have your money."

"You must hate Americans; they occupied your homeland after the war and gave you that asshole Marcos," said Louis to Haribon, trying to emphasize his freedom fighter politics.

"Baseball and Coca-Cola," said Haribon exhaling a huge ball of sweet-smelling smoke.

"I don't understand," said Louis waving away the smoke.

"The U.S. gave us baseball and coke. We gave you sex and our treasures. I think you guys got a good deal, no Louis?"

"Not me, I'm no Yank. My family's real home country is still occupied. Same as you except we give 'em bombs and bullets, rather than lap dances and the clap," Louis replied arrogantly.

"They're Catholic in Ireland too, no....? But from what I hear, girls never fuck even their own countrymen unless they're married to them... let alone British soldiers." Haribon paused. "If more Irish girls had looked like you, the British would have left ages ago."

Louis didn't crack a smile, but once again Haribon burst into laughter his jet-black hair falling over his forehead as he rocked to and fro.

"Louis don't be so serious," Stefan chided, holding back his laughter. "I might have fucked you had I been a soldier." He too collapsed in fits of laughter.

"One day, those in the struggle will appreciate me as much as my grandfather. I want revenge for what happened to my family... I want...."

"OK, OK, you win. I want the same.... We got fucked by occupying forces. So how we gonna do it, get revenge....?" asked Haribon.

"I need a drink before I can answer that," said Stefan.

The three young men stayed up most of the night, drinking almost a whole bottle of Tupay, while swapping stories of their imperfect pasts and their dreams for the perfect future.

It was dawn when they fell asleep and despite the rain that started to fall, slept right through the day. They awoke to a firestorm.

Although barely used in the final edit of the movie, the director had scheduled to blow up the set of Colonel Kurtz's (Marlon Brando's) village, known as the 'Monkey Camp' in a series of special effects explosions that were one of the largest ever filmed. Today was the day. The whole sky ignited with a huge burst of white-hot magnesium and the ground shook as explosion after explosion flashed across the heavens.

"Let's get out of here," cried Louis.

Wide-eyed with fear they scrambled to escape the massive blasts that added to the pounding in their heads from being hungover. Louis turned from the crevice where they had slept to run down towards the river. Haribon grabbed him.

"No, this way, we need to take cover in the rock and caves above us," Haribon said. "A rockfall would crush us."

Stefan had already realized that was the safest option and was rushing ahead to take cover.

Louis' instinct was to run, and he pulled away from Haribon. He started down to the water's edge where massive gasoline charges were shooting flames into the air. He ran a short distance before the large Filipino grappled him to the ground.

"Not that way. Up there," he said pointing to the rock face above them.

Stefan looked to see the two men clambering over the rocks and boulders. Another enormous blast overhead threw them to the ground.

"Look out," cried Haribon. A widening crack in the mountainside seemed to be crumbling and a small avalanche of rocks was now thundering towards them. Haribon managed to pull himself clear but Louis was too slow and slid down the hillside, pulled along in a shower of stones. He stopped after a hundred yards, his ankle caught beneath a boulder and badly twisted.

"Stefan," cried Haribon, "come help me get him out!"

As Stefan scrambled down, Haribon looked for something to

use as a lever to lift the rock and let Louis scramble away.

Another series of explosions filled the air and more of the rock face above gave away, revealing a small cave. A metal cylinder rolled out and bounced down the hill towards Haribon and Louis.

There was horror on their faces as the big brass shell, clearly marked with a chrysanthemum on one side and the rising sun on the other, picked up speed. A moment later it was followed by another shell, then another. Haribon turned, his sense of self-preservation urging him to run before the shells crashed into the rock-strewn ground and exploded.

Louis yelled at him, his eyes fixed on the rolling shells, "For God's sake, help me!"

Haribon threw himself over Louis covering his ears, bracing for the inevitable explosion and certain death. Nothing. All he heard was a long and piercing scream.

He leaped up as Louis' terrified cry turned into hysterical laughter. A carpet of precious stones and small gold bars littered the ground. More shells rolled down the hill and broke open, spilling their valuable contents over the rock-strewn ground.

As Stefan scrambled down to join Louis and Haribon, a round boulder rolled out from the cave and came to a halt among the precious treasure. It was the carved stone head of a Buddha.

Soaked to the skin, the air still ablaze with explosions, Haribon and Stefan eventually managed to haul Louis' leg out from under the rock.

"Jesus, what the hell is all this?" asked Stefan.

Forgetting the searing pain in his foot, Louis tried to scramble up to the crack in the cliff that had opened above them.

"I'm going to find out….," he panted, gritting his teeth in pain. Stefan and Haribon quickly caught up to him and helped him towards the entrance.

The F/X's team flares and the flashes of magnesium threw

moments of light into a small chamber. All three peered in.

"What the hell is in there?" asked Louis, craning his neck.

"Yamashita," whispered Haribon.

They briefly glimpsed inside. A dusty mound of rag covered skeletons, a tripod mounted rusting machine gun, part of an old wooden crate stamped with a 16 Petal Chrysanthemum and a metal box on its side were all they could make out.

Within seconds there was a rumble. Looking up, Haribon and Stefan yanked Louis out of the path of a massive avalanche. Stones rained down obliterating the cave from view, burying the entrance once more under tons of rock and rubble.

There was silence.

"We three. We take a vow right now. We come back one day. Until then we divide what came out of that cave into equal shares," Haribon said firmly.

"But it doesn't look like there is anything to come back for," said Louis.

"I couldn't see properly, and who cares?" said Stefan. "What we have here is enough to set us all up. I'm not digging through all that for what looked like some rags and a machine gun."

"There's more… we need to get out of here, then I'll explain. First, we shake. Right now. We clear everything up. Shells and every last jewel," said Haribon.

He held out his hand, Louis and Stefan shrugged, then clasped it.

"And Stefan, you take that Buddha head," added Haribon.

"Why him?" asked Louis.

"Do you know anything about antiques?" asked Haribon.

"Fine, but if you can sell it, I want my share, said Louis.

"I don't think it's worth much. Just a big paperweight. Come help me, it's damn heavy," said Stefan, straining under the weight as he tried to lift it.

With Louis still nursing his ankle, Stefan gave up and waited for Haribon to come back with the truck. The contents of those shells were more than enough to set them all up in business.

What Haribon told them on the drive to Manila was why they knew one day they had to come back.

It would take them years to set it all up.

CHAPTER 60

MANILA, PHILIPPINES

Rizal and Joselito had arrived at the hotel while Mako and Marcus were at the Fort. Rizal quickly entered the foyer while his sidekick waited in the car. They had strict instructions from their employer, Haribon Guinto. Be quick. They had a plane to meet.

"They're at the Fort, right?" asked Rizal.

"Yes, and I have this," the concierge said holding up a small security sack locked with a tiny padlock. "We offer these to guests as an alternative to the safe in their room and lock them in the hotel safe. We tell them they have the only key…." He shrugged and with a smile, promptly took a key from his pocket and unlocked the bag. He pulled out the red USB and stacks of paperwork.

"What's on it?" asked Rizal looking at the USB.

"No idea. That's for you guys."

"Courier it immediately to Mr. Guinto," said Rizal. He looked around, went over to the newspaper kiosk, and returned with a fat magazine and a pack of chewing gum.

"Put these in for now. It'll feel the same."

The concierge dropped them into the bag and reset the lock. "Let's just hope they don't open it…"

"His compliments for your loyalty," whispered Rizal, handing the concierge a thick envelope, and turning to go.

"Wait," the concierge said, "One more thing. There was someone else asking after Mr. Guinto; he was in the foyer a few minutes ago, but I don't see him now. Name and room number is the best I can do," he added handing over a piece of paper.

Rizal nodded thanks and headed towards the exit.

"Got any more gum?" asked a tall, fit, well-dressed man, who had appeared next to him from behind a column. "My name is Lorne, and I come with compliments from Tyler Gemmell." Rizal would have swatted him away, were it not for the gun poking him in the ribs.

"Just a moment of your time, please," Lorne added politely. "We need to talk…."

CHAPTER 61

MANILA, PHILIPPINES

"It was treasure… not weapons… not drugs…." Marcus leaned his head against the seat back as he and Mako returned to the hotel, crawling through the late afternoon traffic.

"What did Sam think *Aqua Regia* was?" asked Mako as she nestled into Marcus' neck, appearing to the driver as if she were whispering sweet nothings in his ear. They couldn't trust anyone.

"Sam knew it meant something. Maybe he saw or overheard a snatch of conversation that made him think it was connected to drugs. Once Sam had that bit between his teeth, there was no stopping him."

"Well, someone did," Mako replied dryly. Soon they were back at the hotel. Marcus offered a tip to Datu. He grinned and refused with a wave. They walked into the lobby and collected their key. No other messages at the desk.

Marcus handed the concierge a tip which he expertly accepted. "Thanks for the guide. She was…"

"A real treasure," chimed in Mako.

As they walked into their room, they picked up a note that had been slipped under their door. It read simply, 'Be ready to leave at 7:00 in the morning, your car will be outside the hotel. You will be met in Pagsanjan'.

Mako pushed the door shut with her heel. "You reckon this shit's going to get clearer tomorrow? Japanese soldiers, fairy tales about treasure, possible dummy accounts from a movie? Are you sure Bill's even dead? We're in way over our heads. We're dead, Marcus."

"I'm not sure of anything anymore....," he replied, the stress just under the surface. "But this guy or group apparently knew the exact moment we rode into town. If they had wanted us dead, we would have been dropped into a concrete coffin, just like Consuela Ramon's dad. Today was lifting a veil, not lowering a shroud. These people have long arms, Mako. We're no safer at home than we are here." Marcus flicked the room keycard onto the table and stretched. "You're right, that son-of-a bitch wasn't exactly delivering a Hallmark greeting card in Nisten," agreed Mako.

"But what happened to us in *Nisten* just doesn't add up. You know what I think?" Marcus yanked open the mini bar and without asking emptied both small bottles of vodka into a pair of tumblers. He picked out a can of tonic then thought better of it, taking a gulp of the spirit neat and cold. He passed her a glass. "If we're not dead here, our new friend wasn't trying to kill us in Europe either."

"But that's crazy. Two Filipino guys are looking for us?"

"Don't get me wrong, I'd be glad never to have anyone looking for me ever again. Period." He raised his glass. "Cheers," he said as he emptied it. Mako did the same.

"It's insane, but it's the only explanation. Two Filipinos, each with different agendas," Marcus sighed.

"Okay, I'll bite... But I need another drink." Mako waved her fingers at the fridge as she flopped into a chair.

He yanked it open and she pointed at a miniature gin.

"At least no one here has asked us for a Buddha head. Is there any ice in there ....?"

A couple of hours later the last of the sun's rays clipped the edge of the room, bathing it in an amber glow. Miniature bottles of vodka, gin, tequila, sake, Bacardi rum, and a split of champagne stood like soldiers on the windowsill. Mako's pedicured feet rested on a footstool, her toes occasionally splaying and closing, a tell-tale sign she was concentrating.

"Tell me, were you ever lonely down there…." Marcus nodded at her, his slightly drunken stare moving slowly from her face to her lap.

At first she was confused, even wondered if he was so drunk, he was being crude.

"In Cannes, I mean," he quickly added, as he realized the possible *double entendre*.

Nice save, she thought.

"Why? Is Producer boy jealous of my life?" Mako laughed at Marcus. Dangerous waters, she thought. Keep it light.

"Seriously?" she asked, her toes wiggling.

She got up and fished once more into the mini bar coming out with two miniature Tupay bottles. "At least it's white spirit. OK for you or do you want me to call room service?"

He shrugged a gesture of 'fuhgeddaboudit' and offered his empty glass.

"Why were you living on your own?" He wasn't going to let this drop.

"I don't plan for the future… makes commitment difficult." Mako shook her hair. "My father scarred me deeply. You?"

"I travel all the time, go to some fucked up places. One of my bags even has a bullet hole in it from when I was working in Colombia on a movie about the drug cartels. Madness."

Mako looked at him, waiting for him to go on.

"It's easy to find a partner to share your life when it's going up, but harder if you have to accept the kind of downs I've been slapped with. I don't mind putting myself through all that, but it's a lot to ask of someone else. It's usually me who ends it…."

"Just find someone who enjoys the rollercoaster as much as you do. They exist," she said in a matter of fact tone.

"Maybe I just give off the wrong vibe?" he said with a lop-sided grin.

She smiled. "You sure do. Beamed right out and smacked me center forehead the moment I first met you," her own palm slapping against her brow as she said it. "Thought you were a jerk!" She grinned and raised her glass in a toast. "To emotional misfits."

He grinned and raised his glass, the booze making him warm and fuzzy. A couple of peas in a pod he thought to himself. "Two emotional misfits," he replied, misunderstanding and assuming her toast was just for them.

She stretched. "I'm a little trashed. You wanna carry me down to dinner?"

"Screw that. Call room service," he replied waving a dismissive hand.

"I don't want to eat in a hotel room again."

"Me neither. I meant call them to bring a trolley to wheel us both down to the restaurant."

"What the hell went on in Pagsanjan?" she asked, the drink banishing all fear.

"Maybe we'll find out tomorrow," he replied.

"Whatever it is, we'll handle it together. C'mon let's eat. Call for our ride," she said clapping her hands.

Marcus reached for the phone.

That was Mako. Head down, butting antlers with the here and now.

CHAPTER 62

MANILA, PHILIPPINES

The sprinkler system was shooting individual bursts of water out over the manicured garden in a steady consistent beat, each spurt a hissing rainbow as it arced across the cloudless sky. A pair of small green *guaiabero* parrots chorused their distinctive '*zeet zeet*' call as they pecked at the figs growing in trees that lined the lawn. Haribon sat in the formally laid out garden of his Manila home reflecting on the character of his ex-partner Louis McConnell.

It wasn't enough for Louis just to succeed, his friends and colleagues had to fail. Haribon now understood that in the end, for Louis to prove in his own mind that he was the better man, he had to steal from everyone else. This was his weakness and would surely lead to his ultimate downfall.

Like Louis, Haribon had defined his own career by ruthless efficiency. Unlike Louis though, he had a set of rules, parameters he would not breach, mainly because he believed they were bad for business. For Haribon information was his lifeblood, pragmatism his code, and the intelligent application of money and power was how he built an empire.

You chose partners and expected them to concentrate on the work at hand, not double-cross you. A gang war was counter-productive. Eventually the police tired of collecting the dead soldiers of rival gangs, sprawled all over the streets like so much litter. These operations were simply closed down en masse. That is why Haribon had survived. Persuasion and bribery worked better than murder and mayhem.

Yet the more he unraveled what had been happening, the more he saw that he had been cheated. Crossing him face to face was dangerous enough, but for Louis to do it behind his back and make him look like a fool....? That was igniting a very dangerous fuse.

The small-town banker, Rafael Satow had helped. He'd given Haribon the start he needed, but there was more. He needed to be sure who had been duped, who had done the stealing, and who had been paid as agreed. Then retribution would be his.

He had decided to stay on for a day in Manila, like a bird of prey circling the city, his eyes constantly searching. With contacts at every level of airline, immigration and passport control, the first call about the arrival of Marcus Riley and surprisingly accompanied by de Turris' daughter, had thrown him. He wondered how they had met, if they could be trusted, let alone trusted each other. He had a plan for that.

The fact they chose his hotel was a bonus, although the odds were in his favor anyway. His company owned that development outright, but he had a part share in nearly every major hotel in Manila. The concierge knew he would be rewarded handsomely. Haribon took a mouthful of *San Miguel* beer as he relaxed into the sun-lounger. He needed to arrange his thoughts and decide what to say to his guest.

Half an hour later, Haribon heard the soft fall of footsteps on the grass and looked round as one of the guards pushed the visitor into a seat opposite him. He looked at the defiant face. The other guard handed him a package.

"From the hotel sir, just arrived," the man said quietly to his boss.

"You can go now," Haribon said to them both as he peered into the package. "Thank you." The documents and a red USB would have to wait. He turned and looked at his visitor.

"*Magandang hapon, Ginang*, Good afternoon Madam. I am Haribon Guinto."

The upturned face glowered at him, then spat.

"You ordered the murder of my husband, you son of a bitch. There's nothing more you can do to me," said Cara with as much defiance as she could muster.

"You are wrong on both counts. However, I need to be sure what you know…. or most probably don't."

At first, she ignored him. Next she shouted abuse so he in turn ignored her. Suddenly she leapt up from her chair and started physically lashing out at him. Hovering in the background by the pool house, his guards quickly sprinted towards the small woman, whose arms were wind-milling blows over Haribon's frame.

"It's OK, it's OK," Haribon shouted at them. He saw the bodyguards hesitate; revolvers drawn.

"Away," he roared at them. They knew better than to disobey and backed off. Cara suddenly stopped. Startled, she looked up, Haribon's hands clamped around her wrists like human handcuffs.

"Let me begin," he said between gritted teeth as Cara still struggled in his grip, "then when I get to the end, you tell me your side of the story and we can try to get justice…."

"Justice? You're just a gangster," she jeered at him, but she had at least stopped resisting.

"Doesn't mean I don't mete out vengeance when I'm crossed. And let me assure you it's a damn sight faster than years in a court room." He stared into her face then suddenly opened both his hands and freed her. His hands ran through his thick black hair and he readjusted the heavy rimmed shaded glasses that had been knocked askew.

She slowly rubbed her wrists.

"Now, please sit down." Haribon gestured towards her chair with one hand as he used the other to straighten his clothes and tie.

"And just a small correction, a gangster is an ignorant bully who uses violence as his only tool. I use my brain. Violence is my solution of last resort. He looked calmly at Cara and smiled. "Let me tell you how I first met Jonathan." Thus he began giving Cara a brief resume of his times with Jonathan.

Cara listened without interruption.

"That's how it was between us; how we started. Money doesn't motivate him. He gets his kicks from figuring out the most direct and effective way to get things done," Haribon explained.

Cara remained expressionless.

"Jonathan was the perfect tool; truly amoral. I, however, am not. A clash was inevitable," said Haribon.

"What's any of this have to do with Bill?" Cara said coldly, speaking for the first time.

"Because his death is what broke our relationship."

Cara flinched slightly.

"I'm sorry, but you knew that. He's gone." Haribon looked intently into her eyes, searching for any flicker that might give Cara away.

She relaxed a little. "He would have come back to me. Yes, I know he's dead, but not how he died. Tell me."

"Do you understand the connection between Jonathan, McConnell, Riley, de Turris, Wood, and Kelso?" asked Haribon ignoring her request.

She looked at him puzzled. "You mean apart from **THE LAST COMPANY**? Well, they all got Sam's script, which apparently is the kiss of death. As if you don't know. Wood, Kelso, Riley, de Turris and his daughter are all dead."

Both answers shocked Haribon, but his poker face didn't betray it. He and the banker Rafael knew very well what bound these people. He had wanted to see Cara's reaction to him naming each member of the group. However he knew nothing about a script and why would she lie about the death of Mako and Marcus, whom he knew were at his hotel in Manila?

"As for Jonathan," she continued, "you know he is a cousin. Family or not, I just thank God we were never close. I knew he had come to work for McConnell. Saw him a few times. He dog-sat my pug occasionally."

Haribon sighed, "Jonathan and small dogs."

"Robert Kelso's partner came to see me. He showed me photos the police in Cannes gave him, saying they were of the man that killed Robert and probably Marcus and the girl. It was Jonathan." Haribon summoned the guards to request Cara's mobile that they had taken from her purse. He looked at the phone, "Forgive me, it appears you have a message from his cell whilst you were… in transit. Turn the speaker on," Haribon directed Cara, "You may not want to hear but I do."

Cara nodded. She dialed her message service. She was surprised though that the voice was not Jonathan's.

"This is Benjamin. Jonathan is no longer living at Mr. McConnell's guest house and left behind his phone that Mr. McConnell owns and pays for. I accessed your number. He left abruptly taking just his passport and his old blue and yellow jump suit. I suspect he has gone looking for a job as he is no longer welcome here. Out of courtesy and before I burn the rest of his belongings, I thought I should see first if you as his only relative, want to send a courier to get any of it."

"He's left McConnell? First I've heard of that. As far as Jonathan's stuff, forget it," said Cara flatly.

Haribon studied her face for any other reaction. There was none. That message had probably saved Haribon's life. His men had hacked her phone and listened to the message while Cara was en route in Haribon's private jet.

"Now, he continued, "did you know de Turris, McConnell, and

I first got together in the rain on a movie set nearly 40 years ago?"

He proceeded to tell a shocked Cara about *APOCALYPSE NOW*, the rock fall and the shells filled with treasure.

As he was talking, two figures emerged from the main house. A huge man gently leading an elderly woman. The driver stood still while Haribon beckoned her to join them.

"You met them?" he asked, momentarily breaking off his conversation with Cara and turning to Consuela. She nodded.

"Cara, this is Consuela Imee Ramon. I consider Consuela part of my family... indeed she helped raise me." Consuela smiled and sat down, resting her cane against her knee.

"Firstly, I should say how sorry I am for your loss. Even though it was so long ago now, I too have suffered," she started softly to Cara.

"May I join you?" she asked quietly.

Cara nodded.

The old lady leaned forward and told Cara about the secrets of her youth and the maps and caves dotted all over the Philippine archipelago.

"Once I had escaped and the war ended, I came to work for Haribon's mother. My job was to raise him. I thought my secret knowledge of the caves and maps was safe until his father Jorge found out. He thought he could bargain with Marcos for my information. Instead the President just took me, to use me for my knowledge. Years later Haribon and I reconnected. It seemed we needed each other."

Haribon broke into the conversation, "I had just reached the part where McConnell, de Turris, and I caught our first glimpse inside that cave."

Consuela looked back to Cara. "The cave... ah yes..." She looked affectionately at Haribon. "This man learned that particular period of our recent history from me. He recognized at once the significance of the 16 petaled chrysanthemum on the side of the shells. It was the emblem of the Japanese Emperor so whatever was hidden in the cave must have been carried out in his name, if not perhaps with his knowledge.

Japanese buried treasure is part and parcel of the fairy stories told to all Filipino children, as much the core of their myths and legends as the story of the bamboo shoot creation of Adam and Eve."

She looked at Cara who nodded; she had heard the same stories at her own father's knee.

"Yamashita…. So, you stumbled across a big find?" Cara asked. "I still don't see how Bill's death fits in?"

"Those three young men, Haribon, Stefan de Turris, and Louis McConnell, had indeed discovered one of the legendary hiding places of Yamashita's Gold," said Consuela.

"Imagine their horror and frustration as they watched another rock fall bury it again before they could do anything. They had to become partners; bound by this secret, they began to make plans to return and recover the rest…." She turned to Haribon, "When you found me years after I left your parents, how much did you have from the shells that fell from the cave?"

"Nothing, maybe $10- $12million."

"In 1978 that was not nothing!" Cara said with shock.

"Cara, I have the deepest respect for money. What I meant was after talking with Consuela we knew it was nothing in comparison to what we might possibly find there."

"Why not just go back and dig it up?" asked Cara.

"Our beloved President Marcos," said Consuela, a hint of disgust in her voice. "He knew all too well about Yamashita's Gold. He had systematically taken a cut every time anyone found anything. If you were powerful enough, like the Americans at the beginning of the digs after the Second World War, or one of his cronies, Marcos took a modest share. Anyone else…." She just left the sentence hanging.

"No one dug up so much as a drain without the President looking over their shoulder," continued Haribon. "With my family history," he said glancing over at Consuela, "there's no doubt of the outcome. The jackal of Malacañang Palace would have picked the cave clean of everything. All that would have remained are the bodies of the first people to have dug it as well as McConnell, de Turris, and me. So, we waited until he was dead and buried. But wolves still prowled in the world of politics. We needed something that would hide what we really wanted to do."

"*THE LAST COMPANY*," breathed Cara.

"Correct," responded Haribon. "It took years of planning before we could set up that movie. Sure, Marcos was history but many of his former cronies weren't."

"But what happened in the intervening years?" queried Cara.

"Louis took his share of that first money and started his talent agency. I got into construction and de Turris bought a partnership in a film bonding company. We built our own lives, waiting for the chance to return.

Louis began to set up a production. It had to look absolutely genuine. He put together a young and eager crew, hired just about everyone from an aging star down to the clapper loader. The key was Kelso. He was the one with the experience, enough to silence any doubters. Louis and Stefan convinced me that Kelso was on board. In addition, a few other crucial people needed to be paid when it was over. We were certain we could pull this off.

Stefan, who by now was running the bond company, told us to find a small local bank and open accounts for ourselves and everyone on the production both here and at their home bank. Standard practice. During the shoot the accounts would operate normally. Once the shoot ended, some of the accounts would remain live but be converted into numbered accounts, though still ostensibly held by those individuals. Jonathan did some digging and found a manager at the local bank who had a few secrets of his own. At last everything was set.

Cara listened in silence waiting for the ending she didn't want to hear as Haribon thought back to the terror of the first day in the cave.

CHAPTER 63

SET OF *THE LAST COMPANY,* THE CAVE, PAGSANJAN

AUGUST 1997

The team of men were standing, staring into the blackness. The work had taken over a week. At last Haribon's crew with its diggers and drills had managed to clear the rubble outside the cave revealing a dark echoing chamber.

Below in the valley the rest of the crew of **THE LAST COMPANY** were working on the day's set-ups, blissfully unaware of the true purpose of the excavation work at the great rock.

"Fire them up," said Haribon. "No one moves until I say so." The generators spluttered to life and the arc lights the men had dragged to the opening threw white light into the void.

The small chamber contained an empty metal box lying open on its side and the remains of a broken wooden crate that held artillery shells. Both stood close to the entrance next to a tarpaulin-shrouded machine gun. Scattered over the floor that sloped toward the exit were many skeletons and three brass shells.

Haribon crossed himself. Everyone hung back as he slowly entered the cave. He reached down and lifted up a shell and shook it. It rattled like a maraca. He then picked up the metal box. Inside was a large piece of waxed parchment that lifted his crushing disappointment at the bareness of the cave.

Someone was planning to come back, he thought to himself as he unrolled the map. He looked back at the skeletal remains of the man that had lain next to the shell crate and the box with the map.

He was a Japanese major. "So, no honor amongst thieves," Haribon said dryly. "This is now *our* key," he said to the others as he raised the waxed scroll."

Haribon was confident Consuela would make sense of the mishmash of symbols and numbers. At last a reward for patience and resolve. Suddenly there was a crack followed by a cry for help.

One of his men had edged along the far wall well away from the remains. The ground underneath him had given way and he was sinking into a pit of loose, fine sand. Within moments the panic-stricken man was stuck fast up to his waist. Death and suffocation seemed seconds away.

"I said to stay back," roared Haribon. "This whole place will be booby-trapped."

He spread-eagled his arms holding back his men who were eager to rush to their stricken colleague's aid.

"Stay still, Roxas, moving makes you sink faster," he said to the man as evenly as possible. "Calm. Now deep breaths.... gently try and raise your arms and hold them out like you are floating," Haribon said, making the same motion himself hoping to encourage the man. He glanced back at the others. "Fetch me that rope," he nodded at the pile of tools and equipment by the entrance.

The look of fear on Roxas' face gradually changed to one of relief as his descent halted. "It's okay," he replied. "I've stopped. I've found something to stand on."

Roxas barely heard the 'click' as the pin of the small anti-personnel mine engaged. It was one of dozens that littered the base of the trap-pit along with ball bearings, nuts and bolts. The explosion spewed out sand and shards of metal that flayed the walls with such force that anyone within ten feet would have been shredded. The top half of Roxas' torso flopped like a rag doll against the rock wall, his legs still held in the sand.

That night, the map lay unfurled before them on the table at Haribon's small house in Pagsanjan. Lit by three desk lamps, it clearly depicted both the small cave they had uncovered as well as a far larger chamber below. The waxed parchment was covered in small, spidery-like icons and signs, evidently drawn by a weak and trembling hand. Haribon leaned over Consuela as she sat and studied the document.

"What does it say?" he asked her anxiously.

He knew that starting to dig in that cave was suicide unless they could understand every cipher.

"This is most important," she murmured as her gnarled index-finger knuckle rested on a small Japanese symbol. "It's the fulcrum point from which all measurements and angles are taken. Quite simple, that icon, is the Kanji symbol for balance. It's common on these maps. It is one of a number of Chinese characters also used in Japanese."

She took a small sip from her silver flask. "Remember your initial disappointment when you saw that tiny cave? I told you it would be like that. These complex hidden vaults are what protected all of Yamashita's sites. I worked on countless caves where people had stumbled about, not understanding that the treasure they hunted for lay either beneath their feet, above their head or behind a fake wall. We are lucky, this map...."

"Lucky to have such a good guide," interrupted Haribon giving the woman a hug.

"Hmmm," she said, not quite so enthusiastic. "Look at the clock face numbers here and here," she continued, pointing at the document, "tell us the depth of floor we need to break through and the angle the original cave is located from the fake floor above. The face with numbers starting at 15 and running anticlockwise up to 150 is for depth."

"But the face has four different pairs of colored hands each pointing at a different number," said Haribon. "Which one do we use to calculate?" There was another clock next to it, which had three hands and the numbers ran clockwise from 0-360 to depict degrees. "Same problem with this one," he added.

"The bird pecking the ground depicted below the first clock tells us to follow the third hand for the correct depth and the bird with wings spread above the degree numbers means the second hand points at the true angle to dig."

Relief that this beloved woman really knew her job was visible on Haribon's face. On and on she went, identifying each tiny icon. There were anchors that depicted metal supports, an open hand that warned of the sand traps. Depending on which way they pointed, flags warned of dead-ends or secret passages.

"These depict mustard gas canisters," she continued pointing at a crudely drawn eye, "and this sign that looks like a snowflake, that's a mine. These flowers mean a water pipe. Fracture that and depending on the source the engineers tapped into, it could easily flood the entire chamber."

Patiently she went through every sign on the map, as if she was reading a book in hieroglyphics. "And these?" asked Haribon, waving his hand towards the bottom of the map. There were at least forty signs spread randomly across the very base of the map. There were stars, squares, pentagons, pendulums, pyramids and sunbursts.

"They all symbolize…. treasure."

The implication of so many symbols was not lost on Haribon.

"So much, is it possible?"

"Believe me, compared to some I was forced to unearth, this is still quite small." Consuela took a deep nervous breath and shakily rested her knuckle in the center of all the booty symbols where there was drawn a pair of crossed arrows and what looked like three coiled snakes, a curved bow and a thunderbolt.

"You may never know," she said, "because those crossed arrows and the thunderbolt. They mean death."

"And the others next to them?" asked Haribon pointing at the faint symbols of snakes and bows.

"Those are ones I have never seen before," she replied looking back at him, fear in her eyes.

The crew spent three days opening up the entrance, cutting back the concrete and porcelain inlay the Japanese had used to fill it in years before.

"We can't wait any longer," warned Jonathan as they stood out under the stars.

Haribon replied, "We start drilling tomorrow, through the floor, but no one enters the actual chamber below until I say so…. after what happened to Roxas they had better do as I say."

Jonathan nodded reluctantly.

"Why not send in some of the Ifugao tribe laborers I've hired? No one would miss them if something happened," suggested Jonathan.

Haribon glared at him. "You are one cold son of a bitch, Jonathan. I said no one."

Despite the tension between them, Jonathan and Haribon were speaking to each other in hushed tones as the crew headed back to the production offices, the day's work completed. As each one walked past Haribon they nodded 'good evening' to their boss.

"See you at the party," one said, referring to the event scheduled that evening.

"A crew and cast get-together. The foreigners and us. We're all invited," said Haribon, his tone making it clear Jonathan was to attend as well. "Even if you just mooch about in the background." With that, he turned and headed down to the valley himself.

As Haribon walked away, Jonathan was more convinced than

ever of his partner's weakness, unlike the man whom he had become increasingly close to, far away in Los Angeles. Their initial contact had been quite by chance when Jonathan answered a call from Louis McConnell intended for Haribon. Jonathan and the Executive Producer now conversed on a daily basis, Jonathan providing progress reports and other information, repeating every conversation he had on the set from complaints about per diems with the star, to the personal family conversations with his cousin.

As Jonathan confided more and more in Mr. Louis, as he now called him, he began to appreciate that this man saw things with ruthless clarity. He wouldn't have blinked at risking a few tribesmen to get at the treasure he thought, as he slowly followed Haribon towards the party.

The next day Jonathan reported back to Mr. Louis the events of the party and Bill's party trick with the keg. Louis saw an opportunity, an advantage he could exploit. He had a plan for ending the movie and it now included a bonus; the death of Bill Baines.

He buzzed the intercom to his PA. "Get me the insurance document."

Over the next few days Louis explained the upside of the plan to Jonathan who saw immediately it was the right solution. However when McConnell explained it to Haribon, the Filipino had strongly disagreed,

"That's not part of the deal. He lives," he said emphatically into the phone. "Or you will answer to me." Haribon slammed down the phone as Jonathan coolly listened outside.

As the days followed, bore holes were carefully sunk in accordance with Consuela's detailed instructions. They revealed a vast array of trucks, tantalizingly laden with cargo. Haribon insisted that all the trucks were off limits.

Cranes and winches were placed over the holes ready to hoist up the hoped-for bounty, but still Haribon held back. He had never seen Consuela so concerned. All those years when forced to help Marcos, she had encountered traps and deathly puzzles and successfully unraveled their mysteries; until a final dig when she had got it all wrong. Fifteen men died that day, gassed to death by an elaborately concealed canister that had been dipped in gold.

Her life became worthless, her record of involuntary success shattered. She fled from the dictator's wrath, reuniting with the boy she had once cared for as his *ya-ya*. A man who could protect her, as she had once protected him. Now he needed her help and unique skills. She wanted to retrieve the treasure for him, but alarm bells were ringing. For the umpteenth time she stared at the strange shapes.

"I can't hold back any longer, we have to start emptying those vehicles," sighed Haribon that evening. "We enter the chamber tomorrow."

That night Consuela's sleep was haunted by the images of men choking and dying surrounded by gold.

"No one starts unloading till I'm sure." Haribon ordered the next morning while he, Jonathan and four men were climbing down a rope ladder through one of the holes punched in the false floor.

Jonathan wandered over to a nearby truck picked out by the lights from above. The tires were flat, the windshield covered by a film of grime.

Ignoring orders Jonathan withdrew his balisong. He slashed at the cords and the dusty tarpaulin draped over the truck next to him dropped away. Row upon row of stacked boxes covered the bed of the truck.

Jonathan glanced at Haribon then put his leg onto the rear bumper, in readiness to haul himself onto the vehicle.

"Stop, stop, don't touch it!" came an out of breath voice from above.

Haribon swung around and looking up saw Consuela's anxious expression as she leaned forward over one of the holes, two Ifugao tribesmen trying to haul her back.

"Let her go," Haribon shouted angrily.

"It was simple. So obvious," she cried. "Underneath."

Jonathan was not prepared to wait any more. With arms spread wide and grabbing each side of the tailgate he bent his knee in preparation to haul himself up, when a crashing blow to his kidney stopped him. He fell to the dirt.

"For now, you still do as I say," whispered Haribon glaring down at him.

Haribon turned and looked up at Consuela, a questioning expression on his face.

"Underneath," she repeated. "Those images, I thought the snakes and bows were symbols…. the hand that drew them was tired; they were the last on the page. But last night…. we were talking about vehicles, trucks…. It's the first location I have heard of where trucks were left behind. I wondered why? Then it came to me. The vehicles are the traps. I misread those signs as symbols. They aren't coiled snakes and the bows. They depict actual things…. the coil and leaf springs of the vehicles. Take the weight out of the back and as the springs decompress or the leaf springs uncoil…."

Haribon bent down on the ground next to the stricken Jonathan. "Follow me," he said, thrusting a flashlight into his hand. The two men wriggled on their backs under the truck's rear axle.

The compressed leaf springs were completely flat. Attached to each were glass vials containing cyanide as well as chargers wrapped to sticks of dynamite. If the loads were lifted off the truck above, the springs would have returned to their bow shape and pulled the plungers out of the vials, releasing the gas as well as triggering the detonators in the dynamite. It was the same story on every vehicle, the compressed suspension, be it coiled or leaf springs, acted as detonator. Emptying any one of the trucks would have killed everyone in the chamber. Once again, his beloved *Ya-Ya* had protected him. He would protect her forever in return.

After five days of continual toil, the men had relieved every vehicle of the deadly traps. It still took a further ten days to bring out their precious loads. Then it was done. It was time to shut down the movie.

CHAPTER 64

MANILA, PHILIPPINES

"How much are we talking about?" Cara asked quietly, "from the treasure?"

"Over the years the holding company received just over $475 million," Haribon said flatly.

"Once out of the country and stored away, Stefan was the expert. Over time he privately sold off the artwork and jewelry or paid me if he or Louis wanted to keep anything for themselves. Stefan sold the bullion, small amounts at a time so as not to raise suspicion. An initial low profile was key to never being detected. The return on that money as well as from investments made with it has been coming in ever since."

Cara's face was frozen in shock at the revelations. "Nearly half a billion dollars?"

"Twice a year I sent a share to all those involved." Haribon looked straight at Cara. "My group, Golden Eagle Trust, kept 30%, Louis and Stefan's accounts received 30% each; around $140 million apiece. The other roughly $48 million was split between the remaining four: Robert Kelso, Marcus Riley, Sam Wood and Bill Baines."

There was a sharp intake of breath from Cara.

"After Bill's death, I insisted his share be sent to you. One of the numbered accounts was meant to be yours, Cara. Over 15 years your cut should be around $12 million."

Cara looked blankly at him. "No... not my Bill. He'd never be a part of this."

"And you…." Haribon stared at her through his heavy framed glasses.

"But I never even knew…."

"And I believe that because…?" Haribon's tone hardened.

"But I never received a penny…." Then of course she knew she had, even if only a small fraction.

"After Bill died, Louis was pressuring me not to ask questions. He even threatened me with legal action. I had no idea about any accounts… but I took his money," she said, her head hanging down in sadness.

"But nothing like $12million…? I suspected as much. A local bank manager kindly put me right," he said still angry at his own reliance on Louis and Stefan's assurances.

"Louis, that lying bastard….," replied Cara, her tone rising.

Haribon held up his hand to stop her. "So, if you didn't get your money where did it go? What about the others? Who received the money, and who never had a clue like you?"

The silence from Cara made Haribon go on. The shock was still clear on her face.

"I'm sorry, you wanted to know what happened to Bill," Haribon said a bit more softly. "To shut down the movie, Stefan and Louis persuaded me that we needed to make sure things didn't go smoothly. Trucks were late, the wrong materials were delivered; we even gave the impression that drug deals were going on. People became jittery."

"Then we took some completed footage and held the reels of film for ransom as we had agreed at the beginning. That was it as far as I was concerned. Job done. Later, I was told Bill and three friends went up to the cave trying to rescue the stolen film. Jonathan must have set it all up and told them they could leave Bill in exchange for the rushes. I was on my way back to the cave and was surprised to see Bill nonchalantly leaning against the shed wall of the little wooden entrance that shrouded the cave. Suddenly Jonathan stepped out from the shadows, pulled out a gun and shot Bill."

That was as close to the truth as Haribon was going to give her. "End of movie."

Cara jumped at his last words and stared at Haribon. There was not a tear in her eye as she said coldly, "He's a dead man."

# CHAPTER 65

PAGSANJAN, PHILIPPINES

The drive the next day was a hell of a lot easier than it had been the last time Marcus had done it. Pagsanjan was in the very southeast corner of *Laguna de Bay*, a vast body of water about thirty miles long by twenty-five miles wide that clung to the southeast corner of Metro Manila.

On leaving the city the road forked, giving the visitor the choice of turning left and taking the northern shore road or keeping right and taking the road that curved around to the south. In terms of actual miles, they were about the same distance to Pagsanjan. When Marcus had last done it, there was not much difference in the roads, just the view.

The northern road that ran along the edge of the bay was still narrow, potholed, and dangerous. It wound through a number of tiny fishing villages with musical names such as *Jalajala*, *Pililla* and *Kalayaan* and it had always been Marcus' preferred route. Exciting and picturesque, the journey took all day; if there was torrential rain, it could last three.

The southern route was now a paved main road though, so there really wasn't any choice, especially as someone was waiting for them. They hooked onto the freeway and were in Pagsanjan just after midday. As they drove along the shoreline in the hired 4x4 SUV, Mako gazed out over the vast expanse of water.

"It's huge. Freshwater, right?"

"Uh-huh. Fresh-ish. I wouldn't drink it... but don't let looks fool you. You could almost walk across it; at least Sam could have.

It's never more than six feet deep."

They turned into Pagsanjan. Marcus looked around in confusion. It didn't look anything like the small village he had left years before.

As their vehicle rumbled into town, they were immediately set upon by *barceros* eager to take them out in their small wooden canoes up the river that flowed into the bay, to the *Magdapio* Falls and site of the 'Monkey Camp' of Colonel Kurtz. The town was now a commercial shrine to ***APOCALYPSE NOW***.

"Let me be your guide. I was extra on movie...."

"My brother and I were personal friends of Marlon Brando...."

The promises of intimacy and secrets about ***APOCALYPSE NOW*** spilled from everyone's lips.

"Sleepy little town," Mako shouted over the riot of car horns and cries from local traders. Souvenir shops lined the main street, with the bullet shaped head of Marlon Brando gazing out from posters that adorned nearly every storefront. Bars, restaurants, even the gas stations all shouted the name of the famous movie.

"We were only vaguely aware APOCALYPSE NOW had been made in this area when we were here," whispered Marcus. "When the hell did all this spring up?" He wondered how, in all this chaos, they would be able to find the person they were to meet.

"You know my father loved that movie," murmured Mako.

The 4x4 slowly edged towards the town center. Marcus leaned over the steering wheel, his head constantly turning from left to right trying to find a building or landmark he recognized from the past. He saw a big hotel, with an eagle carved over the door. A memory fluttered in Marcus' subconscious.

"It's weird Marcus, but you know....," started Mako.

Marcus slammed on the brakes. The Diet Coke can Mako was sipping from banged against her top lip and spilled its dark sticky contents onto her cotton shorts and thighs.

"Thanks a lot, the bugs will love that," she said yanking his baseball cap off his head, trying to mop up the droplets. There was a sharp rat-a-tat at the windshield that made her jump.

"Tell 'em we're not interested in whatever they want to sell…" continued Mako still inspecting the stains.

"He's not going to take 'bug off' as an answer. I think we have met our guide," Marcus replied grimly.

The tall reed-thin man was nonchalantly leaning against the vehicle, discreetly using the barrel of a snub-nosed revolver to rap on the window.

He pointed the weapon at the door lock button. Marcus hesitated just long enough for him to point the gun at Mako. Marcus had no choice, quickly pushing the rocker switch on the console. The locks snapped open and the sweat-stained man got in.

"Silence. Drive out of town on this road," he instructed, "Should be memory lane for you….," he said, nodding towards Marcus.

With the lake now behind them to their left and leaving Pagsanjan, the 4x4 hugged the road next to the river on their right, as it headed towards the falls.

"He doesn't look much like a big shot hotel owner to me," said Mako loudly, ignoring the man's instruction for quiet, once again her bravado edging out her fear.

The man ignored her remark. "Slow. Now, up there," he said directing them with a flick of the weapon to drive out across the plain and away from the river's edge. Marcus turned the vehicle off the track, engaged low gear, and it slowly growled its way up towards the small rocky outcrop that the man was pointing to.

"Why are we going this way… and who the hell are you?" Mako asked.

"Heaven and hell," replied the voice in the back. "And it's Rizal."

They pulled up at the foot of a tall rock. Marcus' attention was held by the sight in front of them. "It's the cave where they built a set for **THE LAST COMPANY,**" Marcus began, before a wave from Rizal's gun silenced him, ordering them out of the car.

"I can't see any opening. Are you sure, Marcus?" whispered Mako.

"Yes. The main production units were below in the valley. Somewhere up here they were digging out a cave for a scene…."

The sun was arcing back towards the horizon as Rizal deftly pulled a large crowbar from the undergrowth and tossed it at Marcus. "Now move that rock," he said nodding at one nearby and pointing the gun directly at Mako.

With a heave, Marcus rolled the boulder to one side. Rizal motioned his gun towards the small opening Marcus had created, making it perfectly clear they were expected to go in.

Marcus took Mako's hand and squeezed it as they crouched under the low entrance. They found themselves in a cave, pitch-black save for the sliver of light coming from the entrance. Rizal pulled a couple of flashlights out of his hip pocket and tossed them at Marcus' feet.

"Compliments of Haribon. Enjoy your tour," he laughed and turned away. Before they knew it, the boulder was rolled back over the entrance leaving them in complete darkness.

"Buried in a cave." Mako spun around, "Fuck you," she yelled at the blocked entrance…. "and screw Harry Bourne too," she added, "whoever he is."

They heard the engine start then the rumble of their 4x4 growing fainter until there was silence.

"It doesn't make sense…. why kill us now?" said Marcus.

"Because they can," hissed Mako.

"Hold it together," reassured Marcus as his arms encircled her gently. "This is not how it ends," but he couldn't hide the doubt in his voice. They were in lethal danger and both knew it.

He reached down to the dirt and felt for the flashlights. He gave

Mako one and switched his on.

"Holy shit….," Her expression was as shocked as Marcus'.

They were standing on the top section of a vast cavern, the floor a frightening lattice work of holes. In the cavern beneath their feet stood the rusting frames of countless trucks and military vehicles.

The words of the old woman instantly came back to Marcus, *"There were 172 by the end…."*

"We were all played like suckers," exhaled Marcus.

As they swung their beams around the black void, Marcus saw something written on the far wall under the image of a painted crucifix.

On turning to make sure Mako had seen it as well, Marcus' beam dropped to the floor, the thin shaft of light shining across the hole-riddled floor. The flashlight picked out something else though. No more than twenty feet away, lying on the ground and bound at the wrists and ankles, was the body of a man.

"Whoa!" Marcus said. He heard a muffled sound and saw the body move. Mako looked at Marcus and they slowly made their way over to the huddled mass.

As they approached the body and the crucifix above that had been crudely painted against the rock-face, Marcus could just make out an inscription.

'R.I.P. Bill Baines. I am sorry."

As Marcus' flashlight beam licked across the wall beside the cross, something glinted, nestling in a small crevice. It was a nickel-plated revolver, its snub-nosed barrel pointing down at the shape lying on the ground.

Tentatively Marcus leaned to turn the body over. As he did so the man's eyes flew open and blazed at him from above his taped mouth. Marcus jumped back.

"Shit!" he exclaimed.

They both recognized the man instantly. It was the bastard who had attacked them in Switzerland.

Mako's mouth dropped open in shock. Pinned to the man's grimy clothing was a handwritten note. "I executed Bill Baines."

# CHAPTER 66

PAGSANJAN, PHILIPPINES

It was 10:00AM and Haribon and guests were leaving the house in the city to go to his home in Pagsanjan. "I need your help to tie up some loose ends, then you can go home," he said quietly to Cara, thinking about the scripts from the hotel he had read the night before and still frustrated at being unable to unlock the USB.

Datu drove the Toyota Land Cruiser. Consuela sat with Cara in the back. Cara said nothing for the entire journey.

The conversation with Haribon yesterday had hurt her, but at least there was no more doubt, and she knew the truth about how Bill died. Her fury at Jonathan was raw and painful. A fellow Filipino, even worse her own cousin and someone whom she had confided in when they had first met. He was an assassin who had calmly shot her husband and thought no more about it. He worked for Louis McConnell. Louis had amassed a fortune and lied to her from the day they met. All she wanted now was to get away from this place and to face these two men one final time.

For Haribon, Cara's initial reaction had confirmed what the banker Rafael Satow had blurted out to him while tied up in the back of the limousine. The money Louis and Stefan had been so insistent needed to be paid by *Golden Eagle Trust* to the individual Philippine accounts did not end up in the hands he had intended.

Cara had admitted to some hush money, but it was a pittance. Sam Wood had clearly only received one payment. So how much had the late Robert Kelso and the seemingly lucky-to-be-alive Marcus Riley received? And how much had de Turris and McConnell stolen?

Situated about a mile to the north of the village of Pagsanjan, Haribon's house was modest in size for such a rich man. The contents and furnishings of Haribon's home were personal and intimate, small mementos salvaged from his youth. There was a silver-framed black-and-white photo of a young woman squinting into the sunlight with a baby in her arms, a signed photograph of Mr. Coppola on the set at Pagsanjan, a well-thumbed copy of Eleanor Coppola's book *NOTES ON THE MAKING OF APOCALYPSE NOW* and an old baseball bat.

Just three bedrooms, a drawing room and a dining room but still with the traditional 'two kitchens'; one for the owner, more a breakfast room with some modern appliances, and one at the back of the house. This was where the real meal preparation took place and where there was a bed for the cook to sleep.

Hidden from the road by thick ferns and Nipa palms, the garden was a riot of the local jasmine sampaguita, some red-spotted orchids and yellow flowered Nara trees. It was the opposite of the manicured lawns and formal flowerbeds of his more ostentatious house in Manila.

There was a small shack for Haribon's bodyguards hidden in the grounds and a large shed next to it. The unkempt grass led down to the edge of the lagoon, where a small turquoise colored fishing boat with a torn white sun awning was moored. The craft leaned against its moorings and the rickety wooden dock that bent into the lagoon. Nearby floated a small Maule seaplane.

Datu drove the car to the front door and a tall man came out to greet them. "Rizal," said Haribon. "Did you drop off both packages?" Rizal nodded.

"And did you receive the package from the hotel concierge?"

Rizal asked in turn. Haribon confirmed he had.

"Datu, take Mrs. Baines inside and see she is well looked after. I believe there is some lunch. Cara, Consuela, I'm afraid I cannot join you; Rizal and I have some business to attend to. We will be leaving again in a few hours."

Cara had no idea what he was talking about and honestly didn't care anymore. "Consuela, I'm tired. I am going to rest," she said leaving untouched the meal prepared by the wild haired cook, Marites. Consuela decided she too would take a rest, but not before she had tasted some of the beautifully prepared food.

"Now Rizal, tell me everything," said Haribon as they walked off towards the shed.

"As predicted Jonathan came in on the flight at Cebu City," said Rizal much to his boss' satisfaction.

In the first year after the excavation, Haribon had needed to regularly smuggle tons of antiques and bullion out of the country for Stefan to deal with. Louis had been in charge of setting up a small cargo company that used an airport at Cebu City, to the south in the Visayan Islands. It had worked and over the years Louis certainly smuggled other goods out along with what they had taken from the cave in Pagsanjan; sometimes even legitimate freight.

The business was sold long ago. Haribon knew the airline's colors were the same as on the jump suits. Once he heard the butler's message on Cara's phone, he guessed Louis must have 'persuaded' the new owners to let Jonathan occasionally hitch a ride back to the Philippines. Haribon smiled at the irony of McConnell's butler inadvertently saving his life. Louis would have been furious.

"We saw him get out when the plane landed," went on Rizal as they walked into the shed. "He tried to make a run for it. A touch of GHB and he went out like a light."

Rizal turned on the light in the shed and there stood two vehicles, a Jeep and a large truck. The truck was the kind used for breakdown and recovery with a winch in the front and a mid-mounted crane as well as a large flatbed at the back.

"Anyone see you?" asked Haribon as he jumped onto the back of the truck joining Rizal who had started to check the mass of ropes and a huge wicker basket.

"Not anyone who would care. We threw him in the Maule. Flew back then dumped him in the cave. The gun and message exactly as you wanted. Done."

"And your call to me after the surprise meeting with Lorne whatever-his-name in the hotel lobby. You did what I told you?" asked Haribon as they continued to check on the contents of the flat bed.

Rizal took a deep breath and nodded. He jumped down and wandered over to the front of the vehicle to inspect the winch.

"Good. And Marcus and Mako? Any trouble?"

"The guy kept his cool."

"And the girl?"

"*Cojones y fuego*, balls and fire." He slapped the winch. "It's all ready to go, boss." He switched off the light as they headed back to the house.

The scent from the garden filled the air that was gently stirred by six-bladed ceiling fans. Haribon sat at the bamboo and rattan dining table with his laptop. He looked at the screen with the locked message from the USB, the scripts he had read earlier on the table next to him. He now had Cara, Jonathan, Mako, and Marcus in Pagsanjan. He was sure at least one of them would give him some answers.

It was dusk when his driver, Datu, came in with the young muscle and side kick, Joselito.

"OK. We go," said Haribon. "Rizal will follow later with Cara. Tell him to get Consuela to look at this when she wakes up," he added pointing to the laptop.

Across town someone else was making final preparations, too.

CHAPTER 67

PAGSANJAN, PHILIPPINES

After a fierce workout in the hotel garden followed by a cold shower, Lorne Maddox slid back the flimsy closet door to pick out the clothes needed for the rest of his day.

Tyler Gemmell's requests for Lorne's services were rare. When Lorne was at 'work', he favored a dark suit, white shirt and elegant tie to set off his toned frame and close-cropped hair. He found that formal dress added gravitas to his image and weight to his message; an authority figure in formal dress definitely provoked a greater sense of danger than a leather jacket and tight blue jeans.

It worked with that thug Rizal at the hotel in Manila. Lorne had been very ominous and equally clear. He was here to see Haribon Guinto. He would come unarmed. Rizal had no choice but to tell Lorne what Haribon's plans were and who he and Joselito were going to collect from Cebu airport that afternoon.

"Your boss can play out his game," whispered Lorne in Rizal's ear "but this conversation is our little secret... oh and in case you want to run and tell anyone or I don't succeed, neither your wife nor your daughter will see their next birthdays."

After Rizal left, Lorne made a call to Tyler Gemmell. "They've got Jonathan." There was a pause. "Understood," Lorne said and hung up.

He laid out on the bed a pair of loose black silk trousers and a white, short-sleeved shirt. He pulled the right-hand pocket from the trousers inside out, so it jutted out from the leg like a white cotton ear. With the point of a box-knife, he deftly opened the two halves of the material that shaped the pocket as if he was shucking an oyster.

He placed a small role of surgical tape, a mini hacksaw and a pair of pliers on the bed by the clothes. Next, he picked up a .25 caliber Guardian pistol. It weighed barely more than a couple of iPhones and at four inches from eyesight to barrel end, it was about the same length. Despite its extremely compact dimensions, it held six rounds in its squat rubber grip frame. With a bit more firepower than an equally sized .22, it packed a lethal punch at close range. He was about to make doubly sure.

Lorne withdrew the magazine and using his surgical glove–covered thumb, ejected all six cartridges into an ashtray. Using the tiny metal hacksaw, he carefully scored a small 'X' at the tip of all six slugs, ensuring their breakup on impact. At the distance he planned to shoot, the disintegrating round would mean any torso or head shot would be fatal. He reinserted the cartridges, snapped the magazine home and picked up the roll of duct tape.

He attached the gun high against his crotch on the inside of his right thigh and felt the cold steel as his testicles brushed against it. He had shaved off the hairs at the top of his leg while showering, not at the thought of the sting from the tape ripping off, but because the heavily matted curls would make the tape sag and he needed the gun to lay flat against his skin. In his experience, the macho attitude of even the most committed body searcher stopped short of the fork under the fly zipper. He admired his handywork in the mirror.

"Unarmed," he smiled.

He put on his watch, buckled his belt, and then slid his hand through the open flap in his right-hand pocket to make sure the butt of the gun was positioned correctly for a swift withdrawal. Neatly placing the tools back in his bag, he shoved it in the closet. He glanced around the hotel room once more to check that nothing was left out that shouldn't be. He blinked in the late afternoon sunshine filling the room and as an afterthought went into the bathroom, opened his washbag and smeared some sun cream over his face careful to remember the tops of his ears.

He slipped on titanium-framed sunglasses, strode purposefully out of the hotel and crossed the road to the river's edge. He dropped down into the hired boat, pulled the cord on the outboard motor and pointing the small craft upstream, set out over the flowing water.

# CHAPTER 68

THE CAVE, PAGSANJAN

Several hours earlier Jonathan had slowly regained consciousness in the cave. He had no idea where he was; it was pitch black. He felt nauseous and there was a salty taste in his mouth. GHB. He knew that drug, he himself had used the instant sedative to take out uncooperative lorry drivers when hijacking their loads.

His first thought was not where he'd been dumped, but why he wasn't dead. When Rizal caught him at the small airport, he had expected a quick twist of a blade or pull of a trigger, not a blow on the back of the head followed by a few drops of liquid into his slack-jawed mouth. Far too much effort had gone into shoving him in here alive.

Yet he could not understand how Haribon had found him so soon. He had used the secure route of the cargo plane to avoid all customs and immigration and it had always worked so effectively in the past.

He assessed his own situation. He was bound hand and foot lying on a stone floor. The blackness was unrelenting, even with his eyes now accustomed to the dark and his retinas fully dilated; no light was getting in.

Trying to sit up, with his heels pushing at the dirt to give him traction, some pebbles rolled across the floor. A moment later he heard a distant clang from below as the stones fell through a hole in the floor and struck metal. In that instant Jonathan knew exactly where he was. The last time he had been here loyalties had changed and he had killed a man.

After the footage had been stolen from the set of **THE LAST COMPANY**, Jonathan had specifically targeted Bill Baines with details of the ransom demands. He was certain how Bill would react. Sure enough Baines and his three-man crew arrived at the cave's outhouse entrance. "Just you, inside," a masked Jonathan motioned to Bill with a gun. The stuntman walked into the shed, unable to see into the main cave as the entrance was covered.

"OK, I did as you asked," said Bill calmly to the masked man in front of him, "My three guys are outside. Now quit this screwing around, give us back the film and I'll get you some money.... but you can forget a quarter of a million bucks. Enough of this bullshit."

"Give those Kanos outside one day's worth of rushes as a gesture of goodwill. Tell them that my partners are keeping the rest as insurance and you're staying here. If they don't come back with the money, we burn you both. And it's still $250,000."

Bill went outside, handing over what Jonathan gave him.

"He's an amateur, doesn't frighten me," Bill said to his friends. "He's nearly a goddamn midget, for chrissakes, but I don't know where his mates are and we can't risk having them destroy the footage. Tell Marcus to stay calm and I'll negotiate on the price," he assured them before returning to the big shed.

Leaning calmly against the shed wall, without an inkling of the danger he was in, Bill heard his guys walk away.

"So now let's make a deal," he said.

In one swift movement Jonathan stepped forward, raised the gun and shot him. Louis had been adamant, a single shot, execution style. The shell crashed through Bill's forehead and exited through the back of his skull. The dead man stood still for a moment then slumped forward onto the floor, his blood mingling in red rivulets with the dirt and dust on the rocky ground.

"I told McConnell 'No'," said a voice at the door seething with anger."

"I thought you were down on the valley sets," Jonathan said calmly, hooking his forearms under Bill's shoulders and dragging him to the cave opening. He kicked aside the board covering the entrance to the cave and with a mighty heave sent Bill's corpse through the nearest hole in the floor.

Haribon grabbed Jonathan and pulled him outside. For a moment he thought his boss was going to crush him with his bare hands. "I told McConnell very clearly that Bill Baines was not to be killed," he hissed.

"Mr. Louis was clear to us both, this is something he wanted done. It's personal. Baines brought it on himself. It ensures the movie stops. It's the best solution. Win-win all round."

"Where the hell is Baines' win-win?" replied a furious Haribon.

"You have your money. Stop trying to confuse what you really are with who you'd like to be. We're all the same, you, me, Mr. Louis. And if you think you're not, it will eventually destroy you. Let's get the hell out as we all agreed." Jonathan threw his gun down at Haribon's feet.

He turned his back and walked down the hill. If Haribon had picked up the gun and shot him, his last thought would have been that he had misjudged the big man and taken up with the wrong side. But Haribon didn't and Jonathan knew Mr. Louis was right. Haribon's moral code made him weak.

Jonathan soon caught up with Bill's three friends returning to deliver the message. He was quick and direct. "The stuntman is dead. This movie is over. However, as far as Marcus Riley is concerned Baines is still alive. He still has 24 hours to raise the money for the ransom."

Gaffer Mike Garland's eyes widened, adrenalin pumping through his body. "You son of a...," he started and leapt forward.

Jonathan easily sidestepped him, tripping him up. A blade

fanned out in his hand. He grabbed cameraman Rory Carmichael, pushing the blade against his neck. He turned to the remaining man.

"Mr. Wallis, isn't it? If you don't want me to slit your friend's throat, very slowly pull out a note in my right-hand jacket pocket." The man did as instructed and pulled out a slip of paper.

"Your home addresses. One word to Marcus Riley outside of my instructions and your wives will be raped then killed." Jonathan pushed Rory away. "Just one call from me. Now go deliver my message. Not another word."

He saw the fear on their faces. They would do as instructed. Tough guys? They weren't in his league. Nevertheless they were still loose ends. He knew he would eventually kill them all.

...Suddenly there were voices, torchlight. Jonathan struggled to regain his thoughts.

"Kill the bastard," said Mako, the shock of seeing the bound figure made her breath come in short bursts. "If you won't, I will," she threatened as she strode towards the gun.

"No," Marcus said as he grabbed the firearm, then turning to Jonathan added, "at least not yet." He bent down and grabbed at the lapels of his filthy blue overalls. Marcus re-read the handwritten note on Jonathan's chest and looked at the inscription and logo on his breast pocket.

"Well, let's really hurt him, make him talk. Threaten to cut his dick off. That always scares the shit out of you guys," Mako snarled, pushing against Marcus, glaring over his shoulder at Jonathan as she spoke.

He glared back at her, breathing through his nose in short bursts but his mind was clear.

"Forget him for now," Marcus said flatly.

Mako looked at him dumbstruck. "Forget him? He tried to kill me, us.... twice! Kelso, Mary, Giles.... He's a psychopath...."

She struggled as Marcus started to haul her away, mindful of the holes in the floor and trying to illuminate them with his flashlight. At the same time he tucked the gun into his waistband.

"I told you, we're here for a purpose," he finally said when out of earshot of the bound and gagged man.

"Yeah, well, by the looks of our welcoming gift," her head nodding at the gun, "it's to drill him."

"Maybe." Marcus was thinking fast, worried what Mako might do. He shook her. "I want to know why... and I can't think straight with you playing some medieval judge, jury, and executioner. Take a breath."

Mako still glowered but grew calmer. He took a deep breath. "We're obviously looking at what must have been one of the hordes of Yamashita's Gold that Consuela had been instructed to tell us about. Yamashita's nickname loops back neatly to the name *Tiger of Malaya Corporation* on the USB. We made **THE LAST COMPANY** here. It's clear now the location was chosen to allow McConnell, this Harrysomething....," he looked at Mako who nodded that she was following his train of thought "And your father to recover the treasure hidden in the trucks down there; all done under the cover of a movie."

"A film to cover up a crime....," Mako continued, her eyes still glancing at the bound body behind them, making sure he hadn't moved. "Bill Baines is killed, apparently by that," she nodded towards Jonathan, "to trigger the bond." Mako glared at Jonathan.

"Then the treasure is slowly drip fed into the black markets so as not to arouse suspicion," continued Marcus. "Every six months the proceeds are paid by Golden Eagle Trust into accounts here in Pagsanjan.... all of which are rerouted via a bunch of accounts back to the *Tiger of Malaya Corporation*."

"Six numbered accounts in Pagsanjan. Bill Baines, Robert Kelso,

Sam Wood, Louis McConnell, my father, and you." She looked at Marcus and stopped.

"C'mon! I sure as hell never got anything!" Marcus answered sharply.

She ignored his tone and continued, "Nor did Sam, which pissed him off when he unraveled why that money arrived in his account in LA. Convinced what was really going on during **THE LAST COMPANY** had something to do with drugs," continued Mako. "He writes that screenplay which he sends to you all, with tiny clues saying either 'I'm on to you', or 'you've been used.'"

"So, Sam wasn't *sure* who was getting money or exactly what was going on?" Marcus said following her logic.

"That's why he sent you **FALL OUT**… not for you to make it…."

Marcus thought back to his promise to Jax, and why he had desperately seized the opportunity to make **FALL OUT** and the potential revival for his stalled career. "Well, at least let's find out the answers for Sam." Marcus turned to the small bundle behind them. "Who is this piece of shit…. who has selected us to kill him and why?" He thought for a moment, "And why here?"

"How the hell did anyone know this stuff was here in the first place?" questioned Mako. "And how did they all know each other?"

Marcus thought for a few moments, "Did you see the name of the hotel in town, with the large eagle on the roof? The Heart of Darkness Bar and Grill Inn. Don't you see?"

"Joseph Conrad. His book *The Heart of Darkness* was the basis for the film **APOCALYPSE NOW**. I was about to say something but that jerk Rizal stopped me… I told you my father talked to me about the films he'd been involved with?"

Marcus nodded remembering their talk at the hotel in Geneva.

"One of the first was **APOCALYPSE NOW**. McConnell and he met then."

More pieces were falling into place.

"My God Mako. That shoot ended in '77. Something happened that must have alerted them all to this. They waited and plotted for over two decades to pull this off? Everything must have been worked out to the last detail."

"You mean McConnell and my father," said Mako with no hint of emotion now.

"And I assume the person who sent Consuela and stuck us in here."

"The local connection?" Mako asked.

"A local boy made good…. stinking rich good…."

"How did they find it, what the hell took them so long, why wait so many years….?" wondered Mako.

"The eagle!" Marcus said a little too loudly.

That provoked a reaction and movement from the prone figure behind them. A puzzled look came over Mako's face and she slowly started to search her pockets.

"What are you looking for?"

"I'll explain… go on. An eagle?" said Mako, relief on her face as she found what she was hunting for was still in her pocket.

"It keeps turning up everywhere. Soon after the collapse of **THE LAST COMPANY** your father renamed the house in Switzerland after an Eagle's Nest '*Nisten*', Golden Eagle Trust is sending out the money, Consuela pointedly referred to an eagle in her telling of the fable and it's Aguinaldo's symbol in **FALL OUT**. Seeing that eagle in town on the hotel today also jogged something in my memory, now I know what it was. The head construction guy on our shoot, who worked on this cave, his nickname was something to do with an eagle and there was an eagle in his company's logo."

Mako handed him the folded piece of notepaper she had taken from the hotel room with the details for their drive. "Like this?" she asked. Sure enough, under the name of the hotel was the same logo of an open winged eagle.

"It's not Harry Bourne. Consuela told us. It's *Haribon*, the eagle. A powerful friend," Mako said quietly.

"OK, so that explains how he knew where we were."

"And what he wants us to do," said Mako looking at the gun.

Marcus pulled back the retaining pin under the barrel and pushed the cylinder out from the center of the gun. Five of the chambers were empty.

"Only one bullet."

"One bullet, one question," said Mako.

"Right," said Marcus. "Help me out here. Clearly Louis McConnell, Haribon, your father and maybe others built up their own fortunes. But why kill Bill…?"

"But surely it's obvious. The insurance document hidden in my certificate that my father kept showed clearly that Bill's death would shut down the movie," answered Mako.

"They didn't need to kill him for that," Marcus said slowly. "We were screwed once the hijacking of the dailies took place. We couldn't pay. The local crew disappeared; we lost all the shot footage. The named star had already threatened to leave. The bond would have been pulled. Baines' death just doesn't fit. It wasn't necessary. You know what's wrong?" he said after a pause. "This had been planned for years. Every last detail. But something happened after the original bond contract was signed; something down here that meant Bill had to die. Something that made Louis add Bill to the 'Essential Element' clause. Your father was keeping the handwritten amendment to say whose idea it had been."

"Still doesn't get him anywhere near to absolution," Mako said flatly.

"Maybe, but even though Bill's death resulted in a surefire way to close the movie, it was an afterthought. A damned convenient one… and why does the note pinned to that thing say 'I *executed*

Bill Baines' not murdered? Why would anyone *benefit* from Bill's execution?"

Marcus stopped, his flashlight now pointing down at the shattered and broken vehicles that lay beneath him and a sudden cold chill ran through his body.

He thought back to Sam's very first introduction to McConnell. Then to Cara's first night on the set with her cousin and the note pinned to the bound figure.

"Oh no…."

It was the only explanation that possibly made any sense.

"I bloody well know what my question is going to be."

He swung round avoiding the holes and went back to the body huddled on the far side of the cave, trying to resist the urge to shove the muzzle of the gun into the man's mouth and pull the trigger.

Jonathan recognized the danger in Marcus' face as he bore down on him. However those extra moments when Marcus had moved away with Mako had given him all the time he needed. As Jonathan had tried to sit up, he had felt a sharp pain in his leg as a shard of metal protruding up through the floor sliced through his jumpsuit gashing his leg. His wrists and forearms were now bloodied from lacerating them again and again against the jagged metal spike until he had finally worn through the rope.

"Sunburst Airfreight. '*Our Day Will Come*' That's why you killed Baines, isn't it?" spat Marcus.

In that moment Jonathan knew that Marcus understood. Jonathan's arms snapped out from behind his back. Before Marcus knew what was happening, he had yanked the revolver out of his hand. A split-second later Jonathan's legs snaked out from under him, viciously catching the back of Marcus' heel. Even before Marcus had hit the ground, Jonathan had pushed the barrel hard into his temple.

"All *I* need is one bullet," Jonathan said, ripping the tape from his mouth. "Because I can kill *you* with my bare hands," he hissed at Mako. "Of course, if I had a syringe here and a bit more time, I'd inject air into your veins... instantly causes an embolism and completely undetectable," he said with a smirk, looking directly at her.

An embolism. Mako looked at Jonathan in horror as what he said sunk in. Her body started to shake, caught in the glare of his triumphant sneer.

"Your father must have been ashamed of you," he jeered at her.

"If that means he was proud of scum like you, I'm glad he's dead," she snapped back, anger making her breath come in short staccato gasps.

"Your father never asked me to kill for him. Might have, though," he taunted her. "It was Mr. Louis who wanted your mother out of the way. Your father's fault though. He told Mr. Louis about the secret of the head after your mother solved it. Once she did that, she became just one more problem to take care of."

Marcus flinched but Jonathan had him firmly in his grasp.

"Now, come here you *bitch*," he snarled cocking the hammer of the gun pressed against Marcus' head.

Haribon sat outside, high up on the rock above the cave, with the drama playing out below. He rotated the stub of his cigar against the stone.

The three of them should be just about cooked by now, he thought as he looked at his watch. "You two start getting things ready," he said turning to his men. "Rizal will be here with Cara any minute."

Lorne was alone on the water. He could just make out the figures on the rock's summit as he shut off the boat's motor and pulled silently up to the bank. He crept onto dry land and waited as agreed, for his ride to the summit.

CHAPTER 69

THE ROCK SUMMIT, PAGSANJAN

With Haribon watching them, Datu and Joselito unlatched the rear gate of the breakdown truck and began organizing the various piles of coiled ropes, chains, cutters, and cables.

They worked quickly, hooking up the cables to the side of the padded wicker basket. They then heaved the basket off the back of the truck and dragged it a few yards uphill from the rear of the vehicle, leaving it next to the boulder near their boss.

"Joselito, go anchor the truck onto something," Haribon instructed.

The young man walked to the front of the cab that was pointing uphill, disengaged the brake on the forward winch and pulled out a steel cable capped with a spring guarded carabiner tow hook. The winch was bolted just below the radiator grill between the large bull bars that protected the nose of the truck.

With the hook in his hands and the cable snaking out behind him, Joselito slowly picked a path over the rock-strewn surface walking a short distance up the gentle incline. He looped the cable a couple of times around a six-foot fin of rock, clicking the giant carabiner back onto the cable, then tramped back towards the truck and the others gathered around it.

Lying motionless in the long grass further down in the valley, Lorne waited for Rizal and the approaching jeep.

"Where are you taking me," asked Cara as defiantly as possible?

Rizal didn't even turn to face her as the Jeep rumbled up from the riverbank to the rock summit where he was to join Haribon and the others.

She looked at his pockmarked face, highbrow, and jet-black hair, such strong native features. Perhaps he didn't understand her?

"*Sann patungo ang sasakyan na ito*?" she repeated in Tagalog. The man remained silent.

Rizal's eyes never left the road. He had understood exactly what she had said, both in English and Tagalog. He had been told to stay silent and knew better than to disobey; the trouble was he now had two sets of orders; each from very dangerous men. He was taking no more risks and following all instructions to the letter. Rizal barely felt the vehicle sink as Lorne silently hopped onto the back as the Jeep slowly bounced over the terrain.

Dusk was turning to dark by the time they reached the summit and Lorne quietly hopped off his free ride about 250 yards before Rizal and Cara's truck came to a halt among the knot of activity on the summit.

Haribon nodded in greeting to Cara. He was holding in his hand a small glass jar. He carefully poured the mild acid solution over the top of the stone 'plug' in front of him that sealed the cave roof. The plastic and plaster painted to blend in with the stone soon melted away. A large eyelet appeared, driven deep into the boulder and cemented in place by Major Okobudo's men years before.

"Found this when working on our movie," he explained to Cara.

Joselito had his fist locked over a tow hook that swung from the end of the crane and was now poised just over the boulder. Jumping into the truck, Rizal took up the slack of the cable that ran from the front winch to the rock and was acting as an anchor. The rock would prevent the truck's mid-mounted crane and the weight it was about to support, from tipping the vehicle back over its rear axle.

With a hand signal from Haribon, the hook from the crane was inserted in the eye. The whole lorry shuddered as the line attached to the finned rock tensed. With Rizal working the controls, slowly the rock 'plug' was lifted from its hole. Using metal spars Datu and Joselito helped edge it away, lowering it back to earth at the side of the hole. Joselito uncoupled the hook from the stone and attached it to the ropes from each corner of the basket that stood next to the opening.

With a nod to Rizal, Haribon watched as the crane suspended the basket a few inches above the hole as if it hung from the hot air balloon it originally belonged to.

"Cara, we are going to repeat history. Let's see who deserves to survive." With that, Haribon stretched out his arm to the basket and helped a nervous Cara aboard, climbing in after her.

He bent down and picked up the handheld searchlight at his feet. He gave a thumbs-up to Rizal who engaged the crane's gears. Haribon and Cara were lowered into the abyss where darkness and history swallowed them up.

CHAPTER 70

THE CAVE, PAGSANJAN

Jonathan's forearm jerked tighter as Marcus tried to turn his head towards Mako. All he could do was swivel his eyes in her direction. She was walking towards them, a flashlight in her hand, his own dropped beam picking out a mixture of subdued fear and determination on her face. He hoped to God she wasn't going to gamble her life against his bravery as she had at Nisten.

"McConnell told you to execute Bill…." Marcus hissed, barely recognizing the sound coming from his restricted voice-box.

"The man had to die," Jonathan said simply.

Suddenly a sound came from high above and stars appeared in the darkness. Jonathan twisted round and pushed the barrel even harder against Marcus' temple.

"Pick the light up Riley. Easy….," he whispered into his captive's ear. Jonathan's grip slackened just enough to let the fingertips of Marcus' right hand brush the stone floor until he found the flashlight.

"Now shine it up there," Jonathan said jerking Marcus' body up toward where the sound was coming from.

There was a grinding of gears as suddenly a blinding light caught him and Jonathan full square in the face. The two were picked out by the white spotlight from the balloon basket, like some double act in the middle of a bizarre circus performance.

Marcus glimpsed Mako killing her flashlight and ducking out of sight behind a pile of rubble.

"And so we come full circle. With those who know the secret of the cave returning either to be buried in it or released by it," said Haribon's distant voice.

Lorne watched as the basket descended into the hole. As the light faded with its descent, he slowly stood up from where he had jumped off the vehicle and walked toward the three men who were focused on guiding Haribon into the depths of the cave.

While Rizal worked the levers of the crane, Datu and Joselito were bent over the hole watching the basket descend, Joselito's outstretched arm guiding the ropes so that the basket remained in the center of the hole.

"That's it. Hold it," Joselito said, raising his arm.

Rizal pulled on one of the red gear levers that extended out of the control box by the cab door and the cable juddered to a halt.

"Thanks for the lift, Rizal," Lorne said quietly as he stepped into view. Rizal whipped round, pulling a pistol from his belt. Lorne raised his hands and continued walking towards them.

"We have an agreement…." Lorne said, his arms raised.

Datu turned to Rizal in astonishment only for Rizal to switch targets and point the gun back at him.

"Stay put Datu. Joselito, search the *Kano*," Rizal ordered.

The young man ran over to Lorne, patting down his torso and legs.

"Clean," he said.

"You are to wait here," said Rizal to Lorne, "until they finish. Then he's yours." The men above the hole stood stock still.

"What you done… who this man?" demanded Datu, concern and worry rising on his face as he looked down at Rizal. "You loco? No one betray Haribon…."

Inside the cave, Jonathan waved the pistol at the light and cocked the hammer.

"I might be more scared if you had a balisong in your hand, Jonathan. But from that distance… and with that gun. No chance," Haribon called down mockingly.

"Then maybe start with an easier target?" suggested Jonathan, returning the gun to Marcus' head.

As the basket gently swung in the humid air of the cave, Cara stared at the drama being played out below her.

"But, Marcus…. he's dead…." she said to Haribon, confusion in her voice.

"Go ahead," continued Haribon, ignoring her. "For all I know you two are working together. Never known you to fail at killing anyone, Jonathan." Haribon paused as he looked at the scene lit up below him.

"And if you really were mortal enemies, Mr. Riley, you should have shot that scheming little bastard when you had the chance, heh? Where's the girl?"

Mako peered out from behind a rock unsure of what to do, or who to believe.

"Let the girl go," shouted Marcus. "She's not involved."

"Oh come now, Mr. Riley. Chivalry may be dead, but my brain cells are not. Her father stole from me, whether she knew it or not. I want my money back. She knows where it is."

"Take it. I don't want it," shot back Mako, coming out from her hiding place. "And you can even have that damned Buddha head people keep on about. In return I want that murdering bastard," her beam flicking over to Jonathan's face.

Now it was Haribon's turn to look puzzled.

Suddenly there was a jolt and the basket began to swing erratically, Haribon's large beam throwing wildly flickering shadows across the vaulted surfaces.

"My God. What's happening?" cried Cara as she grabbed one of the supporting ropes.

Outside there was panic. With a reverberating metallic twang, the cable that Joselito had anchored around the finlike rock snapped. It flew across the ground, neatly slicing a deep cut into Datu's left calf.

Without its anchor, the truck juddered backwards towards the hole, the noise of the tires scrabbling over the loose stones and rocks drowning out Datu's bellow of pain.

Lorne and Joselito were galvanized into action. They scrambled to the skidding truck.

"You did this?" Rizal yelled at Lorne from the cab in panic.

"That wasn't the deal I made. You know why I am here," Lorne shouted back.

The truck juddered again; the tires unable to grip the surface, the stones rolling like marbles under the tires.

"Rizal," cried Lorne, "Slacken the brake on the crane's winch. Release some of the tension. Let the basket lower to the ground or this whole rig will tip into the hole and crush everyone."

The truck lurched again.

"Do it now!" shouted Lorne, banging his fist on the side of the vehicle.

Haribon was beginning to regret his flair for the theatrical. Come what may though, Jonathan was going to explain and confess to Louis and Stefan's treachery. Then it would end.

But what did the girl know? Why had she mentioned a Buddha head? What was all that about?

The truck slipped relentlessly towards the open airshaft only shuddering to a halt as the rear wheels tumbled into the hole, the rough lip of the opening gouging the vehicle's exhaust pipes. For a moment the nose tipped up and it looked as if the whole thing would be swallowed up by the gaping maw of the airshaft.

"Done," cried Rizal.

Haribon looked up through the hole, hearing the grinding of cogs and the skidding of the tires. He understood what the men above needed to do if there was to be any chance of saving them. Cara pulled at Haribon's sleeve as they swung wildly above the cavern floor.

"If you had wanted to kill me, it's one thing," she said gritting her teeth in anger. "Even ending it here with Bill…. But for all eternity with that piece of shit?" she cursed pointing at Jonathan.

"Brace yourself," Haribon said giving Cara a last look of assurance. He killed the light and the basket gave a jerk followed by a high-pitched whining as the cable unwound. The basket dropped into the darkness, the wire acting as a break against free-fall much as it had for Bill Baines during so many of his stunts.

The release of the tension worked and the truck's nose crashed back to earth.

Rizal jumped down from the truck and slid two distress flares into his belt. "This is really screwed up. Follow me," he said to Lorne. "And Joselito, you stay here, look after Datu and if anyone climbs up that cable other than Haribon, shoot 'em'," he shouted as he disappeared down the craggy pathway to the rock's base.

Marcus knew it was now or never. He threw his head back smashing it against the bridge of Jonathan's nose, which broke with a sharp crack. He felt the grip weaken and quickly pulled away. As he killed his flashlight, he yelled at Mako.

"Hide!"

The cave went dark again, the rear of the truck plugging the cave roof and blocking out any flicker of light from the stars. Five people all fighting for their lives clung to the darkness as their only security.

Mako fought to control her breathing. This could not possibly be going to anyone's plan. She desperately wanted to call out to Marcus but was afraid her voice would give her away. The only thing worse than being on her own, was being in the darkness waiting to be caught by that assassin.

Marcus needed to draw the killer's attention and give Mako a chance to get further away. The floor was riddled with holes and he knew that at any time he could drop right through one and crash onto the twisted metal below. The safest thing to do was crawl, so he lay flat on the floor. No sooner was he down, than he felt something grab his ankle. There was no way Mako could be that close. Praying he was correct, he lashed out with his other foot, rolling to his left as he did. There was a man's grunt as his heel drove into something. Good he thought, happy to hurt that son of a bitch any way he could; but a moment later his smile turned to a grimace as the top of his torso suddenly fell into nothing.

He managed to fling out his right arm just in time to grab the edge of the hole. His upper body was pointing straight down; his right arm twisted at nearly vertical. Marcus' fingertips were all that stopped him from diving headfirst into the void. With every muscle in his arm burning in protest, he managed to haul himself back from the brink.

"Run if you like but I *will* find her," hissed a voice.

Marcus didn't want to think what that bastard would do to Mako if he caught her. One man was trying to kill him, while another seemed only to threaten it. Consuela had said he was a powerful friend. Marcus needed an ally and choice was strictly limited. With one arm stretched out in front to feel for holes, he crawled over to where he judged the basket had crash-landed, hoping Haribon had been armed.

The slackening of the winch had saved both the truck and the people in the wicker basket. Cara and Haribon hit the ground at reduced speed with the padded interior absorbing much of the impact.

Nevertheless the basket had tipped on its side, throwing Cara and Haribon onto the cave floor. Temporarily winded, Haribon had quickly come round, his weakened right arm throbbing, his forearm broken once again. He looked around but was unable to make out anything in the darkness. There was no sound from Cara, whose inert body he could feel next to him.

His gun was no longer on him, lost somewhere in the darkness. All he could do was wait for help to arrive. The numbers were in his favor and so long as Jonathan didn't grab Mako or Marcus as a hostage, the killer would not succeed. Haribon got as comfortable as possible. He was going nowhere.

Rizal scrambled the last few yards to the foot of the great rock followed closely by Lorne, who was deftly picking his way down. Rizal picked up the crowbar he had left there earlier and planted it under the rock at the entrance.

"My associates are grateful for your cooperation," Lorne said.

Rizal nodded, hoping he had made the correct decision. Haribon's plans so far had gone spectacularly wrong and there was no time to lose.

Jonathan reckoned he was close to where the basket had landed. A few more yards and he would have Haribon.

Rizal and Lorne burst into the chamber and Rizal lit the flares, handing one to Lorne.

Jonathan was up in a flash, darting behind rocks. Rizal raised his own pistol only to have it knocked from his grasp by Lorne.

"That's not what was agreed," Lorne admonished him. He turned and strode purposely towards the back of the cave where he had glimpsed movement, side-stepping the gaping holes in the floor with stealth and agility, the flare held in front of him.

Haribon felt a gun in the small of his back.

"Up," hissed Jonathan.

Jonathan stood behind Haribon, his bloody nose at an awkward angle and gun nudging Haribon towards the exit. But Lorne was nearly on them by then.

"Who the hell are you?" Jonathan asked him.

"I come with the compliments of Tyler Gemmell," he replied, still coming.

A flash of recognition at the name and a sting of hurt pride hit Jonathan. However, he had now fixed things. He was back in control.

"You can clean up the others," said Jonathan dismissively. "Tell Mr. Gemmell there is no need on this one, the job is taken care of." He came around in front of Haribon and placed the muzzle right between his former partner's eyes.

"You lose," Jonathan whispered and pulled the trigger.

Only yards from the two men, Marcus flinched as the hammer clicked against the dummy round.

Jonathan stared at the gun in shock and pulled the trigger again.

"A test. Marcus passed," murmured Haribon. "You failed, Jonathan. You think I'd seriously put a live round in that gun?"

Jonathan stared in shock. Lorne was still walking towards the two men. He slid his hand into his pocket twisted his torso slightly, withdrawing and raising the little pistol.

Seeing the movement, Marcus leapt at Haribon, bringing him down behind cover. He needed him alive.

Lorne ignored Marcus as his swing continued in a smooth arc. A hollow point bullet flew from the gun and exploded into Jonathan's collarbone spinning him round for one complete pirouette.

Jonathan's entire shoulder seemed to peel away from his

torso. Another shot rang out an instant later as a second round fragmented in the center of Jonathan's chest, silencing him mid-scream.

His body flew back across the floor, his eyes still wide open in shock, as he skidded towards a large circular opening in the floor.

A second later there was a heavy crash as Jonathan's corpse impacted with the rusting machinery below. A rusted spar poked out through his hip; his left elbow bent backwards at a vicious right angle. His body gave a final twitch.

"I'm done," said Lorne, breaking the shocked silence. "Whatever issues there are between the four of you have nothing to do with me or my associates." He turned to Haribon. "Call this a gesture of good faith on behalf of my clients. Jonathan's presence was a gesture of bad faith from Louis McConnell. We've both had enough of that man. If there's no honor among thieves, there's only death."

"Who told you I had Jonathan," asked Haribon?

Rizal looked nervously at the departing Lorne.

"Who," Haribon demanded?

Lorne carried on walking, "The past told me, Mr. Guinto. I suggest we all concentrate on the future." With that, Lorne ducked out through the exit into the cool evening air, heading back to the boat tethered at the riverbank below.

Haribon eyed Marcus. Without saying a word, he got up and returned to Cara's still form. He bent down and heard her moan. With his good arm he gently lifted her to her feet. She was bruised and had a gash on her forehead just below the hairline. As Haribon carefully walked her towards the exit, he turned to Rizal who still looked tense.

"Thank you, Rizal. Loyalty is everything. Your daughter is safe. That man is certain you never warned me. You did the right thing. We look after our own. Now close this place up for good then come get us with the Jeep."

"How were you so sure that man wouldn't harm you?" asked Rizal.

"We are the opportunity, not the threat. I did my own checking on Tyler Gemmell and his associates. I suspect that they have had enough of Louis McConnell. They just wanted to let me know who they were. Let's just say Jonathan was in the wrong place at the right time."

But I suspect we haven't heard the last of Tyler Gemmell, Haribon concluded to himself.

# CHAPTER 71

THE CAVE ENTRANCE, PAGSANJAN

After rolling the boulder over the cave entrance, Rizal walked back up the incline to where Joselito had bandaged Datu's wound. Datu glared at Rizal, "If anything happened to Haribon, I tear you apart my bare hands," he threatened.

"I don't have time for this now," interrupted Haribon. "It's fine Datu. I knew."

Rizal climbed into the Jeep and with Joselito's help, managed to pull the truck out of the crater. After they had lifted Datu into the passenger seat, Joselito drove the truck away with the injured man. Rizal drove the Jeep down to the cave entrance.

Still in shock, Marcus and Mako gave each other a reassuring embrace. Haribon sat opposite on a rock nursing his arm, his jacket thrown over Cara's shoulders.

"I didn't want them to kill him," Haribon said quietly.

"I would have," glared Mako. Cara nodded in agreement.

"I meant Bill, not Jonathan," Haribon replied.

With his arms still around Mako, Marcus turned to Cara. "'*Our day will come*'," he said looking at her.

Cara stared at him. "You mean today?"

Marcus shook his head.

"That's what really killed Bill... Sam knew that. Jonathan's jumpsuit proved it."

"What are you talking about?" asked Mako, confusion in her voice.

"In the cave. It suddenly clicked. Bill's death had nothing to do with **THE LAST COMPANY** at all. It was never part of the plan. To Louis McConnell it was a surprise bonus too good to miss. I am so sorry, Cara."

A puzzled look appeared on Cara's face.

"That's why Bill was added as a rider to the 'Essential Element' clause so late in the game?" Mako whispered, starting to understand.

"Let's start with the facts from both Sam and Bill's past. The rest is pure hunch. But it fits."

"Mr. Riley. Please, if you would explain," asked Haribon.

Marcus took a deep breath.

"When Sam first sent McConnell a writing sample to try and get his agency to take him on, he sent him a book, a thriller. Louis did indeed take Sam on. However the book was never published. Sam eventually sent it to me after we had worked together to see what I thought."

"I still don't see any relevance," said Cara, the look of confusion now mixed with exhaustion.

"Sam's book was based loosely on the true story of NORAID, the Northern Irish Aid Committee, the former Chief of Staff for the IRA, Joe Cahill, and a Boston-based IRA veteran Ronan O'Neale. In Sam's book, the plot focused on a fictitious gang who were smuggling weapons from the U.S. to Ireland by ship. When I saw Jonathan's jumpsuit, I remembered something from Sam's book. Sam mixing reality with fiction as he would do later in **FALL OUT**. He named the ship in his fictional version of the story after the IRA emblem, *The Morning Sunburst*. A golden sun on a bright blue background."

That got everyone's attention.

"The IRA?" said Mako.

"Louis was obsessed with them," said Haribon, recalling

the drunken and drug-infused conversation on the set of *APOCALYPSE NOW*.

"Haribon, the airline, was it Louis' idea?" asked Marcus.

"It was. We needed our own air freight company to get things out of the country. The local company was useless. Louis was keen to handle this, so Stefan and I left the job to him."

"I thought so. Maybe in defiance, or out of misplaced romanticism for 'the cause', Louis named his airline after the emblem and the ship in Sam's book. He even had the old battle cry of the Republican struggle as his company's motto, '*Our day will come*'. Sam must have somehow found out about the airline when he came back here. He would have immediately seen the relevance of a connection between the IRA and Louis."

The photo in the banker Rafael's office, thought Haribon.

"But this was after Bill's death," said Mako.

"Bear with me. It established for Sam a connection between McConnell and the IRA," said Marcus. "Cara, that first night here on the set. You told Jonathan all about yourself and Bill…?" Cara's eyes widened as she understood the implications of what she had set in motion when she had sat and talked with her cousin.

"Oh my God," she said, visibly shaken. "I told Jonathan in detail all about Bill's time in the British Army. The ambush…."

"Jonathan must have been reporting everything back to Louis. Cara's conversation and the bit about the stunt Bill performed at the party," Marcus added. "Sam repeated that stunt in *FALL OUT* to underline Bill's bravery and ruthlessness. His patented booby-trap damn near killed Mako and me."

"The killers that ambushed Bill and his unit in Ireland…?" Cara's question hung in the air.

"Louis McConnell is closer to his roots than we thought. My hunch is McConnell decided to execute Bill in retaliation. Some kind of delusional retribution. Louis saw an opportunity to stop the film, pull the bond, and get revenge for his IRA heroes. Three birds with one stone," Marcus quickly explained to Haribon and Cara about the 'Essential Element' clause they had found hidden in Mako's certificate.

"Of course, to prove I'm right we need to find an actual connection between Bill, the men he killed in retaliation and Louis' 'cause'… or get McConnell to tell us."

There was a long silence. Finally, Cara spoke up.

"I'm sorry, Marcus, for what I said to you. McConnell forced me to try to get you to drop the movie. I didn't know or understand then. That man…."

"Cara, it doesn't matter. Really. Please forget it. I'm the one who's sorry."

"At least your conscience is clear now," she whispered to him. "They were going to kill Bill anyway. His bravery is what sealed his fate, not your rashness."

Marcus felt a huge sense of relief as Cara's words sank in.

There was a long pause in the conversation, everyone mulling over the implications of what Marcus had said.

"I am so sorry, Cara….," Mako finally said, breaking the silence. "But I still need a lot of answers," she continued looking directly at Haribon. "The Buddha head and my mother for a start. I wanted that bastard in there to explain," she said nodding her head back towards the cave.

The Jeep rumbled round the base of the rock, Rizal at the wheel.

"I know who can answer your questions Miss de Turris," Haribon said, "Come," he added, motioning to the 4x4.

"You want us to go with you? Marcus, is he crazy? After what he just put us through? I don't think so." She pulled away. "And who the hell was that other guy, Tyler someone-or-other's little angel of death? I'm not going anywhere."

"I insist," said Haribon, his face a deadpan expression. "At my house here in Pagsanjan, you will get your answers."

They were in the middle of nowhere. Marcus looked at Mako. There was no choice but to get in.

"You never know," whispered Marcus. "We might even get to the truth."

"Let's just hope we survive long enough to hear it," answered Mako out loud and staring at Haribon.

# CHAPTER 72

PAGSANJAN, PHILIPPINES

"Find what you wanted?" Mako asked Haribon with as much sarcasm as she dared as she surveyed the scene in Haribon's neat drawing room back at the small house.

She was glaring at Consuela huddled over the laptop, the red USB in the port and an open copy of *FALL OUT* on the table next to it. Mako watched in frustration as the computer screen filled with the numbers, she and Marcus had spent so much time deciphering.

Consuela turned around. "Nü-shu," she said. "Clever." Haribon sat down next to Consuela. He scrolled through page after page of the spreadsheet on the computer.

"Nothing in here about a head, but it's clear McConnell just couldn't resist skimming from me. It looks like no one else except de Turris kept any part of a share, unless you have anything to add, Mr. Riley?" Haribon said, still looking at the laptop.

Marcus looked shocked. "I've no money."

"So you keep saying," said Haribon without looking up.

"My father's money; take it back. The art. All of it," snapped Mako.

"And the damned head," added Marcus. "Whatever its meaning. People were killed for it."

"Including my mother," added Mako, her memory still raw from Jonathan's revelation in the cave.

"Where is it anyway?" asked Haribon.

"It's in Kenwood," replied Mako dryly.

"Go back," Consuela said to Haribon, pointing at the computer and totally ignoring the conversation.

The image of the black and white tiger filled the screen. "Freeze now." Consuela stared at the image. "In Hunan, where Nü-shu came from, the religion before Buddhism was *Tujia*. They worshipped the white tiger."

Mako peered at the screen in astonishment. Marcus leaned over the back of the rattan chair examining the image in front of him.

"We were looking at this image of the tiger the wrong way. It's like a negative from a photograph; the stripes are black and the rest of the fur white. This tiger is a white one," Marcus said, the implication dawning on him. "It's not just representing the Tiger of Malaya; it must mean more."

"Exactly," said Consuela. "Mako, my dear. You want to know what this is all about? You are the only one here who holds the key."

Mako looked at her, unsure, caught off guard by the gentleness in her voice. This frail woman seemed to have answers and wanted to help her. Consuela smiled, beckoning to Mako as she turned back to Haribon and the computer.

"Run that sequence again."

Haribon followed her instructions, the tiger dissolved and then the jumbled lines about to form the tiger once more reappeared on the screen.

"Stop again. Right here," directed Consuela. With a glint of satisfaction, she turned the screen towards Mako.

The animated jumble had occurred so fast that Marcus had barely noticed it when they had previously unlocked the security code; they'd been so eager to see the actual files. The lines that morphed so quickly into the tiger weren't random. It was a form of script.

"It's Nü-shu isn't it?" murmured Consuela, looking at Mako.

"I've only ever seen it once before, but I don't know how to translate it."

"But you can," Marcus said looking at Mako hopefully.

"Help us," asked Consuela, "or at least see if you can find the answer to why this nearly killed you."

"I need some paper," Mako whispered as she stared at the frozen image.

Thinking back to the strange scratches Marcus had noticed on the statue when he held it briefly at the house he said, "The Nü-shu writing on the screen, I think it may also be what's etched on the base of the Buddha head."

Mako squinted at the screen and the delicate script. It took her nearly an hour to decipher but she slowly pulled from her memory what her mother had taught her.

"OK," she said looking up, a triumphant look on her face.

Everyone gathered around as she read.

"To my dear sisters," she started hesitantly, *"the secret I give to you is no longer fit for men. Long ago, when the tribes of Tujia were founded we expressed our beliefs in the worship of nature, veneration of our ancestors, and the adoration of our totems of Ba Wuxiang.*

Ba Wuxiang was our first chief. His spirit became the Great White Tiger. Over centuries we hoarded our gold, dug it out from our mine in the hills and our cache grew and grew. All the gold we collected went to make up our prize, our two statues by which the Tima our priest would help us communicate with our forefather; the cub and the resplendent mature lord of the jungle.

But men became greedy. The warlords enslaved us; tried to force us to change our beliefs and they started to hunt for our tigers.

The priest hid the full-grown golden beast in the holy lake, killing himself afterwards to protect the location of the sacred lair. But he had told his secret and given the cub statue to someone whom he deemed to be all that was left that was pure and innocent, a young lowly peasant girl. The priest's words were passed from mouth to mouth of specially selected women. As we developed our own secret script our sisterhood grew. We still hoped to reclaim the large statue depicting our ancestor one day in the future, when the evil done by man stopped and we had returned to the values of our forebears.

But as the time passed one warlord changed to another, none worthy of our secret. Now we are overrun with invaders from overseas. They have tortured, raped and killed. Most villagers are dead, our own warlord fleeing to the hills instead of protecting us. The Wa loot all they find, always hunting for more. The last of us here alive, we await certain death, but we hide in this head the smallest of the totems, a golden cub. Carved on its belly is the location where lies its majestic older form. We pray one day a woman will return and reunite the statues, our beliefs and way of life. Hunan 1944"

They looked at Mako in stunned silence.

"Who are the *Wa*?" asked Marcus, breaking the quiet.

"It's the word the Chinese use to describe the Japanese. This must refer to the *Zhijiang* campaign and the Rape of Hunan… " said Consuela.

"A life-size tiger in gold… worth finding," said Haribon quietly.

"How on earth can you mount an excavation at some lake in China without anyone knowing what you are doing," began Marcus but then he stopped. China was now attracting movie productions with cheap labor and locations. He had no doubt what Louis and Stefan's plan had been. They'd done it before.

"No, no!" Mako made everyone jump. "This time the works of art go back to the people who owned them. All this death, the stealing. These tigers are to be reunited and returned to their rightful owners."

Haribon raised his hand, but it was Consuela who spoke.

"That isn't the head's only value," she said softly. "It is insurance. The Chinese will ensure immunity to anyone who can prove that Yamashita's Gold was no myth and contained items looted from China. That's why McConnell's so desperate to get it."

"Are you saying McConnell killed Mako's mother, because he not only wanted that gold baby tiger for himself but, even more importantly, indemnity from prosecution?" asked Cara.

"Louis McConnell is only interested in one thing…. he has no loyalty to anyone but himself," sighed Haribon. "Even to your father. I suspect that is why Stefan kept those insurance documents should Louis double cross him. Unfortunately…."

"My father was a thief but no murderer. Sam, however, found out about the money, the murder, and the deception," said Mako, with some relief in her voice.

"And Sam thought I might have received some of this money, along with Cara and Robert….," said Marcus.

"Maybe. I certainly wondered," said Haribon. "It's clear to me though you did not, despite my gentle tease just now. You behaved with honor and courage in that cave. Even now you have no desire to find the tiger for yourself."

"You never bothered to check if we were paid. Might have saved some lives," replied Marcus with rising incredulity.

"Louis and Stefan said you all had to be paid. For silence. Why would I not believe them? Tracing the funds once they left the Pagsanjan accounts was impossible anyway. They bounced through dozens of accounts. Those payments reaching the right destination? Not my circus, not my monkeys. In a way, sending the money eased my conscience. I insisted on Cara getting Baines' share. Once the banker Rafael Satow told me about Sam, I guessed. Before I could act though I had to be sure who had and who hadn't been paid."

"What do you mean, act?" asked Mako dryly.

Haribon did not answer.

"And Kelso?" asked Mako.

"On balance I bet he got screwed too," said Haribon. "In the immediate aftermath of Bill's death, I was furious. Tried to get hold of McConnell, but he kept avoiding my calls. It took days before we connected. By that time Jonathan was firmly holed up in Los Angeles. Louis refused to discuss Bill, it was over and done with as far as he was concerned.

As for Kelso, Louis had been worried the drugs might get him talking despite the money we'd be sending him. I told Louis if he touched Kelso or anyone else, he would answer to me." Haribon paused for a moment. "Louis laughed. He told me not to worry. Before Jonathan disappeared to LA, they scared the shit out of him. Strung out on coke, the day after Bill's death, Kelso was grabbed by Jonathan in Pagsanjan, blindfolded and dragged to a local graveyard. Kelso stumbled to the ground and Jonathan pulled off the bandana covering his eyes. He shoved his face into some foul-smelling purple flowers tangled around the gravestones. Told Kelso what they signified. A dead body. If he ever thought about saying anything, the last thing he would remember before he died would be a gift of purple flowers," said Haribon. "They are a symbol I have used myself on occasion…"

"Did you ever go back?" asked Cara. "To where all this happened."

"I returned only once. On the wall I left my message of apology to Bill and painted a crucifix. I then sealed it up for what I thought was forever."

"And Tyler Gemmell and his messenger?" asked Mako.

"Came out of the blue," deadpanned Haribon. "One McConnell double cross too many, perhaps?"

Marcus suspected there was more to it, but Haribon was clearly saying nothing else.

"We free to go?" Marcus said after a pause.

"As Miss de Turris noted, we have your bags. I have booked you on a first-class flight back to Geneva tomorrow," said Haribon as he headed towards the door.

Mako had a puzzled look on her face. "Geneva... how did you know that?"

"Miss de Turris, not only could I tell you the seat number you flew in on but what you had for lunch and the movie you watched." He turned to Cara. "And you're on a flight to LA. My offer is still open."

"Thank you, but no thank you," she replied.

Cara had earlier rejected Haribon's financial help. It was blood money and always would be. She owed Bill more than that. In fact, she knew exactly what she owed him.

"And Louis McConnell? Is he just to go free in the wind?" Marcus asked.

"I have no doubt his greed will ultimately undo him long before the law catches up. He'll screw over one person too many," Haribon replied.

Marcus looked skeptical. However, Cara was sure of it.

"And now, goodnight," said Haribon. He turned towards his bedroom.

"One thing. The money that developed Pagsanjan?" Marcus asked.

"It was I who insisted," said Consuela. "One place where real people could benefit from that treasure."

"She held out for twenty-five percent of my share. Schools, roads, electricity, jobs, water supplies, roads," replied Haribon, looking fondly at the old woman.

"The art and treasures in London and Habkern, along with whatever is left in my father's accounts, I'm returning to you," Mako said looking directly at Consuela." She turned to Haribon.

"Not impressed. You're still a thief."

"Only seventy-five percent of one," replied Haribon raising his index finger at her.

"Me? I'm zero percent," replied Mako.

# CHAPTER 73

HABKERN, SWITZERLAND

Less than 48 hours after leaving the cave, Mako and Marcus were driving back to Nisten. "We've done what Sam wanted, found the guilty parties. You have closure…." said Marcus.

"You don't think we owe it to Sam to nail McConnell? That man was responsible for the death of my mother, Sam, Bill… so many."

"Mako, it's not our world. He's far too clever for conventional justice. Haribon seemed to think his past will catch up with him."

"You mean leave it to divine retribution? I want him to suffer in the present," she responded firmly.

"Cara seemed pretty certain," replied Marcus. "I suspect retribution will find him long before the law does…. and I doubt it will be divine," Marcus added, as he got out and walked with Mako to the house.

"Hey, I forgot," she said, leaning over to kiss him, "Thanks. I'm sorry it had to be three."

He looked puzzled, jet lag still fuzzing his brain.

"You've saved me three times," holding up three fingers to emphasize the point.

He smiled back at her and put his arm over her shoulder.

"I want to stop fighting my father. Close this chapter. Not so much start again but be who I should have been. I'm selling the business. I want to try something more lasting, more fulfilling…."

Marcus hoped that would include him but knew better than to ask. Mako called her own emotional shots.

She opened the front door.

"Bastard," she cursed.

The house was ransacked.

Tables and chairs were overturned, pictures torn from the walls. Some of the priceless china was smashed, a tiny jade figurine lay in pieces at the foot of the curved stairway. Mako looked at the devastation.

"Jonathan venting his rage," Marcus consoled her putting his arms round her.

Mako bent down and picked up the shattered photo of Xavier, her teenage self and her mother all smiling outside the shop in Habkern.

"When he met me outside Xavier's shop, as soon as he said, '*I recognized you from that photo in the hall I saw a few years ago, when I last visited*', I knew he was lying."

"How come?"

"It always hung in my room…." Mako replied

"But your father could have shown him….?"

"…. It always hung in my room in *Pied à Mer*. I sent it to my father about a year ago…. after we had agreed to meet…. just to remind him of what he'd lost."

"It worked. He hung it up. He wanted you back in his life," Marcus said calmly. "Face it, it helped save you."

Mako would keep that sentiment as the last thought of her father. "Let's not mention his name again." She kissed Marcus long and hard. She wanted to reassure herself that Marcus was the only thing she was taking from this part of her life.

"All this stuff. Everything that survived or is not too damaged is going to Consuela. Robin can arrange for everything in London to be packed up. I have already instructed the money in my father's accounts be sent to Consuela as well." Mako sighed, "Poor but honest."

"Agreed, get it out of your life," Marcus said firmly. "Now, time to go get that head, dig out its last secret. After that, we take a break, sort out your future, go find something else to challenge us," he grinned.

Mako shook her head in mock frusutration.

"Life with you is never going to be boring," she said as she followed him into the kitchen. The electric motor whirred as the mixing bowl slowly rose from below the work surface, the Buddha still nestled safely inside. The Nü-shu script was visible at the base of the head.

"You can just see the join in the underside where a stonemason cut the plug for the hollowed out hiding place for the cub," Marcus said as he rolled the head onto the aluminum work surface.

"OK, let's do it," said Mako determinedly.

Marcus found the tools he needed. He carefully started to gently hammer at the base with a chisel.

"Look at this," she said, as she picked up a tiny shard that fell away from the back of the head as he was chipping at the base. It revealed a glimmer of gold inside the head. "It must've broken off some time in the past. Looks like it was crudely reattached."

It took Marcus nearly an hour to carefully chisel away the base but eventually he was able to remove the plug. Nestled inside was an exquisite golden sculpture of a baby tiger cub.

"It's beautiful," Mako whispered, as Marcus carefully removed the statue.

The cub crouched on its stomach with its tail curved around its left haunch, the animal's left paw drawn back to the shoulder and its right leg extended forward. The proud head was resting on the outstretched foreleg, its expression alert, the body coiled and ready to pounce. The tiger's body was made from solid platinum, the stripes on the fur a deep yellow gold. The sculpture filled most of the head. It weighed as much as a medicine ball. They gently turned it over. Sure enough on the animal's belly was more of the delicate spidery writing.

Mako held a magnifying glass up to it. After a few minutes of intense scrutiny of the script, she said, "This seems to be saying the other tiger is hidden in Yongjiang."

"A life-size one like this....?" Marcus gasped. The thought was awe inspiring.

"They need to be reunited and people allowed to see them," said Mako, "Yongjiang is in Western Hunan, where Nü-shu originated." She turned back to the writing.

"*He lies at peace in shallow water in a cave on Dongting Lake under a heaven of Hunan's eternal chrysanthemums.* Marcus, they buried the tiger under chrysanthemum stones."

"What are chrysanthemum stones?" he asked, still looking at the cub.

"Beautiful. Fossilized petals of flowers from thousands of years ago that seem to cling only to Hunan stone. They aren't found anywhere else... quite rare.... Wait here."

Two minutes later she reappeared with a black oval-shaped stone, the size of her fist. The smooth surface was unmarked on one side but when she turned it over, blazing out from the underside was a perfectly formed silver colored chrysanthemum head.

"It's ironic. That flower was the symbol of both the Imperial Chinese as well as Japanese royal family," she said. "From above it must just look like a pile of stones in a lake. Below, from the tiger's point of view, his sky is a bouquet of flowers."

"Amazing," said Marcus admiring the stone.

"Keep it, it was my mother's. Brings good luck." She dropped it into Marcus' hand, at the same time giving him a quick kiss. "You think the cave exists, let alone anyone will find him?"

"We will make sure Haribon convinces them," Marcus said wryly.

"Let's hope so," she replied, stroking the baby tiger's back.

"He has a vested interest in making the Chinese happy, as Louis knows only too well," said Marcus. He turned and went to start organizing the shipping of the treasures to Consuela.

A few days later, after the last of the packing cases had been sent to Consuela, they drove back to Mako's home by the sea. They both needed a break and Marcus knew something was waiting for her there.

Garance met them as the electronic gate opened. After an emotional reunion, he pulled himself together. "This way, if Madame pleases." He pointed towards the long stone staircase to the jetty. Mako looked at Marcus. He smiled back with a shrug of his shoulders.

Slowly she began to descend the stairs. Then Marcus heard her whoop for joy.

Tethered to the mooring post was a Riva Aquarama S. Sheer joy lit up Mako's face.

"I didn't tell you. We wanted it to be a surprise," Marcus said as he followed her down.

"We?" Mako asked looking at Marcus.

Garance nodded. "The insurance money was sufficient, Madame. It was the question of finding a replacement. That was *plus difficile*… more difficult. Via a friend…. *une amie de* Monsieur Riley, we discover in *Porto Cervo*. This used to belong to the Aga Khan."

"I felt so bad about what happened. Garance agreed to help… and kept it a secret, in case we couldn't track one down. I had yacht brokers scouring every port," explained Marcus. "They told me this one may be for sale. I once knew someone very close to the owner… and she persuaded him."

Mako mouthed "Who is SHE…? eyes wide in mock surprise.

"We all have a past…." Marcus reminded her.

Garance handed her the keys.

"Here," she smiled at Marcus. "You take her out first."

That afternoon Marcus made the call to Jax.

"That was Sam," she said after a pause when he had finished telling her the whole story. "Marcus, you found out what he wanted you to. If you want them, those rights are still yours."

Marcus breathed a sigh of relief. Their relationship was whole once more.

"Thanks, Jax. I'll see. Let's stay in touch."

"You think Haribon will keep his word? I don't exactly trust him, Marcus," Mako said lying in bed that evening. "I so want to believe the art; treasure and the tigers will be returned…."

"You remember that picture in his house. The young girl and the toddler? It's Consuela. She brought Haribon up. *The hand that rocks the cradle….* that's what binds them, and what keeps him honest…. more or less."

 # CHAPTER 74

CATALINA, CALIFORNIA

Louis stretched out on the wicker chaise-longue on his balcony, sunglasses on the end of his nose, newspapers on his lap. His empty breakfast tray lay on a table next to him as he watched the gulls swoop and cry over the rocks below.

He had just finished his call with Tyler, who confirmed the message had been delivered in Manila. In fact, as a small thank you, he was sending Louis a gift. And Louis had a pretty good idea what that meant.

No word from Jonathan. Louis guessed he was in hiding now, licking his wounded pride that Gemmell had dealt with Haribon. Louis could breathe easy.

The door to his suite rang and two statuesque nurses entered his room. By the shortness of their skirts and the depth of their cleavage, Louis could tell at once what kind of treatments they would be giving him. He never ceased to be in awe of Tyler Gemmell's resourcefulness, which was matched only by his appreciation of the female form.

"Clothes off," said the first.

"Treatments first, fun later," said the other, as she went outside and wheeled in a massage bed and a large trolley filled with a variety of jars, towels, lotions and potions.

"The latest kelp wash and wrap with aromatherapy oils," continued the first.

"Invigorates. Makes Viagra seem like a vitamin supplement. And afterwards.... well, you'll take us both with ease," added the second with a wink.

Louis was in shell-shocked heaven and rooted to his chair.

"That's if you want to…. we can always tell Mr. Gemmell you'd rather not….," said the first, making as if to leave.

Louis was up in a flash, the semblance of an erection already protruding from his robe.

The two girls giggled.

They eased him out of his robe and told him to stand with one arm bent against his chest, the other at his side.

"Now we pop this over your mouth," she said, sticking some tape across his lips, "as you need to breathe through your nose. The treatment tastes yucky."

A blown kiss melted the initial look of consternation on Louis' face.

Slowly the girls wound the bandages all over his body, except his groin which they left exposed, occasionally brushing their scarlet red nails over his crotch with promises about the future in their eyes. Next, they helped him onto the massage table dropping a cool wet towel over his eyes.

They went around to each side of the mattress and, leaning over in unison, quickly grabbed straps underneath and before Louis knew what was happening, had him tightly secured to the massage table. As they walked out the door, hearing his muffled cries, they were more than happy to leave, glad it wasn't them who would have to perform anything on, near or with him. Their job was done, and they'd been well paid for it.

A short nurse with a surgical mask over her face and a small cut on her forehead entered the room. She locked the door, activating the *Do Not Disturb* light outside by flicking the switch at the bedside table.

"Now we are quite alone," she said, as she raised the towel from Louis' eyes.

The look of fury on his face slowly changed to fear, as Cara peeled away her mask and took a glass jar from the trolley placing it carefully on Louis' chest. She then reached into her handbag and brought out Bill's service revolver. She opened the weapon and made sure Louis saw there was only a single bullet inside.

"I learned this from Haribon," she smiled at him, "when I saw him a week ago…" Louis' eyes stretched wide in fear, "and watched as Tyler Gemmell's man shot dead the bastard you had kill my husband." She never raised her voice. If anything, she spoke to Louis with the cadence and pitch of a mother to a young child.

As Louis struggled against the straps, Cara lifted the jar for a moment until he stopped struggling.

"Gently does it," she cooed.

She had tracked Tyler down on her return, made it plain there was only one solution to the 'Louis problem' and that she wanted to deliver it. He had been more than happy to help her.

"You know your vanity about heritage is what screwed you, Louis." She was standing over him, beads of sweat forming on his forehead. "Just a bit of research, a click on Google. Your house, named after your grandfather? *Roneale*. Ronan O'Neale. A gunrunner from Boston. No wonder you killed off Sam's book. And those bastards that ambushed Bill and his comrades in Ireland so long ago…. the ones he subsequently blew through the gates of hell…. what where their names? Eamon, Sean and Michael… O'Neale. All part of the same happy family… so you saw a chance for retribution for death in the family," she looked at him sharply, "I can empathize."

She picked up Louis' gold *Patek Philippe* watch which the girls had taken off before performing their mummification.

"Let me show you something," she said holding up the jar and filling it with a liquid from one of the glass containers. "You know what this is? *Aqua Regia*. About the strongest acid you can find. Only one able to dissolve gold, which is why it's used to test its purity…. But silly me, of *course* you know that." She placed it back on Louis' chest and he immediately stopped struggling, his eyes fixed on the container.

With that she lowered Louis' watch into the glass jar. Within seconds, the liquid began to bubble, and Louis stared as his watch dissolved like an Alka Seltzer.

"Need a new one now," she chided. She reached over again to the trolley and pulled out an identical liquid-filled jar and a smaller one filled with a milky liquid.

"The first…. well now you know what that is. This smaller one here…. snake venom. The kind that killed poor Christo… in agony. But of course, you know that too." Louis' breathing became short.

"Now, don't go having a coronary before you've had the full treatment," she admonished him gently.

She poured the snake venom into the other liquid. Louis would never guess that unlike the first which really was *Aqua Regia*, the second was merely a mild solution of capsicum; the 'venom' she added to it just acetic acid and bleach. The mixture would sting like hell on exposed skin, but barely leave a rash.

"Now," she said slipping the suicide note onto his bedside table, "here's the last decision you are going to make. Slow or quick?"

She screwed a silencer into the end of Bill's revolver then shoved the elongated barrel under Louis' chin. She forced the butt of the pistol into Louis' hand that was bound tight against his chest and put his forefinger on the trigger.

"Let me help you, that looks awkward," she whispered as she bent down and cocked the hammer.

"Hair trigger, so be careful."

Cara held up the liquid and looked him dead in the eyes. "When

I pour this onto your crotch, it will take the acid about a minute to burn off your cock and balls… maybe another three minutes of agony before the snake venom kicks in and attacks your lungs, unless you just bleed to death first. Either way you die here in agony. Or if you prefer quick, just pull the trigger."

Without another word she dumped the liquid over his exposed groin and within seconds the capsicum and bleach started to burn his skin.

Louis made his choice and blew off the top of his skull.

# CHAPTER 75

MANILA, PHILIPPINES

Several months had passed since the events in the cave. Haribon looked around the new apartment which he had recently moved into. The views across the city were magnificent and he watched the crowds as they scuttled and scurried past gaudy fairy lights to enjoy Christmas Eve celebrations.

He had been sanguine about the supposed suicide of Louis McConnell who had been found at a luxurious spa all alone, stark naked, a simple suicide note, and a fatal gunshot wound to his head.

Haribon had spent much of October in China with his new partner, Tyler Gemmell. They had struck a number of lucrative deals for the supply of motion picture equipment. Furthermore, it looked as if production of film and television was to be a major commitment from the Chinese government over the next few years. The new joint venture between Gemmell Group and Golden Eagle Trust, EagleGem, was going to be at the forefront and the search was already on in Hollywood for suitable scripts.

Haribon remembered smiling when Tyler had mentioned one night over dinner how Louis had been wrong on several counts.

"I now see the value in reading scripts, and recognize in you, Haribon, a man I can do business with …. On top of that I finally got Benjamin to work for me," said Tyler raising a glass.

"To men like us… honest. Just not fanatics." Haribon toasted his new partner.

The unraveling of the mystery of the Buddha lead to the discovery of the golden tiger. It was a triumph of Chinese archaeological techniques and made front page headlines the world over. The Chinese Government agreed that much like the Terracotta Army, the two wonders would remain where they belonged, in Hunan Province.

"So *ya-ya*," Haribon said, "have I atoned at all for my sins?"

"Probably not," she chided him. "However, as I was there while you grew up, it's arguably my fault you turned out as you did. I'm not even sure about this apartment. Too flash," she said with a mock frown.

Haribon stretched then ran his fingers through his hair. "The McKinley Road house is yours now, or I'll buy you another anywhere you like as your *balato*," he smiled at her, referring to an old Philippine tradition that when one comes into good fortune a *balato*, or share, be given to close family or loved ones.

"Thank you. I'm happy where I am. However, there is something I would like. A first-class return ticket to see those tigers in Hunan, then a visit to the museums filled with all the treasures that Mako returned. While I'm away, just keep an eye on the foundation we set up with her father's money. Make sure the right people benefit."

"Done," he laughed. He glanced across expecting to see a smile on her face but instead was greeted by a frown. "Why the *tampo* (sulk)?" he asked.

"Where are your manners?" she admonished him. "That is what you can do for me. Now what are you going to do for them?"

CHAPTER 76

PIED À MER, CANNES

The wind was blowing fiercely, the halyards slapping and clinking against the masts of the yachts in the marina below. The sea swirled in eddies reflecting gunmetal grey from the brooding rain-filled clouds that hung over it.

Mako was curled on the sofa in front of the fire, a pencil holding her long hair in a knotted bun at the back of her head. A balloon glass of Calvados was in one hand.

The doorbell rang. A few moments later Garance entered the room.

"A courier, Madame. *Une enveloppe.* Most insistent I give to your hand, Monsieur Riley," he said.

Marcus smiled a thank you. He looked at the sender's address and stood still.

"Anyone we know?" asked Mako.

He slowly opened the envelope. He drew out a sheet of heavy and expensive writing paper. At the top was the familiar gold embossed logo of an eagle, wings raised but this time its claws clutching a diamond gem.

Attached was a five-page distribution contract as well as details of a full studio facility and crew in a new production complex in China. Neatly stapled to the top right-hand corner was a check from *EagleGem Distribution* for an advance against all rights in the Pacific Rim and Europe for **FALL OUT.** It was for $40 million.

"What do you know," Marcus smiled bending down to give Mako a kiss on her forehead. "We're back in the movie business," he said.

The End

 # BIBLIOGRAPHY

Much of the content of this book is based on historical fact.

Asian Loot: Unearthing the Secrets of Marcos, Yamashita and the Gold - Charles C. McDougald, San Francisco Publishers, 1993

America's Boy: The Marcoses and the Philippines - James Hamilton-Paterson, Granta Books, 1999

Notes: The Making Of Apocalypse Now - Eleanor Coppola, Faber, 1995

Balisong: The Lethal Art of Filipino Knife Fighting Paperback – Gary Cagaanan, Sid Campbell and Sonny Umpad, Paladin Press, 1986

Philippine Culture Manual for Foreigners: Understanding the Culture of the Philippines - Bob Martin, CreateSpace, 2015

Tagalog Down & Dirty: Filipino Obscenities, Insults, Sex Talk, Drug Slang and Gay Language in The Philippines - Emmett Henderson, CreateSpace, 2011

Lonely River Village: A Novel of Secret Stories - Norma Libman, Rio Granata Press, 2014

Food of the Philippines: 81 Easy and Delicious Recipes from the Pearl of the Orient - Reynaldo G. Alejandro and Luca Invernizzi Tettoni, Periplus, 2017

Culture Shock! Philippines: A Guide to Customs and Etiquette Paperback – Alfredo Roces and Grace Roces, Kuperard, 2000

Asian Art (The World's Greatest Art) - Michael Kerrigan, Flame Tree Publishing, 2017

Art of the Korean Renaissance: 1400-1600 -Soyoung Lee, Yale University Press, 2009

Asian Art: India China Japan - Berenice Geoffroy-Schneiter, Assouline, 2002

Classic Chinese Furniture - Wo-Lap Lam Willy, Formasia Books Ltd, 2006

Chinese, Celtic & Ornamental Knots - Suzen Millodot, Search Press Ltd, 2012

The Art of War - Sun Tzu, Pax Librorum, 2009

General Yamashita's Dream Book : How to successfully find hidden treasure in the Philippines - Aquila Chrysaetos, New Generation Publishing, 2013

 # ACKNOWLEDGEMENTS

My thanks to Bette Anne Berg, Sherry Landrum, Kathy Freeman, Kim Whyte, Georgina Jackson Sytner, Paul de Vos, Sheila Morris, Wayne Stanley and Irondome, the friends and family who encouraged me in dark moments and partied in the light ones, Matthew Smith, Kerry-Jane Lowery and all at Urbane Publications.

Thanks to Aquila Chrysaetos for the signs and symbols.

Please enjoy this excerpt from M.N.Grenside's thrilling new novel
The Bastion, publishing in 2021.

THE BASTION

CHAPTER 1

LOS ANGELES

Detective Jake Meadows had attended dozens of homicides. He'd
seen countless bodies and witnessed an infinite variety of methods
to kill; stabbed, shot, strangled, poisoned, suffocated, hung,
beheaded and even skinned. The grisly sight at a crime scene no
longer had any effect, but after twenty years the stench still got to
him. He had a delicate sense of smell. He could pick out individual
perfumes in a crowded room or alcohol on breath at twenty paces.
Decomposed bodies were the worst, quickly followed by burnt
ones. This victim ticked both boxes.

"Kind 'a puts you off your food," said Sergeant Benny McAllister
as he bit into the bacon cheeseburger he had bought from a stand
across the street, the ketchup and mustard oozing over his fingers.
Jake glowered at him. "I love the smell of bacon in the morning,"
teased the younger man, well aware of his boss' one weakness.
"Did ya' wanna bite?" Benny added as he licked the goo off his
fingertips, looking for somewhere to throw the wrapper and paper
napkin of his burger.

"This is a goddamn crime scene, Sergeant McAllister. Stow
it." Jake rebuked him. Reluctantly Benny used his index finger to
gently poke the sticky paper mess into his leather jacket pocket
grimacing at the thought of resulting stains. The love of clothes

was Benny's weakness and Jake knew it. The Detective smiled to himself. One weakness each. Both exposed. Now they were even.

The two men were standing in a puddle of water at the entrance of the half burnt out interior of a small industrial unit. The whole building was a sixty by forty-foot rectangular room with a double door entry and no windows. To their right against the far wall stood a row of steel cabinets, filled with racks of burnt out electronic machinery. Next to these was the buckled remains of a walk-in vault, the door looking more like a huge bar of chocolate that had been left too long in the sun. The room was being lit up by the flair from an oxyacetylene torch.

"How long till you cut the door off?" called out the detective. The man lifted his visor.

"Another five minutes. Whatever heat source caused this you know nothing's gonna remain of what was inside ..."

On the ground in front of Jake and Benny lay a corpse being examined by two Crime Scene Investigators. A cell phone was in an outstretched hand, a pair of handcuffs still attached to the left wrist while the other wrist was horribly deformed and broken. The body was puffy and bloated, yet where the skin was not blistered, it was ghostly pale; but the worst were the eye sockets. They were a hollow mess of crushed eyeball and the jellied vitreous that once filled them.

"So how do you see this went down? Somebody must 'a wanted something," Benny asked Jake.

"Whatever it was, the victim didn't give it up without resisting," said Jake dryly. "Popped his eyes like they were squishing grapes."

"Soundproof and no windows. If you're gonna torture someone, this is ideal," grimaced the young man looking up at his boss.

Benny McAllister walked past the body into an annex leading off to a small kitchen with a fridge, coffee machine and microwave. It ended with two individual floor-to-ceiling heavy cupboard doors. One was still closed and marked 'Storage. Downloads. Dolly and Master Shots'. The other was open, a fireman and CSI both closely examining it. Benny peered inside. The top shelf was a mangle of wrecked electronic equipment. In the center was a void behind which sprouted a mass of wires and cable trunking. Benny turned and went back into the main room.

His boss was standing by a long desk that ran the entire width of the unit. At regular intervals several different control panels were sunk into it. A rail ran along under the desk on which was once mounted a single high back chair but now twisted on its side. An empty handcuff hung from one of the chair arms.

The other arm had snapped away from the frame.

The husks of burnt out monitors clung to the walls while the wiring from individual light fittings hung down like twigs, the false roof where they had been housed completely burnt away.

"Finished with the vic?" Detective Meadows shouted back to the CSIs who were still leaning over the body. They don't even wear a mask, he thought to himself. Being that close they must be inhaling bits of him. Jake really wanted them to take the corpse and the smell away.

"Yeah but moving him might be difficult. He's pretty ripe. All his insides are bloated. He could split open, then everything would pour onto the floor...."

Jake waved a hand at them signalling that was enough. Benny McAllister's phone rang. He listened.

"Detective. This guy is was some kind of a legend. He's a multi Oscar winner...worked with everyone."

There was a crash and they both whipped round. The vault door was now on the floor.

"Told you," said the man with the oxyacetylene torch as he peered inside the vault. "Just a hardened puddle of metal in here."

Sergeant McAllister shook his head then turned to the burnt-out glass and steel cases that lined the wall.

"Get whatever that mess is out of the cases and get 'em to the labs," Detective Meadows ordered as he started to walk towards the door. "Let's get out of here before the press arrive. I can't stand the smell any longer," he glowered at his younger sidekick.

A CSI officer walked over to Jake as he headed towards the exit.

"That entry camera and all the internal cameras record via Wi-Fi onto a separate hard drive. I suspect that was located in this cupboard by the kitchen. The contents have been ripped from the wall. Maybe your puddle of metal in the safe? The intruders knew what they were doing. Disconnected the police and fire alarm systems. Turned off the water system. Looks like they used some kind of accelerant on the equipment and assumed the rest of the place would go up in flames."

"Thanks," said the Detective. "You finished with the bathroom. I need to take a leak before I go," he said to the agent returning to the crime scene.

"Can't see one here. Must be outside."

Jake thought for a moment. "There must be one. You think he just pissed in a jar?" he mumbled. "McAllister, get the dead guy's phone details and find out who he called and when." Jake looked round at the white suited CSIs carefully sifting through the debris.

"Why did this place not totally burn down? The firemen told us the sprinklers were disabled," countered Benny.

"That kitchen extension. It's new. Look at the sprinklers. Different, they halted the damage at the entrance end of the building. Lack of air and the rest of the fire in the main part of the building just dies down. Still I reckon it was damn hot in here, so over the weekend the vic just rots," Detective Meadows answered.

"Three days in that heat, hence the wonderful 'bouquet' coming from the body," continued Benny.

"Outside it still looks normal, inside though," said his boss.

"Monday morning and a cleaner opens up and throws up," concluded Benny, remembering the scene when they got there after the frantic call and the heap they had found her in.

"I think we found something. You still wanna take a leak?" came a voice behind them.

The CSI agent had forced open the cupboard door, marked 'Storage. Downloads. Dolly and Master Shots'. Inside was no storage room but a small bathroom. "There's fecal matter in the bowl and the window's open," added the CSI agent. "Maybe hairs or DNA."

"We have a witness," said Jake.

"Maybe more than you know ... there's a monitor in here," said the agent.

"How do you know it's not the vic and he, er, just was airing the room," asked McAllister.

"He didn't flush. We'll run tests but my bet is it's not the vic. Someone else was here, heard it all, may even have seen it, and got out through the window," concluded the CSI.

"The data from the vic's phone is coming through," Benny said to his boss. "Seems his last call was local, in fact very local."

"Where?" asked McAllister.

"This one," said Benny pointing to another cell phone that had already been bagged as evidence and was still laying on the kitchen table

"Who makes a call to a phone no more that fifteen feet away?"

"Beats me as the call before couldn't have been further away. Some Brit called Marcus Riley. But he's lost in France."

CHAPTER 2

INTERIOR CAR

TWO DAYS LATER

"We have to work out where the shooting took place," said Marcus Riley, concentration clear on his face as he held his 60's classic sports car, an electric blue Maserati Mistral spyder, in a power-slide, the tires wailing in protest. The car straightened and then rocketed on down the tree lined road.

"C'mon Mako, the others are gaining. We can work this out" he said glancing in the rear-view mirror while encouraging the 35-year-old woman seated next to him.

Sure enough, a moment later two other cars careered round the same corner, the drivers both fighting the skid Marcus had skilfully pulled through. The sunlight shone brightly through the trees on the dead straight road, as Marcus drew away from the two cars still in his mirror.

"Read it again," said Marcus.

"*South from Montbard, towards Venarey-Les-Launes and Poullenay left to Flavigny then on to Val-Suzon via Thenissey. There take the D971. If you cut the mustard you've missed it, and you are done. From Wilcox Field to Idlewild was where which shooting took place for a fee?*" Mako read out loud. "Makes no sense to me," she added.

Marcus furrowed his brow as he quietly repeated what she had said trying to make sense of it.

"Isn't *Idlewild* what they used to call JFK?" Mako asked, trying to make herself heard above the noise, the wind whipping the few strands of her long black hair not secured by a red bandana.

"Uh-huh," Marcus nodded, "And *Wilcox Field* is what they used to call Miami International Airport and yet …we're in the middle of France. There's something we're missing."

Mako slapped the clipboard in frustration. "Marcus, this is impossible." Marcus shrugged and turned to Mako, her Eurasian features remaining calm and serene despite the speed at which they were travelling.

"It's all logical, we just need to puzzle it out together. *Cut the mustard* must mean Dijon, we're not far, about 60 kilometers. There was a sign back there. So we know if we reach it, we have gone too far. It must be before … read the clue one more time."

As Mako repeated the instructions a smile spread across Marcus' face. "Devious bastards, whatever shooting that they are referring to happened I know where they mean," he said with certainty. "Right now we don't need them following us," he said glancing in the rearview mirror. "Let them work it out themselves."

A road sign notified Marcus of an approaching danger; a dip in the road causing a blind spot. He could see a small turn off at the base of the hill.

"Now's our chance," he said looking again in the mirror.

The cars behind momentarily lost sight of Mako and Marcus as they dropped down into the hollow and Marcus swung the car left into a tiny lane, the thick hedgerow growing up from each side and joining above the narrow strip of blacktop to form a dark tunnel. Marcus killed the engine. Sure enough, the two pursuing vehicles shot straight on.

"OK, no hangers on. Can you get us to *Flavigny* on this road?" Marcus asked, looking at Mako who had the map.

"No phone, no sat nav …"

"Those are the rules."

Exhibition stand designer Melinda de Turris, who preferred her nickname 'Mako', and her partner feature film producer Marcus Riley were competing in *The Grand Tour*, an invitation only four-day charity car rally from London to Monte-Carlo. Running through the more remote byways of France, the roads were closed to the public for the event but interspersed in each day's directions were cryptic clues that needed to be answered.

This was Mako's first time and she was still feeling her way around the hieroglyphics on the route map as well as trying to decode the questions hidden within. Having previously won twice before, Marcus was a marked man, with other competitors eager to stick close to him, hoping he would lead them to the answers, or could somehow be persuaded to part with the information on how to solve the puzzles.

"But why *Favigny*? Explain Marcus," she asked gently, swatting him with the clipboard in mock frustration.

"Miami airport to Idlewild which is now JFK, so that's Florida to New York. So what are the state abbreviations?" he started, trying to get Mako to connect the dots.

"OK, FLA to NY. But I still don't see..." she began.

"For a fee ..." continued Marcus.

There was a pause.

"Of course," Mako said with a clap of her hands "A *vig. FLA VIG NY*?" she said triumphantly.

"OK but who the hell was shot here?"

"No idea but let's go find out," Marcus said as he gunned the car out from under the hedgerow and Mako pointed the direction he needed to take.

Half an hour later their car purred under the crenelated ramparts of a medieval stone gateway which was book-ended by two round towers; a sign greeted them announcing they had arrived in *Flavigny*.

They entered the tiny village and Marcus nosed the car into a small cobblestone square with a fountain at its center and dominated by the spire from a nearby monastery. Hunched round the square were narrow houses of pale sandstone hung with either lilac wisteria or white flowering jasmine, and in the far corner was a small bar. Apart from a few people sipping drinks at the tables shaded by parasols, the rest of the town seemed quiet, an oasis of calm after a hectic and hot morning at the wheel.

Marcus decided to park in a small back alley, discreet and out of sight.

Apart from a black cat who was imperiously licking his paws while keeping an eye on Marcus' grime covered car, the narrow street was empty. It was July and already getting too hot to be out in the midday sun. Marcus quickly pulled his cap low over his face, his sunglasses covering his eyes.

"C'mon, let's go walkabout," he smiled as he opened the door for Mako. "See who got shot."

"People getting shot is not my idea of a good time," she replied as they slowly walked back towards the main square now filling up with other competitors from the race.

Mako and Marcus had met nearly two years earlier under very different and dangerous circumstances, when a man had indeed been shot. The bond they had formed during that time had remained tight and they had managed not only to survive threats to their lives but unravel a long-buried mystery. Marcus' stalling career had re-ignited and together they had recently completed producing a motion picture in Asia. Thankfully it had been a commercial hit at the box office and they were now enjoying a well-earned rest. They had a number of projects in development but there was nothing that needed immediate attention, apart from recently arranging for the filming on location in Malta for some establishing shots for a new action movie.

"Remind me again why I agreed to do this?" asked Mako

"You like treasure hunts," Marcus replied. "And if we win it's your charity that gets the prize money."

"Bullshit! You just like a chance of legally driving too fast," she grinned.

They spent over an hour walking around the town but apart from the local monks producing a small aniseed sweet there was nothing either could see about this tiny village that was special, let alone where somebody was shot.

"Is there a plaque or anything somewhere to commemorate Resistance fighters?" suggested Mako as they entered a cemetery. Sure enough, a wooden clog, or 'sabot' hung near a grave, a not uncommon sight in France. The sabot had been adopted as the secret insignia for the Resistance and indeed was where the word sabotage came from. However the grave did not seem remarkable enough to warrant a stop and for such an elaborate clue.

"You know there is something about this whole place that's familiar," said Marcus, "yet I can't pin it down."

They returned to the square,

"Let's have a drink," said Marcus, waving at other competitors who were milling about, many with puzzled looks on their faces.

Marcus went into the tiny bar and ordered a couple of *Perriers* and a small calvados for Mako as she wasn't driving that day. As the elderly owner bent down to get some more ice, Marcus noticed a small framed photo under the row of assorted spirits crammed onto a wooden shelf behind the counter. The same barman was grinning back, his arm around one of the most instantly recognizable faces in the world.

Marcus quickly paid for the drinks trying to hide the triumph on his face. "Drink up, we're leaving," he said quietly as he went to the table where Mako had only just sat down, another competitor sitting very close by.

She looked up at him with a quizzical expression and Marcus leaned forward to whisper in her ear, "Behind the bar. The barman has a photo of himself with Johnny Depp. I knew I recognized this place. *Chocolat*. A movie. That's what they shot here and that's the answer. Let's go."

"OK but a bathroom break first," pleaded Mako.

A moment later Mako returned a sheepish grin on her face. "He's a favorite of mine," she sighed theatrically.

"Who?" said Marcus as he rose to leave.

"Johnny of course. You ever work with him?" she said batting her eyelids in mock star-struck euphoria.

"Not yet, I hear he's wildly creative though," replied Marcus not rising to the bait.

"I will treasure this and put it by my bedside." She swooned as she waved the photo at Marcus. "Told *Le Patron* he could get another printed tomorrow. All he wanted for this was a kiss. Gotta love the French."

"Mako! This is cheating and then some! The clue is for everyone."

"The clue is for charity."

"Tchyeah...." Marcus playfully snatched at the photo and as they left the square to return to their own car, surreptitiously slid it under the wiper blade of one of the cars that had been following them all day.

A few moments after they sped off to complete the day's route leading to their final destination, their hotel, the car's owner returned to his vehicle, tossing the photo away. He had blond hair and blue eyes contrasted by deeply tanned skin. A rope and a baton were tucked inside his shirt. All he needed was a moment alone to grab Mako and he'd get Marcus to talk.

Mark Grenside began his working career straight out of school at Lloyds of London, specializing in Kidnap, Ransom and Extortion Insurance. At 25 it was time for a career change and to dump the suit and tie, so he started his media career working for Jim Henson and The Muppets©. From that moment on he has been involved in Entertainment and nearly every aspect of it.

He went on to create and produce several television series and mini-series. At the same time, he started a music management company launching million seller artist Neneh Cherry.

In 2004 he arranged a $250 million buy-out of the Hallmark Channel International which was then successfully sold to NBC. He returned to producing a number of movies and mini-series.

He recently has somehow morphed into a serial entrepreneur and is now a co-founder of seed to shelf CBD producer Dragonfly Biosciences (www.dragonflybiosciences.com) and a founder in two separate digital companies…. but has also seen a very good return from his love of cooking in an expanding waistline.

A probably unhealthy amount of time and money is lavished on a collection of classic cars that he has raced all over the world. He enjoys risk and has parachuted in New Zealand, scuba dived in the Pacific, hang-glided in the Himalayas and even tobogganed down the Cresta Run. In nearly every case chasing after his wife who is utterly fearless!

He is now writing the follow up to *Fall Out*, entitled *The Bastion*. In addition, he writes a humorous blog with subscribers in more than 40 countries. **www.andanotherthing.com**

He has two grown sons, two daughters' in law, three grandchildren and lives with his wife, his classic cars and two French bulldogs in Malta.

Urbane Publications is dedicated to
publishing books that challenge, thrill and fascinate.
From page-turning thrillers to literary debuts,
our goal is to publish what
YOU want to read.

Find out more at

urbanepublications.com